The Amish Widower

The Men of Lancaster County
(by Mindy Starns Clark and Susan Meissner)

The Amish Groom
The Amish Blacksmith
The Amish Clockmaker

The Amish Widower
(by Virginia Smith)

The Amish Widower

VIRGINIA SMITH

A continuation of the original series created by
Mindy Starns Clark and Susan Meissner

HARVEST HOUSE PUBLISHERS
EUGENE, OREGON

Scripture verses are taken from

The Holy Bible, New International Version®, NIV®. Copyright © 1973, 1978, 1984, 2011 by Biblica, Inc.® Used by permission. All rights reserved worldwide.

Die Bibel, Die heilige Schrift, nacht der Ubersetzung Martin Luthers, in der revidierten Fassung von 1912. (The Bible: The Holy Scriptures, as translated by Martin Luther in the revised edition of 1912.)

The King James Version of the Bible.

Cover by Garborg Design Works

Cover Images © Chris Garborg; Andrea Izzotti, captured by carol / Bigstock

Published in association with the Books & Such Management, 52 Mission Circle, Suite 122, PMB 170, Santa Rosa, CA 95409-5370, www.booksandsuch.com.

THE AMISH WIDOWER
Copyright © 2017 by Virginia Smith
Published by Harvest House Publishers
Eugene, Oregon 97402
www.harvesthousepublishers.com

ISBN 978-0-7369-6865-2 (pbk.)
ISBN 978-0-7369-6866-9 (eBook)

Library of Congress Cataloging-in-Publication Data

Names: Smith, Virginia, author.
Title: The Amish widower / Virginia Smith.
Description: Eugene, Oregon : Harvest House Publishers, [2017]
Identifiers: LCCN 2016039333 (print) | LCCN 2016047410 (ebook) | ISBN
   9780736968652 (softcover) | ISBN 9780736968669 (ebook)
Subjects: LCSH: Amish—Fiction. | Widowers—Fiction. | Amish Country
   (Pa.)—Fiction. | GSAFD: Christian fiction. | Love stories.
Classification: LCC PS3619.M5956 A84 2017 (print) | LCC PS3619.M5956 (ebook)
   | DDC 813/.6—dc23
LC record available at https://lccn.loc.gov/2016039333

Printed in the United States of America

17 18 19 20 21 22 23 24 25 / BP-SK / 10 9 8 7 6 5 4 3 2 1

To Ted,
the inspiration for every hero I write.
I love you.

ONE

The rumble from someone's stomach on the bench behind me stirred up an answer in my own empty belly. As was often the case in the winter, this church meeting had lasted longer than normal. I forced myself not to shift my weight on the hard wooden bench and tried to ignore the numbness that had overtaken my backside a good hour ago. Instead, I focused on Bishop Beiler's message. Or attempted to. The bishop had made his point multiple times, but he had yet to run out of different ways to say the same thing. *Ya,* we understood that true peace came only from God, and we knew that complete commitment, patience, and constant prayer were the keys to living in that peace. How many times did he have to repeat the point?

A sudden rush of guilt washed over me, and I did fidget then. My thoughts had just proved the bishop's point. Patience was a virtue I struggled to attain, and more often than not I lost the skirmish with my restive nature. And what was the result? Irritation with others and with myself, which demolished the very divine peace Bishop Beiler spoke of at such length.

Gott, *forgive me. Teach me patience, beginning now.*

With a renewed awareness of my own shortcomings, I spared a glance across the room, where the women's dresses formed a harmonious rainbow of quiet color. The Schrocks' house possessed a room large enough for the community to attend the twice-monthly church services, though we all sat shoulder-touching-shoulder. No one minded. This arrangement was far better than a cold barn, which was where some of us hosted the service when our turn came around. My gaze settled on Hannah, my wife of just four months. Proof that the Lord I served was, indeed, a merciful God. Her lovely face was turned upward as she focused her attention forward, her brow slightly furrowed as though in deep concentration on the bishop's words. No doubt she was compiling a list of questions to ask me on the way home. She always did, insisting that we discuss the details of the sermon, asking my opinion on various points. Some of which, to be honest, I hadn't heard.

That the good Lord had given me a woman as intelligent as she was lovely was further proof of His mercy for me. The fact that He'd refilled my tormented heart and empty bed…

Swallowing, I forced my thoughts away from the lingering pain that would forever accompany reminders of the loss three years ago that shook my world to the very foundations. Instead, I made myself focus on the words of the man standing at the front of the room.

Thankfully, he chose that moment to wind up the lengthy sermon with one final admonition—a quote from the *Confession of Faith*.

"May the Lord through His grace make us all fit and worthy, that no such calamity may befall any of us; but that we may be diligent, and so take heed to ourselves, that we may be found of Him in peace, without spot, and blameless. Amen."

The last word served as benediction as well as permission for a moment of fidgeting, and the men all around me shifted on their benches to relieve the stiffness of muscles denied the luxury of movement for nearly three hours. Bishop Beiler took his seat, and a communal breath was drawn and held. Would any of the other ministers feel led to add to the main sermon? A long silence stretched on as we waited. Breaths were expelled cautiously as we realized none of the other men gathered in the front of the room intended to speak on the subject. I formed a grateful prayer in my mind, further proof that my struggle to attain the patience of which the bishop spoke was not yet won.

Apparently, I wasn't the only one whose patience with the overly long sermon had expired. We hurried through the remainder of the service with unusual haste, and were then dismissed.

Jacob Schrock, the host of today's church service, addressed us as we rose. "We welcome you to share our lunch of meat and cheese, along with some of Abigail's *gut* bread and apple butter."

Indeed, the yeasty aroma of recently baked bread lingered in the air. The smell had plagued my empty stomach during the entire service. I glanced across the room at Hannah, who had stood and was brushing at a wrinkle in the lilac fabric of her skirt. She met my gaze, and I raised an eyebrow in an unspoken question. At the quick shake of her head, I smiled. The communal meal following a worship service was an enjoyable part of church Sundays during the summer, when the children could be let loose to run in the grass and burn off their energy, while the adults visited and the young people flirted. In the cold months of winter I was just as happy to miss the meal and hurry home to a lunch of sandwiches and chunky applesauce. Even more so because Hannah's parents and younger *schweschders*, with whom we lived, would probably take advantage of Abigail Schrock's hospitality. Rare were the times Hannah and I had the house to ourselves.

A small number of the community filed outside with us, our breath forming clouds of steam in the frigid air. While I waited for Hannah, I stamped my feet on the frozen ground and clasped the edges of my coat together against the cold.

"*Guder mariye,* Seth." Josiah Graber approached and stood beside me. "A *gut* main sermon today, *ya*?"

His lips twisted into a teasing smile that told me he, too, thought the bishop's sermon had lasted far longer than his message. We were of an age, Josiah and I, and because his family's farm bordered my father's, we had spent much of our childhood together. We'd enjoyed many a riotous outing during our *rumspringas* and had shared our deepest thoughts with one another, our reserves lowered and our words fueled by large quantities of the beer we both eschewed when we joined the church. Sometimes I knew the way Josiah's thoughts ran simply by the expression on his face. No doubt he knew the same about mine.

"*Ya*," I answered with a nod, my own lips curved into an answering grin. "The bishop has *much* wisdom, and is generous to share it with us *fully*."

The glint in his eyes told me he understood my comment, and we both broke into laughter. We were still laughing when Hannah and Ella, Josiah's wife, exited the house and joined us.

"Sorry to keep you waiting in the cold," Hannah said, coming to my side. "I wanted to hold the Yoders' new *boppli*."

"She's a precious little baby, isn't she?" Ella shifted her two-year-old from one hip to the other and pinned a teasing look on Hannah. "I thought for a while you weren't going to give her back to her *mamm*. You had that baby hungry look in your eyes."

Hannah and I exchanged a quick glance, and then she lowered her gaze. About her lips hovered a secretive smile that sent a tingle of fear through the base of my skull. I pushed the emotion away as the five of us headed for the pasture, where forty or so buggies waited in more-or-less straight lines.

When we approached Josiah's buggy, he took his son from Ella and I helped her climb up.

"How is that new Saddlebred working out for you?" he asked.

I glanced at our rig, where my new horse, hitched to the buggy, stamped his hooves on the frozen ground much as I had moments before.

"He's a bit skittish," I admitted. "The *Englisch* man I bought him from said he'd been trained to pull, but I don't think he's spent much time in the harness."

Ella reached down to take the toddler from Josiah, a scowl carving creases at the sides of her mouth. "You can't trust the *Englisch*."

"Oh, that's not true." My softhearted Hannah shook her head. "Most of them are as honest as Amish men. And besides, Lars is a fine horse." She smiled toward our rig. "He's just young, that's all. He needs time to become accustomed to his new job."

The confidence in her gaze as she looked at the horse she'd named Lars soothed the nagging doubt that I'd been hoodwinked by the *Englisch* horse salesman. Hannah had accompanied me to select the animal, and she had taken a shine to Lars immediately. I had my eye on a different animal, several years older with a sturdier build, but she argued that Lars—she'd named him on the spot—would fill out as he grew. The good news she'd shared with me only the night before had created a tender spot in me for my beautiful wife, part excitement and part fearful anxiety, so that I could deny her nothing that day. Lars had come home with us, hitched to the back of the buggy pulled by her *daed*'s horse.

"Besides," Hannah went on, "we've only hitched him to our courting buggy, which is pretty light. When he's used to that, we'll let him try *Daed*'s family wagon. The heavier load will settle him."

We bid Josiah and Ella goodbye, and made our way toward our own rig. Hannah gave Lars a gentle rub on the muzzle as we passed, and he responded with an equine nod and a welcoming nicker. I couldn't help but laugh. The animal was obviously as fond of Hannah as she was of him.

I placed my hands on her waist, still slender beneath her thick black coat, and lifted her onto the bench. As Hannah had mentioned, we owned only a small courting buggy that seated two. Because of its open carriage it was a pretty cold ride in the winter, but it did provide the option of riding alone with my wife.

Someday soon I'd need to look into an enclosed buggy, suitable for a family.

While I rounded the front, my gaze swept over the fittings, and I gave a tug to the leather pocket to make sure the shaft was settled securely. When I climbed up beside Hannah, she scooted close and covered my lap with the thick quilts she'd already spread across herself. I clucked my tongue and gently shook the reins, and Lars lurched forward.

The buggy jerked, and Hannah gave a startled laugh. "Looks like Lars was eager for the service to end too."

I looked sideways at her. "Too? Did you think the bishop's sermon was a little long?"

"Not me, silly. You. I saw you fidgeting."

She shifted nearer, whether for warmth or simply to be closer to me, I didn't know or care. The feel of our sides pressed together the length of our bodies, even with several thick layers of clothing between us, settled a comfortable feeling in the pit of my stomach that generated a warmth all its own.

"I didn't fidget. I made a point of not fidgeting."

"Maybe, but your eyes were fixed more often on me than on the bishop." She tilted her head and displayed a charming dimple. "I always notice when you're watching me."

"And who could blame me? You're much prettier to look at than Bishop Beiler." I grinned as I applied the reins to steer Lars from the Schrocks' property onto the road just behind Josiah's rig. Soon the *clip-clop* of a dozen horses' hooves on the pavement filled the chilly air as the line of buggies carrying people who had opted not to stay for Abigail's bread and apple butter made their way home.

Hannah broke the silence. "I think Ella guessed our secret. She watched me with such a knowing expression while I was cuddling the baby."

Again, the familiar shaft of fear shot down my spine. As though she sensed my reaction, my wife slipped a hand onto my thigh beneath the cover of the quilt and gave my leg a comforting squeeze.

"There's nothing to fear, Seth. Doesn't the Bible say, *Fear not?*" With a final squeeze, she withdrew her hand. "I will be fine. You'll see."

How I longed to share her confidence. But though she had developed an uncanny knack for guessing my thoughts, she could not see the vivid memories that haunted me, nor feel the depth of my horror at the sight of my first wife lying in bed, white faced and weary, the coverings around her stained with the evidence of yet another miscarriage. Sweet Rachel, whom I'd loved since childhood, had not survived the night. A few days later, another grave was dug in the community's cemetery, and Rachel was buried holding our tiny but perfectly formed son.

But that was three years ago, and God had been gracious to me. I'd never thought it possible to love another woman until Hannah's family moved to Lancaster County and bought a farm in our small district. What she saw in me, a grief-stricken widower, the second son of his father with few prospects besides working as a hired hand on the family farm, I could not imagine. But I thanked God for her, for my second chance at happiness, every day of my life.

Still, when Hannah revealed to me that we would welcome a child of our own in the summer, I couldn't stop the fearful thoughts that coursed through my mind. What if she miscarried? Rachel's gut-wrenching sobs in the night after the first two losses haunted my dreams. And my own inaction, which caused her death. Why hadn't I overruled her and insisted on taking her to the hospital when the bleeding started in the third pregnancy? Why had I allowed her to continue with the household chores?

That's why I insisted that Hannah not share our good news with anyone, even family, until the evidence became obvious in her thickening waist. And I had already determined, though I had not yet told her, that at the first sign of distress I would hire a car and take her to the hospital. No dallying around, waiting for spotting to stop, drinking herbal concoctions that the midwife brought. I would take no chances with my Hannah.

The road climbed a slight incline, and Lars responded with a surge of energy and an increase in pace. Josiah's buggy was several lengths ahead of us, and I preferred to maintain a safe distance.

I reached for the brake lever. "Whoa, there," I called in a low voice, at the same time applying the gentlest force. Lars responded with a toss of his head, and his hooves clapped loudly against the pavement as he pranced against the restraint.

Hannah laughed. "Maybe he was trained to be a racehorse before he learned to pull. He wants to be in the front, not following tamely behind."

"He needs to learn who's in control." I pulled a bit more firmly on the brake lever.

The roar of an engine behind us heralded the approach of a car. A loud rattle gave evidence of a damaged muffler, and as the automobile approached the line of buggies, the driver revved the engine, filling the air with a thunderous clatter. I glanced back. A rusty green vehicle with two occupants zoomed toward us, close enough that, when it passed the rearmost buggy, less than a yard's space separated the side window from the buggy's wheel. The horn began to honk, and the passenger window lowered.

"Hey, *Aim-ish*," a young man shouted. "Pretty cold outside. You got heaters in them things?"

The car passed the second and third buggies, both of which edged as far to the right of the buggy lane as possible.

"What are they doing?" Hannah's voice held a note of concern.

"*Englisch* teenagers." I tugged on the leather strap to direct Lars closer to the edge of the pavement. For the most part, *Englisch* and Amish lived a peaceful coexistence in Lancaster County, but every so often we were subjected to jeers and taunts about our simple ways.

Lars snorted, his ears jerking to stiff attention as his neck shot upward like a giraffe's. The car gained speed as it neared. Laughter from the young *Englisch* man leaning halfway out the lowered window was drowned out by the loud rattle of the inoperative muffler, which roared through the cold afternoon air. Lars tossed his head, clearly jittery, and I wrapped the leather reins firmly around my hand as the car approached us.

"Easy now," I said in a tone as soothing as I could make it, but the nervous horse probably couldn't hear because the driver chose the moment he zoomed past us to lay on his horn.

Lars bolted. The buggy shot forward, and Hannah gave a startled shout as she grasped the edge of the bench for balance.

"Whoa!" I called, pulling back on the reins with one hand and the brake lever with the other.

In response, Lars issued a high-pitched neigh that sounded eerily like a human screech. He tried to dash forward, but the buggy's brakes and my firm grip on the reins impeded his progress. Instead of forward, he bolted sideways. The front wheel of the buggy slid off the pavement, and the resulting lurch jolted Hannah and me across the bench. The horse's hooves tromped on the frozen ground beside the road. Fighting desperately to regain control, I couldn't be sure what happened next. Perhaps Lars's hooves slid on a patch of ice, or maybe it was the wheel. I found myself pitched sideways, my body crashing into Hannah's, as the buggy tilted at an impossible angle.

We're going to flip.

The certainty struck me a second before the horse fell, taking the buggy with him. Hannah screamed as the buggy teetered and then careened sideways. Her hands flailed the air, reaching for something to anchor her as she was pitched forward. Releasing the reins, I grabbed for her while holding on to the brake lever for stability. Our hands grappled for each other, but my fingers closed around nothing. Hannah became airborne. For a split second I saw her, terror plain on the face she turned my way, and then she tumbled headfirst toward the icy ground for a heartbeat before the buggy crashed. Her scream, high and piercing, cut off abruptly.

I managed to kick off the floorboard and flew through the air. With a jolt that knocked the breath from my lungs, I hit the ice a few feet clear of the overturned buggy. Something in my shoulder snapped, and I was dimly aware that pain shot through my body. I climbed to my feet, trying to gulp air into my paralyzed lungs, and staggered toward the place where my wife lay unmoving, pinned beneath the front wheel.

"Hannah!"

My cry came out as a choked sob as I reached for her, intent on freeing her from the buggy's crushing weight. My right arm refused to cooperate, but I grabbed for her with my left.

"Seth, no." Strong hands halted me. Josiah's. "It's not safe to move her."

The sense of his words cut through my stunned brain. If the fall had damaged her spine, moving her could prove disastrous. Instead, I fell to my knees beside her, dimly aware that we were surrounded by black-garbed people. A woman's quiet sobs rose toward the frigid sky as Josiah directed someone to run quick for the nearest phone and call an ambulance.

I crept forward, my eyes fixed on my wife's face. Her *kapp* had been torn off, and I reached to smooth a lock of honey-blond hair away from her eyes. As my finger touched her skin, a terrible realization struck me with the weight of a millstone, dragging me down into a dark despair that was both devastating and horribly familiar.

No ambulance could help her. My Hannah was dead.

Two

One Year Later

Milk streamed into the pail in a rhythmic pattern my hands performed automatically. My right shoulder ached, and I paused for a moment to stretch my arm. Though I'd regained full range of motion after the surgery that repaired the tendons and bones injured during the accident, a nagging pain in the damaged muscles persisted. The *Englisch* surgeon said it probably always would. It was an ache I must learn to live with, to ignore and move on.

I had many such pains, my shoulder the least of them.

The cow stood patiently as I drained her udder, her tail giving a periodic swish as if to shoo a fly from her flank. The gesture was habit only because flies were rare during the winter months. At least Caroline took care to avoid my head resting against her warm side. Our other milk cow, Delilah, lived up to her name. She maintained a far less accepting attitude toward milking. More than once I'd felt the painful flick of her tail across my cheek.

My *bruder* Aaron laughed at me when I once told him that Delilah took a perverse pleasure in slapping at me, but he didn't know our cows as well as I did. Though they looked nearly identical, they had distinct personalities. Delilah, outwardly as docile as a proper milk cow should be, harbored a pent-up streak of rebellion that occasionally broke free in small but frustrating ways. I'd learned to place the bucket carefully and keep a sharp eye on her hind legs, ready to grab the handle and rescue the milk from her well-aimed kicks.

I never had to worry about mild-natured Caroline, who always seemed grateful to be relieved of the pressure in her heavy udder. As if to prove my point, Caroline turned her head and fixed a deep brown eye on me. Her placid expression was almost kind, as if to say, *I would never hurt you, Seth.*

With a smile at my own fanciful thoughts, I gave her girth an affectionate slap. My mind often wandered down wayward paths during this quiet time of milking. I always began the twice-daily chore intending to spend the time in prayer, and felt guilty when I ended up pondering something frivolous, such as bovine personalities.

But better shallow thoughts than the dire memories that returned so often to plague me, bringing with them the pain that carved fresh gouges in my heart every day.

Gott, *show me the way to peace. I beseech You for mercy.*

I shut my eyes against the two visions that haunted me so often they had become intertwined. Two beautiful women. Two wives. Two tragic deaths.

And both my fault.

Forgive me. The often-repeated prayer cried out from an agony rooted deeply in my soul. But relief did not come. It never did.

The creaking of the barn door alerted me to someone's approach. I lifted my head and leaned sideways on my stool, craning to see around Caroline. Night had fully fallen during my time in the barn, and the light from the oil lamp cast a warm glow on my sister-in-law, Saloma, as she slipped inside.

"Hello." She cradled a steaming mug between her hands. "I thought you'd like some coffee to warm you."

"*Danke.*" I didn't tell her that my hands were already warm from their labor, but I took the mug with a grateful nod and sipped from it before returning to my chore.

Saloma leaned against the shelf where the lamp flickered and rubbed her upper arms briskly. The roundness of her belly showed starkly in the golden light, the cause of yet another stab of pain that I experienced a dozen or more times a day.

"Where is your cape?" I asked, my tone slightly chiding. "You shouldn't be out in the cold without it."

She gave me a soft smile. "I'll be fine for the short walk to the barn and back. I wanted to ask you something. A favor."

The flow of Caroline's milk slowed. I made sure each teat had been fully emptied, and then moved the nearly full pail to rest beside the others, ready to strain and run through the separator.

"What do you need?" I asked as I resettled my hat on my head.

"Can you take *Mamm* and Becky and me to Strasburg tomorrow? I want to shop for a gift for my *schweschder*, and *Mamm* would like to stop by the fabric store."

Saloma's *schweschder* and brother-in-law, who married last October, had spent the winter months visiting their relatives, as was our tradition for newly married couples. Because Johann's family cabinet shop had received several large jobs and could not spare him every weekend, the couple had been forced to limit their visits and were only now finishing the rounds. The host family customarily bestowed wedding gifts during these visits, so naturally Saloma would want to find something nice to give her *schweschder*.

A string of memories flitted through my mind. Gifts I'd received from Rachel's family, and later, from Hannah's. I'd left them all with my former in-laws. I didn't need them, and certainly didn't want the visual reminder of my failure as a husband. The memories were painful enough.

In an instant, the impact of Saloma's request slammed against me, nearly knocking me from the milking stool. My body turned to stone. An unbearable weight pressed against my chest, making breathing impossible. I was being asked to drive a pregnant woman. The warm glow of the oil lamp disappeared as a heavy darkness descended over me, and the barn became as black as the cavern in my soul.

Why would they ask this of me? Do they not know? Can't they understand? What if…

I could not finish the thought. Drive the women to Strasburg? No. I could not do it. I *would* not.

With the hard-won control that I had nearly perfected over the past year, I kept my features rigid while I battled the panic that gripped my chest. Amish men must exercise strict discipline, regardless of the strength of the emotions that raged inside.

Forcing my chest to expand, I drew in a deep breath. When I could move, I turned my back on Saloma under the excuse of retrieving the post-milking disinfectant from the shelf on the back wall.

"I'm sorry, but tomorrow we are doing repairs to the chicken coop. Aaron needs my help."

"I asked Aaron, and he said between him and Noah and *Daed*, he could spare you if you don't mind the trip."

Aaron, my oldest *bruder* and Saloma's husband, ran the farm. Two years ago, *Daed* had suffered a stroke, mild enough that he could still function, but he moved slower, and with a shuffling step that wasn't as steady as before. Aaron had slowly taken over more and more of the management of the farm since that time. Ownership of the family farm would have come to him eventually anyway, so *Daed*'s condition merely accelerated the transition in leadership.

Of course Aaron could spare me. Between him, *Daed*, and my brother-in-law, Noah, they could handle everything that needed to be done. I was nothing more than an extra pair of hands, largely superfluous except during the growing season, when tending the land required more effort. The widower *bruder* who took up space in the overcrowded house.

Using slow, measured movements at odds with the turbulence in my soul, I applied the disinfectant to Caroline's teats. Only when I was certain I could speak in an even tone did I answer.

"I am happy to hitch the buggy for you, but the trip is only nine miles. Between you and Becky, I'm sure you can manage the driving."

I returned the disinfectant to its place on the shelf and turned to find that Saloma had crossed the distance between us. She stood a mere foot away, peering up into my face with eyes so full of compassion that something twisted in my chest.

"It is time, Seth."

Her low tone was infused with an unspoken message. She knew full well what she was asking. How stupid of me to think that my family, those with whom I spent my daily life, had not noticed that I had not driven a buggy since the accident. I'd ridden with others, but not once had I taken up the reins myself.

A wild rage rose up from the dark emptiness in me. Angry blood heated my face, and my pulse pounded in my ears. It was not their place to decide when the time had come for me to do *anything*. What business was I of theirs?

Immediately, I stuffed the anger down. Of course I was their business. I was family.

And maybe they were right. It had been a year. The fact that they trusted me—that Aaron trusted me with his wife and unborn child—snuffed out the last flicker of fury. Maybe it *was* time.

Drawing a deep breath into lungs that still resisted, I managed a nod. "*Ya.* I will drive you." Did Saloma have any idea the effort those words cost me?

If so, she gave no sign. A soft smile curved her lips. "*Gut.*" Then she clapped her hands and grinned. "We can treat ourselves to lunch at Katie's Kitchen."

For her benefit, I forced a smile. "That will be fun."

When she'd left the barn, I untied Caroline and carried the milk pails to the attached shed, where we kept the separator. Working hard to clear my mind of turmoil, I focused instead on the task at hand. First I poured the fresh milk through the strainer and then into the separator. While I rotated the handle, I kept an eye on the cream spout, which had been known to leak if the cream screw loosened. Cream trickled in a steady stream into the pail I set in place, while the skimmed milk ran into a bucket below.

When Naomi and Johann visited, I'd need to stay in the *daadi haus* with my *grossmammi* so they could sleep in my room. To be honest, I'd thought a lot about moving there permanently. When Saloma's baby arrived, that would bring the total number living in the main house to ten. The three little ones—two belonging to Saloma and Aaron, and one to my *schweschder* Becky and her husband, Noah—occupied the nursery already. Noah had plans to buy a farm of his own, but that was a few years away. My *grossmammi, Mammi,* would welcome me in the *daadi haus,* which was connected to the big house by a breezeway, but there was only one bedroom. I didn't mind sleeping on a pallet on the floor for a few nights, but permanently? And one day she would be gone, and *Mamm* and *Daed* would live there.

The separator can emptied. I moved the skim milk to one side, ready to feed to our hog, and then proceeded to strain the other pail of whole milk for the family's use. The cream would be picked up by the milk truck in the morning, ready for sale.

What I needed to do was find another place to live. Aaron didn't need me here. Oh, he would never say that. I would always be welcome, and especially once Noah and Becky left. I could even build a small house on the property next to the *daadi haus* where I could live alone, out of everyone's way. Though Aaron was perfectly capable of running the farm on his own, he'd be glad of the extra pair of hands.

But that's what I would always be—an extra.

I awoke the next morning to a tightness in my chest that was familiar, but more intense than usual. Today I would take the women of my family to Strasburg. I would hitch up the horse, take up the reins, and guide our family buggy down nine miles of paved road. My hands trembled as I slipped my suspenders over my shoulders. Darkness hovered at the edge of my thoughts like a storm cloud, black with rain and rumbling with thunder.

Light of the world, shine on us this day.

With an effort, I stilled my trembling hands and descended the stairs.

An air of excitement hovered around the breakfast table. The women anticipated the treat of the day's outing. *Mamm* smiled brighter than usual as she wished me *"Guder mariye."* She set a platter of thick-sliced fried ham in the center of the table, the source of the savory aroma that filled the house.

Daed had already taken his place at the head of the table, where he perused the latest issue of the *Budget*. At the stove, Becky ladled gravy from a skillet with one hand and bounced little Sadie on her hip with the other.

The thunder of small footsteps pounded down the stairs, heralding the arrival of my three-year-old nephews. Saloma turned from her place at the work counter, a pan of gooey cinnamon rolls in her hands, and leveled a stern look on her twins.

"No running in the house," she commanded. "Did you wash your hands?"

Mark nodded, while Luke extended his arms and splayed his fingers as proof.

"Okay, then. Go to the table and practice sitting still."

"Wike at church?" Luke asked.

"*Lllllllike,*" she repeated, emphasizing the proper way to pronounce the *L*. "Exactly like at church."

Both boys groaned as they climbed onto their chairs. Putting my discomfort out of my mind, I hid a grin as I slid onto my own. Three hours was a long time for little ones to sit quietly. Especially boys with as much energy as these two. I sympathized completely. Many were the times Aaron and I drew stern, disapproving glares from *Mamm* when we were young and failed to contain our boyish restlessness during the service.

"At least now you only have to sit still for a few minutes," I offered by way of consolation.

Identical grins flashed onto their faces as Becky set a huge bowl of creamy gravy beside the ham. Next followed *Mammi* with a dish of fried potatoes and onions.

Noah and Aaron descended the stairs together just as Saloma added a bowl of fluffy scrambled eggs.

"Did you wash your hands?" she asked her husband with a playful smile as he took his seat.

With the same gesture as his son, Aaron held up his hands for inspection. "Yes, ma'am. Even used soap."

The table laden with food and the full complement of family seated, a comfortable silence fell. *Daed* lowered his head, eyes closed, and we all did the same. I mentally formed a prayer of thanksgiving, for the bounty of food and for each person around the table. I'd just moved on to the topic most heavy on my heart, our safety during the day's journey, when the silence was broken by eighteen-month-old Sadie babbling a string of unintelligible words. I cracked open an eye to see Becky put a finger over her daughter's lips and make a show of closing her eyes and bowing her head. The toddler did fall silent, but her bright eyes circled the table. She giggled when she caught me looking at her, and with a quick grin I shut my eyes and continued my prayer.

"Amen." *Daed* ended the prayer and reached for the eggs in front of him. "While you're in town, would you stop at Zimmerman's and pick up a can of creosote conditioner?"

An everyday errand, one such as any man might perform during a perfectly normal outing to town. The task gave me a measure of comfort. "*Ya,* sure."

"Oh, good!" Becky grinned across the table at Saloma. "I love Zimmerman's."

Zimmerman's Hardware Store stocked a huge variety of items, everything from kitchen mops to tractor parts. A person could wander up and down the aisles for hours, though I hoped Becky didn't plan on spending that much time there. At least they offered a few well-placed benches up near the front where I could wait until the women were finished browsing.

"I want to stop by Eldreth Pottery for sure." Saloma ladled a helping of gravy over the fried potatoes on her plate. "I think I can find something nice for my sister there."

Mark raised his head and fixed an eager glance on his *mamm.* "Can we go?"

Hope sprang into his *bruder's* eyes as well as they awaited the answer.

Without hesitation, Saloma replied with a firm, "No. You and Sadie will stay with *Mammi* and *Grossdaadi.* This shopping trip is for grown-up women only."

A forkful of eggs hovering in front of my mouth, I cleared my throat.

She shot an apologetic look toward me. "And *Onkel* Seth because he is driving us."

Both boys drooped.

"On the way, I'd like to stop by Lettie Miller's to return a book I borrowed from her," *Mamm* said. "Would that be okay, Seth?"

Something in her tone put me on alert, and I looked toward her. She calmly sliced a bite of ham and speared it with her fork, her expression serene. A bit too serene, perhaps? I intercepted a quick glance between Saloma and Becky, and then they, too, became absorbed in their plates. The three definitely had a plan, something they'd not shared with me.

It didn't take much pondering to figure out what that plan might be. If I remembered correctly, Lettie Miller had two unmarried daughters living at home.

A shock of certainty slapped at me. I laid my fork on the edge of my plate and sat back in my chair. Recent comments rose up from memory, innocent enough at the time that I had not put them together. *Mamm*'s soft gaze as she said good night and added, "I worry about you, Seth. I do not want you to be lonely." And yesterday, Saloma's comment as I swooped one of the twins up into the air and his giggles pealed. "The boys love you so. You are good with children." She had not added, "It's a shame you don't have any of your own," because that would have been too hurtful, but I saw the unspoken comment in her eyes. Innocent and caring remarks in themselves, but combined they led to a conclusion.

The women in my family were plotting to find me a third wife.

I waged a private battle while staring at the food in front of me, taking care to keep my face frozen into a placid expression. So driving was not sufficient progress toward my recovery. Apparently, they had decided that one year of being a widower was long enough. Pain and anger flared in equal measures. Anger, because I could not believe these women who loved me could be so blind to my still-raw grief. Didn't they know that the agony of Hannah's tragic death had not receded even a tiny bit? That the sound of Rachel's last, unsteady breath haunted me when I lay in my bed listening to the night sounds from the other rooms in the house?

Pain, because I relived the moments before the accident over and over, torturing myself with questions.

Had I pulled too hard on the brake lever, and thus aggravated skittish Lars's panic over the sound of the automobile's horn? Had my weight crashing against Hannah as I grappled for her hand proven to be the tipping point, like the proverbial straw that broke the camel's back? What if, instead of leaning toward her, I'd thrown myself in the opposite direction and used my weight as a counterbalance? Would it have made a difference and kept the buggy on all four wheels? Or what if I'd done the reverse—flung myself toward her, grabbed her by the waist and kicked off the floorboard with enough force that we both would be thrown far enough that the buggy wouldn't have crushed her?

An awkward silence around me drew me from my torment, and I realized everyone was staring at me, waiting for an answer to *Mamm's* question. Fighting for a controlled tone, I nodded, "*Ya*, of course we can stop by the Millers'."

Let *Mamm* return her book, and let all of them take a moment to visit with the Miller women. I would wait in the buggy.

THREE

After breakfast Aaron helped me hitch our buggy to Rosie. We worked in silence, outwardly in the comfortable companionship of a lifetime of laboring side by side. Inside, though, the storm cloud with which I'd awoken threatened to break. I fastened the collar around Rosie's neck, and then Aaron buckled the harness. I followed him, checking the snugness of the straps and testing the security of each buckle. We fastened Rosie in, and again I checked every connection.

When I began a third inspection, Aaron laid a hand on my arm. "It is *gut*, Seth."

His soft voice and the understanding in his brown gaze struck me like a hammer, and I struggled to remain composed. Swallowing hard, I nodded and stepped back. It was then that I noticed the women had exited the house and stood watching.

"Are we ready?" Saloma asked brightly.

"*Ya.*" Aaron helped the three women into the buggy while I battled a compulsion to check the fittings one more time.

When all were seated in the back, I climbed up and took my place in the front. If a slight tremble had returned to my hands, my family kindly said nothing. I took up the reins, piling the extra length on the bench beside me. Rosie's ears flicked back, waiting for me to tell her what to do. An irrational fear seized me, clenching my insides with a fist. I could still refuse, make up an excuse of sudden illness. Too much gravy at breakfast. My mouth opened, the words on the verge of being spoken.

A movement at the kitchen window drew my eye. *Mammi* stood there, watching from inside. When our eyes met, she smiled and raised a hand in farewell. At the simple gesture, one that might be given on any ordinary day to any ordinary buggy driver, a bit of the panic that had gripped me receded. With a soft *chuck-chuck* and a slight shake of the reins, I prodded Rosie forward.

The world did not end. I did not collapse from nerves, nor did terror stop my heart from beating. Instead, the buggy bounced the length of our rough driveway. The slight jolt when the wheels left the dirt and found the pavement set my teeth on edge, and I fought to ignore the awful resurgence of that fateful afternoon a year ago.

But this was a different day. Rosie was far steadier than poor Lars, whose presence I could not tolerate since the accident that had taken my Hannah from me. He had been sold at a mud auction a few weeks afterward. This buggy was heavier, more solid, and enclosed. Realization struck me, the force of it almost taking my breath. I could do this. A cautious sense of victory swelled, and my grasp on the reins relaxed.

The Millers lived in the district just south of ours. The oldest Miller son, Joel, was several years my senior, but I knew him from various gatherings when our districts combined for things like barn raisings and singings. Because their farm was on the way to Strasburg, we headed there first.

Mamm spoke from behind me, where she sat between Saloma and Becky, swathed in quilts for warmth. "I hope Lettie isn't in the middle of a chore. I don't want to disturb her, but it seems a shame to drop off the book and not spend a few moments visiting."

Hospitality being what it was, Lettie would stop any task she was involved in and invite us to sit down for coffee and a slice of cake or pie or whatever she had to offer. The interruption would not pose a hardship, either. The districts in this part of Lancaster County consisted mostly of farmers, so our lives were led in isolation, necessitated by distance and the all-encompassing work of running our farms. Visits, planned or spontaneous, were an occasion to be enjoyed.

Except by me, in this case. I may have taken a giant stride toward conquering my fear of driving a buggy, but the idea of sitting across the table from the Miller sisters, idly sipping coffee and pretending I didn't know the scheme of every woman in the room, left me colder than any February wind.

I answered in a mild tone. "The longer we stay, the less time we'll be able to spend in Strasburg."

The comment was met with silence. I fought the impulse to turn my head and see their expressions but focused instead on guiding Rosie down the long, frozen path leading to the Miller house. Snow covered the fields on either side of the driveway, shallow enough that the pattern of straight rows plowed into the land beneath was clearly visible. As I pulled the buggy to a stop in front of the house, I scanned the area and, with a surge of relief, found my excuse to avoid the uncomfortable encounter. The doors to the nearby barn stood open, and inside I glimpsed Joel crouching beside a piece of equipment.

After I'd lifted the three women from the buggy and set them on the ground, I nodded toward the barn. "Enjoy your visit. I'll go and see if I can help Joel with whatever he's doing."

Clearly disturbed, *Mamm*'s forehead creased. "But don't you want to come inside and say hello?"

"Just for a minute," Saloma added. "We won't stay long."

"You go ahead." I kept my smile guileless. "Give me a shout when you're ready to leave."

I left them standing there and headed toward the barn, congratulating myself on avoiding what would surely have been an awkward situation.

Parts of a disassembled plowshare lay scattered around the floor. Joel, who rubbed at a gauge wheel with a cloth, looked up at my approach.

"Seth. *Guder mariye.*"

When he started to rise to greet me, I stopped him with a wave and instead squatted beside him. Nodding at the plow parts, I asked, "Can I give you a hand here?"

"Nah. Just cleaning everything up before I put it back together." He held up the spoke-shaped object. "This gauge was starting to slip a bit last year. I thought it might need to be replaced, but I think it was just loose."

During the winter months, when the land lay dormant beneath a covering of snow and ice, farmers took advantage of their free time to maintain their equipment. We'd done the same with ours, making sure everything was in good working order for the coming planting season.

The gauge clean, he set it down and picked up the jointer knife and a pad of steel wool. "What brings you here?"

"We're heading to Strasburg, and *Mamm* wanted to return a book she'd borrowed."

A female voice I recognized as Joel's wife called from the house. "Joel, why don't you and Seth come inside? There's fresh coffee."

He tossed the wool pad on the ground and, opening his mouth to answer, started to rise.

I stopped him with a hand. "I'd rather not, if you don't mind."

With a startled look, he studied my face a moment. Realization dawned on him, and he gave a quick nod. Retrieving the pad, he shouted an answer. "I can't right now. I'm in the middle of something."

"Thanks," I mumbled. "I got the impression that the book wasn't the only reason my *mamm* wanted to stop by."

His features softened, and he tossed the steel wool toward me. "Here. You do this while I check out the moldboard."

Glad for something to do, I picked up the jointer knife, and we worked for a while in companionable silence. Not five minutes had passed before the sound of shoes crunching on snow alerted me to someone's approach.

Turning, I spied one of the Miller girls heading toward the barn with a steaming mug in each hand. I didn't bother to hide a low groan. Apparently, *Mamm* would not have her plan thwarted and had decided on a different approach. Joel gave me a sympathetic look.

To ignore her would be unforgivably impolite, so I stood and turned as she entered the barn.

"I brought something to warm you." The young woman handed Joel a mug first and then turned to me.

Joel performed the introduction, his tone resigned. "Seth, you've met my sister Hannah, haven't you?"

The name hit me like a brick, and the hand I'd been in the process of extending shook so violently I shoved it behind my back, afraid to take the mug. Hannah. A common enough name, but hot anger flashed through my skull. How could *Mamm* be so unfeeling as to confront me with someone who shared the name of my beloved wife?

This Hannah must have seen my emotions in my face because her eyes widened and she took a backward step. Guilt flooded me, dousing the angry flames. I plastered on a calm expression. The poor girl before me had done nothing wrong, and it was rude of me to make her uncomfortable.

With rigid control, I halted the trembling and extended a steady hand toward the coffee. I even managed a quick smile. "*Danke.*"

Her hesitation clear, she stretched her arm to hand me the mug without coming closer. "*Mamm* said to tell you there's warm biscuits and apple butter in the house if you'd care to join us."

Her gaze failed to meet mine, and I experienced another stab of remorse. She was young, probably not yet twenty, with round eyes and wisps of curly dark hair showing beneath her *kapp*.

"Tell her I appreciate the offer, but I had a big breakfast. I couldn't eat another bite." I sipped coffee and then lifted the mug. "But *danke* for bringing this."

She stood hesitantly a moment longer and then hurried from the barn. I watched her cross the thinning layer of snow and disappear into the house, and then I turned to find Joel studying me.

"How long has it been since…" He cleared his throat. "Since the accident?"

"A year." I clipped my answer short, not out of ill manners but because whenever I spoke of it, an invisible fist griped my throat and threatened to squeeze it shut.

"I'm sorry."

I answered with a nod and looked away from the pity in his face. Crouching again to the floor, I set the coffee mug down and picked up the steel wool. Joel returned to his task. This time, though, the silence that fell between us as we worked was heavy and uncomfortable. I forced my thoughts to focus on the task, rubbing the jointer knife with smooth, even pressure.

By the time *Mamm* and the others exited the house, ready to continue our journey, that was the cleanest jointer knife in all of Lancaster County.

Strasburg was a sprawling town that bustled with a bizarre blend of Amish and *Englisch* trade. Many of the businesses were built for the benefit of *Englisch* tourists, and thousands flocked there each year to visit Amish country. The historic town had been built centuries ago by French immigrants. The Amish came later, attracted by the lush farmland that sprawled in all directions from the town. Now, those who shared my faith lived and worked side by side with the *Englisch,* separated by virtue of our beliefs, our culture, and our ways. In the world but not of it, as the Lord instructed.

A tourist attraction called the Amish Village offered visitors a look at life inside an Old Order Amish farmhouse and a one-room schoolhouse. Though some of my friends laughed at the idea of a sterile house furnished to look as if someone might really live there, I'd been through the place a couple of times and thought it pretty well done. There were even real animals in the barn. And, of course, before the visitor left, they were invited to browse a gift shop, where they could purchase a variety of souvenirs to remind them of their trip to Amish land.

Another of Strasburg's popular attractions was the Choo Choo Barn, a gigantic model train layout where the Pennsylvania Dutch countryside had been re-created in miniature. Trains traveled around the layout, past animated figures that depicted the local culture and lifestyle, including even a barn raising. When Rachel and I were dating, she loved to visit the Choo Cho Barn. Thankfully, that attraction lay on the far side of Strasburg, and we would not be going that way today. One less set of memories to haunt me.

We rode past the Amish Village on our way into the town proper, and I noted in passing that the parking lot held a small number of automobiles. Tourism would pick up when the weather warmed, but apparently a few hardy folk didn't mind braving the cold Pennsylvania winter.

"Zimmerman's first?" I asked. The hardware store was the logical first stop because we would encounter that establishment on our way into town.

"I thought we could we go to Eldreth Pottery first. That's the farthest, and then we can work our way back and stop at Zimmerman's last." Saloma leaned forward to touch my shoulder. "Is that okay with you, Seth?"

I shrugged. On this trip I was the driver, nothing more. Other than picking up the creosote conditioner for *Daed*, I had no agenda besides chauffeuring the women around.

Not true. My second goal, a new one and of the utmost importance to me, was to avoid any marriageable females they might attempt to introduce me to. I hoped the Millers were the only trap they intended to spring on me today, but I couldn't be sure.

"Eldreth Pottery it is," I replied, and urged Rosie into a slightly quicker pace.

In my peripheral vision I saw Becky lean forward to speak to both me and Saloma. "Before we go to Eldreth's, maybe we ought to stop by that new place Lettie Miller told us about. I'd kind of like to see what they have. We know what Eldreth's has to offer, so we can always go there if you don't find anything you like."

"*Ya,* it's a good plan," *Mamm* agreed.

"What new place?" I asked.

Becky leaned even further forward so I could see her scowl. "If you'd come inside the Millers' to visit with us, you would know."

I did turn my head then, just to give them all a chance to see my stern expression. "Joel appreciated my help with his plowshare. I felt more comfortable lending a hand with that than sitting in a kitchen with the women."

Before I turned back, I held *Mamm*'s gaze for a long moment, until I was sure she took my meaning. She looked away first, her eyes lowering to the quilt on her lap, but not before I caught a glimpse of loving determination in those brown depths. Sighing, I faced forward. Someday soon I would have to confront her. She needed to understand that I was not interested in marrying again. Not now. Not ever.

"Where is this place?" I asked.

"Out toward Ronks, Lettie said." Saloma's hand appeared beside my head, pointing. "Turn left on Star Road."

I followed her directions, navigating the turn onto the well-kept two-lane road that was, at the moment, free of traffic, Amish or *Englisch*. I'd been out here before, of course. There were few places in Lancaster County I had not seen. During my *rumspringa*, Josiah and I bought an old Ford from an *Englisch* guy who let us keep it at his house because neither of our families would allow us to bring it home. For a couple of years we spent nearly all of our free hours in that car, once even driving as far as Philadelphia. I don't know which of us was sorrier to sell it when the time came to turn our backs on the world and make the lifelong commitment to our faith.

Rosie pulled us past a harness shop and a mower service, both surrounded by wide-open farmland. Because the sun was out and the temperature tolerable today, the dairy farmer on the right side of the road had turned out his cattle, which stood in the snow clustered around several mounds of hay.

I saw the place at the same time *Mamm* announced, "There it is. Plain Man's Pottery."

A squat, wood-and-stone building, that years ago had housed a small general market, now bore a sign hanging above the wide window to the left of the door. *Plain Man's Pottery.* In smaller letters beneath, *Handcrafted Amish Earthenware and Stoneware. Lessons Available.* Inside the window, a display of bowls, pitchers, and other dishes had been artistically arranged on shelves.

A buggy stood at one side of the building, a car parked beside it. I guided Rosie in that direction, our wheels crunching on frozen gravel.

We rolled to a stop beside the car. Behind the building, a brown mare stood in a small paddock, apparently having been unharnessed after she had delivered her charge to the store. The owner, probably, because a customer to this small establishment wouldn't expect to be here long enough to unhitch the horse.

I helped the women climb down from the buggy and then walked to the front to inspect Rosie's harness.

Mamm stopped on her way to the front of the building. "Aren't you coming in?"

I slipped my hand beneath the back pan and ran it across the horse's warm back. "How long are you planning to be?"

She planted her hands on her hips. "We won't know until we get inside and see how much they have to look at, will we?"

Chuckling, I checked the throatlatch and crown. Secure but loose enough to be comfortable for the mare. "Okay, I'm coming in."

We followed Saloma and Becky through the door, a dangling bell announcing our entry. The store was even smaller than I expected. Including the one in the front window, the room contained a total of five display shelves. I'd been inside Eldreth Pottery's showroom many times. This place was barely the size of one corner. The pieces lining these shelves lacked the variety of painted designs for which Eldreth's wares were known. Yet I liked the look of these plain pieces. There was no absence of color here, and the muted browns and rich rusts and dark reds appealed to me. Their hues were natural. In a way, they were even peaceful and comforting.

I approached the nearest shelf and picked up an earthenware bowl. The inside was smooth, while the outside held a circular grooved pattern that gave the design an unmistakable handmade appearance. Browns and muted blues blended in a pleasant, sedate color. A design had been carved into the clay—a wheat spike, simple but intricate in its detail. Turning the bowl over, I read the potter's mark on the bottom. A simple set of initials, EB, inside a circle, and the year in neat numbers beneath. This bowl was made last year.

A curtain hung over a doorway situated behind the high counter holding a cash register and a few odds and ends. A hand swept the curtain aside, and a dark-haired *Englisch* woman appeared, apparently alerted to our presence by the bell.

"Hello. Can I help you find something?" Her smile, though pleasant enough, disappeared after a few seconds, and her face settled into a serious expression that looked natural to her.

She wore her hair pulled back into a tail that hung down her back. No makeup, which surprised me. Most *Englisch* young women wore lipstick and such to work, didn't they? But what drew my attention was the scar that ran from her left cheekbone to her chin, slashing across one corner of her lips.

Her gaze flicked toward me, and her eyes narrowed. Aware that I had been staring, I looked away and replaced the bowl on the shelf.

Saloma stepped up to the counter. "I'm looking for a gift for my sister. She recently married." She offered a friendly smile. "We didn't know this place was here until this morning."

"We just opened a few months ago. We're a bit out of the way." The young woman, who I gauged to be close to Saloma's age of twenty-four, gestured around the room. "As you can see, we're starting small, but we hope it won't take long to outgrow this building, and then we can move to a place more accessible to visitors."

Becky lifted a mug and turned it in her hands, inspecting it. "This is beautiful. Did you make all of these?"

The woman laughed and shook her head. "Not a single one. My pieces are so clumsy they would have to be sold as boat anchors. I don't have the skill or the patience to master the art."

Her laugh, low and rumbling, fell pleasantly on my ears. I risked an upward glance, careful to avoid staring at her scar, in time to see the smile fade and her solemn expression return.

A second person appeared through the doorway, an Amish man. The owner of the horse and buggy outside, no doubt. He was of an age with my *grossmammi,* his full, dark beard sprinkled liberally with gray. Over his broadfall trousers and white shirt he wore a thick canvas apron stained with splotches of gray.

"*Guder daag.*" He greeted us with a nod, the brim of his banded straw hat dipping low. Then his hands, which were covered in clay, spread wide. "Welcome to Plain Man's Pottery. I am Elias Beachy."

I stepped forward to perform the introductions. "Seth Hostetler. My *mamm* and sisters—" I gestured toward each of them, "—are shopping for a wedding gift."

"Your work is beautiful," Saloma commented as she turned a canister in her hands to examine the piece from all sides.

He smiled. "*Danke.* With the Lord's help, I do my best."

"Do you create custom pieces?" Becky asked.

Elias's head bobbed "*Ya,* of course. Did you have something in mind?"

"Not really. Not yet, anyway." Her lips curved into a bashful smile. "Someday my husband and I will build a house of our own, and then I might want something made just for us."

Saloma turned and extended the piece she held toward him. "How much is this canister set?"

Elias splayed his hands and took a backward step. "Leah can answer any question you have. I'm merely a potter. I'm happy to leave the business to her. I have a bowl on the bat, so I need to get back to work, but I didn't want to miss the chance to greet a new friend." His gaze slid toward me. "You're welcome to watch while they shop."

I returned his knowing smile. Men understood one another. Though the shop was not large and the displayed wares small in number, the women of my family could easily spend an hour fingering and discussing every one.

"*Ya,* I'd like that."

Leah stepped aside to give me room when I rounded the counter and followed Elias through the doorway. Now I saw that the biggest part of the building had been dedicated to his workshop. Wide racks lined the walls, full of metal trays containing plain, dull gray pottery in various sizes and shapes. Unfinished, obviously. The center of the room was occupied by four low tables, deeply rimmed and each with a round steel disk below. Though I claimed no knowledge of the craft, even someone as uneducated as I recognized them as potter's wheels. At the back of the room sat a cylindrical container that stood nearly as high as my waist, with an electronic control panel on the front. A steel hose ran from the back of the cylinder to a vent in the wall.

Elias followed my gaze. "My kiln. One of them." He shook his head with a sardonic smile. "I've given in to electricity, but only for certain pieces. I still prefer the wood kiln out back."

He sat on a low bench before one of the tables, straddling the rimmed platform. A lump of wet clay rested on a round plate inside the rimmed area. A bowl of cloudy water sat in front of the plate. With a booted foot, he kicked the steel disk near the floor and the plate began to spin.

"Do you live in Strasburg?" He dipped cupped hands into the bowl and spread water over the spinning clay.

"Our farm is a few miles north, near Upper Leacock."

His hands and feet appeared to move independently. He kicked the disk at regular intervals, and the speed of the spinning plate remained consistent. But his hands were what drew my attention. They cupped the clay, firmly but almost lovingly, pressing the sides so it rose from the center to form a small tower, and then he used the heel of one hand to push the top down into a rounded lump. One hand stayed on the sides of the clay while the other scooped more water, and then the process began again. Mold a tower. Press it down. Wet the clay. Mold a tower.

Though he didn't look up from his work, he must have been aware of my stare, for he offered an explanation.

"I'm centering the piece on the bat. If it's even a tiny bit off center, the bowl won't spin true and I'll have to start again."

I noticed then that the plate on which the clay rested—the bat, he called it—was marked with a series of circles extending from the center to the outer rim. I pointed. "Those markings let you know when it is centered?"

"No, they let *you* know when the clay is centered." A small smile appeared beneath his clean-shaven upper lip. "After a while, a potter can tell by feel. And this one is."

The clay now formed a thick disk in the middle of the bat, spinning in perfect symmetry. With another splash of water, Elias held both hands above the clay, one grasping the other, and pressed the curved joint of his thumb downward. A hollow appeared in the disk and his thumb pressed further, sinking into the clay to form a deep cavity.

Fascinated, I watched as the clay became a bowl, wide and deep, the kind that would be used to serve a dish of vegetables at a family table. Without taking my eyes from Elias's work, I lowered myself to the bench of the wheel that faced his, crouching in an imitation of his posture. His tools were simple—an oblong piece of wood with one rounded edge, a small sponge he used to smooth the clay, a tiny metal pick with a wooden handle. Applying the smooth piece of wood, which fit neatly into the palm of his hand, he formed a rim on the bowl and then with the lightest touch, held the wet sponge against the lip so that it was perfectly level.

When the bowl was finished to his satisfaction, he picked up a piece of thin wire and ran it beneath the bowl, across the surface of the still-spinning bat. Then he straightened and leaned back to eye his creation. A satisfied smile twitched the corners of his lips upward.

"It is *gut*."

He lifted the bat, still holding the bowl, from the platform. I stood when he did, and followed him to one of the racks lining the walls, where he slid the bat onto a metal tray. On this side of the room, the trays held several bats, each with its own clay creation. Besides bowls, I saw pitchers and mugs, dinner plates, jugs, and pots with lids resting beside them. The pieces in the racks along the back walls were of a different color, a chalky white, and a quick inspection showed me that they had a more finished look, a few even with carved designs similar to what I'd seen in the showroom.

"Would you like to give it a try?"

I turned to find Elias smiling at me. He gestured toward the wheel he'd just vacated.

"I doubt I'd even be able to produce a boat anchor."

He dismissed my objection with a wave. "I have plenty of clay. And whatever you ruin, I can salvage and reuse. We have very little waste here."

My fingers twitched, eager to feel the wet clay, to mold and shape it as he had done. I balled my fists, sorely tempted.

Leah stepped through the curtained doorway and addressed me, her expression unsmiling. "Your family is ready to leave."

The decision made for me, I nodded and then turned to Elias. "*Danke* for letting me watch you work. I may stop by again and see what that bowl turns into when it's finished."

"It's always a joy to view the finished product." He smiled. "When you return, you could take a turn at the wheel. The first lesson is free."

He and the young woman followed me through the doorway, where *Mamm* and the others waited. Saloma held a box, and as I took it from her, I saw three well-wrapped bundles inside. The canister set no longer rested on the display shelf. Apparently, she'd found her sister's wedding gift at the first place we stopped.

We bid Elias and Leah farewell, and I escorted the women to our buggy. Elias's offer occupied my thoughts as I secured the box and assisted them up onto the bench. What would it feel like to dip my hands in the water and press my fingers into the clay? I felt an urge to know. The next time I could take a few hours away from the farm, maybe I would find out.

FOUR

Mammi met us at the door, little Sadie in her arms. One glance showed me that the hours of tending the little ones had taken their toll. Wisps of hair floated free around her *kapp,* and her face held a grayish pall that I had not noted at the breakfast table. The wrinkles on her cheeks seemed deeper, heavier than they had that morning.

"*Mammi,* you shouldn't be holding her." Becky rushed forward to take the toddler.

"She's missing her *mamm* and needing a little extra attention," *Mammi* said, though she gave the child over quickly enough.

As though to prove her claim, Sadie threw her arms around Becky's neck and squeezed, babbling a string of mostly unintelligible words that ended in, "No bye-bye."

Becky hugged the child back. "Well, you shouldn't pick her up. She's getting heavy."

"Where are the boys?" Saloma looked toward the empty front room as we filed inside and into the kitchen.

Mammi pulled out a chair from the table and sank into it. "In the barn with Silas. They were getting restless inside, and Aaron and Noah are working on the roof of the chicken coop."

I caught the worried glance Saloma cast toward the door. Though they treated *Daed* with the respect due their *grossdaadi,* they could run him ragged without intending to with their high energy and constant activity.

I set the box containing the canister set on the table. "I'll go see if I can lend a hand."

She cast me a grateful smile. When I left the house, she was unwrapping her purchase to show *Mammi.*

I found the three of them not in the barn, but standing outside the chicken coop, their heads thrown back as they watched Noah and Aaron work. *Daed* stood with his hands clasped behind his back, while the boys had hooked their fingers through the wire fencing that surrounded the chickens' yard. Noah stood on the rung of a ladder leaning against the coop, while Aaron knelt on the roof, nailing a board in place.

At my approach, Luke deserted the fencing and raced toward me. "*Onkel* Seth, I painted the barn."

Not to be outdone, Mark charged after his brother. "Me too! Wanna see?"

Both their coats bore splatters of white paint that would no doubt bring scolds from Saloma, and Luke had a splotch across his forehead. "I think I see already," I teased, and tilted the rim of his straw hat, a miniature version of his *daed*'s, to rub at the white spot.

"No, the barn." He settled his hat back on his head before grabbing my hand and tugging me in that direction.

Daed fell in beside us. "I've been meaning to repaint that door in the back for a while now. They were a big help."

Mark turned a wide grin up at me. "We were a big help."

"I'm sure you were." I couldn't help but return his grin.

"*Grossdaadi* used a rowwer," Luke explained. "We used a brush."

It took me a second to translate. "He used a *roller.*"

The little boy nodded. "And we used a brush."

We had not yet reached the barn when the sound of a car on the road drew our attention. A red vehicle slowed and turned into our driveway. As the car approached, I noted there was only one occupant.

Aaron and Noah had also seen. Noah hopped off the bottom rung of the ladder, and Aaron followed him down as the car rolled to a stop not far from where *Daed* and I stood. The engine stilled and the driver sat for a moment. Through the windshield I saw his hands clutching the top of the steering wheel as he looked at us. Then the door opened and he emerged.

Both boys drew back to stand behind me, suddenly and uncharacteristically reserved. They'd seen cars pass by on the road, of course, but rarely did one come to our farm.

The young driver closed the door and stood looking at us, his posture hesitant. *Daed* approached, a broad smile on his face.

"Hello. Welcome to our home."

He was a slender youth, tall and almost gangly, with a thick shock of dark hair that stood awry when he snatched a knit hat off his head. I judged his age at nineteen or twenty. He stood for a second, wringing his hat in his hands, and then he stepped forward. With a slow and somewhat timid gesture, he extended his hand. *Englisch* people were often unsure how to greet an Amish man. When *Daed* readily shook the offered hand, a relieved smile settled on the boy's face.

"Hello. I'm Robbie. Uh, Robert Barker."

"I am Silas Hostetler." *Daed* turned as the others approached, and nodded toward each of us as he performed the introduction. "My son-in-law Noah, and my sons Aaron and Seth."

It might have been my imagination, but the young man seemed startled when *Daed* spoke my name. I did not imagine the way he stared at me through wide eyes while barely glancing at the others. Then he cleared his throat and looked back at *Daed*.

"I was just wondering if you need any help. You know." With a jerky gesture he swept a hand toward the field behind us. "On the farm. Or anything."

It wasn't unheard of for Amish to hire *Englisch* in their businesses. Elias Beachy employing the solemn Leah to help in his shop was a good example, but it was certainly unusual for an *Englisch* man to approach an Amish farmer looking for work. Either young Robbie was ignorant of our ways, or he was desperate enough for money that he hoped we would make an exception.

Aaron stepped forward then, his expression friendly. "Thank you for the offer, but as you can see, we have four strong pairs of hands to handle the work here."

Robbie swallowed and jerked a nod. "I get that. I just thought maybe…" His gaze slid toward me for a moment and then back to Aaron. "I know sometimes your people need a lift somewhere. Like if you have to go a long way." He reached into the back pocket of his jeans and pulled out a slip of paper, which he extended. "I'll drive you wherever you need to go."

Aaron took the paper. "We will keep that in mind."

A long moment passed, during which the young man stood still, as though waiting for Aaron to say something. Then he straightened and offered his hand again.

"Well, goodbye. Nice to meet you."

Aaron shook it, and then Robbie practically leaped forward to shake Noah's hand as well. His manner was so odd, so edgy, that when he turned to me I found I'd clasped my hands behind my back. I let go of them. What was this young man up to? Was there something more to this visit than a search for employment? Still, when he stood in front of me he seemed nervous, but I couldn't detect any signs of insincerity. His gaze traveled over my face while never making contact with my eyes. He barely touched my hand before releasing it, and then he lowered his eyes to look at the ground between our feet.

"I mean it," he repeated, scuffing a tennis shoe. "If you need a ride, call me."

With the flash of a smile at the boys, who had ventured out from behind me, though they still stood well clear of the stranger, he whirled and hurried toward his car.

We all stood watching the red vehicle retreat down our driveway and turn onto the road in the same direction from which it had come.

Mark's childish voice broke the silence. "Who was that?"

A good question.

Daed turned a smile on the boy. "A man looking for work."

"Can he help us paint?" Luke asked.

"Why would we need his help?" *Daed* answered. "We have two good painters right here."

Identical grins broke out on their faces.

"Come on, *Onkel* Seth!" Luke shouted. "Wook what we did."

The twins raced toward the barn and disappeared around the side. Aaron and Noah headed back to the chicken coop to finish their repair work, while *Daed* turned to enter the house. With one more glance at the road in the direction the red car had gone, I followed my nephews, ready to praise their work.

🙢🙠

We needed Robbie Barker's car sooner than we expected.

I was in the pigpen, up to my ankles in mud, when the rumble of an engine nearby reached me. The beginning of March had brought an unusual bout of warm weather, melting nearly all of the snow and turning the pig's yard into a sloshy mess. Our sow, Schwein—so named after the German word for "pig"—was housed behind the barn as far from the house as possible while still offering her a bit of shelter from the elements. She was due to farrow soon, and she'd begun to exhibit the telltale signs of preparing for her approaching litter. I made sure she had plenty of straw in her pen, all the while keeping a sharp eye on her. Though generally a placid animal, Schwein tended to get cranky as her time for farrowing approached. She'd been with us for a number of years, and each year we sold her piglets, retaining a couple to feed the family. She'd learned to anticipate the removal of her young, and her maternal instincts kicked in as their birth neared. Four hundred pounds of charging sow was enough to keep any man ready for a quick dash for the fence.

When Schwein's pen was as dry as possible and covered with a layer of clean straw, I let myself out of the enclosure and headed around the barn. An *Englisch* car had parked in front of our house, and a couple emerged. I'd seen Saloma's *schweschder* Naomi and her husband Johann once or twice, though it had been quite a while. Saloma and Naomi greeted each other, hands clasped as they grinned into the other's face. The rest of the family had lined up for the introduction, the little ones standing politely still between *Mamm* and Becky. I approached as Saloma finished.

"And you remember Seth, *ya*?"

Johann nodded. "It has been a while since we met."

Naomi opened her mouth to speak, but she appeared to change her mind and closed it again. Instead, she merely smiled and bobbed her head in my direction.

I recognized a touch of pity in her shy smile, and the reason struck me like a hammer. The last time I'd seen her had been at my Hannah's funeral.

Saloma looped an arm through Naomi's. "Come inside. We have coffee and fresh rolls ready."

Johann followed the *Englisch* driver, an older man with a serious disposition, to the trunk of the car and lifted two bags out. He set them down and then extracted a leather money clip from one.

The driver took the bills, folded them, and slid them into the pocket of his jeans. "You're all set to get to your uncle's place, right?"

Johann turned to Aaron. "Wayne can't pick us up tomorrow. Do you have a driver who could take us to my *onkel*'s farm in Wakefield?"

"There's a man down the road who is kind to drive us when we need. We'll ride over to Kevin Cramer's after lunch."

I shook my head. "At church on Sunday Joel Wagler mentioned a trip to Akron this Saturday. He said Kevin was driving him." The nervous young man from a few days ago rose in my mind's eye. "What about calling that Robbie Barker? He seemed eager for work."

"*Ya*, he did." Aaron turned his attention to Wayne. "If you have a phone, we can call him now."

Wayne nodded. "Sure thing."

While the driver retrieved his cell phone from the car, Aaron went into the house and returned in a few moments with the slip of paper the young man had given him. Wayne punched the numbers on the phone and then handed it to Aaron. I hid a smile. *Englisch* often thought that just because we chose not to own technology, we didn't know how to use it. During Aaron's *rumspringa*, he'd owned a cell phone of his own, as had I. But because I never remembered to bring it with me, mine had not seen much use. Unlike the car, the phone had been an easy thing to give up.

Apparently, Robbie Barker answered, for Aaron identified himself and proceeded to describe our need. He nodded at Johann and Wayne, and then thanked the young man on the phone before disconnecting the call.

He handed the phone back to the driver. "He will be here at two o'clock tomorrow."

"Fine." Wayne faced Johann. "I will pick you up in Wakefield on Sunday and take you home."

"Thank you."

The man got back into his car, and the engine revved to life. With a final wave, he drove away.

Johann picked up one bag, and I grabbed the other. "I'll show you to your room."

My room, of course. But my things had been removed and the bed linens changed this morning in anticipation of their arrival.

Aaron took the bag from my hand. "I'll carry it. *Mamm* will have a fit if you go inside like that."

He ducked his head toward my muddy work shoes, which I'd forgotten. Suddenly aware that my clothes were covered in mud and worse from my work in Schwein's pen, I yielded the bag. "I might as well clean the barn while I'm dirty, but save me a roll."

That brought a boyish grin to his face. "You'd better hurry. I'm hungry, and those are *Mammi*'s *gut* pumpkin rolls."

I couldn't help but return the grin. As boys, we had once snitched an entire pan of *Mammi*'s pumpkin rolls and hid behind the well house to eat them. We were finishing the last one when Becky found us. I'm convinced that if we'd saved one or two for our *schweschder*, she wouldn't have taken such joy in reporting our crime. *Mammi* would have discovered the missing pan eventually, of course, but we blamed Becky for the whupping we'd received from *Daed*. Honestly, the rolls were so good that we both agreed later they were worth the punishment, though perhaps not the lecture and Bible reading we endured while sitting on our raw backsides.

"Make him save me one, Johann," I said with a grin, and when he nodded, I turned toward the barn for yet another smelly job.

The addition of Johann and Naomi made supper that night a festive affair, and the women outdid themselves in the kitchen. Our table never lacked for food—a farming family worked hard and used a lot of energy, and therefore required plentiful nutrition—but the variety of dishes that *Mamm* served that night almost bordered on prideful gluttony, something of which Bishop Beiler would most definitely not approve. No one mentioned the overabundance, of course. And there would be no waste, though we would enjoy leftovers of chicken, pork roast, beans, corn, stewed tomatoes, potatoes—both sweet and white—turnips, and fried cabbage for days to come. Even though our bellies were full of the good food, no one refused a slice of *Mamm*'s apple cake or a wedge of *Mammi*'s squash pie topped with thick, sweet cream.

When everyone had eaten as much as they could hold, the men retreated to the living room, leaving the women to clear the table.

"Business is good at the cabinet shop?" Noah asked of Johann as we settled around the room.

The children played on the floor between us, the boys building a structure with the smooth wooden blocks Aaron and I had played with when we were younger. When Sadie would have joined in and no doubt destroyed whatever the twins constructed, Mark turned a cautious eye on his *daed* before handing her two blocks and sending her to a far corner to play on her own. I hid a grin. Only three, and already Mark was becoming adept at keeping the peace without drawing the disapproval of his elders.

"*Ya,* too good at times." Johann leaned forward, elbows propped on his knees and hands clasped. "We have orders we won't be able to fill until summer, and have had to turn away customers who need cabinets sooner."

"Is it new houses or replacement cabinets?" Aaron asked.

"Some renovations, but mostly new construction. Lancaster County is growing, especially the western part of the county. More *Englisch* are settling there."

Furrows appeared beneath the thinning shock of *Daed*'s gray hair. "I hate to see it."

Johann looked surprised. "Why is that? They bring more business to the county. And besides, it isn't Amish land they're buying but *Englisch*."

I kept my eyes fixed on the growing tower of blocks between Mark and Luke, afraid I'd not be able to filter the surprise out of my gaze if I looked at the young man. Was he really so ignorant of our situation here in Lancaster County?

Aaron explained in a patient tone. "Because your family owns a business, you benefit far more from the *Englisch* than those of us who farm. If the *Englisch* buy up all the viable farmland in the county, where will our young men go?" He gestured toward my brother-in-law. "Take Noah. He hopes to buy a farm of his own in a year or two. If there is no land for sale in Lancaster County, he will have to look elsewhere."

Noah nodded. "My *daed* can divide our family land in half but no more. Three of my older brothers are saving, but the way things look now, Becky and I will have to move away when the time comes." His gaze settled on little Sadie, who was quietly babbling to herself while trying in vain to balance one block on top of the other in imitation of her older cousins. The day Becky and Noah and Sadie moved away from the family would be a sad one indeed. Especially if they were forced to move far away.

I felt the weight of a stare and looked up from my niece to find Aaron's gaze fixed on me. Heat prickled beneath my shirt and threatened to rise into my face. I, too, was one of those younger *bruders* who, if I were married, would find myself with no land to farm unless I married the daughter of a farmer with no sons. I had done that once, but could not bear to stay with Rachel's family after her death and so had returned home. My family's farm had been divided for three generations, the most recent between my *grossdaadi* and his *bruder*. To reduce the size any further would be to render the farm unable to support a crop big enough to make farming worthwhile.

Of course, I was not married and *would not* marry. What need had I of land?

The women entered the room then, all smiles and chattering. Naomi held the box from Plain Man's Pottery, the pottery pieces inside released from their newspaper wrappings. She hurried across the floor to sit between me and Johann.

"Look what they've given us." She settled the box on the floor and lifted one of the canisters. "Isn't it lovely?"

Johann made a show of examining the piece, nodding his approval. "*Ya*. We will make good use of this." He caught her in a teasing sideways glance. "I can use it to store nails in the shop."

"Oh, you!" Naomi leaned sideways and shoved his shoulder before taking the canister from his hands. "They'll never see the inside of that shop. These are for flour, sugar, and barley in *my* kitchen." She smiled. "When I have one, that is. And look here." She replaced the canister in the box and lifted out a piece of fabric. I recognized a set of dishtowels that my sister and *Mamm* had sewed.

While Johann made a show of admiring the gifts and thanking everyone for bestowing them, I leaned forward to lift one of the canisters out of the box for a closer examination. A perfectly round cylinder with a quarter-inch foot that would rest solidly on a tabletop without wobbling. The outside contained the slightly grooved design that I'd noticed on most of Elias's pieces. Instead of a wheat spike, a trio of simple wildflowers decorated one side, their petals small and delicate. The lid, which I lifted by a knob, fit so perfectly as to be nearly airtight. How did Elias make it fit so snugly? Inside the canister was smooth, the lid slightly concave. I turned it over and noted the familiar encircled EB with the current year carved in neat numbers beneath.

In my mind's eye, the potter's hands rose, shaping the clay, dipping the water, molding the mound into a tower, and gently pressing it down again. The patience, the sheer artistry required to turn that lump of gray clay into the item I held in my hand captivated me.

Daed's voice interrupted my thoughts. "It is time to read." He picked up *die Bibel* from its resting place on the table beside his chair.

The boys began putting the blocks into their wooden crate, and Sadie toddled across the room to add her two. I replaced the lid and set the canister inside the cardboard box containing Naomi's wedding gifts. Elias's offer echoed in my mind. *The first lesson is free.*

Because the day had been warm, a good bit of snow had melted. Tomorrow we planned to walk the roofs of the main house and the *daadi haus* and perform any minor repairs that might be needed. But maybe I could slip away for a few hours the day after that.

Daed laid the big book in his lap, moved the oil lamp closer to the edge of the table so he could see, and began to read. I forced my thoughts away from spinning wheels and wet, pliable clay and focused on the nightly reading.

"You'll sleep hard and cold, I fear."

Mammi stood with her arms folded across her apron, worry carving heavy lines at the sides of her mouth as she examined the pallet where I would spend the night. No less than five quilts, carefully folded and layered atop a foam cushion on the rough-hewn floor, lay before the hearth where the fire had burned low.

"I've no doubt I'll sleep more comfortably here than in my bed in the big house. And sounder, too, because I'll not have to listen to Aaron's snoring."

That brought a smile to the face etched with years of love and laugh lines. "Often were the times your *grossdaadi* kept the house awake with his snores."

"I remember."

Grossdaadi's snoring was renowned. Many a night as a boy I lay in bed and imagined I felt the mattress beneath me rumble with the vibration from his snores. My own *mamm* took to plugging her ears with cotton wool in the days when we all lived in the big house together. The day *Grossdaadi* and *Mammi* moved into the *daadi haus,* my *mamm* celebrated with perhaps a touch more exuberance than the situation warranted. I'd spied upon her when, after bidding her elders a fond farewell, she took two screwed-up pieces of wool and dropped them ceremoniously into the trash bin.

Since that time I believe she had acquired a new collection of cotton wool. The tendency toward noisy sleep had missed my *daed* and settled instead on Aaron. These days they said that snoring was bad for a person and indicated health problems, which gave Saloma no end of worry. Aaron merely laughed at her concern and continued his nightly serenade of the inhabitants of the main house.

"*Ach*, but I miss him." In the waning firelight I caught the glimmer of tears in *Mammi*'s eyes.

The admission disturbed me more than the tears. *Grossdaadi* had died nearly fifteen years ago when I was a boy of eleven. My Rachel's death four years ago, and Hannah's last year, still lay like raw wounds in my soul. Would they always, even ten years from now?

"Still?" I asked, and a touch of my agony must have seeped into the question, for the next tear that slid down her cheek seeped from eyes so full of compassion that my heart squeezed painfully in answer.

Taking me by the arm, she guided me to a pair of chairs situated before the hearth and bade me sit in one. When she had lowered herself next to me, she clasped her hands and rested them on the skirt of her black dress, her gaze fixed on the glowing embers.

"For thirty-seven years I lived as his wife. Too many memories crowd this old head of mine to ever forget him."

"A long time," I agreed.

She glanced sideways at me and bit her lower lip as though hesitant to say more. I knew what was coming, of course. The inevitable comparison. Gott, *don't let her say it.*

Apparently the Almighty did not see fit to hear my plea.

"Your pain is no less, my Seth. I know that."

I nodded, grateful for the acknowledgment. *Let her stop there.*

She laid a hand on my arm, an unusually intimate gesture for an Amish woman, and one that spoke to the depth of her compassion. "But you are young. You have more life ahead than behind you."

My feet itched inside my boots. I wanted to stand, to stride across the room and escape not only the caring touch upon my arm but the words I knew were coming.

"*Es ist nicht gut, daß der Mensch allein sei.*"

The quote from *die Bibel* wasn't unexpected, but the stab of pain that accompanied it was. I shot to my feet and paced three long steps to the window, where I stood looking out at the unplowed field, white moonlight reflecting on the few patches of snow that remained. *It is not good for man to be alone.* How often had that verse replayed itself in my mind when loneliness clawed at my insides? But I'd come to the conclusion that the verse was written for other men, not for me.

Without turning, I quoted another, one that I'd taken as my own. "Did not the apostle Paul say, *To the unmarried and widows, it is good for them if they abide even as I?*"

"*Ach.*" A dim reflection in the glass showed me that *Mammi* had thrown up a hand in dismissal. "I'll not enter a battle of verses with my own *kinskind.*"

I hid a grin at the typical *Mammi* reaction. If she couldn't win the battle one way, she would switch to another approach.

"Besides, if I ever saw a man less like the apostle Paul, it is you."

I turned and fixed a teasing grin on her. "Should I be offended that you think so little of me?"

"I only meant you should look elsewhere for your role model. Your namesake, for instance. A farmer who followed the Lord's command to be fruitful and multiply."

She could not know how the words hurt, how they conjured images of my disastrous attempts to multiply. Therefore I answered in as gentle a voice as I could manage. "I do not intend to marry again. The Lord blessed me with two wives already."

I did not add my thought, *And I caused both their deaths. Why would He entrust me with another?*

"You think the Lord's blessings have limits?"

She placed her hands on the edges of the wooden seat and heaved herself up. I was about to answer with a quick rejoinder when she wavered on her feet. Her hand flailed wildly behind her, landing on the high chair back, and she half turned to lean heavily upon it.

I crossed the room in seconds and slid an arm around her waist. "Are you all right?"

I searched her face. Was she paler than normal, or was that a trick of the dim light? There was no mistaking the trembling in her body, which felt frail and almost weightless within the circle of my arm.

"Fine, fine." She tried to wave off my concern with a weak gesture, but didn't step away from the security of my arm. "I stood too quickly, that's all."

Something in her tone alarmed me. She sounded almost feeble, something my *grossmammi* never was.

Suspicion crept over me. "Has this happened before?"

"*Ach,* it is nothing. The excitement of the day and too much apple cake. I should have insisted on a smaller piece."

She'd avoided answering my question. "It *has* happened before, hasn't it?"

"I get dizzy every so often when I'm tired." She straightened then and gave me a sharp look. "When you are seventy-four, you'll see. Help me to my room, Seth."

For the first time, I noticed how shrunken she was. I knew she tired more easily than in the past, of course. The other day, for instance, when we returned from Strasburg to find her fatigued from tending the little ones. Afterward she'd retreated to the *daadi haus* and slept for several hours, emerging fresh and as energetic as usual.

But she *was* seventy-four years old. I'd not considered my vigorous *grossmammi* frail until this moment, and the realization left me reeling. I'd lost too many women I loved already. Surely *Gott* would not take another from me.

Mammi leaned heavily on me as we slowly made our way to the single bedroom, and I helped her sit on the side of the quilt-covered bed. I struck a match and lit the candle on the bedside table and then stood back, watching her and feeling more useless than a bull in a milking barn. Should I fetch *Mamm* from the house?

As though she sensed my thought, *Mammi* smiled up at me. "It is passing. I'll just sit here a minute and then get ready for bed."

A close inspection showed that her face had regained some color, and her breath didn't appear as shallow as a moment before.

"Can I bring you something? A cup of tea, maybe?" I found that I was actually wringing my hands, and whipped them behind my back.

"I don't need nursing, Seth." She laughed, and the sound did more to put me at ease than anything. It held the ring of her trademark humor. "After a full night's sleep I'll be good as new. You'll see." She flipped her fingers at me in dismissal. "Go. Make yourself as comfortable as you can on that pile of quilts. And put more wood on the fire, please. It's cold in here."

I left her bedroom door cracked open on the pretense of allowing heat from the fireplace an avenue to warm her room. But mostly I didn't want to miss hearing if she called for help.

Five

The festive atmosphere remained the next morning as our family continued to host the newly married couple over a bountiful breakfast. Naomi had taken quite a liking to little Sadie, and dandled her on her knee, trying to teach her the game of pat-a-cake. Laughter pealed from both of them as Sadie's chubby hands tried and failed to imitate the rhythm.

When *Mamm* called them to the table, Naomi stood and settled the child on her hip. It was then that I spied the telltale thickening of the young wife's waist. Well, she had been married five months already, so that was perhaps inevitable. My Hannah, for instance, had—

I ripped my thoughts from that devastating direction. Naomi must have seen something in my expression, for she placed a protective hand over her round belly, and her peachy cheeks stained with a blush. I tore my gaze away, fighting to calm my expression.

By a sheer act of will, I managed to hold the memories at bay. Would I forever be haunted by the sight of women in the family way? If so, then I was doomed to experience the familiar ache daily for the rest of my life.

During the silent prayer before our meal, I prayed for the health of Naomi and her baby. And for Saloma and hers. And for every other expectant woman I knew. Maybe, by praying for other men's wives, I could achieve some relief from the guilt of not praying hard enough for my own.

It was with a sense of relief that I followed the men outside the house after breakfast. The cold air cooled my face, a welcome relief from the warmth of the house generated by *Mamm*'s wood-fired oven, which had been cranking out heat since long before sunup. While *Mammi* accompanied the twins to the chicken coop to oversee their daily chore of egg gathering, Aaron retrieved the ladder from the barn.

Johann gladly joined in our work for the day, following Noah up on the roof while Aaron held the bottom of the ladder steady. When he was at the top, I handed up the long chimney brush. We'd decided that while we were working on the roof, we might as well perform the messy job of ensuring the chimney was soot- and creosote-free.

"Any ice up there?" Aaron called.

Several years ago we'd replaced the old roof of the main house with a newer metal roofing material, which came with a forty-year warranty. The steep pitch, especially of the second floor, would be dangerous if icy.

Noah's voice answered. "Not a bit. The sun has done its job."

I heard two pairs of boots trod upon the metal above as they moved toward the first of the chimneys. When I grasped the ladder and started to plant my foot on the bottom rung, Aaron stopped me.

"It won't take four of us. Why don't you go give *Daed* a hand inside?"

Though his smile was kind, I once again felt the sting of being the extra. Of course Aaron was right. Only one man could apply the chimney brush at a time, and it certainly didn't take three others to inspect the length of the roof. They didn't need me up there.

On the other hand, neither did *Daed* need my help inside, where he had laid cloths around the living room hearth and had no doubt already begun to scrub the bottom half of the chimney with a brush of his own. The task was one he was pleased to be able to handle because there were so many around the farm he could no longer perform.

I glanced toward the barn, but nothing in there required my attention. I'd been up and dressed since long before breakfast to milk Delilah and Caroline and had turned them out in the small side pasture to enjoy the day's sunshine. The milk had been separated, and Schwein had been fed.

I forced a smile for my *bruder*. "Sure."

Inside, I drew curious glances from Becky and *Mamm,* though the other two women didn't stop their talk as they worked together to clean up from the morning meal. The sounds of boots on the roof above was nearly drowned out by Naomi's recounting of some story about a family she and Saloma knew from their home district. Bypassing the kitchen, I headed for the living room.

I found *Daed* on his knees before the hearth, applying the chimney brush with industry.

"Could you use a helper in here?" I asked.

He turned to me, and I stifled a grin. His face bore evidence of the volume of soot he'd managed to dislodge in a short period of time.

Instead of answering my question, he pointed to indicate the mound of soot in the bucket he'd placed inside the fireplace. "That creosote conditioner you picked up last week? We got it not a moment too soon. Might have had a fire if we'd waited any longer." He backed away and jerked a nod toward the bucket. "Want to empty that for me?"

My mood dipped even further. So this was to be my role for the day. Emptying buckets of soot and probably cleaning the drop cloths and tools used by the other men. *Maybe I should help the boys gather eggs next.*

I kept my expression clear of the dour thought. "*Ya,* sure."

A steady stream of soot rained down from above, proof that one of the men on the roof had begun their work from the top. I grabbed the metal bucket and set an empty one in its place, and then I headed outside to perform my chore.

A little before two o'clock, Luke and Mark, who had been stationed outside with the important task of watching for the arrival of the driver, galloped into the house shouting, "He's here!" I picked up Naomi's bulging bag and followed the rest of the family through the door in time to see Robbie Barker's red car roll to a stop in front of our house. The engine shut off, and for a moment the young man didn't move. Through the windshield I saw him stare at us. I supposed we did look like a spectacle, all lined up in a row, staring back at him.

He broke the tableau when he opened the door and exited the car. Rather, he unfolded himself from inside. He rose to his full gangly height and stood, somewhat hesitantly, hands shoved in the pockets of a Chicago Cubs jacket. His gaze slid down the line of us, and when his eyes met mine, his Adam's apple, prominent in his long neck, bobbed up and down a few times.

Johann, who clutched his bag in his left hand, stepped forward and extended his right. "Thank you for being on time."

"Oh, yeah. No problem."

A nervous smile flashed onto his face and then disappeared just as quickly. I caught the exchange of a glance between Naomi and Saloma, their eyebrows forming nearly identical arches. A wave of sympathy for the boy swept through me. I remembered being an awkward teenager, unsure of myself around strangers. Especially *Englisch* strangers. I supposed Robbie might feel the same around Amish strangers.

Stepping forward with a wide smile, I hefted Naomi's bag. "Do you want to put this in the trunk?"

Robbie jerked upright, as though just now reminded of his reason for being there. "The trunk. Yeah. Let me just make some room."

Johann and I followed him to the rear of the red car and stood by as he punched a button and the trunk lid released. The inside was littered with items—a set of orange jumper cables, a plastic milk crate packed with a mishmash of things, a wooden box that rattled when he shoved it aside, several articles of clothing, a large bag of dog food. These he pushed toward the back, clearing enough room for the two bags to fit.

Aaron approached carrying the cardboard box containing the rewrapped canister set. "Is there room for this?"

We eyed the full trunk. It was clear nothing else would fit in there.

"Sorry," Robbie mumbled. "I shoulda cleaned some of my stuff out."

Had this young man never acted as a driver before today? If today was his first time driving the Amish, it would explain his nervousness. I caught sight of concerned lines on Saloma's forehead as she studied Robbie. Apparently, the same idea had occurred to her, for she clutched her sister's arm in a protective manner.

Johann awarded Robbie a wide smile, and I sensed that he was trying to put the nervous young man at ease. "No need. The box can sit on the seat beside us."

Gulping again, the driver nodded and slammed the trunk closed with such force that Becky jumped. A note of doubt crept into my mind. Maybe I'd been hasty to suggest that we call Robbie. After all, we had no idea of his driving skills, having seen them demonstrated only on our own driveway. As nervous as he appeared to be, would he be reckless on the road? Or would he calm down once he got behind the wheel of his car and began the journey?

I followed him around the bumper to the rear door. "What route do you plan to take to Wakefield?" Maybe if I drew him into a conversation, he would relax a bit.

"Uh, I thought I'd take 896 down to 372, and then 222." He looked directly into my face, and I saw uncertainty in his gaze. "Is that okay?"

"*Ya,*" I assured him. "That is how I would go."

Gulping again, he nodded as though relieved. I glanced around at my family. Robbie's nervousness was spreading. Even Johann had begun to look hesitant. They could change their minds, of course. The distance to Wakefield wasn't more than thirty miles. If we hitched Rosie up to our buggy, I could deliver the newlyweds to their destination in about four hours.

But how would Robbie react if we sent him on his way? We would offer to pay him for his time, of course, but I sensed this young man's need was for more than money. Something about his nervousness touched a tender place in me. I would hate to send him away feeling rejected and useless.

My gaze lit on the box in Aaron's hands. The route Robbie had outlined would take him directly through Strasburg. Maybe if I asked to accompany them, Johann and Naomi would feel more at ease. Not that the young driver would, because I seemed to make him more nervous than anyone else. But if I rode along for the nine miles between our farm and Strasburg, at least I could ascertain his driving abilities. If he turned out to be unsafe behind the wheel, I would insist that Johann and Naomi get out of the car with me in Strasburg, and I would find another way to get them to their family in Wakefield. Surely I could find an *Englisch* driver willing to take on a last-minute job.

I clasped my hands behind my back and spoke in an even tone. "Since you're going that way, I wonder if I might ride along as far as Strasburg. There's a pottery studio I've wanted to visit there."

Robbie jerked upright, his eyes darting to my face. "Uh, yeah?"

Mamm stepped to my side. "Why, Seth?"

"You heard Elias Beachy the other day. He offered me a free pottery lesson. I'd like to try it." I looked up at Aaron. "We've finished the chimneys and inspecting the roofs, *ya?*"

My *bruder* cocked his head to give me a speculative look. "*Ya.* There is some small work to be done on the *daadi haus,* but nothing Noah and I can't handle."

Though Johann and Naomi both looked relieved at my suggestion, *Mamm* was clearly not supportive of the idea. Her forehead a field of crevices, she asked, "How will you get home?"

"I'll find a driver," I assured her.

Robbie stepped up beside me. "I'll bring you home. I have to come back through Strasburg anyway. It's right on my way."

For the first time since he'd arrived he appeared eager, less nervous than a moment before. Why would driving me put him at ease, when driving Johann and Naomi clearly made him nervous? Was it the idea of the extra money for performing a second service? Or maybe he just wanted to feel useful. Being of use for two errands instead of one meant he was doubly needed.

I certainly understood that feeling.

I smiled at *Mamm.* "You see? It's arranged, then."

While Aaron settled the box containing the wedding gifts on the backseat, Johann and Naomi expressed their thanks to my parents and said their goodbyes. I went into the house to retrieve my money clip. Elias Beachy had promised a free lesson, but I had no idea how long that lesson might last, and I might want to purchase a sandwich for my supper before I returned. I might even offer to buy one for my hungry-looking young driver. I exited the house to see Robbie standing politely beside the open back door as Johann helped Naomi into the car. With a farewell nod at my family, I opened the front door and slid onto the passenger seat.

On the floor lay a crumpled fast-food bag and an empty can, which I pushed out of the way with my foot. A second can sat in the cup holder in the center console. I recognized the black-and-green logo of an energy drink favored by the *Englisch* and indulged in a smile. No wonder young Robbie fidgeted so. He was full of caffeine.

He slid behind the wheel and, I was glad to see, immediately fastened his seat belt. His glance fell to the trash at my feet, and red spots erupted on his cheeks.

"Sorry about that. I didn't think I'd have anyone up front."

"It's fine," I assured him as he turned the key.

The engine rumbled, and as the car backed up to turn around, my family all waved. Johann, Naomi, and I returned the gesture and, the turn completed, began the journey with our new driver.

The first few miles of our trip were silent. I doubt I was the only one who paid close attention to Robbie's driving. A tense stillness emanated from the backseat, and though I didn't turn my head, I saw Naomi's stiff posture and tightly clasped hands in my peripheral vision.

Our nervous worries were unfounded. The young man drove with a light foot, several miles per hour under the speed limit, and the little red car rolled smoothly down the road without swerving. Well in advance of the first turn, he put on the turn signal and looked into all the mirrors.

When we approached a buggy, he slowed even further and edged to the center line to put a wide distance between his car and the buggy. The muscles I'd held rigid relaxed.

"Do you live nearby?" I asked.

He answered without taking his eyes from the road. "In Lancaster, so not too far."

Not far, but that meant taking me home would be out of his way. Further evidence to support my earlier conclusion about his desire to feel useful. I glanced sideways at him. The nervousness he'd displayed earlier had not completely disappeared, evident in his tight grip on the steering wheel and the convulsive gulping. But his driving was good, and I had no qualms about allowing him to take Johann and Naomi on to Wakefield.

"I appreciate your being willing to bring me home," I said.

"It's not a problem." He did glance away from the road then, just for an instant, and met my gaze. "I mean it. Any time you need to go anywhere, you can call me. If I've got something else going on, I'll work it out."

In some people, such eagerness would tend to make me suspicious. For some reason, Robbie's didn't. What was it about this *Englischer* that piqued my curiosity? His willingness to help seemed sincere. The reasons were a mystery I found myself wanting to unravel.

Suddenly aware of the line my thoughts had taken, I gave myself a mental shake. The personal life of an *Englischer* was no business of mine. Settling myself more firmly in the seat, I faced forward and put further questions out of my mind. Other than my directions to Elias Beachy's shop, the rest of the short drive to Strasburg was silent.

The same buggy and car as before were parked on the side of the building. Robbie glided to a smooth stop directly in front of the door. Unfastening my seat belt, I turned to wish Johann and Naomi goodbye and safe travels. When I exited the car, Robbie jumped out as well.

"What time should I come back?"

I had no idea. The bowl I'd watched Elias make had taken less than half an hour, but no doubt my efforts would be fumbling. In fact, I wasn't even sure he had time for me. My spur of the moment idea of riding along on this trip may have been ill advised without a phone call first.

I rubbed a hand over my beard. "Give me a moment, please."

He followed me inside, the bells on the door announcing our arrival. A quick glance around the storefront revealed that the shelves held several more wares than on my last visit. The canister set had been replaced by a similar one. Seated behind the counter on a high stool, the young woman—Leah, her name was—looked up from a ledger. Recognition flashed in the eyes that lit on me, though her solemn expression did not change. Her gaze slid to Robbie and then moved again. At the same moment, I heard the bells announce the entry of someone else. Naomi and Johann had decided not to wait in the car.

Catching sight of Naomi, Leah did smile a greeting.

Interesting.

"Hello."

"Hello," Naomi answered in her cheerful voice. She moved immediately toward the first display shelf and picked up a mug. "I received a wedding gift from here, a beautiful canister set, so I was eager to see where it came from."

Leah looked at me again and gave a small nod in acknowledgment of our purchase several days before. "I'm happy to answer any questions you have."

I cleared my throat. "Is Elias here?"

As though summoned by the mention of his name, the curtain behind her parted and Elias stepped through. He caught sight of me, and his smile widened. "Ah, young Seth Hostetler. *Velkumm.*"

At least someone smiled when they saw me. I avoided looking in Leah's direction and returned Elias's greeting. "I came to accept your offer of a lesson if you have time."

He spread his hands wide. "Of course! I'd love the company and the opportunity to share my craft." His gaze lit on Robbie. "And you've brought another student with you?"

The young man's eyes went round. "Uh, no. I'm just driving them, that's all."

"When should he return for me?" I asked.

Elias tapped a finger on his lips, considering. "Give us two hours. *Das gut, ya?*"

I nodded. I'd be home in time for supper, which would make *Mamm* happy. "Is that okay with you?" I asked my driver.

"Sure." Robbie glanced at his watch. "I'll be back around four thirty."

Leah had come out from behind the counter and was showing Naomi and Johann a set of bowls. When Robbie opened the door, Naomi gave him an imploring look. "May we have a moment here, please? We won't be long, I promise."

Shrugging, the young man said, "Take as long as you want. I don't have to be anywhere until four thirty."

He left the shop, and Elias turned his infectious smile on me. "Come with me and let's get started."

Nervous excitement took me as I followed him through the curtain. On one of the benches sat an unfinished pitcher. A set of tools lay on the tray beside it, and I walked over for a closer look. Elias was in the process of carving a design in the soft clay.

I turned to him. "I don't want to interrupt your work."

"*Ach.*" He dismissed my comment with a wave. "I can finish that later. Teaching is more fun."

Taking up a sheet of heavy plastic, he loosely covered the pitcher and then indicated that I should follow him to a high work surface beyond the benches. From a row of pegs on the wall he took a canvas apron—similar to the one he wore, only cleaner—and indicated that I should put it on. While I did, he retrieved a huge brick of dull gray clay from a corner and unfolded the plastic wrapping. Taking up a thin metal wire, he sliced off a sizable chunk, divided it in half, and set one section on the scale that rested on the corner of the table. Seeing that the other portion weighed approximately the same, he gave a satisfied grunt and, rewrapping the brick, returned it to the floor.

"This," he said, holding a chunk in each hand, "is clay."

Such a serious expression. Like Becky explaining to little Sadie, "This is a spoon." I couldn't hold back a chuckle.

He raised a finger. "You laugh, but there is much to learn about the type of clay a potter chooses."

I furrowed my brow. "There is more than one type of clay?"

"There are hundreds of varieties of clay bodies, each with its own benefits and drawbacks. This"—he hefted one of the lumps—"is a basic stoneware clay, inexpensive, soft, and easy to work with. It has minimal impurities, and the iron content makes it durable after firing." He slapped a lump on the surface in front of me, where it landed with a *splat*. "First, I will teach you to wedge."

A familiar term, but obviously when applied to clay it had a different meaning than the one I knew. Perhaps explaining the process of making pottery as if to a small child was not a bad idea.

Elias placed his own chunk on the work surface and covered it with both hands. "Put your hands like so, with the heels of your palms on the top edge closest to you."

I arranged my hands like his. The clay felt moist but firm beneath my fingers.

"Now, roll the clay away from you, pushing down with equal pressure on both hands."

He demonstrated, and I watched a few times before attempting it myself.

Elias shook his head. "No. You must cup the sides of the clay as well. Roll down and cup. Roll down and cup."

Imitating his movements, I applied more pressure to the sides, pushing the clay down and away from me while pressing in on the sides, and then rolling it back toward me and pressing forward again.

After watching me for a moment, he gave a nod. "*Das gut.*"

"I feel like my *mamm* kneading bread."

He smiled. "Something like that, and for a similar reason. This process removes pockets of air that may crack when the pot is fired. Also, wedging the clay forms a spiral that will make it easier to work with on the wheel. See here?"

Lifting his lump, he turned the side to me. The repetitive pushing and rolling had produced a circular design visible on the edge. I picked up my own, and was disappointed to see that my spiral looked more like uneven ripples.

"Cup more firmly," Elias advised, "and keep wedging."

I did. As with most new things, the master beside me made the process look easier than it was. He finished wedging long before I did and then waited patiently as I continued to roll and cup, roll and cup.

When he deemed my lump sufficiently wedged, he instructed me to ease up on the cupping pressure until the clay formed a rounded pyramid, with the spiral most evident in the base. I stepped back, examining my work while rubbing away an ache in my right shoulder. Elias's creation looked like a smooth gumdrop. Mine resembled a squat, malformed carrot.

"It will do," he pronounced. "Now we go to the wheel." From a shelf on the wall he took two plastic discs and held one up. "This is a bat."

"Why is it called a bat?"

A good-humored grin hovered around the corners of his mouth. "Why is an apple called an apple?"

I took that to mean he didn't know the origin of the word and returned his grin. "I guess it doesn't matter."

With a nod of agreement, he approached one of the benches. "You fit the bat on the wheel like so."

Indicating that I should sit on the bench, he fixed his own bat in place on the wheel next to mine. Elias taught by example, using few words but patiently demonstrating the techniques again and again until I grasped them. I learned the proper way to slap my cone-shaped lump of clay in the center of the bat, or as close as I could manage, how to kick the footplate to achieve and maintain a consistent spin, and how to hold my hands as I manipulated the whirling lump of clay. Several times he left his bench and placed his hands over mine, pushing to show me how much pressure to apply, how to mold with the heel of my hand, and to plant my elbows on my thighs to keep my arms steady.

The consistency of the clay changed as I applied more and more water. At first gritty, when I added water and worked it through the mass, it became smoother and more pliable.

As the clay drank in the water, so it absorbed my thoughts. The world narrowed to the size of Elias's workshop, my focus to the spinning object taking form between my hands. Under his guidance, my thumb pressed into the center, pushing its way down to create a cavity, and then my fingers expanded the hollow into a basin. The clay felt soft and pliable, susceptible to the slightest change in pressure. The sole of my shoe kept the kick plate spinning, and after a while I forgot to notice the movement of my leg, so fixated was I on forming the bowl taking shape on my bat.

And then I pressed too hard. Or perhaps my arm slipped, or I forgot to move with the slow, unhurried movements Elias advised. My bowl began to wobble and before I could steady it, the sides collapsed inward.

I sat back, my foot returning to the floor, and stared in dismay at the malformed object before me.

Looking at the disaster on my wheel, Elias nodded toward it. "The sides were not uniform thickness. See there." He pointed to the strip where the upper two inches of my bowl had separated from the rest. "Look how thin the clay is there, and how thick directly below. Go ahead. Feel it."

I did, and immediately saw the problem. By not applying consistent pressure as I worked the sides upward, I'd created an area that was thinner than the rest. That section had been unable to withstand the strain of further molding.

The older man wore a wide smile that touched off an itchy irritation in my mood. I didn't bother to soften my tone. "You need not be so delighted with my failure."

To that, Elias merely laughed. "But that is how we learn, Seth. How else do we gain knowledge except through failing and trying again?"

His words struck me as particularly wise and applicable to more than pottery. But I was not in the mood to think deep thoughts at the moment. Instead, my hands itched to mold the clay once again.

"How do I fix it?"

Elias shook his head, still chuckling. "There is no fixing that. But don't worry about waste. We will reclaim the clay. For now, put it in that barrel over there"—he pointed to a thick plastic trash can behind me—"and begin wedging another piece."

I did as instructed, though I experienced a stab of melancholy as I scraped my ravaged bowl off the bat and into the barrel.

When the curtain was swept aside and Robbie stepped through, I looked up in surprise. "You came back early?"

He halted a step inside the workroom, confusion apparent on his face. "It's four thirty."

Astonished, I looked at Elias, who nodded. I couldn't remember ever losing track of time so completely.

"Hey, that looks pretty good." The young driver approached, eyeing the bowl on my bat. "I thought you'd never done this before."

"He is a *gut* student." Elias awarded me a wide grin. "Only two mishaps and three successes."

He waved toward the shelves, where my three bowls sat beside the seven he'd made during the same time. Though pride was a sin not to be tolerated, I couldn't help feeling a sense of accomplishment. Not a single one of my three was in danger of being called a boat anchor.

"I'm almost finished with this one," I said. "Do you have time?"

Robbie shrugged. "I've got nowhere to be."

He straddled the bench of the wheel facing mine and watched as I put the finishing touches on my final bowl. When I had formed the rim exactly as I wanted it, I set down the wooden rib and saturated a small piece of sponge in the now-cloudy bowl of water. Applying the sponge, I smoothed the surface, both inside and out, and then separated the bowl from the bat by running a thin wire beneath it. Then I straightened and examined my creation.

"Looks great to me," Robbie said.

Elias came to stand beside me and bent over for a closer inspection. With a nod, he remarked, "It is usable."

Over the past two hours I'd learned enough about him to recognize the remark as approval. Satisfied, I stood, removed the bat, and slid the bowl on the tray beside the other three. Now that I examined them with a critical eye, I noticed something I had not before.

I turned toward my teacher with a frown. "They're not the same."

"No. They are not."

I'd started with the same amount of clay each time, but looking at the bowls now, I saw that one was taller than the rest, and one thicker. The third's sides bulged wide, and the lip of the bowl I'd just finished appeared more round. Perhaps my satisfaction of a moment before was unfounded.

Robbie had come to my side. "I like that one best." He pointed to the tall bowl. "You should make a few more like it, and then you could sell them as a set."

I was about to protest that I was a long way from producing anything that would be worthy of selling, but Elias spoke before I did. "A good goal for a future lesson. But on Monday we will trim these."

"Monday?"

"*Ya*. I like to trim the next day, but tomorrow is Sunday. I'll cover these in plastic to keep them moist, and we will trim on Monday."

I hadn't considered when I would return, but I certainly saw his point. My creations were recognizable as bowls, but they lacked the finishing touches of the products on Elias's shelves. The lower portions were uneven and thick where they squatted on the bats. The bottoms would need to be shaped to look like regular bowls. And if I wanted to carve a decoration into them, as Elias sometimes did, I'd need to do that before the clay was hardened in the kiln.

"Monday it is. I'll come after morning chores."

Robbie jerked to attention. "I'll bring you. What time should I pick you up?"

I eyed the young man. Though I hated to monopolize his time, I also hesitated to ask Aaron for use of the family's buggy for a personal errand such as this one. It was enough that I would be asking for permission to leave the farm and any work he had planned for the day. Noah would no doubt lend me the use of his buggy, but again, I hesitated to ask. Driving myself did not produce nearly the anxiety of driving the women of my family, and yet I found myself wanting to avoid taking up the reins. And besides, Robbie seemed eager.

"Will ten thirty work?" I included Elias in my question, and both agreed.

I cleaned my work area and my hands, and then we exited the work-room. Beyond the curtain we found Leah sweeping the showroom floor. She glanced up at me, and I felt myself the subject of an intense stare that lasted a few seconds. Then she gave a slight nod, whether in dismissal or acknowledgment of my work with her employer I didn't know, and returned to her sweeping.

An odd woman. She'd certainly displayed a friendly side to Naomi this morning, but though I'd gone out of my way to be pleasant, I had yet to see even a hint of a smile directed toward me. Nor Robbie either. Was she uncomfortable with men? Had her scar, perhaps, been caused by a man?

Pondering the disturbing thought, I bid Elias farewell and followed my driver out of the shop.

Six

The following day was a church Sunday, and this time the meeting was held at the Graber home. My friend Josiah lived there with his *mamm* and *daed,* along with Ella and their two children and a few younger brothers and sisters. As eldest son, Josiah would one day run the family farm, but for now his *daed* remained in full control.

The service lasted the usual three hours, but today the main sermon was delivered by James Troyer. Our district was fortunate to have such an engaging speaker among our ministers. James loved to laugh, and though he controlled himself during his sermons, he couldn't completely restrain his natural tendency toward humor. Often during his sermons the community struggled to maintain an appropriately solemn and worshipful attitude, and Bishop Beiler had been known to cast a disapproving glare around the congregation, daring anyone to laugh out loud.

As we filed outside, where the early March sunshine was putting on a surprising and most welcome display of the approaching spring, every face wore a smile. I stepped from the porch to the grass, and a herd of children ran past me, their delighted laughter filling the air. Mark and Luke raced after the older ones, intent on keeping up as they galloped toward the barn.

"We have a new litter of kittens," a familiar voice said behind me.

I turned to greet Josiah, with whom I'd not spoken before the service. "That explains the excitement."

"I warned them to take care. That barn cat doesn't take kindly to people approaching her kittens." He shook his head. "No doubt we'll see blood drawn before the day is over."

Bishop Beiler exited the house, scanned the gathering, and when he caught sight of us, headed our way. With a nod at Josiah, he addressed me. "Seth, I want to speak with you. You are aware of Laura King?"

I'd heard *Mamm* and Saloma discussing the sad news only the day before. Laura, the daughter of one of the families in our district, had been enjoying her *rumspringa* for several months. Last week Laura had shocked the district by running away from home. Her parents found a letter on her pillow in the morning, telling them she had decided to leave the Amish.

I scanned the crowd gathering on the grass as more people exited the house. Susan King stood in the center of a small knot of women. She held a handkerchief to her eyes, her shoulders heaving, and my own *mamm* rested a hand on her arm in a gesture of comfort.

"*Ya,* I know of Laura."

The bishop rocked back on his heels, hands clasped behind his back. "We are going on Tuesday to bring her home. I would like you to come with us."

"She has decided to come back?" I had not heard that bit of news.

Bishop Beiler's lips tightened. "Not yet. But she will."

Now I understood. When a young person chose to leave the Amish, it was the district's responsibility to convince them of the error of that decision. No doubt Laura had already received letters written by many in our community. In fact, that was the conversation I'd heard yesterday. Saloma had written a letter to Laura, telling her how her absence had affected the entire district and particularly Laura's parents. If the campaign of letters from those who loved her and were concerned for her failed to bring about a change of heart, a delegation was often sent to try to persuade the lost sheep in person.

"I don't see what I have to offer," I told the bishop. "She barely knows me."

"You are respected and liked more than you know. You can speak of the comfort of the Lord through faithful adherence to our ways."

Ah. Now the reason for my inclusion became clear. Because I had experienced tragedy and remained faithful, my opinion might hold some weight. At least that was the bishop's hope.

Was I seen as having a strong faith among my community? I glanced at Josiah, who wore a thoughtful expression and whose head nodded slowly as though in agreement with the bishop's explanation. Did no one know how often I had questioned my faith after the loss of my wives? How often I still did?

The bishop's gaze became piercing. "I believe you should join us."

In other words, the invitation was not one I could refuse. Accepting the inevitable, I nodded. "*Ya,* I will go. Of course I will."

He smiled. "We will pick you up at eight. Laura is in Philadelphia, so I expect to be back before the evening meal."

The drive would be less than two hours each way. Laura had not gone far from home, which could mean she was reluctant to desert her family and her community completely.

The bishop's gaze focused on something behind me, and he left with a determined step. I turned to see him approach Abigail Schrock, no doubt to recruit her for the same mission.

"That was a surprise," I said to Josiah.

He cocked his head and peered at me from beneath the round brim of his hat. "It shouldn't be. You're the perfect person to go, for several reasons."

Something about the way he spoke set off a flicker of concern. "What reason besides the one he gave?"

"You really don't know? Laura was riding home from the singings with Daniel Schrock. Now Katie Zook rides home with Daniel."

He indicated a place to our right with a jerk of his forehead, where Daniel and Katie stood a good distance apart from everyone else. They stood close together and, as we watched, Daniel lifted his head and laughed at something Katie said. Their attraction for one another was obvious to anyone who happened to glance their way.

I turned back to Josiah. "So Daniel threw Laura over for Katie. What does that have to do with me?"

"Seth." Josiah spoke softly. "Laura is now without a prospect for a husband."

His meaning slapped me like a physical blow. I reared back and stared at him, incredulous. "Do you think the bishop intends me to court Laura King?"

"It has been discussed."

"Discussed?" Now I was incensed. Was I a topic of conversation among my community? "By whom?"

My friend shrugged. "Ella said it has come from several sources."

I could not believe what I was hearing. Josiah's own wife had participated in gossip about me, her husband's friend? "But Laura is a teenager, little more than a child."

"She is twenty. You are twenty-six. The age difference is nothing." His tone softened. "It has been a year since the accident, Seth."

Hot anger rose up inside me. I spoke through clenched teeth. "Do you think I don't know *exactly* how long it has been?"

Compassion flooded his face. "Of course you do. I didn't mean to suggest otherwise."

So it was not only my family who had decided I'd had enough time to grieve. My entire district apparently believed grief expired after one year.

Well, I would put a stop to their scheming. Josiah was my closest friend. Let him be the messenger.

"I do not intend to marry again. Ever." I looked him directly in the eye. "Please tell Ella to do me the favor of informing her sources."

Josiah looked at me, shaking his head. "You may think so now, but you will change your mind."

Seeing pity so clearly in the eyes of my friend fanned the anger smoldering inside me into full flame. My hands clenched into fists.

"I know my own mind, and it will not change," I retorted with more volume than I intended. "I won't marry again. I have no right to do that to another woman."

Josiah's eyes widened, and I snapped my mouth shut. I hadn't intended to say that. My anger had gotten the better of me. I wasn't prepared to discuss my deepest guilt with anyone. From the look on Josiah's face, he was about to prod the issue, something I would not allow. Before he could reply, I turned on my heel and stomped away.

I would wait in the buggy for the rest of my family. Alone. The way it should be.

Trimming my bowls turned out to be an exacting and extremely rewarding task. Once again I sat next to Elias and watched him closely as he demonstrated.

"It is important to center the bowl on the wheel." He lifted one of his bowls from its bat and placed it upside down on the wheel, then began to kick. "Concentric lines on the wheel help, but again, you must develop an eye."

The spinning bowl looked perfectly centered to me, but Elias rested a hand on the rim of the basin and extended a finger until the tip barely touched the clay. Using that technique, I saw that his fingertip did not touch the bowl consistently, but one side moved slightly away. He stopped the spinning and made a slight adjustment to the bowl's placement. After repeating that process several times, he sat back with a satisfied smile.

"Now you do it."

My bowl, which had been so pliable and soft in my hands on Saturday, had hardened somewhat. The clay felt firmer, and though I could still press it inward if I applied pressure, I was able to place it upside down on the wheel without fear of damaging the rim. Of course it took me three times as long to center my bowl than it had Elias, but eventually he gave me a nod. We then pressed small pieces of clay onto the wheel on three sides of the bowl to hold it in place while we worked.

I learned to apply a faceting tool—a new word for me—to trim away the excess clay on the bottom of the bowl. Clay carved away in ribbons as I created the foot on which the finished bowl would rest. Elias demonstrated the proper way to apply a soft rib—another familiar word with an unfamiliar application, this one for a rubber wedge with rounded edges—to smooth out the foot and the sides of the bowl.

That finished, Elias said, "Now you must mark your work." He picked up a wooden-handled metal pick and, with a deft movement, carved his initials and the year into the bottom of his bowl.

I retrieved my own pick and sat staring at the neat bottom of my bowl. What should my potter's mark be? Initials, like my teacher? No, I could not mar the perfectly smooth clay by carving my initials into it. Something else representative of me, then. But what represented me? A cow to indicate my work as a farmhand? Inwardly, I indulged in a sarcastic laugh.

I leaned over the piece on my wheel, lowered the pick, and carved a straight line. In my mind rose an image of Rachel on our wedding day. A distance away I carved another line, a picture of Hannah laughing at something I'd said so clear my heart twisted. In the center of the two, I carved a third line, this one a diagonal slash that did not quite touch the other two. I was the lopsided line, hovering in the middle, no longer anchored on either end. Drawing in a deep breath, I blew it out slowly as I set down my tool.

Elias inspected my mark for a long time. Finally, he gave a nod. "I like the simplicity."

So did I. An immense feeling of satisfaction settled over me when I leaned back to inspect my work. "It looks like a real bowl."

Elias laughed. "It *is* a real bowl, and a fine one." The laughter faded, and he eyed me sideways. "You have the touch, a feel for the clay. You could be a good potter."

I was still attempting to battle a flare of pride when he lifted his head and shouted toward the showroom. "Leah, come and see what Seth has done."

The curtain parted and Leah entered. I scooted back on the bench as she approached and tilted her head to inspect my bowl. Though her solemn expression did not change, I detected a slight…softening, perhaps?

Was that her way of showing approval? A moment later my assumption was proven true.

"You did a good job." Her low voice held a note of affirmation that set off an answering flutter in my stomach. I doubted if compliments came often from Leah's scarred lips. Then the sardonic tone returned. "It would bring a good price as long as you don't mess it up when you glaze it."

Judging from the glance she gave me, she fully expected me to botch the glazing process.

Elias leaped to my defense. "He will do fine."

I ignored both the accusation and the affirmation, and answered the first part of her comment. "I don't intend to sell it. This will be a gift for my sister, Becky, for when she has a home of her own."

"Then we must work on turning this bowl into a matching set," Elias said. "After we trim the rest, we will have time to throw several more before your driver returns."

I remembered his comment from Saturday, how he liked to trim the day after a piece was created. "I'm not sure when I can come back. Tomorrow I'm traveling to Philadelphia, and on Wednesday I'll need to help my *bruder* with the farm after being absent for two days."

"Philadelphia?" He raised his eyebrows. "There is a ceramic supply store there with a particular glaze I like. Would your errand in the city allow you time to bring back a gallon or two?"

Leah left my side and headed toward the front as I answered.

"I'm not sure. If I have time and the others don't mind, I would be happy to. But I am going with a group to convince a young woman to come home."

At my words, Leah halted and jerked around to face me. "You're going on a delegation visit?"

The question sounded like an accusation. I returned her piercing stare with a curious nod.

Her lips twisted, making the scar appear more pronounced. "I will say a prayer for the poor girl." With that she swept out of the room.

What did she mean? Not that she would pray for the success of our mission. Did she mean she would pray for Laura to be persuaded to the truth and return with us? From her sharp tone, I didn't think so. It sounded as though Leah intended to pray that Laura would stand firm against us.

I turned to Elias, questioning him without words.

He shook his head slowly. "She experienced many such visits herself in the days when she went *Englisch*."

"Leah was Amish?"

"*Ya.*" A sad expression rested heavily on his features. "My wife and I raised her in our faith when our son and his wife died. But she has suffered much, our Leah. In the end she chose to leave."

"Wait." I put a hand on top of my hat, trying to make sense of the words whirling through my brain. "Leah is your *granddaughter*?"

"Did you not know?" I shook my head, and Elias heaved a sigh. "The only one of our family who has rejected our ways. But she has not rejected us." He cast an unreadable glance toward the closed curtain and continued in a soft voice that could not have been heard from the other room. "And we never cease to pray that one day she will return, embrace a Plain life, and be baptized."

So many questions burned in my mind. What suffering had Leah endured that caused such damage to the faith of her upbringing? Was her scar a part of that suffering? And what of her relationship with Elias and his wife? Apparently, Leah had not yet been baptized when she chose to leave the Amish, which meant that while her family must certainly grieve her decision, she was not under the ban, and they could still associate with her, even eat with her. Still, most young people who rejected our way of life moved away so they could engage in worldly pursuits without the disapproving eyes of their families.

Elias had moved to Lancaster County from Ohio, where districts often adhered to an *Ordnung* much stricter than ours. I'd heard, for instance, that in some communities bicycles were not permitted or, if they were, that the tires may not be rubber. A visitor to our district a few years back had expressed surprise that we were permitted to ride in cars in the seat behind our *Englisch* driver. In his community, they were required to all ride on the passenger's side, even in the backseat, lest the view from the driver's side tempt them to drive themselves.

Had Elias's district adhered to such a strict *Ordnung* that his relationship with his granddaughter was affected? Was that why he came here, to Lancaster County, to set up his pottery shop?

I might have asked some of my questions, except Elias rose from his bench and picked up the bowl he'd trimmed as I'd worked on mine. By his manner he dismissed the subject from further discussion.

"This"—he lifted the bowl—"is called greenware. It is a piece that is ready for the bisque firing."

His attitude was once again that of the teacher instructing his student. Though my questions about Leah and the reason behind his move remained unasked, I had plenty more of a less personal nature.

"Bisque firing?" I repeated the unfamiliar term, weighing it on my tongue. Leah's comment returned to me. "Because it is not yet glazed, I assume there is more than one firing."

He nodded. "A pot is fired twice. The first firing dehydrates the clay, removing all remaining moisture, which changes the clay into ceramic material. A gradual increase in temperature is very important. If the kiln becomes hot too quickly, the water in the clay will turn to steam before it leaves the material, and the bowl will crack."

I glanced toward the back corner of the room where the kiln rested. "How hot does it get?"

"Around one thousand seven hundred degrees. But slowly." He held up a finger. "Very slowly. Then the pot is sintered, and the gradual cooling begins."

I shook my head. So many new terms, I almost felt as though I should write them down in order to remember them all. "What is *sintered*?"

"That means the composite material of the clay has been transformed enough to fully adhere. Look here." He set his trimmed bowl on one of the wide metal trays along the back wall and moved to a separate section to pick up a pitcher. Handing it to me, he said, "Feel the difference."

Was this the same pitcher I'd seen on Elias's wheel the day I brought the women of my family to shop here? If not, it was certainly similar.

Having just trimmed my own creation, I turned it over in my hands, admiring the evenness of the sides, the uniformity of the thickness. The clay of which this pitcher was made had become chalky white and firm. I ran a finger down the sides, which felt smooth but not yet slick and polished like the ones in the showroom.

"It is hardened, but still porous enough to accept the glaze." He took it from my hands and returned it to the shelf beside several other white pieces. "These are all ready to be glazed. The ones waiting for the bisque firing are kept there." He pointed toward the shelf where he'd just placed his newly trimmed bowl. "Put yours there and get the next. We have more trimming to do."

I did as I was told, eager to practice the trimming techniques I'd just learned.

Once again, Robbie's appearance surprised me. I had trimmed all four of my bowls from Saturday and had thrown three more. Though I'd picked up speed, my technique still lacked Elias's skill. Two of my new bowls were close enough in size and shape to my favorite from the previous batch, but I had not yet managed to achieve a set of four that matched.

"You will have to keep trying," Elias said, his lips forming a wide smile.

I grinned in return. "I suppose I will." With another glance at my bowls, I found myself unwilling to wait three days to return to the wheel. Surely, Aaron would not begrudge me a few hours if I rose early and finished my chores before I left the farm. I faced Robbie. "Are you free to drive me on Wednesday?"

The young man shrugged. "Sure. Around the same time?"

I looked at Elias, who said, "*Ya*."

After I'd cleaned my tools and wheel, I bid my teacher *guder daag* and exited the workshop. In the showroom, Leah was engaged in conversation with a pair of *Englisch* ladies, holding up a sturdy earthenware mug and pointing out something on its side. At our appearance she looked up, and her gaze locked onto mine. At least today I knew the reason for the disapproving twist of her lips. No doubt she was thinking of my task tomorrow in light of her own past. I dipped my head in a silent farewell and left the shop.

The clock on the dashboard of Robbie's car read fifteen minutes before one. My stomach rumbled. It had been a long time since breakfast, and I'd missed the noon meal at home.

I turned in my seat toward my driver. "Have you eaten lunch?"

"I haven't had a chance yet," he said as he steered the car out of the parking lot and onto the street. "I was gonna grab something after I dropped you off." He glanced sideways. "You hungry?"

"I did not realize how hungry until just now. What were you planning to grab?"

Without removing his hands from the steering wheel, he shrugged. "I don't know. A burger or something."

A fast-food hamburger would not be my first choice. Because we raised our own meat on the farm, beef prepared commercially always tasted a bit off to me.

I offered an alternative. "There's a Subway on Main Street. Let's go there if you have time." He was silent a moment, and I noticed him biting down on his lower lip. A possible reason occurred to me. "I will buy your lunch."

His head jerked toward me. "You don't have to do that."

"*Ya,* I know. I would like to." My stomach growled again, louder this time.

Apparently loud enough to be overheard. Robbie laughed, and his grip on the wheel relaxed. "Since you put it that way, okay."

The short drive to the restaurant was spent in an easy silence. Inside, we joined the line of those waiting to place their sandwich orders and studied the menu board. Though fast-food hamburgers held little appeal to me, I didn't mind deli meat. One of my favorite sandwich meats was Stoltzfus Sweet Bologna, made and sold locally. *Mamm* sliced it thick, fried it, covered it with plenty of melted Swiss cheese, and served it between two slices of her homemade potato bread. Because Subway didn't offer

Stoltzfus bologna, I settled on ham and watched with admiration as the girl making my sub piled on a generous amount of vegetables and managed to deftly fold the sandwich in half and roll it in a wrapping of paper.

After a slight disagreement at the register, I paid for both meals, and Robbie and I claimed a table near the front door.

He unrolled his sub. "Thanks for this, but I still feel bad about your buying it."

Before answering, I folded my hands in my lap and bowed my head. In silence I thanked the Lord for the food and for granting me the ability to bless the young man sitting across from me. When I opened my eyes, I found that his hands, too, rested in his lap as he waited for me to finish my prayer.

"Amen," I said. "And you shouldn't feel bad. You've been good to me. I'm happy to do something for you."

He didn't smile, but instead his expression became even more solemn as he smoothed the wrapping from his sandwich out on the table like a place mat. "I haven't been good to you. You pay me for driving you."

"Not very much." I'd intended to discuss Robbie's rates with him today anyway. I had no way of knowing how much he had charged Johann and Naomi for delivering them to Wakefield, but when he dropped me off at home Saturday afternoon, I'd been stunned when he would accept only a few dollars from me. "Since it appears that I may visit the pottery shop a few more times, I'd like to know how much I should expect to pay my driver."

The young man shrugged before taking a huge bite out of his sandwich without answering.

"Really." I leaned toward him. "How much will you charge me?"

After he had chewed, swallowed, and washed down the bite with a long draw on his straw, he said, "I haven't really thought about it. How about three dollars?"

I'd picked up my sub, but now set it back down to stare at him, incredulous. "Three dollars? That's outrageous. Kevin Cramer would charge five times that amount."

One eyebrow quirked upward. "Then you should definitely call me instead of Kevin Cramer. It's only seven miles. In my car it doesn't even take a gallon of gas both ways."

"But you drive from Lancaster," I pointed out.

"Just south of Eden, actually. Our house is only about ten miles from yours."

"Unless your car gets forty-five miles to a gallon of gas, that means you're losing money every time you pick me up."

He glanced through the window at his little red vehicle. "It gets almost thirty, so the whole trip doesn't even use two gallons. So then let's say five dollars."

I sat back against the hard booth. "You're forgetting about your time."

That drew a blast of laughter. "Believe me, I don't have anything important to do with my time."

My idea about the reason for Robbie's visit to our farm to offer his services as a driver had been wrong, then. Apparently he was not in need of money. Why, then, would he offer to drive the Amish?

"Do you work?" I asked.

His mouth full again, he shook his head. I picked up my sandwich and bit into it, waiting for him to answer.

"I ought to get a job, I guess, but…" He shrugged. "My parents aren't pushing me to. Not yet, anyway."

So he lived at his parents' home. Perfectly normal for an Amish man of Robbie's age, but not so much for the *Englisch*.

"How old are you?" As soon as the question left my lips, I wanted to take it back. We did not typically express curiosity about our *Englisch* neighbors. We kept to ourselves, separate from the world. But something about the young man across from me compelled me to know more.

"Nineteen." His lips twisted into a sardonic line. "Yeah, I know the next question. Why aren't I in college?"

I would not have asked, but now that he'd brought the subject up, I couldn't help but wonder. Amish children stopped their official schooling at the completion of eighth grade, but *Englisch* went on for another several years. Still, I took another bite of my sandwich, an excuse to remain silent.

"I'm taking a couple of online courses to keep my dad happy. But I… wasn't ready for college." The lightness of his tone a moment before had disappeared. He set his food down on the makeshift place mat and stared at it, a struggle plain on his face. "I barely graduated from high school. Just couldn't concentrate those last few months of my senior year. My counselor felt I needed to take a year off to get my head straight."

Though I'd never attended any school but the one-room schoolhouse within walking distance of our farm, I was aware of the purpose of guidance counselors. My general impression was that they helped *Englisch* teenagers decide on a suitable profession and steered them toward the education that would help them achieve it.

What could he mean by *get my head straight*? Had he gotten off track, as so many young people did these days? Gotten mixed up in drugs or alcohol? We knew that drugs were a growing problem in the world. Thanks to some who carried the freedoms of *rumspringa* too far, the insidious stuff had even snaked its way into our community, though the bishops worked hard to stay on top of the issue.

Whatever Robbie's problem had been, clearly he still struggled with it. His downcast expression could almost be described as haunted, something with which I could relate. Compassion welled up in me. If he had been on drugs, I was confident that he no longer was. I'd never detected a hint of impairment in him, and his driving skills were excellent. He had never even displayed the effects of a hangover, something I was familiar with from my *rumspringa* days.

With a visible effort, his countenance cleared and he picked up the remaining section of his sandwich. "Anyway, I guess my job is driving you people around. So if you hear of anyone else who needs a driver, I hope you'll give them my number."

"I will do that."

We finished our lunch and Robbie drove me home. When we arrived, he balked at my offer of payment, claiming I had bought his lunch and that was payment enough. I tossed a twenty-dollar bill onto the passenger seat and hurried into the house before he could return it.

SEVEN

My ride arrived to pick me up a few minutes before eight o'clock on Tuesday morning. Bishop Beiler had rented a van to accommodate the number of people included in this visit because Kevin's automobile could only seat five. Besides Susan King and me, Bishop Beiler had included Laura's younger sister Irene and, to my surprise, Daniel Schrock. My conversation with Josiah on Sunday played again in my mind, along with the sight of Daniel's infatuated attention on Katie Zook. An odd choice for the day's errand, to be sure. His mother, Abigail, was not in the van, and the reason for the bishop's conversation with her on Sunday became clear. He had enlisted Abigail's help in convincing Daniel to join us. The young man sat alone on the rear bench, a morose expression darkening his features. Apparently, he had not agreed to participate willingly.

I gave Kevin the slip of paper on which Elias had written the address of the ceramic shop in Philadelphia, and he verified that the place was not far out of our way. We would be able to perform the errand.

Mamm followed me out of the house and handed a basket to Susan. "I made lunch. Sandwiches, cookies, and a few odds and ends."

Susan's eyes flooded with tears. "*Danke,*" she managed as she accepted the basket. Anyone with eyes saw immediately that her emotions were not stirred merely by the kind gesture and gift of food. The fate of her daughter's eternal soul rested on the success of the day's errand. What mother would not be emotional?

The bishop occupied the front seat beside Kevin, while Susan and Irene sat on the middle seat. I slid onto the back bench and nodded a greeting at Daniel, who returned the gesture and then immediately plastered his face against the opposite window.

The drive to Philadelphia was made mostly in silence. Occasionally, the soft sound of sobs drifted back to me from the middle seat, and once Irene unfastened her seat belt to slide to the center of the bench, where she could sit closer to her *mamm*.

When the skyline of the city rose before us, Bishop Beiler twisted around in his seat. "We must agree on our approach. I will speak to Laura first and remind her of the community's love and concern for her."

Susan's sobs returned, louder this time, and Irene leaned toward her so that their shoulders touched.

The bishop spared a compassionate glance for her and then addressed Irene. "You must tell her how it has been at home since she left. Do not soften your words. Describe how her decision has hurt your family and you."

Irene nodded, and the bishop raised his gaze to Daniel. "You will apologize for hurting her."

The young man's head shot up, defiance glaring from his eyes. "I have done nothing to apologize for. We never had an understanding. *Ya*, I drove her home from the singings a few times, but we never..." He bit his lower lip. "...touched. If she thought more would come from our relationship, that is not my fault."

More sobs from the middle seat, and Irene tossed a quick glare over her shoulder.

I watched the bishop closely and was impressed to see not a hint of disapproval at Daniel's rebellious display. Instead, his smile softened.

"I am not suggesting that you are to blame, Daniel. I have no doubt that your treatment of Laura has been honorable at all times. But her letters to her *schweschders* mention you as one of the reasons for her unhappiness in our district." When the young man drew breath to interrupt, Bishop Beiler held up a hand to stop him. "Through no fault of your own, you played a part in her departure. Therefore, you may also have a part in her return. Our task today is not to throw blame toward you or Laura or anyone else. It is to remind her that a Plain life is God's will for her, and to convince her that great comfort can be found in our way of life."

Daniel's head dropped forward so that his chin nearly rested on his chest. He accepted the bishop's logic with a barely perceptible nod.

Our leader's gaze slid lastly to me, and my spine stiffened. If he dared to suggest that I offer a romantic reason for Laura to return, I was not sure I could control my temper. I might even desert the group and find a phone to call Robbie to come get me.

I don't know if my guarded expression halted the words he was about to speak, or if his long silence was due to his uncertainty about my role in the upcoming confrontation. We stared at one another for moments that stretched longer than was comfortable.

Finally, I drew a resigned breath. "And what of me? What have I to say that may convince her?"

"You can speak to her of the comfort of our Lord." His tone was so soft that the rigid place in my chest melted. "Tell her how our community has supported you, and of the strength you've received through adherence to our way of life."

His words were well spoken. Not once did he mention the double tragedy I had suffered, which would certainly have raised my carefully constructed defenses and closed in my emotions. Instead, he spoke of the comfort found in being part of a faith community. I dipped my head in acknowledgment, and the bishop faced forward once again.

Kevin's cell phone directed us through the streets of outer Philadelphia with a pleasant, if stilted, female voice. The neighborhood through which we drove was not a wealthy one. Though the time was midmorning, I spotted a group of school-aged youth clustered in an alley, a cloud of smoke rising above them. Trash littered some of the dirt-packed yards we passed, and grass grew only sparsely. When the phone announced that we had arrived at our destination, Kevin parked the van in front of a narrow three-story house. At least this building appeared clean and well maintained. Frilly white curtains showed inside a large front window, and a rainbow of colors covered the others.

As we piled out of the van, Kevin opened a thick book and propped it on the steering wheel, apparently prepared to wait as long as necessary. Our little troop filed up the short walkway and onto a small covered porch. Plastic chairs sat on either side of a round table, where an ashtray filled with cigarette butts emitted a pungent and unpleasant odor.

An *Englisch* woman answered the door. She had short hair, which was mostly gray but with enough red locks still to see that her hair had once matched the liberal spray of freckles covering her face. She wore jeans and a T-shirt covered with a bright yellow apron with a giant smiley face.

Her gaze swept our group, and the smile left her lips, replaced by a caustic line. "Who are you here for?"

The question and her manner surprised me. Obviously, she'd received delegations such as ours before. Did she have several Amish people staying there?

"Laura King," answered the bishop in a firm tone.

"Hmm." The lips pursed while she nodded. "Well, you're in luck. She hasn't left for work yet." She swung the door open and swept a hand inside. "Come on in. I'll get her."

Daniel and I exchanged a glance as we followed the others into the house. I don't know what he'd expected, but I thought we'd find Laura living in a cheap hotel room, or maybe sharing a shabby apartment with someone else. I'd not often had reason to visit *Englisch* houses, so I glanced around curiously as the woman led us through an entry hall and into the front room, the one with the white curtains. The walls were covered with decorations, including photographs, that would never be found in an Amish home. Above a carved mantelpiece hung a huge painting of a cottage beside a stream, surrounded by trees beneath a brilliant sunset that nearly took my breath away.

"Have a seat," our hostess instructed. "I'll tell Laura you're here."

When she'd gone, we stood frozen for a moment. The furniture in this room was all so, well, *fancy*. Cushioned and covered in brightly patterned fabric, with matching pillows in the corners of the sofa. On a highly polished table in the center of the room rested a gleaming vase full of flowers amid sprigs of greenery. Flowers in March?

The bishop moved first, selecting perhaps the plainest seat the room had to offer—a high-backed chair with upholstered arms. He perched on the very edge, not allowing himself to lean against the padded back. The rest of us did likewise, spreading ourselves around the room. Before I sat, I bent to inspect the vase. Its shape was beautiful, delicate with a graceful curve at the top. Ceramic, certainly, though not the earthenware Elias produced in his workshop. I also noted that the flowers, though pretty, were not real. What a shame to use such a beautiful vase to hold something unnatural.

I'd just settled on a soft chair when Laura entered.

At the sight of her, Susan leaped off of the sofa and flew across the floor, her sobs filling the room. She gathered her daughter into a hug, weeping on her shoulder. Irene, too, went to her sister's side and wrapped her arms around them both. Laura returned the embrace and her shoulders, too, heaved with tears. I glanced at the bishop. Perhaps our task would not be so difficult after all.

When the torrent of the women's emotions slowed, they stepped apart, though Susan grasped Laura's hand and pulled her back to the sofa where she maintained her grip after the three had been seated. Glancing around the room, Laura acknowledged first the bishop and then me. When her gaze fell on Daniel, who did not look up from his close examination of the carpet between his shoes, her face crumpled and tears once again filled her eyes.

Though she was still our Laura, she wore the clothing of an *Englisch* girl. Her T-shirt bore a bright zigzag pattern of orange and green, and she wore jeans that clung rather too tightly to her slim frame. Her feet were bare, not at all unusual for the Amish, but each toenail had been painted a bright red, as had her fingernails. Her lips also bore color, and the makeup on her eyes had run down her cheeks in black streaks with her tears. Her hair flowed loose down her back, with no *kapp* covering her head.

Bishop Beiler cleared his throat. "We've come to bring you home."

"I know." Swallowing hard, she nodded. "I've been expecting you."

Hope sprang into Susan's eyes. "Then you are ready to come home?"

The look Laura gave her mother was filled with pity. "No, *Mamm*. I am staying here."

Susan leaned forward, her face to her knees, as sobs took her once again.

On Laura's other side, Irene grabbed up her free hand. "Look at her. She's like this always. How can you do this to her? To all of us?"

I knew in the moment before Laura's face hardened that her sister's approach was the wrong one. Guilt was no way to convince a person to embrace faith.

"The whole community misses you," Bishop Beiler said. "You are part of us. When one part goes missing, the others suffer."

Laura lifted her gaze to him. "It's not my intention to make anyone suffer, but I must make my own decisions." She squeezed her mother's hands. "I have a job here, a good one. And a nice place to live, thanks to Marilyn."

"You have jobs to do at home." Irene's tone held an unrelenting note of accusation. "But now the rest of us have to do them. We work twice as hard to make up for you."

I interrupted, mostly to relieve the mounting tension. "What job do you have?"

Laura gave me a grateful look. "I'm a waitress at a pizza restaurant. Besides my paycheck, my meals are free." The hint of a smile appeared. "And I must be a good waitress, because my tips are always good."

The bishop straightened. "Did not our Lord say, 'Ye cannot serve God and mammon'?"

Her expression became contrite at the reminder. "*Ya*, but I am not serving mammon. I am serving people." She looked down and lowered her voice. "Which the Lord also commanded us to do."

Daniel gasped, and even I widened my eyes at her boldness. To quote *die Bibel* to her own bishop? Had rebellion taken such a deep root in her?

When she looked at Daniel, her expression hardened. "What are you doing here?"

"I…" He cleared his throat. "I came to apologize if I have hurt you in any way."

"No apology is necessary." She gave him a brief, chilly smile that convinced no one. "There was no understanding between us."

The glance Daniel cast at the bishop held a not-so-subtle *I told you so.* "Still, I would hate to think I had any part in your deserting your family."

The woman who had opened the door interrupted any answer Laura might have given by entering at that moment, carrying a silver tray. "I know you've driven a long way, so I thought you might like some coffee." She set the tray, which held a coffeepot, mugs, and a plate of cookies, on the low table in front of the couch. "I also have tea if you prefer."

Susan, who had managed to stop her flow of tears, cast a cautious but grateful look at her. "That is very kind of you."

The woman gave her a smile that held a measure of compassion and then left us alone.

Laura began pouring coffee into mugs. "That is Marilyn, my friend. She let me stay here free until I found a job. Now I'm able to pay rent like the others."

Bishop Beiler took the mug she handed him. "Others?"

"*Ya.* Five girls are living here."

Marilyn's comment at the door returned to me. "Are all of them leaving the Amish?"

"Not all." Laura brought coffee across the room to me. "Only three of us. The other two are *Englisch.* They fell on hard times, and Marilyn offered to help."

I glanced at the empty doorway through which Marilyn had disappeared. She opened her home to girls in need. Admirable, and in fact an act of Christian charity. I shook myself. Well, the Amish knew there were Christians living in the world. But we were called to express our Christian faith in different ways than them. And Laura, having been born and raised Amish, needed to understand the difference.

Bishop Beiler obviously felt the same. He began to speak then, telling

Laura of the grief her community felt over her departure. Had that not become evident to her in the many letters she had received? Did she think she could find the same sense of belonging in the world?

As he spoke, my thoughts drifted to another woman who had left the Amish. Had Leah found a sense of belonging in her *Englisch* life? Judging by her solemn countenance and sarcastic comments, I didn't think so. Yet she still enjoyed the love and acceptance of her family. Watching Laura's face as she attended to the bishop's lecture—for there was no other word to describe the diatribe he now began—I wondered if Elias and his wife had truly acted in their granddaughter's best interests. Had they been less accepting and instead insisted on her returning to the Amish, would that have been a deciding factor in her decision?

Of course, there was also the suffering Elias had mentioned. Christ Himself instructed us to ease the suffering of others. I could do nothing but respect Elias for supporting one he loved who was caught in the midst of such pain as Leah must have experienced to cause such a life-changing decision.

With a quick shake of my head to dislodge the thoughts, I drained the last of my coffee. Such questions were for men much wiser than I, who couldn't get through even a single day without being tormented by my own pain.

At last the bishop seemed to have exhausted his store of reasons for Laura to return to those who loved her. She rose, her expression solemn, and picked up the silver tray. As she circled the room so each of us could place our mugs on it, she didn't meet anyone's gaze.

"I'll take this to the kitchen," she said before leaving the room, her head lowered.

Bishop Beiler looked at me. "Talk to her, Seth."

I scrubbed at my beard, overcome by a fit of nerves as they all stared at me. I'd been included in this delegation for a reason—my mind skittered away from the second reason Josiah had mentioned—and the time had come to fulfill my commitment. Dread settled in my stomach as I rose and followed Laura from the room.

The kitchen lay at the end of the short hallway through which we'd entered the house. The same cheerful jumble of brightly colored items filled this room, and I glanced around at an assortment of appliances that would never be found in an Amish kitchen. The countertops were covered with electric gadgets, each connected by cords to outlets in the walls. I knew their purposes, of course, having seen *Englisch* appliances on the shelves at Zimmerman's often enough. A mixer, blender, and toaster sat side by side next to the stove. Red curtains, even brighter than Laura's toenails, hung at a window above the sink.

Laura jumped when I came to her side, and then she gave an embarrassed laugh. "You startled me."

"I didn't mean to." I pointed to the tray of dirty coffee mugs. "Could you use some help cleaning up?"

Her eyes narrowed. "Is that why they brought you? So you could wash the dishes?"

The look she gave me was filled with such shrewdness, and more than a little belligerence, that I couldn't help but laugh. This girl was smart and not one to fall for vague platitudes. Nor was she likely to be convinced by tearful pleas, though clearly her *mamm*'s sorrow touched her deeply. The approach Laura would respect the most would be complete transparency.

Which, of course, was the attitude that made me the most uncomfortable.

I forced an easy tone as I took a half-filled mug from the tray and emptied it in the sink. "I think I'm supposed to convince you that the best way to overcome grief is to draw on the depths of your Amish faith and the support of your community."

She took the empty mug from my hand and placed it in the top rack of an electric dishwasher before giving me a sharp look. "What grief? Ah. You mean losing Daniel to my closest friend."

Bitterness saturated the words. She looked quickly away, but now I understood. Josiah and the bishop had been right. She felt angry and betrayed that her friend had taken up with her beau. Was that her only reason for leaving home? I had no way of knowing, but the loss of a loved one was a reason to which I could speak. My throat tightened at the thought. Though I much preferred to keep my grief to myself, if a word from me could comfort another hurting soul, was that not my duty as a man of faith?

"I lost someone I loved too." I couldn't look at her but focused on emptying another mug.

She placed the mug carefully in the rack and spoke in a quiet tone. "I know. I am sorry."

How I'd grown to hate those words in the months after the deaths of my wives. Of course everyone was sorry, but was their expression of sorrow supposed to lessen mine? Now I was more accepting, and even sympathized with those who were, after all, only attempting to acknowledge my pain.

"Thank you. The point I believe I've been brought here to make is that faith is what…" I'd been about to say *overcomes the grief*, but that would not be true. Grief still gripped at my very soul. I cleared my throat. "Faith provides the comfort necessary to move forward. That, and the work we do in service to our families and our community, which is an outward expression of that faith."

"I have work." She set the last mug in the dishwasher and slid the rack inside. "I work hard at my job, and I do my share of work here." A hand waved to indicate the house around her. "We all do."

"But your family is not here," I pointed out.

"We are like a family." She lifted her chin. "And besides, as I told the others, I am not grieving over the loss of Daniel or even of Katie. I was hurt, yes, but I'm over it. I'm happy here. I even have a boyfriend."

"An *Englisch* boyfriend?"

"He is *Englisch* and honorable. He treats me well."

That piece of news had not been mentioned in my hearing. Did the bishop know? Did Susan and Irene? Attachments to people of the world were among the most dangerous things that could befall an Amish person. Of course there were honorable *Englisch* people, but the fancy ways they embraced were so contrary to ours. Could someone raised Plain ever find true happiness in the world?

I could see how a young woman such as Laura, hurting over what she no doubt felt as the betrayal of her friends, would be vulnerable enough to fall for anyone who showed her kindness.

"Laura, you are an attractive young woman. There are plenty of men back home who would treat you well."

She whirled on me, eyes blazing. I was stunned at the anger in her face. What had I said? I'd spoken only the truth.

"Is that why you think I should return? So I can find an honorable Amish man to marry me?"

"I…no." I took a backward step away from her sudden fury. "I just meant—"

"I know what you meant." She jerked her head toward the front room. "What the bishop meant. What my *mamm* and Irene mean. You want me to come back home, find a husband, and become a good Amish wife!"

She was shouting now, and I countered with a low, reasonable voice.

"What is wrong with that? The Plain way is a good life, the one you were brought up to live. A quiet life of faith, and—"

"Wait a minute." Sparks snapped from her eyes as she raised a finger and stabbed it in my direction. "I just realized why you're really here. You need a wife."

Fury, hot and fierce, rose up in me so quickly it sounded like fire roaring in my ears. "I do *not* need a wife! I will never marry again, never! And if I did, I would not choose a rebellious child like you!"

My declaration came out louder than I intended. The words bounced back to me from the kitchen walls, pounding against my ears. Laura opened her mouth to snap back a reply, but I didn't want to hear any more. I turned on my heel and left the room. Marching down the short hallway, I glanced into the living room, where the others sat staring at me through wide eyes. That they had overheard at least the last part of our conversation was obvious.

I slammed the door shut behind me and winced when the glass rattled. Though I'd intended to sit in the van, the sight of it changed my mind. At the moment the idea of sitting in a confined space was suffocating. Instead, I stomped away from Marilyn's house, down the cracked sidewalk, breathing deep gulps of air that tasted like exhaust. In my mind I tried to form the words of a prayer—any prayer—but the flames of my temper were not so easily extinguished.

I didn't know how much time had passed before my anger lessened enough that I became aware of my surroundings. The houses along the street were not familiar. I had not made any turns so I knew I was on the same street. All I had to do was turn around and go back in the direction I'd come.

Which is what I *should* do. My outburst had probably damaged the day's mission. I should go back and apologize to Laura for my unacceptable lack of control.

The idea left a sour taste in my mouth. I'd spoken the truth, but not all truth needed to be spoken. If only I'd held my tongue and my temper, the others may have been able to convince her to return to her family, her community. Instead, I'd probably driven her further away.

I was saved from the decision when the white van pulled up to the curb beside me and stopped. Through the windshield I glimpsed Kevin and Bishop Beiler, whose face was as blank as a sheet of unlined paper. The side door slid open, and I scanned the interior. As expected, Laura was not inside. Susan sat with her head bowed, her face covered with a handkerchief. Irene did not meet my gaze but stared at the floorboard. With a sigh, I climbed inside and slid onto the back row.

Daniel looked at me. "She says she's never coming home."

A muffled sob sounded from the center row, while the bishop twisted around in the front to face us.

"What did our Lord say when a sheep has wandered away from the flock?" He paused, but no one answered. "He said the shepherd would leave the others to go after the lost sheep, and there will be rejoicing when that sheep is restored." His gaze softened as it rested on Susan. "We will not abandon our lost sheep. We will try again and again until she is safe at home."

Susan looked up from her handkerchief, but being behind her I couldn't see her expression. Still, she must have taken some comfort from the words, because her sobs quieted.

Kevin pulled away from the curb as the bishop again faced forward.

Daniel and Irene turned away from me to look out their respective windows. I did the same, guilt twisting in my gut. There would no doubt be another delegation sent to convince Laura to return to our community, but I would not be invited to be part of it.

EIGHT

When I entered the shop the next day, Leah looked up from the computer screen with a hard glance. "Well?"

I set down the two buckets of glaze I'd purchased in Philadelphia and turned to pull the door shut before facing her. "Well what?"

She rolled her eyes. "Did you convince the wayward soul to return to the safety of the fold?"

A half dozen sharp replies to the sarcastic question came to mind, but I'd spent much of the night praying for the ability to better control my tongue. So I answered simply, "No."

A half smile, half smirk settled on her face, and she returned her focus to the computer.

I started to slide past her into the workroom, but curiosity stopped me. Leah obviously harbored a lot of painful memories behind that hardened exterior and caustic tongue, memories that were none of my business. But one question did burn in my mind.

She raised an expectant expression up to me.

"Do you hate the Amish?"

Clearly, I had surprised her. Her eyebrows arched, and for perhaps the first time since I'd met her, the sneer that always hovered around the edges of her nostrils disappeared.

"Of course not. My family is Amish." Her gaze flickered toward the curtain leading to Elias's workshop.

"Yet you seemed happy just now that our mission to bring Laura home failed."

Her head tilted sideways, and she studied me through narrowed lids, as though trying to decide whether to answer me honestly or deflect with yet another derisive comment. Apparently she settled on the former.

"I don't hate the Amish in general, but when I made the decision to leave, there were those who didn't treat me kindly."

"I'm sorry."

She gave me a sharp look, as if to judge the sincerity of my words, and then nodded. "That meeting you had yesterday? I sat through five of them, and the last few did not end well."

Laura's shouted accusations and the echoes of my own voice sounded again in my ears. "Yesterday's didn't end well either." At her openly curious glance, I shrugged. "I lost my temper."

"Ow." Her features scrunched in a wince. "Did you tell her she was dooming herself to eternal damnation if she didn't pack her bag and come home with you immediately?"

My head jerked upward. Never could I imagine anyone in my community, from Bishop Beiler on down to the least patient farmer in our district, saying that to anyone who had not been baptized into the Amish faith.

My surprise must have showed on my face, for she grimaced. "That's what I was told. And since I've never been one to hold my tongue, my reply was not the least bit, uh, *Plain*."

Her expression made me laugh. I imagined that Leah knew quite a few un-Plain expressions that would have blistered the ears of conservative men.

"Our discussion was heated, but nothing like that," I told her. My laughter faded, and I hung my head. "I became angry, but not for reasons of piety or even in an attempt to convince her to come home. She said something personal that hurt."

I could have bitten my tongue off for those last words. My private pain was not a topic I wanted to discuss. Not with the woman before me or with anyone else.

Leah's expression softened. "I'm sorry." Before I could react, her habitual smirk reappeared, though perhaps not quite as overtly as before. "But I'm glad for her. If she's meant to return to the Amish, she'll come to that decision in her own time. If not, then forcing her will only end in her being miserable for the rest of her life."

Though that logic flew in the face of the common practice of our people in trying to bring a lost soul home, I saw her point.

The curtain opened and Elias appeared. "*Guder mariye,* Seth." His gaze settled on the two buckets resting beside the front door, and he brightened. "You were able to get my glaze. *Danke.* Leah, would you pay him from the cash register?"

I waved aside the offer. "How about a trade? Glaze for lessons. I saw some beautiful pieces yesterday and want to learn how to make them."

"And you still need to learn to glaze your bowls." He rubbed his hands together. "What are we waiting for? Let's go throw some pots."

He disappeared behind the curtain. I touched the round rim of my hat and nodded to Leah as I followed, but she had already dismissed me and returned to her work on the computer.

I suppose I should have expected Bishop Beiler's visit the following day, but the sight of his buggy pulling down our long drive toward the house Thursday morning surprised me. The women were still cleaning up from breakfast, and the arrival of our bishop sent them into a flurry of activity.

"Saloma, make some fresh coffee," *Mamm* directed. "Becky, slice some more of the apple bread and arrange it on a dish. Are the mugs clean yet?"

She addressed the question to *Mammi,* who replied by applying a final swipe with a towel and holding up a clean coffee mug.

Over supper Tuesday night, my family had questioned me closely about the trip to Philadelphia. I had described the meeting, though not my private conversation with Laura in the kitchen. They knew that our mission had not been successful, but I didn't see the need to describe my part in angering the young woman or my outburst. They had clucked their tongues at Laura's determination to stay in the world, and commiserated over the King family's grief.

Daed opened the door before the bishop knocked. "*Guder daag*," he said as he threw the door open wide. "Come in. Always a pleasure to see our bishop."

My father and the bishop had been friends from childhood, back before the lot fell to him and he was merely Amos Beiler. I remembered Amos coming to our house many years ago, when I was a boy, shortly after our former bishop passed away. It was a Saturday night, the night before the church service where our new bishop would be chosen. Aaron and I had hovered at the top of the stairs, spying on the adults. We'd overheard Amos tell *Daed*, "Though I dread the idea, I feel in my gut that the lot will fall to me tomorrow." My father had asked the reason for his dread when serving as bishop to the district was such an honor. Amos had answered, "An honor, yes, but what changes that would bring to me and my family. Selfishly, I am happy with my life as it is. But, of course, I will honor *Gott*'s will if that is what He deems best."

One of my most vivid memories is of the service the next day, when Amos Beiler opened the book that held the slip of paper identifying him as our new bishop. I would never forget his expression of utter humility.

The expression he wore as he entered our house was wreathed in smiles, though perhaps only I detected a hint of strain around his wide-set eyes.

"*Danke.*"

The bishop's straw hat bobbed as he ducked his head at each of us in turn. His gaze lit on me for only a moment before moving quickly on to Aaron. I had no doubt I was the reason for his visit.

Mamm emerged from the kitchen wiping her hands on a towel. "We have fresh coffee and apple bread."

"I've just finished breakfast." He patted his stomach and then grinned even wider. "But how can I turn down a slice of your apple bread?"

"Come into the living room." *Daed* extended a hand to guide his friend farther into the house.

The children had lined up along the wall and stood watching with wide eyes. Bishop Beiler awarded each a smile as he passed. The twins didn't move, but little Sadie giggled and waved a chubby hand.

I followed the men into the living room and took a seat between Aaron and Noah. I kept quiet during their conversation. They discussed the unexpected warm weather, and debated whether or not planting could be done early this year as a result. When the women joined us and passed around coffee and thick slices of sweet bread, talk turned to news of the district. A new teacher had been appointed for the school, a young woman from the next district over.

I cupped the hot mug in my hands and let the voices flow around me. Once I looked up to find *Mammi* giving me a shrewd look, which I deflected with a quick smile. After all the news had been discussed, a brief silence fell as everyone waited for the bishop to reveal the reason for this visit.

Finally, he set his empty mug on the floor beside his plate and looked across the room toward me. "I wonder if I might have a few moments alone with Seth."

All eyes fixed on me.

I dipped my head. "*Ya,* of course."

Curiosity erupted on my family's faces, all except *Mammi*'s. Everyone stood, prepared to leave us alone, but Bishop Beiler also stood and waved toward the front of the house.

"I thought maybe we could walk outside and enjoy some of this pleasant weather we've been talking about."

Out of the range of prying ears. I nodded, relieved at the suggestion.

We donned our coats and left the house. Though the sun shone brightly in a blue sky that promised another warm day, the morning chill had not yet released its grip on the air. Our breath steamed as we walked side by side toward the barn. I'd thought to take him inside, where we would be shielded from any cold breeze that happened to blow, but the air this morning was still. And besides, I felt suddenly reluctant to confine myself inside any structure. The vastness of the bright morning sky and the frosty air felt more appropriate for the conversation I knew was about to take place. Instead, I walked to the far side of the barn, where Schwein lay on her bed of straw, her huge belly swollen with unborn piglets.

"Looks like you'll have a new litter soon," the bishop commented, hands clasped behind his back.

"*Ya,* any day." I came to a halt a few feet from the fencing, wrinkling my nose against the pungent odor that permeated the air around her pen.

"You heard that Nathan Yoder will divide his farm and portion it out to his sons?"

I had heard mention of that at the last church meeting and nodded.

"Young John will have need of livestock soon."

"I'll let Aaron know."

He became quiet, and I battled impatience while waiting for him to get to the reason for this talk. I glanced at the position of the sun. Robbie would arrive to pick me up in an hour to drive me to my next pottery session.

His chest expanded with a breath, and he spoke while keeping his gaze fixed on Schwein. "Yesterday did not go as I had hoped."

A sarcastic reply about his penchant for stating the obvious rose to mind, but I swallowed it and said instead, "I am sure all of us wished for a different outcome."

"After you left the house, we spent some time convincing Laura that you were not there to declare your interest in her." He cleared his throat. "Romantic interest, that is."

For a long moment, I battled a flare of temper. After Josiah's revelation on Sunday, how did Bishop Beiler expect me to respond to that? Should I tell him I felt as Laura did, that I'd been manipulated and used as a romantic lure? And that the idea not only infuriated me but also dishonored the memory of my dead wives?

When I could speak calmly, I said, "I hope you succeeded because I have no interest in her or any other woman."

"That I gathered from your…" He seemed to grasp for a word. "Your conversation in the kitchen."

"My outburst, you mean." I turned to face him. "I apologize for losing my temper, and I will gladly apologize to Susan and Irene and Daniel too. I will even write to Laura asking her forgiveness if you believe that will help." I drew in a breath. "But I meant what I said. I will not marry again." I did not add *and the sooner everyone realizes that, the better.*

He, too, turned, so that we stood face-to-face. Being several inches taller, I looked down on him, which forced him to tilt his head back to see me from beneath the round rim of his hat.

"I have spent much time in prayer for you, Seth Hostetler." My surprise must have shown in my face, for a small smile curved his lips. "I pray for every person over whom the Lord has given me authority through my position, but the plights of some lie more heavily on my heart than others." His voice became little more than a whisper. "You have suffered much pain in your young life."

I would far rather be lectured or even shouted at than to face the heartfelt compassion of my bishop. To my surprise, tears began an unwelcome prickle in the back of my eyes, and I fought hard to douse them. My answer came out gravelly. "*Die Bibel* says the suffering we have in this life will be forgotten in the next."

"I know what *die Bibel* says."

Just yesterday Laura had dared to use the Bible to answer the bishop, and I was chagrined to realize I'd done the same thing.

But his smile became softer, letting me know that he was not offended, and I relaxed a fraction. Then he turned away again, facing the pigpen, and spoke seriously. "You ask my forgiveness for your outburst, and I give it freely. But I must also ask your forgiveness. The reason you were included in yesterday's visit was not merely to offer wisdom concerning the comfort of our Amish ways in the face of loss." He straightened and lifted his head. "I hoped that the plight of an unmarried young woman would soften the heart of a grieving widower."

Did he think I had not already figured that out? Judging by his shamefaced expression, apparently so.

I worked hard to keep my tone even but didn't bother to stop a caustic reply. "I did not realize it was part of a bishop's role to play matchmaker for the community."

He ducked his head in acknowledgment of my accusation. "I listened to the advice of others and did not spend sufficient time in prayer before making that decision. And that is why I must ask your forgiveness."

So even the bishop was not immune to gossip. Apparently, Ella Graber's "sources" had a wider reach than I realized. But I couldn't doubt the sincerity of the man's request.

"I forgive you." I spoke the words required by our Lord, and as they left my lips I realized I meant them. I held no ill feelings for Bishop Beiler, who sincerely wanted the best for those the Lord had placed in his spiritual charge.

"*Danke.*" He drew in a breath and released it.

He was quiet for a few moments, and I sensed that our conversation was not yet over. Finally, he faced me again. "Seth, I cannot forget the anger I heard in your voice yesterday. Such anger is not pleasing to God."

My emotions slammed shut like a door. The inner turmoil with which I struggled was a private battle, not one I cared to discuss with the bishop or anyone else. He waited for a reply, which I did not give.

"I believe there is something unresolved related to the tragic deaths of Rachel and Hannah. Their deaths were not your fault, Seth."

Though the words stabbed at a raw place inside, I snapped, "I know that!"

"Do you?" Wise eyes tried to pierce mine, but I refused to return his gaze.

Eventually, he realized I would not answer his query. With a nod, he stepped away from Schwein's pen and we began our walk back to the house in silence. When we rounded the side of the barn, the door to the house opened, and *Mamm* appeared holding a wrapped bundle. The rest of the family filed out after her.

Just before they came into earshot, Bishop Beiler whispered, "I will continue my prayers for you."

I was saved from replying when my family gathered around us.

Mamm pressed the bundle into the bishop's hands. "For Sarah and your family. Fresh loaves of apple bread and some apple butter we put up last year."

The man's wide smile held no trace of our conversation. "Sarah will be delighted. *Danke* for your kindness."

I stood off to one side as the rest of them gathered around the buggy to bid him farewell. *Daed* and my *bruder* did not act as though anything out of the ordinary had occurred, but the women threw curious glances my way as the buggy pulled down the long driveway. *Mammi* studied me with a shrewd stare, which I ignored.

A private battle raged in my mind. I should be pleased that my bishop took the time to pray for me, but I found the thought more disturbing than comforting. Exactly what did he pray? For my soul, or for me to find a new wife?

I kept my promise to the bishop and wrote a letter to Laura that night. I struggled over the wording. Would something I said make a difference in her decision on whether to return to her Amish home or remain in the world? Probably not, but as I wrote, her angry face hovered in my mind, and guilt gnawed at me for causing such anger with my own lack of control. My pain was private and should remain that way lest it hurt others.

On Friday, when Robbie drove me to the pottery shop, I took my letter with me. I wasn't sure why, but I wanted Leah to read it. Maybe because she'd been in Laura's place, and I wanted to make sure nothing I said offended the girl. In the back of my mind another reason hovered. Though I refused to think about the explanation why, I wanted Leah to know I regretted my part in causing Laura any discomfort.

She smoothed out my letter on the counter beside the cash register and spent some moments studying it.

Dear Laura,

I have not been able to forget our conversation in the kitchen. I hope you will accept my apology for losing my temper and forgive me for shouting at you. I would hate to think that anything I said caused you pain.

When I said that there were many men who would be honored to court you, I was telling the truth. But I hope you know I was not talking about myself. I meant a number of other young men, both in our district and in the neighboring districts. I do not have a particular man in mind, but I am certain many will be happy to court an attractive girl like you if you decide to come home.

I am not writing to try to convince you to come home. I know if you decide to, it will make your family very happy and everyone in our district too. And I do think that you will be able to find happiness in a Plain life because that is how you were raised. But that is a decision you will have to make on your own.

Sincerely,
Seth Hostetler

My stomach tensed awaiting Leah's verdict. Her expression was hidden from me. Today she wore her hair unbound, and waves of brown locks fell forward as she read, creating a dark veil through which I could not see.

Finally, she looked up, her lips curved into their typical cynical arrangement. "Your handwriting is terrible. She'll be lucky if she can decipher it."

An unexpected comment but completely in character for Leah. The tension in my gut erupted in a laugh.

She smiled in response, and the unusual expression warmed my insides. "It's a good letter, Seth. Heartfelt and caring. Not at all the kind of letter I received. If I'd gotten one like this, I might even—" The sardonic grimace returned. "No, I wouldn't have." She refolded the letter and handed it back to me. "I think you should mail it."

"*Danke.*"

When I took the paper from her hand, our fingers touched. She jerked her arm back as though I'd burned her. A spasm erupted in her scarred cheek, and she turned quickly away. The momentary peace that had settled between us fled in an instant, leaving me confused and more than a little curious. The harsh line of her spine and rigid set to her shoulders repelled any question I might have posed.

The curtain parted, and Elias emerged, his wide smile in sharp contrast to his granddaughter's scowl. "I thought I heard your voice out here. Come and see how your bowls have turned out. I think you will be happy with that glaze."

With another glance at Leah's stiff back, I followed Elias into the workshop.

The glaze had turned out much better than I'd hoped. I lifted one of my bowls and turned it in my hands to examine all sides. I'd been hesitant to try the color my teacher suggested, because it looked blue in the bucket, and I wanted a more natural look. But the second firing had transformed the unnatural blue into a darkened hue that resembled a stormy winter sky. Accent colors had appeared, a truly beautiful blend of browns and rusts that rimmed the lip and highlighted the rougher portions of the bowl's sides.

"Becky will like these." I set down one bowl and picked up a second, nearly identical one. I turned the object over and noted with a sense of satisfaction that the stain inside the carving of my simple potter's mark had been transformed into a dark rust that stood out starkly.

"*Ya,* any homemaker would." Elias took the piece from my hands and returned it to its tray. "Now let us make her a serving bowl to go with it. The concept is the same, but working with more clay to produce a bigger piece requires a deft touch and a different skill."

Though I itched to try my hand at throwing something besides a bowl, I deferred to my teacher and set about gathering my tools for another instructive lesson.

NINE

My pottery sessions with Elias continued, and though my family said nothing, I was always careful to finish my chores at home before leaving for the shop. By late March we no longer called my time with Elias lessons. I'd gained enough skill that the pieces I made were added to the display shelves and sold. At first I refused payment, insisting that any profits from my pieces would hardly come close to reimbursing my teacher for his time and the supplies I used since he refused to let me pay for his tutoring.

"That's not true," Leah told me when I thrust my hands behind my back as she tried to force money on me. "We sold a set of six of your bowls, plates, and mugs yesterday, and we made more from that one sale than any single week since we arrived in Strasburg."

I refused to take credit. "Word of Elias's work is spreading. Sales are bound to increase as more people become aware of the shop's existence." I tapped the top of the computer screen. "And your work on the computer has no doubt raised awareness as well."

Leah's work, besides that of handling sales and customers in the showroom, had been a mystery to me until a few days before, when she showed me the pictures of my work she'd placed on the Internet. Elias had paid an *Englisch* man to create a website for his shop, and that man had taught Leah how to place pictures of the items for sale. She called the procedure *uploading* and seemed to take a great deal of pleasure in the process. Just as I took pleasure in creating the bowls and cups and pitchers she displayed.

Elias raised his hands, shaking his head. "It was not my work the customers bought yesterday. It was yours." He awarded me a kindly smile. "Take the money, Seth. *Ein arbeiter ist seines lohnes wert.*"

That particular Scripture from *die Bibel* was one Bishop Beiler was fond of quoting. *The worker deserves his wages.*

"Besides," Leah added in her usual acerbic tone, "I am not giving you *all* of the money from the sale. I'm keeping a portion to cover our expenses and a nice profit besides."

I threw up my hands in defeat. "How can I argue with *die Bibel* and your making a profit?"

She actually laughed as she pressed a stack of bills into my hands.

"*Gut.*" Elias rubbed his hands together. "Now, let us get to work. You must trim that canister you threw yesterday, and I have an order from an *Englisch* customer for a pair of large pots for her front porch. This will require the larger wheel and wooden bats. You will learn a new technique today, my skillful student."

The door's jangling bells stopped me as I turned toward the workshop. Robbie rushed in, his face white and eyes round as *Mammi*'s donuts.

"Is something wrong?" I took a step toward him, his alarmed expression creating instant tension in my chest. "Did you have an accident?"

"Not me." The young man held up his cell phone, his gaze fixed on me. "It's your grandmother. You need to get home now."

My heart stuttered, and for a moment I couldn't move. Then I sprang into action and raced through the door after Robbie.

Robbie drove like a maniac while I clutched the dashboard and wished he would go faster. We arrived at the farm in time to see an ambulance turning from our driveway onto the road. The little red car sped toward the house, where my family stood gathered outside, watching the vehicle with flashing lights disappear in the distance.

I leaped out of the car as soon as it was stopped. "What happened?"

"She just fell." Saloma's face was the color of the bleached sheets hanging on the line stretched across our backyard. "She picked up a dress from the wash basket and started to hang it, and—" Her voice broke.

"It was my dress." Tears squeezed Becky's voice tight, and Saloma placed a comforting arm around her shoulders. Sadie clung tightly to her *mamm*'s leg, her face hidden in the dark fabric of her dress.

Daed, who held a twin's hand in each of his, cast a sympathetic glance at my *schweschder*. "Your dress had nothing to do with the fall, *dochder*. She must have tripped on an uneven place on the ground."

"I am sure that is what happened." Saloma gave Becky's shoulders a final squeeze before releasing her. "The ambulance driver said she might have broken her hip."

Though a broken hip in a woman *Mammi*'s age was nothing to take lightly, a few of the tense knots in my stomach unwound. After the episode I'd witnessed in the *daadi haus*, I'd feared worse.

The door to the house opened, and *Mamm* bustled out, holding her cape closed beneath her chin. Aaron followed with a small overnight bag in his hands.

"I will call the Cramers as soon as I know anything," she said as she hurried toward Robbie's car. "Doris Cramer said her husband would bring a message here."

Robbie took the bag from Aaron and placed it in the trunk of his car while I opened the back door for *Mamm*.

She addressed Saloma as she settled herself on the seat. "Ham for supper, and don't add wood to the oven too soon or you'll burn it."

"I won't," Saloma promised.

"And don't start the potatoes too late or everything else will get cold waiting for them to cook."

"Don't worry about our supper," Aaron chided. "Save your worries for *Mammi*."

Daed fixed a hard stare on him before turning a soft expression toward his wife. "Do not worry at all. Instead, pray, as we all will be doing."

Pray. I had not done so, too obsessed with my concern for my *gross-mammi*. I formed a quick, silent plea for her health and safety as I rounded the front of the car and opened the passenger seat.

Mamm leaned forward and asked, "You are coming too?"

"Did you think we would let you go alone?" I shot back.

Everyone nodded, and Becky shot me a grateful look as I climbed inside.

Robbie opened his door. "Which hospital did they take her to?"

"Lancaster General." Saloma switched her gaze to *Mamm* and raised her voice to be heard through the closed window. "Call the Cramers as soon as you know anything."

Mamm nodded as Robbie turned the key. The engine caught with a rumble, and we took off in the wake of the ambulance.

Robbie pulled the car to a stop in front of the emergency room doors and then jumped out to help *Mamm* from the back. I sat frozen in the front seat, unable to move. All the way here my mind was focused on praying for *Mammi*. I hadn't anticipated the wave of sudden panic that gripped my lungs with fists of steel and left me gasping.

The last time I was here, I'd watched my Rachel die.

My mind replayed the scene as though it had occurred mere moments before. The feel of the asphalt beneath my shoes as I leaped from the back of the ambulance and scurried to get out of the paramedics' way. The sight of them pulling the stretcher out. The sound of metal snapping into place as the collapsible framework expanded so they could wheel her inside. The antiseptic smell when the glass doors slid open and I followed them in. But especially her deathly pale face, the only part of her visible beneath the sheets and straps that bound her to the stretcher. Her breath had been horribly shallow then. Not long after, it stopped completely.

The car door opened, and I tore my gaze from my memories to focus on Robbie's face.

"Are you going in?"

Mamm had already hurried inside, and the doors slid shut behind her. My legs felt wooden as I swung them out and placed them on the asphalt. I sat for a minute, willing my lungs to relax enough to take in air.

"Seth?" Concern creased Robbie's smooth forehead. "Are you feeling okay?"

My response was, perhaps, indicative of the depth of my distraction. Normally, I would have merely nodded. To my horror, I found myself uttering, "My wife died here."

A moment later I had a new concern, for Robbie's face went a ghostly white, and he swayed on his feet. I stood quickly and grabbed his arm to steady him.

"Are *you* feeling okay?" I asked, noting his pale skin and round, darting eyes.

"I—" He swallowed several times in rapid succession. "Yeah, of course. I'm fine. I just—" With an unreadable glance thrown over his shoulder at the hospital entrance, he shook himself. "Give me a call when you and your mom are ready to go home."

Promising to do so, I watched as he climbed in the car and pulled away. A puzzling young man. Why would mention of my grief cause such a reaction? The explanation occurred to me a moment later. Robbie must have lost someone here too. Someone close to him. My thoughtless comment had brought the pain back to him as vividly as the sight of the emergency room doors had done to me. My young driver and I had more in common than I'd realized.

How I wished I could hop in a car and run away too.

Instead, I steeled myself to follow my *mamm* inside. I held my breath as I passed between the doors.

"Here you are, Mrs. Hostetler." A white-garbed woman carried a tray into the hospital room and set it on the rolling bedside table. She pitched her voice high and smiled with exaggerated brightness at my *grossmammi*. "The doctor said you could have some broth and yogurt. And here's some nice apple juice to drink."

Mamm, who was seated in a chair close to the bed, rose to inspect the food when the woman lifted a plastic dome. I remained in the corner—a position I'd selected an hour ago because it was tucked out of the way of the steady stream of nurses and aides who paraded in and out of the room, checking monitors and adjusting tubes and jotting notes on their clipboards.

"Broth?" *Mamm's* nose curled. "How can she get strong again on a diet of broth and yogurt?"

The woman smiled. "Doctor's orders. You don't want anything heavy this soon after surgery." She switched her attention to *Mammi*, and her voice again resumed the irritating, high-pitched tone. "It wouldn't be much fun having your dinner come back up, would it, Mrs. Hostetler?"

Mammi opened one eye to look at the woman and then closed it again without answering. Since being wheeled into this room, she had yet to say more than a few slurred words, still groggy from hip replacement surgery.

"Someone will be by to pick up the tray in a little while," the woman told *Mamm*.

She left, her sneakers squeaking on the spotless hospital floor.

Without opening her eyes, *Mammi* whispered, "Is she gone?"

"*Ya,*" *Mamm* replied.

Mammi's chest inflated as she drew in a breath and then blew it out. "I hope she does not come back. Her voice goes through my ears."

I piped up from my corner. "I think she works in the kitchen."

"That's right." *Mamm* smoothed the blanket around *Mammi's* shoulders. "She is not a nurse. Now you should have some broth. I will help you."

When *Mammi* agreed, *Mamm* looked at the buttons on the bed rail and then turned toward me in a silent plea. After studying the device for a moment, I figured out how to raise the head enough that *Mammi* could sip from the spoon *Mamm* held to her lips.

After a few swallows, she waved away the rest with a feeble gesture, her brow wrinkling when she noticed the IV line puncturing the back of her hand and taped to her wrist. Her gaze followed the clear tubing up to the pole beside her bed, where a bag of fluid dangled and glowing numbers showed on an electronic box.

"What is that they are giving me?"

We had asked the same thing. "Mostly fluids to keep you from becoming dehydrated," I told her. "And some medicine. They want to make sure you do not get an infection, and there is something to help with the pain."

"The last is not working." Her tone was as cross as my soft-spoken *grossmammi* ever sounded.

Mamm recovered the tray and rolled the bedside table away. "I will tell the nurse. Maybe they can give you something else."

She left the room, and I stepped to the bedside.

Mammi closed her eyes. "What did they do to me?"

The surgeon had explained the procedure to us in detail, though most of what he said was lost on both *Mamm* and me because we had little experience with implant prostheses and the other unfamiliar terms he used.

"You broke your hip, so they gave you a new one."

Her forehead creased. "I have a fake hip?"

"An artificial hip," I corrected her. "One that will work well for the rest of your life. He said he was surprised you had not complained of pain before now because he found evidence of osteoarthritis."

Again, a feeble wave of the hand. "What does complaining do other than make us discontent?"

So she *had* been suffering pain that she'd not mentioned.

"In this case, you might have had this surgery before and avoided breaking your hip to begin with. In fact, the doctor said he would like to take X-rays of your other hip as well."

"So he can charge us for two surgeries?"

Such an uncharacteristic attitude for one who always sought to see the best in people. She must be in real pain. I glanced toward the open doorway, where *Mamm* had gone in search of more pain medicine.

"He is a very good doctor," I answered softly. "This hospital has an entire program dedicated to helping people with osteoporosis and fractures and joint replacements like yours." I did not mention the name of the Geriatric Fracture Program, lest in this cranky mood she would take offense at the reference to her age.

The doctor had also spent a good deal of time discussing *Mammi*'s heart, having noted some concerning symptoms during the surgery. He'd insisted on calling in a cardiologist, who would examine her tomorrow. I decided not to mention that either.

Mamm returned then, followed by a nurse with a rolling cart.

"I understand you're experiencing some pain, Mrs. Hostetler." Thank goodness she spoke in the soft, soothing tone of a normal person, not the offensive, squeaking shout of the cafeteria woman.

The nurse tapped on a computer keyboard, scanned the wristband on *Mammi*'s free arm, and then took up a syringe with clear liquid inside. When that had been injected into a port on her IV tube, she smiled at her patient.

"That should take effect almost immediately. You'll feel better very soon."

"*Danke.*"

Indeed, before the nurse had even left the room, *Mammi* uttered a soft sigh and her eyes drooped shut.

Mamm turned to me. "Seth, call the driver and go home."

I looked at her in surprise. "You are not coming with me?"

"I will stay here. The nurse said that chair unfolds into a bed." She pointed at the chair in which I'd been sitting. "Besides, I expected we would not be home tonight, so I came prepared with a clean dress and other things. I will not be able to sleep at home anyway. What if she wakes in the night and needs help?"

I could have pointed out that the nursing staff seemed perfectly capable and attentive, but it would not have done any good. Besides, I too felt reluctant to leave *Mammi* alone. I would stay myself, but given the circumstances it made sense for *Mamm* to stay instead. It would be far more appropriate for a woman to give the care and attention *Mammi* might need than a man, even a relative.

Conceding to the inevitable, I used the telephone in the room to call Robbie. When I explained that *Mamm* would stay the night but I needed a ride home, he said he would be right over. Less than twenty minutes later, he strode through the door, carrying a reusable grocery bag.

With a quick glance at the bed, where *Mammi* dozed, he spoke to *Mamm* in a whisper. "I would have been here sooner except my mother insisted on sending your supper."

Surprise lit *Mamm's* features. "She sent food for me?"

"Yes, ma'am." He set the bag on the floor and extracted several plastic containers to show her. "She said she's eaten in this cafeteria enough to know the food is good, but nothing beats homemade. She was just taking our supper out of the oven when Seth called, so…" He shrugged.

I looked at the clock on the wall. The hours had evaporated, and it was now nearly six o'clock. Between the uncertainty of waiting for X-rays and doctors' reports and then the tension of pacing in the waiting room while the surgeon operated on *Mammi*, the day was nearly gone.

Tears appeared in my *mamm's* eyes, fueled by exhaustion and the gesture of an *Englisch* stranger.

"Please tell her I am touched by her kindness."

She pried open the lid on one of the containers, and a delicious aroma filled the room. My empty stomach rumbled in response. I hadn't thought of food throughout the day, but my breakfast was long gone. Cold ham and potatoes at home would make me a welcome late supper.

"I will." Robbie looked at me. "Are you ready to go?"

A quick glance at *Mammi* revealed that she slept. I told *Mamm*, "I will be back tomorrow."

We wound our way through the hospital corridors, the smell of antiseptic stinging my nose. I was relieved when Robbie led me to the main doors, bypassing the emergency room. My weary brain was too tired to combat the memories that area held.

Once we were on the road, he slid a quick glance in my direction. "My mother told me to bring you to our house for supper before I take you home."

"That is not necessary."

His hands tightened on the steering wheel. "I told her you would probably be tired and in a hurry to get home, but she kind of insisted. Our house is only a couple of miles from here, and it's on the way." I opened my mouth to voice another refusal, but he spoke first. "I think she wants to meet the guy I've been driving around so much."

A natural desire for the mother of a teenager. Robbie had spent a lot of time in recent weeks taking me back and forth to Elias's workshop. We'd come to an agreement about a payment schedule, though he still refused to accept an amount I thought was fair.

"In that case, I accept."

"Cool."

The sun hung low in the sky behind us, casting long shadows from the tree-lined avenue down which we traveled. I watched the landscape outside the car. Wide lawns spoke of professional care, green and immaculate even in late March. We drove by a golf course on the left, and the houses facing it were large and ornate, even by *Englisch* standards. Apparently, my young driver came from a wealthy family.

He turned onto a long driveway that looped in front of a brick house three stories high. A sunroom on one side consisted of tall, multi-paned windows, and behind that lay a garage that had been designed to look like a miniature of the main house. A fit of nerves overtook me. This place was far too fancy for a Plain man like me.

Robbie parked in the circular driveway, and I sat for a moment gaping through my window. The words were on the tip of my tongue to say I'd changed my mind, and would he please take me home now? Then the front door, made of carved, gleaming wood, opened, and a woman stood in the doorway smiling in our direction.

"There's my mom."

He opened his door and exited the car. What could I do but follow?

As I drew near, I detected the family resemblance. The same thick, dark hair, though she tamed hers into a stylish arrangement favored by *Englisch* women. She was thin, too, though not gangly like her son. She smiled at me with Robbie's smile, and extended a hand.

"You must be Mr. Hostetler. I'm Amanda Barker."

I clasped her hand with a quick, gentle touch, and then released it. "I am pleased to meet you."

Her smile widened. "You must call me Amanda. And is it okay if I call you Seth?"

I nodded.

"My husband is sorry he can't join us. He's in Philadelphia on a business trip and won't be back until tomorrow. Oh! What am I thinking?" A quick laugh emerged, and I thought then that she was a touch nervous herself. "Please come inside. I didn't mean to leave you standing on the porch."

She backed up, swinging the door wide, and I hesitated. If her husband was not home, would it be inappropriate for me to be in her house? Of course, we would not be alone. I waited for Robbie to enter first and then followed him inside.

A large, sweeping staircase drew my attention, the dark wooden steps and polished banister gleaming with care. Wide, arched doorways on either side of the entry hall led into other rooms. On my left, a living room filled with color and furniture that bore no resemblance to the sturdy wooden furnishings that stood in my family's home. The walls displayed many paintings, and though I was reminded of my visit to Marilyn's house in Philadelphia, these paintings were noticeably different. Some were no more than multihued splashes of paint on giant canvasses. What they were supposed to represent, I couldn't imagine.

At a glance into the room on my right, my heart stuttered. A huge, glass-topped dining table dominated the space, surrounded by ornate white chairs. The largest flower display I'd ever seen rested in the center of the table. Would we eat our supper in there? I was certain I would not be able to force down a single bite in such fancy surroundings.

Instead, Amanda led us past the staircase and down a short hallway. The entire rear of the house was open, one giant room that could easily have housed our entire district on church Sundays with plenty of room to spare—if it were not stuffed with furniture, that is. Why did the *Englisch* feel the need to crowd their houses with so much *stuff*?

But even I, with my Plain sensibilities, could see that this giant room, unlike the two in the front, was meant to be informal and comfortable. A large kitchen area lay to the left, a granite-topped island the only thing that separated the cooking space from the rest. A second glass-topped table sat tucked into a windowed alcove, this one round and just large enough for four chairs. To my relief I saw that this table had been set for three. Still fancy, and not at all what I was accustomed to, but at least it felt less formal than the giant one in the front room. To my right lay another living room, though the furniture in this one appeared to be of overstuffed leather. Above a fireplace on the far wall hung the biggest television I had ever seen. The screen was dark, and from somewhere soft music played.

"I hope you like chicken piccata," Amanda said as she rounded the island.

I attempted a smile to break the tension that had clenched my jaws so tightly together. "I will tell you after I have tried it."

She laughed, this time an easy sound. "Robbie, find out what Seth wants to drink, would you?"

My young driver looked as relaxed as I'd ever seen him. Well, that would make sense. He was at home, a place where he felt comfortable.

"We've got Coke, Diet Coke, Dr Pepper, green tea." He ticked off fingers as he listed them.

Though Aaron enjoyed soda, I'd never developed a taste for it. "I would like water, please."

"Okay." He opened a shiny, stainless steel refrigerator and bent to inspect the contents. "Hey, Mom, where's the Dr Pepper?"

Amanda turned from the stove with a platter of delicious-smelling chicken in her hands. "You'll have to get some out of the fridge in the garage."

They had a refrigerator in the garage too?

Robbie left through a door I hadn't noticed. The moment he was gone, Amanda set the tray down and pierced me with a look across the island.

"I hoped I'd have an opportunity to thank you for all you've done for Robbie." She spoke quietly, holding my gaze without looking away. "My husband and I are more grateful than we can say."

I shook my head. "I have done nothing except take advantage of his services and pay him too little."

A shadow appeared in her eyes. "You've done a lot more than you know. He needs to feel like he's helping. It's..." She bit her lip. "It's important."

Though I itched to ask for more details, Robbie returned at that moment with a can of soda.

Amanda's lips widened into a bright smile. "Seth, I'm going to put you to work too." She slid the platter toward me. "Would you carry that to the table, please, while I get the potatoes?"

I did as she asked, curiosity burning. Though Robbie seemed like a sensible, friendly young man, obviously his parents were concerned about him. Whatever trouble he'd gotten into during his last year at school must have been serious.

When I finally arrived at home, I was peppered with questions about *Mammi*'s condition.

"Will she be able to walk again?" Tears sparkled in Becky's eyes.

"According to the doctor, she will walk better than before." I eyed her and Saloma. "Has she mentioned pain in her hips?"

"Mentioned?" Saloma shook her head. "But she moves more slowly than before, and I have noticed she sometimes winces when she stands after sitting awhile."

I explained what the doctor said about a possible second hip replacement, and how *Mammi* had scoffed at the idea.

"We will insist," *Daed* said.

Sitting in our familiar living room, surrounded by Plain furnishings, some of the tension seeped out of my taut muscles. The children were already upstairs in bed, and the rest of the family sat working quietly, waiting for me to arrive home with news. Becky stitched at a colorful patch of fabric, her latest quilting project, while Saloma mended one of the boys' shirts. *Daed* and Aaron shared a yellow circle of light from an oil lamp to read, and Noah applied a sharp-bladed knife to a piece of soft wood, whittling away at what would probably become another set of toy farm animals to be offered for sale at one of the Amish craft stores in Strasburg.

"Worse than her hip, though, is the doctor's concern about her heart." I told them briefly about the cardiologist's visit in the morning.

"She tires more easily than before." Becky glanced at Saloma, who agreed with a nod. "We've noticed and have tried to involve her in tasks that require little effort, like peeling potatoes while she sits."

Aaron leaned forward, forearms planted on his knees, his book forgotten. "Did the doctor say when she will come home?"

"She could leave the hospital as soon as in four days, but he wants her to stay in a nursing facility for several weeks where they can take care of her."

Saloma straightened. "We can take care of her here."

I saw *Mammi* again in my mind, looking fragile in her hospital bed. The doctor did say we would be surprised at how quickly she recovered from the hip replacement, but what of her heart? If the wave of dizziness I witnessed several weeks past recurred, she could easily fall again. The next time she might break something harder to repair.

"I worry about her being alone at night and us not able to hear if she calls for help. Especially if the cardiologist says her heart is as fragile as her bones."

Daed studied me for a long moment, his fingers absently stroking the bristly hair of his beard. "Perhaps it is time for a change." Though he spoke softly, the intensity in his words caused everyone to stop working at their individual tasks and fix their attention on him. "For some time Joan and I have discussed moving into the *daadi haus*." He looked toward Aaron. "We thought to make way for you and Saloma to take our room and *Mammi* to take yours, but perhaps that move will need to wait a while longer."

I immediately saw why. Our house had only one bedroom on the main floor—*Daed* and *Mamm's*. The rest were upstairs. With *Mammi's* increasing age and now fragile joints, a bedroom upstairs would not be advisable. The best place for her would be on the first floor of this house, where all of us would be nearby if she needed help in the night.

But such a move would officially accentuate the fact that the family farm would now be in Aaron's complete control. While *Daed* and *Mamm* occupied the large main-floor bedroom, he was still the acknowledged head of the family and the farm, at least in name. A move to the *daadi haus* would send a clear message to our community that *Daed* was retired and Aaron in charge.

Aaron and Saloma exchanged a look full of unspoken meaning. Not only would management of the farm fully and officially transfer to Aaron, the running of the house would become Saloma's responsibility. When a husband retired, so did his wife. Of course, Saloma would no sooner wrest control from *Mamm* than *Mamm* had from *Mammi* when the previous move occurred. The change would be gradual, but it would also be inevitable.

Daed closed his book and set it on the table beside his chair. "The move makes sense in many ways. It is time."

"Before we make any decisions, let us see what the doctor says tomorrow." Aaron, too, closed his book, though he held his in his lap. "And *Mamm* should be included in our discussion."

The suggestion held wisdom and acted as a dismissal for the night. Saloma and Becky began folding their sewing projects, and Noah stowed his knife and wood in the box where he kept them.

"Do I need to milk the cows?" I asked.

Aaron shook his head. "I took care of them."

Saloma looked up from her sewing basket. "Seth, have you eaten? I can fix for you a sandwich."

I shook my head. "I was invited to eat by Amanda, young Robbie's mother."

Everyone halted in the midst of whatever they were doing to turn curious gazes my way.

"And how was that?" Noah asked.

I tilted my head, considering how to answer. The meal had threatened to be awkward, but Amanda proved to be a gracious and lively hostess. She kept me entertained with stories of Robbie's mischievous childhood, and once I laughed so hard I had to cover my mouth with my napkin—paper, something not used at our table—to stop myself from spraying my plate with water.

"Fancy, but enjoyable."

Becky's eyes gleamed with interest. "What did she serve?"

"Chicken piccata." The term felt odd on my tongue. "Thin pieces of tender chicken covered with a sauce of lemons and butter and capers. Also roasted potatoes and beans and salad, much like we would have here."

"Capers." Saloma's forehead wrinkled. "What did they taste like?"

I shrugged. "I pushed them to the side. But the chicken was very good. She sent some to *Mamm* at the hospital, too, so she would not have to eat in the cafeteria."

"And for dessert?" Becky asked.

"No dessert. She apologized and explained that she did not typically have dessert."

Saloma stood and scooped up her basket in the crook of her elbow. "Then I will fix you a piece of peach pie and a glass of milk."

The words were on the tip of my tongue to refuse, but at the mention of peach pie, anticipation flared on my taste buds. A slice of pie before bed would be good.

"Would you fix two?" Hope showed in Aaron's eager expression.

His wife planted her free hand on her hip. "You ate a piece after supper."

He shrugged and ducked his head, managing somehow to look as wishful as one of his sons even with the beard.

Saloma returned his look with a stern one, which broke into a smile after a moment. "Oh, all right." She left the room chuckling.

Standing, *Daed* picked up his book. "Is your driver coming in the morning?"

"*Ya*, at nine o'clock."

"I will go to the hospital tomorrow." He doused the light. "Then I can speak with Joan and *Mammi* together. I will have this thing settled."

How like my *daed*. Once he set his mind to a thing, he did not rest until it was accomplished. It would not surprise me if the move were completed by this time tomorrow.

His plan made sense and would resolve every issue except one—the fate of the younger *bruder,* the extra. It was time I had a plan for myself that made sense.

TEN

Robbie drove *Daed* and me to the hospital at nine o'clock as arranged, but when we arrived, *Daed* informed me that he would like to have the conversation privately with my *mamm* and *Mammi*. Feeling slightly rebuffed, even though I understood his reason, I went up to *Mammi*'s room long enough to say hello and assure myself that her condition was no worse. In fact, she seemed much improved for her night's sleep, sitting up in her bed and awarding smiles all around. I left the hospital encouraged.

Before climbing into Robbie's car, I eyed him across the roof. "Do you have the time to take me to Strasburg?"

"You bet," the young man assured me. Then a shadow fell across his face. "But I have an appointment at one o'clock. It'll last about an hour."

He'd just arranged to pick *Daed* up at two thirty for the drive home.

I waved a hand. "I will find someone else to take me home. Either Kevin or someone in Strasburg."

"No." Robbie's expression became almost injured, as though I'd hurt his feelings by even suggesting another driver. "It's just that I'll either have to come get you at noon or it'll have to be after I drop your father off."

Amanda's words returned to me. *He needs to feel like he's helping. It's important.*

I aimed for an easy tone. "All right. How about I expect you around three?"

Relief lightened his features. "Sounds good." A boyish grin appeared. "Or as your people would say, *Das gut.*"

Laughing, I slid into the car.

When I entered the pottery shop, Leah was helping an *Englisch* couple select a set of dishes. At the jangle of the bells she looked up at me, and a smile lit her face. The gesture was so unusual, my heart skittered. Today her Plain upbringing showed. She wore a simple dress, and though it buttoned at the neck instead of being pinned like an Amish dress, the pale blue color might have been worn by any of the women in my district. She'd pulled her hair back and wound it into a knot secured at the back of her head. No *kapp*, of course, but without the distraction of flowing dark hair, her eyes appeared clearer and bluer in her face.

Blue. I hadn't noted the color until this moment.

Without the sarcastic curl of her lips I was accustomed to seeing, she looked lovely. Even the scar, though still apparent, didn't detract from her appearance.

"And here is the potter who created these," she said to her customers.

They turned and voiced appreciation for my work. My cheeks burned as I acknowledged their praise, and then I turned my back to shut the door.

Leah did not leave the couple when she directed a question at me. "How is your grandmother?"

"Better. A broken hip, which the doctors replaced."

I didn't go into the extent of our concerns for *Mammi*'s condition. Instead, I made my way across the room and left her to her work.

Elias looked up from his wheel when I stepped into the workroom. "I did not know whether to expect you or not. I hope your presence means things are going well at home?"

"*Ya,* better. At least for now."

As I moved about the now-familiar workshop gathering my tools, I went into more detail describing *Mammi's* condition to Elias. He shook his head in sympathy when I spoke of my concerns about her heart and the acceleration of *Daed's* retirement.

"Age can be unkind, and not only to the elderly."

An insightful comment. I agreed with a nod as I set my tools on my favorite wheel and headed toward the shelf to retrieve one of the canisters I should have trimmed yesterday. My gaze fell on a table along the back wall containing two huge pots that had not been there before.

"You threw the planters." I almost added *without me.* I'd looked forward to learning a new skill, working with something as large as this.

"*Ya.* I promised to get them done as soon as possible."

I drew near to inspect them. They were nearly identical, with the differences being so minute that no one with a casual eye would notice. Each stood around four feet tall, the lines smooth with a graceful curve around the middle, the widest part. A rounded ridge formed the lip around the top. I bent close to study one. Though I detected no break in the clay, there was only one way Elias could have managed to achieve a lip that thick and so perfectly formed.

"You added the lip after the pot was finished?"

"A coil of wedged clay. I added many coils, in fact, one at a time, each achieving additional height."

So that's how the process went. I understood in a flash. Wedging and centering so much clay at once would be a trying and difficult task. Instead, he'd started small and built the pot a bit at a time. How I wished I could have seen him work.

Elias laughed. "Do not look so downcast. You will have a chance to throw your own one day, I promise. Leah will post these on the computer, and perhaps that will bring orders for more. In the meantime, go trim your canisters. We sold the last finished set yesterday."

I retrieved my pieces from the shelf, noting that Elias had wrapped them in thick plastic to keep them from becoming overly dry. Taking one from beneath the covering, I tested the consistency by pressing a fingernail into the thick bottom edge, which was about to be sliced off.

The clay was leather hard, perfect for trimming. Satisfied, I returned to the wheel I'd come to think of as mine and centered the piece. When its spin was perfectly even, I applied the trimming tool. An immense feeling of satisfaction settled on me as the thick, ugly, unwanted ridge sliced away in clay ribbons that curled as I severed them from the pot. The result, when smoothed with a damp bit of sponge, was a perfect foot that would sit firmly without wobbling on a table or counter.

When I was pleased with the foot, I turned the canister right side up and examined it with a critical eye. Unlike Elias's pieces, the outer sides of mine were always smooth and even. Something about achieving a perfect sleekness appealed to me. The clay itself was porous enough to allow for the separation of colors in the glaze to achieve the subtle multi-hued finish I desired.

But something about this canister seemed wrong. I sat back, fingering my beard, and tried to pinpoint the cause. Not wrong, exactly. Unfinished? Yes, that was it. Somehow the perfect symmetry and precision of the shape did not fit *this* canister. It was too…well, too plain.

Though Elias nearly always added a simple carving to decorate his pieces, I had not yet attempted the technique. I opened my mouth to ask for advice, but my teacher had slipped out of the room while I worked. I heard his low voice, muffled through the curtain, and Leah's quiet response.

I took up Elias's carving tool and tested the sharp end with my thumb, all the while studying the smooth surface of my canister. Though I'd watched him many times, I'd never handled the knifelike tool myself. With my breath caught in my chest, I lowered the metal edge until it barely rested against the clay. What design to carve?

A pattern appeared in my mind, and with it pain stabbed at my heart as though I'd turned the tool on myself. The pattern was from the quilt my Hannah had made for our marriage bed.

I closed my eyes and let pain wash over me while the design burned the insides of my eyelids. When I could see nothing else, I opened my eyes and pressed the sharp tool into the clay.

Time slipped by unnoticed. The canister became my focus, duplicating Hannah's pattern in every detail. Finally, I carved the last piece of clay away, smoothed the final rough edge, and set down the tool. I straightened, pressing a fist against an ache in the small of my back. My vision, focused so long on the close work in front of me, blurred when I lifted my head and glanced around the workshop. What was the time?

I called toward the curtain. "Elias?"

He and Leah appeared.

"You're finished, *ya*?" The old man's smile melted from his face when his gaze lowered to my work. "Seth, what have you done to the canister?"

I looked at the piece on my wheel. The pattern was precisely what I'd hoped to achieve. If this piece were placed beside Hannah's quilt, no one could doubt that the designs were identical. But instead of etching the decoration on the outside of the clay, I had cut all the way through. Ornamental, perfectly shaped holes covered all sides of the piece that could no longer be called a canister.

"I—" Words deserted me. The piece looked exactly like I wanted, but it was useless.

My perfect canister, ruined.

"Nothing can be stored in that." Elias waggled his fingers in the pot's direction. "It will pour out the sides."

A knot formed deep in my throat, threatening to block the breath from my lungs. Why had I spoiled my work? My palms itched to snatch it up and dash it to the floor, the urge strong to see it lying in broken shards at my feet.

Leah stepped away from her grandfather, her gaze fixed on my pot. "Maybe that's the point."

"What do you mean?" Elias asked. "What point?"

She reached out, her hands halting inches from the piece while she turned an unspoken request for permission my way. When I nodded, she picked up the ruined canister and turned it slowly around, examining it from all angles.

"The design is beautiful. So intricate and delicate."

Just like the quilt that had covered my wife and me as we learned to love one another. The lump in my throat expanded, and I struggled to breathe past it.

"If you put a candle inside, light would spill out all around." Leah turned sparkling blue eyes to me. "Imagine how beautiful that would look in a dark room."

Whether because of her enthusiasm or the reverent hush in her tone, my breath eased. The image she described showed clearly in my mind's eye. My Hannah's pattern, projected all around a room, casting a beautiful light to illuminate the darkness.

Elias cocked his head and studied the piece critically. "Who would want to buy such a thing?"

"I would." Leah pulled the canister to her chest, though gently. "In fact, I will." Her gaze slid to me. "If you will allow me to?"

For a long moment I stared at the clay creation she cradled. How I longed to see light spill from the carvings, to gaze upon the pattern the light made on the dark walls of my bedroom late at night, when the loneliness was almost too much to bear.

But Hannah's quilt was gone, left with her parents, and no doubt by now used by her *mamm* or one of her *schweschders*. I had not wanted the reminder of her quilt on my widower's bed.

Nor did I want the pattern on the walls of my widower's room.

I forced a nod. "*Ya*, but I will give it to you. A gift. You may select the glaze you want and make it your own."

She seemed especially pleased by my suggestion. "Then would you make another one so I can put a picture on the website?" Holding up the canister-turned-candleholder, she smiled wider than I had yet seen. "This one is not for sale."

A thrill of pleasure at her obvious delight over my work dissolved the last remnant of the lump in my throat. I glanced at my teacher, seeking tacit permission. Though skepticism still saturated his features, he shrugged. "What can it hurt? It is only clay, and clay is cheap."

Smiling, Leah set the pot carefully on my wheel and returned to the front of the shop. I rose and, after placing it on the shelf beside the rest of the pieces ready for the bisque firing, retrieved a second canister. Could I do it again? And even if I could, did I want to?

I wasn't sure of the answer to either question, but I set to work anyway.

Daed and *Mamm*'s move to the *daadi haus* did not happen as quickly as I'd projected. Instead of one day, it took three. *Mammi* proved stubborn against *Daed*'s efforts to convince her that the move was a good idea. In the end, he sternly informed her that if she continued to refuse to move back into the main house, he would have no choice but to agree with the doctor's recommendation and have her released to a convalescent center, where she would receive round-the-clock care. Fuming, she finally agreed.

In fact, moving to the big house turned out to be the only logical solution in light of the cardiologist's report.

"The Doppler results indicate a significant thickening of the arterial wall." The heart doctor, a young man with a no-nonsense manner and a pair of thick eyeglasses, directed his words to me, though *Daed* and *Mamm* and Becky were also present in the hospital consultation room. He spread a file folder open on his lap and tapped on a paper inside. "Her blood pressure is high, there's a marked difference in the systolic and diastolic readings, and her pulse pressure is elevated. Those symptoms usually indicate a serious stiffening of the arteries, and the onset of a number of cardiovascular disorders common among the elderly."

The unusual words spun in my head, and from *Daed*'s expression, he'd understood even less than me.

Becky, who sat quietly with her hands folded in her lap, asked, "Does she need heart surgery?"

The doctor glanced at her. "Unless we do more extensive tests, I couldn't say. But from my conversation with Mrs. Hostetler, she isn't willing to undergo more tests."

Daed's lips pressed together. "If she needs the tests, she will have them."

I knew from the set of his jaw that he would win any argument on the topic. And I was in full agreement.

But the doctor shook his head. "At this point, given her recent surgery and her osteoarthritis, the tests may cause more harm than good. Once she's fully recovered…" He shrugged.

"Then what can we do for her?" Becky's lower lip quivered, and her voice broke.

The doctor gave no indication that he noticed her emotional state. His manner did not change. "The conditions I've mentioned can be treated with medications. I'm starting her on blood pressure meds. Also statin therapy has been shown to help, along with a consistent exercise routine."

"Exercise?" I'd been present that morning when the hospital's physical therapist came to work with her. "She can't walk across the room without gasping. Even before this surgery, she had dizzy spells and was sometimes short of breath."

He looked at me over the top of his glasses. "I'm not suggesting she lift weights or run a marathon. But after her hip has healed, she should be able to handle mild to moderate exercise." He slapped the folder closed. "Dr. Cassel is referring her to a physical therapist on an outpatient basis. I'll write an order for cardiac therapy as well. And I'll leave orders for the meds with the nurses." A question appeared in the deepening of the crease between his eyebrows. "She will take medication, won't she?"

I understood the question immediately. Some Amish districts resorted to medications only if there were no other alternatives, preferring natural options. Our community had no regulations on medicines prescribed by doctors, though *Mammi* was fond of the home remedies passed down to her from her own *mamm*.

"She might balk, but she will take them," *Daed* assured him.

Without saying goodbye, the doctor scurried from the room, no doubt already thinking of his next patient. We looked at one another, and I didn't think mine was the only mind reeling from the conversation.

Finally, *Daed* placed his hands on his thighs and pushed himself upright. "If medicine and exercise are what she needs, then that is what she will get. The entire family must be in agreement." We nodded, and he muttered, "She can't fight us all."

I hid a smile. If he thought that, he did not know *Mammi* as well as I did. But in this I thought she would cooperate.

Mamm and *Daed*'s move was accomplished before *Mammi* came home the following day. Saloma was sent to the hospital to sit with *Mammi* in the morning so *Mamm* could oversee things. There was not much to be done. The beds were the same size, so *Mamm* said she would only change the bedding. The *daadi haus* was furnished with everything necessary for an aging couple to live comfortably. *Mamm* insisted on taking some of her own cookware, though she left the larger pieces for Saloma, who would be cooking for a greater number of people.

I carried the box containing *Mamm*'s dishes and set them on the small table in the miniature kitchen while she clucked her tongue over the state of the oven.

"You will still eat with us, *ya*?" The idea of a family meal without my *mamm* and *daed* set off ripples of discomfort in me.

"At first." She opened the oven door, shoved her head inside, and uttered, "Spiders! Seth, hand me the broom."

I did as requested and she applied the straw end to the oven cavity with an energy that reminded me of the wooden spoon she'd applied to mine and Aaron's backsides during our misbehaving childhoods. Then she removed the metal racks and attacked the oven again, just to be sure.

"*Mammi* ate with us even though she lived here."

"*Ya*. Well, it is certain she has not cooked in this oven for a while." She straightened and gave me a soft smile, along with the broom. "When your *grossdaadi* was alive, they took their meals here except on Sundays."

I'd forgotten. It wasn't until the death of her husband that *Mammi* became a constant at our family table. When I was a boy, having her and *Grossdaadi* at our table gave the meal a holiday-like feel. Now, we were merely family, and in our culture the most important thing a family did together was eat.

"Besides, it is important that Saloma be permitted to lead in her own kitchen. With me there, she is second."

"But—"

Mamm stopped me with a finger held to her lips. "Seth, the change will not happen all at once. For a while we will take our meals with the rest of the family. Then I will begin to cook breakfast and lunch for my Daniel here. After a while, we will come to the big house on Sundays only. It is the way of things."

I knew she was right but couldn't help grumbling, "I do not like the way of things."

The oddest expression came over her face. She tilted her head and studied me for a long moment. I fought the urge to shuffle from one foot to the other. Then the reason for her expression struck me with force. She had taken my words as having a larger meaning than I'd intended. I only meant I did not like to think of meals without my parents seated around the family table.

Or had I? In a bigger sense, *things* had certainly not turned out to my liking. Life itself had not turned out to my liking. One of Robbie's sayings came to mind. "Life stinks sometimes." I agreed wholeheartedly.

Her expression cleared. *Mamm* reached into the box and pulled out a black iron skillet. "You are always welcome to take your meals with us, Seth." She pointed the skillet at the two benches tucked beneath the table, a miniature version of the one in the big house. "There is plenty of room at our table for you."

Because I knew the offer was kindly meant, I smiled my thanks. But my smile faded when I turned to put the broom away. With *Mamm* and *Daed* gone from the main house, my presence as the extra *bruder* would become even more apparent. And awkward. If Saloma deserved a chance to lead in her own kitchen, then Aaron also deserved to lead his own household. I was making a little money now with my pottery, though I'd contributed most of it to the family budget, with a bit to Becky and Noah for their farm savings. Perhaps I'd best start setting some back for myself.

By the time Saloma and *Mammi* arrived from the hospital, the move had been accomplished. No evidence of *Mamm* and *Daed* remained in

Mammi's new bedroom in the big house. Her dresses and aprons hung on the pegs on the wall, and her lamp and *Bibel* rested on the small table beside the bed. Her quilt, slightly frayed at the corners and faded with years of washing, gave the room a homey feel. We'd moved a chair into that room, and Becky had stitched a soft cushion stuffed with lamb's wool for the seat, something we'd learned would make her more comfortable over the next few weeks until her recovery was complete.

When a strange car pulled up to the house, I thought we had a wealthy visitor. Though I could not tell one car brand from another, this one's sleek appearance and gold trim indicated a high price tag. Then Robbie leaped out and ran around to the other side to open the rear door. We all filed out of the house, the children hopping with excitement.

"Stay back," Becky warned the three energetic youngsters. "If you jump on *Mammi*, she might fall again."

The threat failed to calm them, though they charged off to the back of the car, well out of *Mammi*'s vicinity, and ran in circles.

Daed hurried over to take Robbie's place in helping his *mamm* to stand, while Aaron opened the door on this side for his wife. The trunk popped open, and I followed Robbie there to lift out a plastic bag with the hospital emblem on it, bulging with *Mammi*'s things.

"Did you buy a new car?" I asked him.

"I wish." He lifted out a metal walker and closed the trunk lid with a care he did not show his own red vehicle. "This is Mom's. She let me take the Lexus because she was afraid my car would be too rough for someone just getting over surgery. This baby rides like you're sitting on a cloud."

Mammi made her way slowly across the grass, leaning heavily on the walker and surrounded by caring family members. The children had become solemn at the sight of the unusual gadget. Sadie hugged her *mamm*'s leg while the twins stood off to one side, eyes round as buggy wheels, and watched the family parade. The porch steps presented a challenge, which *Mammi* tackled with extra caution while Noah stood behind, his hands extended toward her back, ready to catch her if she should stumble.

When they disappeared into the house, the boys came to my side.

"*Onkel* Seth, what is that thing?" Luke asked in a hushed voice, his gaze fixed on the closed door.

"It will help *Mammi* walk until she is strong enough to walk on her own."

"It had green balls," Mark said. "Did you see them?"

"Green balls?" I had not looked that closely, being more concerned with *Mammi*.

Robbie enlightened us. "Tennis balls. They put them on the front legs so the walker moves more easily across the floor."

Mark turned an eager grin up to me. "Can we play with them?"

"Maybe when she is stronger." It did not take much imagination to envision an episode when this pair of mischief-makers decided on their own that *Mammi* was strong enough. "But unless she gives them to you, stay away from them."

They both nodded, and then Mark took off running toward the barn, one hand on the top of his straw hat to keep it on his head. Luke did not hesitate a moment before racing after his brother. Schwein's piglets were a week old now, and the boys never tired of watching them.

Robbie jingled the car keys. "So I guess you're not going to Elias's today, huh?"

Enough eager hands were ready to help *Mammi* any way she needed, but I hated to leave during such a big family change. Besides, the afternoon was half over.

I shook my head. "I need to stay."

"Bummer. I like driving the Lexus." He grinned. "Maybe I'll tell Mom Mrs. Hostetler needs to go somewhere tomorrow."

I leveled a stern look on him and prepared to deliver a lecture on dishonesty, but he laughed and punched my shoulder with a light shove. "I'm kidding, Seth. Mom would freak out if she caught me in a lie like that."

Robbie's language was so expressive, and so unlike the talk of my family, that I laughed. "I would hate for Amanda to *freak out*. But I would like to go to the shop tomorrow if you are free to drive me."

Though tomorrow was Saturday, and whatever pots I threw would have to wait until Monday for trimming, my hands itched to mold clay.

"See you at ten thirty, dude."

I stood watching as the fancy car pulled down our driveway. *Dude*, he had called me. I thought of the nervous young man who had first approached us and offered his services. Robbie had certainly become more comfortable around me in the ensuing weeks. Maybe driving me and my family was helping him get over whatever it was that worried his mother.

The Lexus turned onto the main road, and then I heard the squeal of tires on pavement as it sped away. I couldn't help but laugh. No wonder Amanda did not often allow her son to drive her expensive car. Shaking my head, I followed my family inside.

Dinner that night would have been a festive occasion with all of us together again, except for one huge change. Aaron sat at the head of the table, and Saloma at the opposite end. The twins were full of questions about the reason for the different seating arrangement, and Sadie kept pointing at Aaron and then *Daed* and giggling.

Saloma had come home from the hospital with a stack of papers outlining a heart-healthy diet, and throughout the meal she chattered about new recipes she wanted to try and the need to do more roasting and less frying.

When the meal was finished, *Mammi* reached for her walker and, moving slowly and with much wincing, rose from the cushion Becky had placed on the bench for her. One hand braced on the walker, she reached for her plate, but Becky took it out of her hands.

"We will clean up tonight. You go and rest."

I thought from the stubborn pursing of *Mammi's* lips that she might refuse. How she thought she could help with clearing the table while using the walker, I couldn't imagine. The same thought must have occurred to her, for in the next instant her expression changed to one of resignation. With a nod, she began her slow way toward the living room.

I picked up the cushion and trailed after her, ready to place it in her usual chair near the fireplace. Instead, she limped through the living room and into her new bedroom. I followed her and placed the cushion in the chair there.

She glared at it. "I never thought I would have to sit on a fancy thing like that."

"It is only for a while."

"Humph." She ignored the chair and hobbled instead to the bed. Her features seemed to be set in stone as she lowered herself onto the edge of the mattress.

"You are moving well for only a few days after hip replacement surgery."

"I hate it." Bitterness that I'd never heard saturated her voice. "The doctor showed me a picture of the device he put inside me, and I hate it. A fancy thing in my body." She waved toward the cushion. "Much worse than a fancy thing in my bedroom."

I seated myself in the cushioned chair and made a show of wiggling to settle myself. The wool stuffing was soft and would no doubt feel much better for someone in pain than unyielding wood. "If you would rather not sit on padding, I can take it away. But it seems a shame to suffer unnecessarily."

"You can't take this *thing* out of my hip, though."

This attitude was so unlike my peace-loving *grossmammi,* even given the discomfort she must be feeling. "You are upset about *Daed* and *Mamm*'s move to the *daadi haus.*" I spoke softly so our family in the other room could not hear.

She did not bother to temper her tone. "And who wouldn't be? I leave for a few days, and when I come back, everything is different."

Because I knew exactly how she felt, I remained silent. After a moment, she heaved a sigh and the bitterness seeped away. Her shoulders drooped.

"This was my room before, you know." She patted the bed with a wrinkled hand that still had a bandage covering the place where the IV had been. "I slept here with my husband. Your father was born in this bed, him and six others. Three did not survive."

The reason for her sullenness became clear then. This room held so many memories for her, memories she'd never thought to face again. What would it be like for her, to sleep in the bed where she'd slept with her husband, my *grossdaadi*?

"You lived with *Grossdaadi* in the little house too," I pointed out.

But she shook her head. "It is not the same. I have stayed there longer without him than with, but here…" The hand caressed the quilt, and a bittersweet smile curved her lips. "I never lived here without him."

Of everyone in our family, I was the only one who had an inkling of the turmoil she must feel. Though I had never lived in this house with either Rachel or Hannah, having moved in with their families after our marriages, we did stay here on occasion. If those few memories haunted me in my room upstairs, imagine how many ghostly visions filled this room for *Mammi*.

"When your hip is well enough to handle the stairs, you can have my room."

The suggestion elicited a laugh, which was at least better than the sad visage of a moment before. "And where will you sleep? Here?"

I shook my head. "I would move to Aaron's room, and they would move here, and when Becky and Noah leave, their room will become a nursery." I hesitated. My plans were not firm enough to discuss with anyone, but maybe *Mammi's* ears were a good testing ground. "Truth be told, I have been considering another kind of move. I have not approached Aaron with my request, but I would like to build a small house here, on our farm."

"Another *daadi haus*?" She shook her head. "Whoever heard of such a thing?"

"Not a *daadi haus*." I grinned. "An *onkel haus*. I can be out of the way there, but still close enough to help with the farm. And maybe the new house can have two bedrooms, one for you and one for me."

She laughed then, the full-throated laughter that was so much like her old self. When the laughter faded, her eyes glistened. "My Seth, you make me proud. But it is not your responsibility to care for me in my old age. Nor is it your lot in life to make your home with an *old* woman."

Her emphasis on the word warned me of what would come next. I stood, ready to flee before she could continue, but she would not be stopped.

"You *will* marry again. I know it here." She pressed a fist against her chest, over her heart. "And when you do, your wife will not want to live in an *onkel haus.*"

I left her still chuckling at the silly term I'd invented. With barely a word for my family, I picked up the slop bucket and left the house, heading for the pigpen. *Mammi's* laughter had turned the good food in my stomach sour. Though I knew she did not intend to be unkind, she had treated my plan as a joke. And now that I had given voice to the idea, it sounded ridiculous in my own ears. Why would Aaron want his *bruder* hanging around his farm forever? Sooner or later I would have to move away. *Mammi* was right about that.

But in one respect she was wrong. I would not marry again, not ever. How long would it take for my family to accept that?

ELEVEN

When I stepped into Elias's, I was struck by the pleasant scent that permeated the shop. I came to a halt, inhaled deeply, and tried to identify the smell.

"Are you baking cookies?" I asked Leah, who stood behind the retail counter jotting notes on a pad of paper.

She shook her head. "Good guess, though. It's a candle called Sugar Cookie."

Pointing with a pencil, she directed my attention to the display table in the front window, where one of my carved candleholders sat. I stepped close to inspect the display.

"You glazed it already." The last time I saw this piece, it had been ready for the bisque firing. Now it was finished.

"I hope you don't mind." She came out from behind the counter and approached. "You said I could glaze mine however I liked, and we had room in the kiln for your three pieces."

Elias liked to fill the kiln completely, which was the most efficient use of electricity. The last time I'd been in the shop, we'd had almost enough pieces for a firing.

"Not at all." I knelt to look more closely at my candleholder. She had selected a red glaze that I'd used on a few of my bowls. Once fired, it darkened to the color of the reddish sandstone soil found in the eastern part of Pennsylvania. Light shone from inside, though the daylight shining through the front window rendered it virtually invisible. This had been the third candleholder I'd trimmed on Wednesday, the pattern not nearly as intricate as the one based on Hannah's quilt. I'd dreamed up the decorations for the second and third myself, designing as I carved. This one, a series of circles that I thought resembled bubbles, was the one I'd been least satisfied with.

I straightened and glanced around the room. "Where is the other?"

"The one with the curves?" She splayed her hands. "Gone. I set it out this morning, and a woman bought it about ten minutes ago."

The door opened and Robbie entered. "I forgot to tell you that I have another appointment this afternoon." He raised his nose and sniffed. "Hey, it smells good in here."

Leah pointed to the source of the aroma. "Look at Seth's candleholder."

Interest showed on his face as he approached. "Wow, that's really pretty. I thought all you made were plates and bowls and stuff."

I didn't answer, because at that moment the door opened again and a trio of *Englisch* shoppers entered. Leah went to greet them.

"So it'll probably be two thirty before I get back here," Robbie said, "unless you want me to come get you early?"

One of the shoppers gravitated in our direction, and we stepped back, out of her way.

"Two thirty will be fine," I told him.

The woman reached for one of Elias's pitchers, but then she stopped, her hand hovering over my candleholder. "Louise, come look at this." She carefully turned it around to examine it all sides. "I've never seen one like this."

Leah cast a grin in my direction as she followed the pair. "It is a custom design, created by one of our potters."

I was glad she didn't identify me. I found the inevitable praise that followed uncomfortably embarrassing.

The woman blew out the candle and, handling it gingerly, held it high to inspect the bottom. "How much is it?"

"Seventy-five dollars."

Though Leah did not bat an eyelash as she quoted the price, I nearly choked. Who would pay such an outrageous price for a canister with holes?

The shopper held it toward her friends. "Do you think Rhonda would like it?"

"She'll love it," answered one of them. "In fact, I love it. If you don't get it for her, I'll buy it myself."

The first woman shook her head. "Too late. I found it first." She handed it to Leah. "I'll take it."

The other lady turned in a circle, her gaze traveling around the shop. "Do you have any others?"

"Not yet," Leah answered as she carried the candleholder to the counter. "But check back in a few days. I'm sure the potter has plans to make more."

She gave me a pointed look as she removed the candle and began wrapping the holder in newspaper. I stood rooted to the floor, stunned. Seventy-five dollars.

Robbie turned to me. "You know what? My mom's birthday is next week. She'd really like something like that. Think you could make one for her?"

His comment overheard, the two ladies closest to us looked at me, their faces alive with interest. I grabbed Robbie's arm and steered him into the workshop before they could say anything. At his questioning gaze, I shrugged.

"I would prefer they didn't know I did the work."

"Most people would be proud to show off something like that." He cocked his head. "You're a weird dude, Seth, you know that?"

Though his odd *Englisch* phrasing was not how I would describe myself, I could not help but agree with the sentiment, for a variety of reasons.

"*Ya.* I am a weird dude."

Elias emerged from the small supply closet. His face brightened when he caught sight of me. "I am glad you are back. Remember the big planters?"

A glance toward the table where they had rested on Wednesday revealed that they were still there, now bisque fired and ready for glazing.

"The *Englisch* lady who ordered them came yesterday to select the glaze, and liked them so much she has commissioned four others." He shook his head, smiling. "She must have a very large porch, that lady."

A few days before I'd been disappointed at missing the opportunity to learn to throw large pots. Oddly, now I found myself frustrated at the delay the huge pots would cause.

I faced Robbie. "If you do not mind, could you come back for me even later? Around four thirty?" That would give me time to work on both planters and candleholders.

"Sure." He started to leave and then stopped. "But you'll make something for my mother, right?"

"*Ya,* I will make something nice for your mother."

The design had already begun to take shape in my mind.

Throwing my first big pot proved to be enough of a challenge that I forgot all about candleholders for several hours. Elias had only one wheel that could handle the weight required for a giant planter, so I worked with him standing beside me, directing my movements.

The pot began like any other, though with a large amount of clay. When I had centered that piece I added a second mound of equal size, which Elias had wedged and ready. Combining the two so that they formed one base took a great deal of effort, and then I was ready to begin forming the pot itself. Several times I paused in my work and left the wheel to inspect Elias's completed planters. The shape of mine had to match them, at least close enough that any differences were not easily detectable.

When the bottom part was formed to my satisfaction, Elias instructed me to score the upper edge, and then he brought over a thick, snakelike coil of clay to lay over the top.

"Now combine the two, but take care to leave no seam. There must be no weak place." He left me to the task and returned to the worktable to roll another coil.

The technique was difficult in a different way than a smaller piece would be. By the time I had worked the final coil seamlessly into the others, sweat poured down my face and dripped into my beard. My sleeves, which I'd rolled up, were stiff and salty from wiping my brow.

Though the work absorbed my full attention, I was aware that every so often the curtain parted and Leah peeked through. She never entered the room. She merely watched me work for a moment and then disappeared again.

At last I formed the rounded lip. When it was as smooth as I could make it, I sat back and inspected the finished pot. All along I'd used my fingers to create the circular grooved pattern along the outside that was Elias's trademark, though he'd corrected my technique a few times. The result was nearly identical to the other two.

Elias bent close to examine the lip, and then he straightened and gave a satisfied nod. "So now you have thrown large." He smiled. "Large and in charge, as my own *daed* used to say. What do you think?"

I arched my back and circled my shoulders. "I think I like bowls better."

"Ha!" Eyes twinkling, he finished wiping his hands on a towel and tossed it to me. "So do I, young Seth. So do I."

The curtain parted and Leah peeked in. "You're finished?"

"*Ya.* Come and see." I waved the towel toward my giant pot.

She entered carrying a covered basket, which she set on our wedging table before making a show of walking around the planter. Bending close, she examined it through narrowed eyes. "It looks good." Then she awarded me one of her sardonic expressions. "It took you long enough. *Daadi* could have done two in that time."

It was the first time I'd heard her refer to Elias by any name, and the use of the Amish *Daadi* for grandfather surprised me. In the next instant, I realized it should not. She had, after all, been raised Amish.

"I am merely a student and not a master like Elias," I told her, a little defensively.

She grinned, an expression I'd seen more and more of late. "I'm teasing, Seth. You did a good job. But I like your candleholders better. Especially mine."

The grin softened, and the glow in her eyes sent an unexpected flood of warmth through me. Becky had been thrilled with my gift of bowls and plates, and she had praised my work to the point that I'd flushed with embarrassment. But the candleholder, so special to me because of its design, seemed to have touched Leah deeply. To think that something I had made with my hands brought such pleasure to another was at once humbling and exhilarating. I returned her smile with a soft one of my own.

She broke the moment by jerking her gaze from mine. The smile evaporated, and she was once again no-nonsense Leah as she turned to Elias.

"*Grossmammi* brought lunch while you were working." She nodded toward the basket. "The chicken is cold by now, but come and eat it anyway."

Elias rubbed his stomach. "Cold chicken is just the thing to fill this empty belly. Come, Seth. Cold or not, once you've tasted my Lily's chicken, you'll never be satisfied with anyone else's."

I hesitated. In all the weeks I'd been working with Elias, I had never shared his meal. Usually *Mamm* packed a sandwich for me, which I ate in hurried bites between throws. But after breakfast this morning, she'd returned to the *daadi haus*, and Saloma hadn't thought to make a lunch for me. Nor had I remembered it myself.

Leah was watching me. "There's plenty. My grandmother always sends enough food for a dozen."

"If that is so, my belly is as empty as Elias's."

"But not nearly so big." He patted his midsection, which did fill out his trousers more than mine.

Leah lifted the basket and indicated that I should wash the table. I did, scrubbing away clay residue left over from the wedging. Then she covered the surface with the cloth from the basket and began pulling out bowls covered with filmy plastic. Apparently, Lily Beachy had anticipated my inclusion in today's meal, for Leah removed three plates.

I must have looked curious, for when she handed one to me, she gave a small shrug. "I noticed you didn't have a lunch sack today, so I called the neighbor's house and asked her to take a message to my grandmother."

The gesture touched me. Twice in one day I'd been surprised by Leah. For the first time, I could see behind that caustic tongue and solemn countenance. Once she must have been a kind and caring woman. What had changed her? Was it whatever had caused the scar on her face?

"*Danke.*"

My tone came out softer than expected, almost tender. She looked startled, and then she busied herself with uncovering the bowls.

Elias took his plate and looked over the food, grinning widely. "Beans and coleslaw too? Seth, I beg you. Forget your lunch every day."

He loaded his plate—which was, of course, made of stoneware with his own potter's mark on the bottom—and then balanced a biscuit on top. Leah had spoken the truth. There was enough food to feed us and several others. Elias seated himself at one of the wheels while I piled modest portions on my plate, though I did select two pieces of fried chicken.

Leah sat at the bench facing mine. When Elias bowed his head for the blessing, she did the same. So she still followed some of the ways of her childhood. Or did she pray only in the company of her grandparents out of respect for them? I realized I was staring at her and quickly closed my eyes, reeling off a prayer of thanksgiving for the bounty of this lunch and for the people who shared it with me.

"Amen." Elias did not begin eating but instead said to me, "Go ahead. Taste my Lily's chicken."

He watched as I bit into a thigh. Though cool, the breading was still crisp and flavored with a combination of spices so pleasing to my taste buds that I chewed with relish. The meat was tender and juicy, and after I'd swallowed I was able to say with perfect honesty, "That *is* the best chicken I've ever tasted."

With a grin that stretched the width of his face, Elias nodded. "Did I not tell you? The Lord bestows gifts on each of us, and He blessed my Lily with the gift of cooking. Wait until you try the coleslaw."

He raised his biscuit to his mouth, but before he took a bite, the jangle of bells in the other room reached us. Leah hurried to put a forkful of green beans in her mouth, and then she set her plate on the wheel, already rising.

"No, no." Elias waved her down. "You eat. I will take care of the customers for once."

Before she could protest, he scurried from the room. With a shrug, she picked up her plate and set it once again on her knees. "He loves talking to the people. He might say he'd rather leave that part of the business to me, but it's not true."

"No?"

She shook her head. "He wants me to feel useful, like I'm an important part of the family business."

The explanation rang true. Anyone had only to watch Elias when he looked at his granddaughter to see his concern for her. Certainly explainable, because she had left the Amish faith, which he obviously cherished. My curiosity about her returned. Her past was no business of mine, but I couldn't help wondering about her present. Maybe in her current softer mood, she would not mind a question or two.

"Do you live with them?"

She looked up from her plate, surprise on her features. "*Daadi* and *Grossmammi*? No. I have a small apartment in town." A grin tweaked the scarred corner of her lips. "With a microwave, so this chicken would be hot if we were eating it there."

"And a lot of other *Englisch* things as well, *ya*?"

"Of course. An electric coffeemaker, a radio…even a television." She scowled. "But I never turn it on. There's nothing but trash showing, and I don't want to fill my mind with that stuff."

I finished the thigh and set the bare bone on the edge of my plate. "What do you do with your free time?"

"I read a lot." She eyed me over a fork loaded with coleslaw, and the grin returned. "I like Amish novels, if you can believe that."

That surprised a laugh out of me. "Why would you read those?"

"Because they're so sweet and peaceful. They remind me of when I was growing up." A faraway look appeared in her eyes, but then it cleared. "Some of them, anyway. Some get it all wrong, and a few are so ridiculous they make me laugh."

I could almost see her, sitting in a cushy *Englisch* chair, laughing with derision over the pages of a book.

She lifted a chicken leg and eyed it with appreciation. "I do eat dinner every night with *Daadi* and *Grossmammi*. I'm their official dishwasher."

"Every night?"

"Mm-hmm." She chewed and swallowed. "I'm a terrible cook, and as you can see, my grandmother is amazing." Her gaze became distant, and she lowered the chicken to her plate. "They, at least, will still eat with me."

A confusing statement. I'd been under the impression that she was not yet baptized when she became *Englisch*. If that were so, then she wouldn't be under the ban. Any Amish person could eat with her.

Regardless of my determination not to pry into her past, I couldn't help it. The question popped out unbidden. "You were baptized, then?"

I thought she might not answer, but finally she shook her head. "No."

"But—"

A blast of air that might pass for a grunt accompanied the return of her bitter expression. "I am sinful and unrepentant. Our bishop back in Ohio thought that a taste of what it would be like to live as one who'd been shunned might convince me to repent." Her head dropped forward. "Most of my aunts and uncles agreed with him."

I slumped backward on my bench. Discipline was, of course, the responsibility of the bishop, and the community was bound to follow whatever measures he decided were appropriate in a given situation. But refusing someone who had not yet been baptized the privilege of eating with their family? Either Leah's sin was a grievous one, or their former district was far stricter than any in our affiliation.

The sorrow apparent in her bowed head and drooping shoulders touched a place deep in my heart. I picked up my second piece of chicken and held it aloft. "I am eating with you. And I will do so again." I took a big bite.

Was that a flash of gratitude in her eyes? I couldn't be sure, because a second later the twisted smile returned. "Only because you want more of *Grossmammi's* fried chicken."

We finished our lunch in a companionable silence.

Twelve

I awoke the following morning with an unnamed feeling of dread and could not for a moment figure out why. As I fastened my suspenders to my trousers, the reason returned. Today was church Sunday, and it was the Schrocks' turn to host.

I had not been in their home since the day of the accident that haunted me day and night.

The last time the hosting responsibility fell to them, I'd made an excuse not to attend. My family had immediately seen through my claim of illness—I knew that from the pity in every face—but no one challenged me. At that time it had been just six months since Hannah's death.

I stared for a long time at my black felt hat hanging in readiness on its peg. Could I do that again? Make up another excuse? Actually, my stomach was churning at the thought of entering the house where I'd attended my last church service with Hannah, so I would speak nothing but the truth if I said I felt too sick to go.

Maybe I could offer to stay home with *Mammi,* who could not yet withstand the buggy ride or sitting on a hard, backless bench for the length of the service. When Becky innocently suggested that she take her seat cushion, *Mammi's* glare could have ignited wet logs.

No. Everyone would see right through my suggestion. They would know it was not a sacrifice I offered, but a self-centered escape. And *Mammi* herself would insist on my going.

Heaving a heavy sigh, I took my hat and coat from their pegs. I had to return to the Schrocks' house sometime. They were part of my community, my extended Amish family. If not today, then when?

I said nothing during the ride to church, and my family seemed sensitive to my need for silence because no one spoke to me. I sat wedged in the front between *Daed* and Aaron, while *Mamm* and Saloma rode on the seat behind us with the twins. We followed Noah, Becky, and Sadie, who had thrown a tantrum because she wanted to ride with her *grossmammi* like the boys and had received a strong scolding as a result.

When we arrived at the Schrocks', I helped the women and *Daed* out in front of the house and then rode with Aaron to park the buggy in the field designated for that purpose. He maneuvered Rosie into a long line of buggies, and we left her happily munching on a patch of new clover that had pushed its way up through the winter-hard soil.

Aaron didn't wait but began walking toward the house while Noah was still settling his buggy. Sensing that he wanted to speak with me, I fell in step beside him.

"This is a hard day for you." He spoke without looking my way, his gaze fixed on the house ahead of us.

Did he realize that on his own, or had Saloma or *Mamm* said something? I had no doubt every one of my family members was aware of the significance of this church service for me.

Seeing no reason to deny it, I nodded. "*Ya,* it is hard."

We covered a few more steps.

"We all have memories, Seth. We loved her too."

Emotion lay raw in his words. It was the first time my *bruder* had spoken to me of Hannah's death. He had never mentioned Rachel to me at all. I dared not look in his direction, lest the bubble of tears that pressed against the backs of my eyes burst.

He waited a moment, and when I gave no answer, he spoke again. "A year is a long time. But not, maybe, enough time. No matter what the bishop says."

Now I did look at him, my jaw dangling in surprise. Aaron and I were not accustomed to voicing personal feelings to each other. To hear him speak in open contradiction to Bishop Beiler, even though I knew how much he respected the man, spoke of the depth of his feelings on this matter.

His comment also revealed another truth to me. Not only had my family discussed the fact that I should be over my grief and ready to find a new wife, they had discussed it with the bishop as well. And who else? Lettie Miller and her daughter Hannah? Ella, my friend Josiah's wife, who was also friendly with Becky? Was the entire district talking about me?

At least Aaron understood. Warmth for my *bruder* flooded me.

"*Danke* for that," I said.

When we neared the house, where people clustered outside visiting before the service began, he stopped. Staring at a group of women that included Saloma, he spoke in a low voice. "Our home is your home. Never think other than that." Then he looked at me, and the depth of feeling I saw in his eyes nearly undid me. "You always have a home with us, Seth. Always."

My throat was so tight that I could not answer. I merely nodded and kept my lips rigid so they would not crumple and betray me.

When I entered the house, my *bruder* was right beside me. Our shoulders touched as we squeezed through the doorway together. I doubt I'd ever been more grateful for anyone's presence as I was for Aaron's that day.

The congregation sang the first song, a slow, unison hymn from the *Ausbund* that I'd never understood. It had been one of Rachel's favorites, though, so I stumbled through the German words with my mind fixed on her and not on the Lord, where it should have been.

While we sang, the bishop and ministers filed out of the room to decide who would preach the opening sermon and who would preach the main sermon. Apparently, they had no trouble with the decision because they filed back in long before we'd sung the last word. And they brought with them a surprise.

At first I didn't recognize the young woman who entered with them. The last time I saw her, her lips had been painted bright red, and black marks from her *Englisch* makeup streaked down her cheeks. Today her face had been scrubbed clean, and a starchy *kapp* covered her hair. She wore a proper Amish dress, and she walked with her head bowed in an attitude of humility.

The song's melody stumbled as the people recognized Laura King. Several indrawn breaths were audible, and at that moment she walked directly in front of me so that I saw her face in profile. Head still bowed, her mouth twitched into a smile. Only for a second, but long enough that I knew she enjoyed surprising some in the community by her return. By the time she reached the women's side on the front bench and stood beside Sarah Beiler, her expression was once again properly humble and penitent.

When the song ended, the bishop gestured for Laura to join him. She stood facing the congregation, hands clasped and head still bowed.

"It is with the joy of the Lord that I tell you a lost sheep has returned to her flock. Laura has made her confession and has been accepted back into our community. Further, she has made the decision to take the classes and be baptized this fall." An excited murmur arose from somewhere behind me on the other side of the room, which Bishop Beiler allowed with an indulgent smile. "I urge you all to accept her and make her welcome."

Laura returned to her place on the women's side. I risked a glance at her mother. Joyful tears flowed freely down Susan King's face. I would have liked to see Daniel Schrock's reaction, but to do so I would have to twist all the way around on my bench, which would be an unacceptable display of curiosity.

No one was surprised when Bishop Beiler delivered the first sermon on the topic of faithfulness to God and the importance of a Plain lifestyle as the way of worshipping Him. The main sermon came from Kurt Miller, and I don't think I was the only one who struggled to find a clear message in the string of seemingly unrelated comments.

Abigail had prepared a light meal of sandwiches and store-bought chips. Acutely aware that the last time I'd attended church in this house I'd skipped the meal to go home and enjoy time alone with my wife, today I took a sandwich of peanut butter and a mug of coffee and headed outside. Though the sky was overcast and rain threatened, the temperature was not unpleasant. Some of the men had moved the church benches to the yard, and I sat to eat my sandwich. I looked around for Josiah, and then remembered hearing Becky say he and Ella had gone to visit her family the next district over for the weekend.

Laura stood near the door, surrounded by a crowd of women who were no doubt following the bishop's directive to make her welcome. Even many of the men stopped by to speak a word to her. Scanning the area, I saw Daniel slumped on one of the benches, shoulders tense and his entire focus on a handful of potato chips. Where was Katie?

I looked closer at the knot of young women around Laura and identified Katie. The two embraced, which brought a smile to my face. Good. Forgiveness had occurred and, I hoped, friendship restored. The Lord and the bishop would both be pleased.

I'd finished my sandwich and was about to drain the last of my coffee when Laura left her group of well-wishers and made her way toward me.

"*Guder daag*, Seth."

She stood in front of me, forcing me to tilt my head back to see her face from beneath the brim of my hat. "*Guder daag* and welcome home."

"*Danke*. Were you surprised to see me?"

"Surprised?" I nodded. "*Ya*, but glad."

She dropped onto the bench beside me. "The last time I saw you, I was rude. I hope you will forgive me for shouting at you."

"I hope the same."

"I already did, the minute I read your letter." She stared at her hands, folded in her lap. "I received a lot of letters, but yours was the only one that didn't try to make me feel guilty for leaving. You said the decision must be mine."

I grinned. "I am glad you made the right one."

She returned my smile, and then her expression brightened. "Will I see you at the singing tonight?"

The question surprised a laugh out of me. Singings were for the *youn-gie*, a time when youth from several districts in our affiliation gathered to sing songs, play games, and flirt.

"I'm too old for singings."

"No, you're not."

"I am twenty-six." I tugged at my beard, a sign of the youth I'd left behind when I married Rachel. "Far too old for singings."

"There is no age limit on singings." A stubborn set to her jaw made her look almost like the twins when they were feeling defiant over an instruction they did not want to follow.

The comparison elicited another laugh from me. "Imagine what people would say if a bearded old man showed up at a singing." If I weren't the object of gossip already, that would assure me a place in many a conversation throughout several districts.

"I don't think of you as one who cares what people say." A sparkle appeared in her eyes. "If I cared what people said, I would never have been able to come home. No doubt many conversations this week will speculate on the details of my confession to the bishop, and I don't care in the least."

I envied her attitude. Knowing that people were talking about me bothered me enormously. I shifted on the bench. No, it was not the talk that bothered me. It was the pity.

"Besides," she went on, "if you really think you're too old, you could come and chaperone."

"That's for the parents to do."

She shrugged. "It doesn't have to be."

I turned sideways to look at her head-on. Why was she so determined to convince me to go to a singing? She returned my stare without flinching, and then she did something that sent alarm bells ringing in my ears. She tilted her head slightly and half closed her lids so she gazed at me from beneath a veil of curly lashes. The merest hint of a dimple appeared in one creamy-smooth cheek.

Laura King was flirting with me!

What had given her the idea that I would be interested in her? Certainly, our heated conversation in Philadelphia left no doubt that I had no intentions toward her, nor her toward me. My mind raced over the contents of the letter I'd written to her. Nowhere in it had I hinted at a romantic interest. In fact, I'd openly stated the exact opposite.

Around us, parents began to call for children, and people wished each other farewell. Men began picking up the benches and loading them onto the wagon, where they would be taken to the bishop's barn and stored until needed for the next church Sunday. We stood when Nathan Yoder and Daniel approached to take our bench. Laura nodded a greeting at Nathan and ignored Daniel completely.

When they had moved out of earshot, she faced me. "Will you drive me home, Seth? We can continue our conversation about the singing."

I was stunned at the bold request. When a man drove a young woman home, that sent a clear message to everyone that they were courting. Normally, the man asked the girl, or if she wanted to make her interest known she might convince a friend to hint to him that she would be open to his offer for a ride.

Though I should make a firm statement that let her know without a doubt that I had no interest in courting her, I found myself mumbling, "I rode with my family. I do not even own a buggy anymore."

At that moment I spied Aaron over her shoulder, striding toward Mark and Luke with their coats in hand. "I must go. My family is leaving now," I hurried to say before she could respond. "Again, welcome home."

Ignoring the disappointment apparent on her features, I jerked a quick nod and made my escape.

On Monday Robbie picked me up at ten thirty as usual and dropped me off at Elias's shop. I intended to stay late again today so that I could trim my candleholders from Saturday and perhaps throw another large pot for Elias.

When I entered the shop, Leah spied my lunch bag.

"You can just take that right back home with you," she said. "*Grossmammi* plans to make our lunch. I'm to pick it up at noon."

Though my mouth watered at the memory of Lily's fried chicken, I shook my head. "I can't eat her food again. I would not feel right."

Leah shrugged. "It's too late. *Daadi* said she was already cooking when he left the house."

Elias emerged from the workshop in time to agree with her. "I have not seen my wife so excited about cooking a meal since we left Ohio. She plans to send lunch every day, so you can leave your sandwiches at home."

"It is not right to take advantage of her this way."

He placed his hands on his hips and awarded me a stern look. "Would you deny her the pleasure of using the gift *Gott* has given her?"

Put like that, how could I refuse? "Then I insist on paying for my meals."

Elias waved away the offer. "You pay us by making more wares for our shelves."

"More candleholders, I hope," Leah said. "I put a picture of mine on the website with a big caption that it was sold. We've already received three emails inquiring when more would be available."

"A canister with holes." I shook my head. "I never would have thought."

"Well, why are you standing here?" Leah pointed toward the workshop. "Get busy!"

Laughing at her bossy command, Elias and I got busy.

The next two hours evaporated, so focused was I on my carving. I repeated the curvy design from last week and also the one I'd begun to think of as the bubble design. The pattern based on Hannah's quilt would never be repeated. Not only did it seem appropriate to honor my deceased wife with a once-only creation, I wanted to please Leah by gifting her with a one-of-a-kind piece.

But I'd seen many quilt patterns, and so I set about replicating the one on *Mammi*'s bed. I wasn't aware that Leah had left the shop until she walked into the back carrying the same lunch basket as before.

"Time to take a break," she told us. "Cold schnitzel is not nearly as good as cold chicken."

"Schnitzel." Elias grinned at me. "You have never tasted anything like my Lily's *schweineschnitzel*."

Because his claim about her chicken had been true, my expectations for the meal soared.

Nor was I disappointed. Tender pork, pounded thin, breaded, and fried to a golden brown, melted in my mouth. The potato salad held a touch of tangy sweetness that reminded me of the German recipe *Mammi* used to make, but with only enough sugar to go well with the lemony schnitzel. We also ate salad and bread still warm enough that the butter melted quickly after being spread on.

When I set my empty plate on the wheel and sat back, my belly bulged almost as much as Elias's. "And to think I would have eaten a bologna sandwich."

Leah rose and began stacking the empty plates. "There's lemon sponge pie for dessert, and I've been sternly instructed to send the leftovers home with you."

I moaned, but Elias beamed. "You've never tasted anything like my Lily's lemon sponge pie."

Leah and I joined in laughter. If there were a man who took more delight from his wife's cooking than Elias, I had never met him.

"I will taste it later," I promised.

While Leah cleared the remains of our meal, I returned to my wheel and inspected my work. This pattern was difficult, being a series of concentric circles. Once a hole was cut in the clay, nothing remained to form the center of the design. I'd modified the quilt pattern by forming the outer circles out of tiny holes. The work was exacting and required a great deal of concentration, but so far I was pleased with the result.

Leah approached and bent to study the design. "That looks like a quilt my aunt used to have."

Pleased that the pattern was recognizable, I nodded. "My *grossmammi* has a similar one."

"It's beautiful." She stood and turned a smile on me. "Not as beautiful as mine, but this one will sell quickly."

Elias joined us. "I like that. An Amish quilt design on Amish pottery."

I didn't point out that this could hardly be called Amish pottery because it would be considered impractical, and therefore too fancy for most Amish homes. But as an Amish man had made it, I supposed that made it Amish pottery.

He excused himself to check on the firewood supply because the big planters would be fired in the wood kiln. Leah finished filling the basket with empty dishes, and I picked up my tool. Today she had pulled her hair back again, though it hung in a long rope down her back. She stood in profile, with her scar hidden from my sight. The skin on the cheek presented to me was creamy and smooth, nearly as smooth as Laura King's. With a start, I realized she could be of an age with Laura.

"How old are you?" I blurted out the question before I could stop myself.

She didn't seem offended. "I'm twenty-two."

Only a few years older than Laura and younger than I'd thought. Her habitual stern expression added the appearance of age. Some Amish people were not even baptized yet at twenty-two, though that would be cause for much anguish for their parents.

She picked up the napkin that had covered the worktable and shook it out. "How old are you?"

"Twenty-six."

"An old man, then." Her teasing grin faded, and her gaze focused on her hands as she folded the napkin. "When I first met you, I assumed you were married because of your beard. Then *Daadi* told me about your wife."

Only once had Elias and I discussed Hannah. He, too, had assumed I was married and had asked my wife's name. I'd given a clipped answer about her being deceased, and he had never broached the subject again. Unless someone in his district had told him about Rachel, he probably didn't know I'd been married twice.

I surprised myself by clearing my throat and saying, "Two wives."

She faced me fully, eyes round. "You were married twice?"

Nodding, I managed to keep my tone even. "My first wife, Rachel, died in childbirth. Hannah died in a buggy accident." I didn't know why, but I added, "She was expecting a baby too."

She completed her task in silence, though I felt sympathy radiating in my direction. When the worktable was clear and the basket full, she asked in a quiet voice, "Will you marry again?"

"No."

My answer was quick and gruff. She looked surprised but only nodded.

I bent over my work, and then I remembered that I had not yet told her of yesterday's church announcement. Glad for a reason to change the subject, I asked, "Do you remember the girl who ran away?"

"The one you wrote the letter to?"

"*Ya.* Well, she came back. She was at church yesterday."

Leah's lips twisted into their familiar acerbic arrangement. "They got to her, did they?"

"I think she came to the decision on her own." I glanced away. "She mentioned my letter and how I had said the decision should be hers."

Something in my tone must have betrayed my discomfort, for Leah's stare became sharp. "Let me guess. She came back for you."

"Of course not!" I said sharply. "She came back for God."

"But she's interested in you." When I didn't answer, she prodded. "Am I right?"

I nodded. Then I laughed in an attempt to lighten the conversation. "She asked me to go to a singing, and when I refused, she asked me to drive her home."

Leah grinned. "I like this girl. She has a mind of her own." Her head cocked sideways. "So did you?"

"Of course not. And I will not make a fool of myself by going to the singings, either."

A sigh escaped her lips, and she fixed an unfocused stare toward the ceiling. "I used to love singings when I was young. We'd play games and stuff ourselves full of *Grossmammi*'s cookies. She always sent cookies."

I was about to point out that she was still young, but Elias returned at that moment.

"Leah, will you make a call for me and place an order for a wagonload of wood? I will need it delivered by Wednesday morning."

Nodding, she tucked the basket's handles in the crook of her arm and left the room without another glance in my direction. The faraway look in her eyes when she spoke of the singings hovered in my mind as I bent once again to my carving.

THIRTEEN

When Robbie left me at home that afternoon, I went inside to deliver the sponge pie—minus three pieces—before going to check on the livestock. The women of my family worked in the kitchen with a perfect harmony they had rehearsed daily since Aaron's marriage. *Mamm* moved from the stove to the cutting board, and the moment she left the simmering pot, Saloma swept into place behind her with a long spoon to give the contents a stir. Becky whirled from the counter to set a bowl of stewed tomatoes on the table, where *Mammi* sat peeling turnips, little Sadie at her side carefully pulling pickles from a jar and placing them in a dish.

They exclaimed over the pie, and *Mamm* fixed a too-innocent look on me. "What a shame we did not have this sooner to offer our visitors."

The sight of her expression, along with the sudden smile Becky tried to hide by bending over the wash bucket, sent my defenses on high alert.

I made the inquiry *Mamm* obviously expected, though with a degree of caution. "You had visitors today?"

She nodded. "Susan King stopped by, along with her daughters."

Leah's comment about Laura having a mind of her own came back to me. She certainly did, combined with a boldness that many would find unappealing in a young woman. I found it disturbing.

Because their silence held an expectant quality, I voiced a vague comment. "That must have been a nice visit."

"Laura was disappointed to find you not here." *Mamm* continued chopping as she spoke, though now she stood sideways to the counter so she could watch me. "She wanted to ask a favor of you."

Saloma turned from her stirring. "Why did you not tell us you sent a letter while she was in Philadelphia?"

A sharp reply nearly shot from my mouth. *Because you would have acted as you are now, as if a simple letter held more meaning than the apology it contained.* Instead, I shrugged. "It was not important enough to mention." Before she could answer, I asked *Mamm,* "What favor does she want?"

"She hopes you will go with her to pick out a puppy. Her *daed* promised to buy her one when she returned."

So that was one of their tactics in convincing her to return. Bribery. Not uncommon, but a puppy?

I actually laughed, though the sound fell hollow in the room. "Let her *daed* help her, or her *mamm* or *schweschder.*"

Mamm gave me a stern look. "She wants *you* to take her."

"I know nothing about dogs. We do not even have one."

Saloma slid the chopped onions from the cutting board into a bowl. "That is one reason you are a good person to take her. Aaron says we need a dog around here to guard the chickens. He's seen a fox and her kits prowling around lately."

Sadie looked up from the pickle jar, eyes sparkling. "Puppy!"

I spared a smile for the child. "Then maybe Aaron should take Laura King. I have no time to shop for dogs."

Becky speared me with a sharp look. "If you spent less time with Elias Beachy, you would have more time to help around here."

The mood in the kitchen became noticeably awkward. The tasks everyone performed suddenly required close attention, and no one looked at me. Because I had not shirked my duties of milking the cows and caring for Schwein and her piglets, I knew that was not an issue. And because I regularly asked Aaron if he needed my help, and he regularly said no, that was not a problem either. No, Becky's complaint had nothing to do with Elias or the time I spent away from the farm. Instead, she had concluded that my focus on my pottery work was interfering with her plans to see me settled with a third wife. The fact that no one spoke to contradict her let me know they were in agreement.

This was a topic I had no intention of discussing, with Becky or anyone else.

I answered in a soft voice. "If you need my help with anything, you have only to ask."

Before anyone could reply, I left the kitchen and the house. The horse stalls needed mucking out, a task I usually disliked but just then looked forward to as a handy means of escape.

✌

With Becky's comment still stinging, I walked up the road to the Cramer house after dinner. The Cramers greeted me with friendly smiles and allowed me to come inside their home to use the phone.

"I haven't seen much of you lately," Kevin said as he handed me the cordless handset. "Heard you've hired another driver. Wasn't anything I did, was it?"

I hurried to assure him otherwise. "A young man who needs the work offered his car." It would not be proper to go into details, but I added, "I think he plans to go to college soon."

Kevin seemed relieved when he nodded. If he assumed from my words that Robbie needed the money for his education, I would not correct him.

I pressed the numbers for Robbie's cell phone. I explained that I would not go to Strasburg tomorrow, and we made arrangements for him to pick me up at the usual time on Wednesday. Then I disconnected the call and dialed the number for Plain Man's Pottery. No one would be there this late, but I could leave a message on the machine.

"Plain Man's Pottery. How can I help you?"

Startled to hear Leah's voice, at first I said nothing.

"Hello?" she said.

"I—" I cleared my throat. "This is Seth Hostetler."

"Hello, Seth." Her voice became friendly.

Words tumbled off my tongue. "You are working late."

A low laugh sounded through the phone. "No, I'm at home. I forward the store's phone to my cell at night just in case someone from the West Coast wants to place an order."

I shook my head at the mysteries of telephones. "I hope I have not interrupted you."

"Not really. I'm just reading."

My grin seeped into my voice. "An Amish novel?"

Again the low laugh that fell pleasantly on my ears. "Actually, this one is a sweet prairie romance."

The words meant nothing to me. "I called to say I will not be there tomorrow. My family needs my help on the farm."

"Oh." She sounded disappointed, which pleased me. "Okay, I'll tell *Daadi*. Is there anything he needs to do for you?"

I'd finished trimming all my candleholders and then had thrown another large pot—the final one to fill the special order.

"He will want to trim the planter so it is ready for bisque firing on Wednesday."

"Will you be here for that?"

I had only seen the wood kiln in operation once and was eager to see it again. "*Ya,* I will be there on Wednesday."

"Okay, good. I'll see you then."

I stood for a moment, the phone still held to my ear. Her voice had warmed when she said she would see me. A list of possible reasons came to mind. She might be concerned for her *grossdaadi* and wanted to make sure he didn't attempt to lift those heavy pots by himself. Or maybe she wanted me to make more candleholders because they seemed to sell well. Another possibility hovered at the edges of my mind—one I refused to think about.

I thanked the Cramers for the use of their phone and left. During the mile-long walk home in the dark, I spent a lot of time *not* thinking about that third reason.

The following day a steady rain drove us all indoors. After my chores in the barn, I joined the rest of my family inside. *Daed* reread the most recent issue of the *Budget,* while Aaron studied the *Old Farmer's Almanac.* I watched Noah whittle more of his wood pieces, envious of his task. My hands itched to be at the wheel, wetting the clay, molding it, testing the thickness with my fingers. I joined in a couple games of Dutch Blitz, but Saloma beat me soundly both times.

Wednesday morning I finished my chores early, eager to be on my way. I was watching the road for the familiar red car when instead a buggy pulled into our driveway. Not one of the large ones, but the same size as Noah and Becky's.

"We have a visitor," I called into the house.

That brought the women out, *Mamm* wiping her hands on a towel. "Saloma, put on the—" She stopped and cast an apologetic grimace toward Saloma. Entertaining visitors at the big house was no longer her responsibility.

Saloma smiled. "I'll put on coffee."

She disappeared into the house. When the buggy neared, I detected two occupants, their white *kapps* visible through the windscreen. It wasn't until they stopped that I recognized them. My stomach dropped toward my shoes. Laura and Irene King. Their mother was not with them this time. Had Laura returned to try to convince me to help with her flimsy excuse of an errand? When I went forward to help them to the ground, I saw that was not the case. In her arms she held a squirming yellow puppy.

She held the animal close to her chest as I lifted her down.

After seeing Irene safely on the ground, I nodded at the creature. "I see you found a dog on your own."

"*Ya,* I did."

The twins emerged from the house and charged toward us as the women of my family came forward to see the puppy. Noah and Aaron were in the field, testing the temperature of the soil, and *Daed* had returned to the *daadi haus* after breakfast.

Sadie squealed with delight when Laura set the puppy down. It bounded over to the boys, who dropped to the ground to pet it.

Robbie's car appeared then, and I waved him over.

"He seems to be a sweet dog," Becky said. "I'm surprised you picked him out so quickly." I detected a frown when she glanced up at me. My sister did not like to have her plans thwarted.

The dog bounded back over to Laura and nosed at the hem of her dress.

"He seems to be attached to you already," *Mammi* commented.

"Oh, he's not mine." Laura turned a grin up at me. "He's yours. I brought him for you."

"Mine?" I slapped a hand to my chest. "I don't want a dog."

"Seth! That is no way to receive a gift." *Mammi*'s stern reprimand accompanied a displeased scowl in my direction.

But Laura laughed—a high, ringing sound that rose into the sky. "I didn't mean the gift for Seth alone, but for the whole family. You said you wanted a dog to keep foxes away, and when we went to pick out our puppy, only two were left."

Irene nodded and stooped to rub the dog's ears. "The people told us these dogs are gentle with children and yet protective enough to guard your chickens."

Robbie's car pulled to a stop a few feet behind the buggy. Though he rolled his window down, he did not emerge.

"We insist on paying you." *Mammi* turned to Becky. "Fetch for me some money from the jar."

"Oh, the puppy was free. The people were anxious to find homes for the last two and gave them to us gladly. But I will let you pay for his food. We bought a bag for you when we bought ours." She turned a smile up to me. "Will you get it from the buggy, please?"

The dog bounded off in the direction of the barn, followed by a trio of laughing children. Irene began a description of the puppy's mother and the people who had raised the litter. When I headed toward the Kings' buggy, Laura followed me.

"This is my family's second buggy," she said as I lifted out a heavy bag of kibble from the back. "I can drive it whenever I want."

"Oh?" I tossed the bag over my shoulder.

She tilted her head and fluttered her eyelashes. "I plan to drive it on the next church Sunday."

I saw where the conversation was going, but short of turning on my heel, there was no way out. Before I could do so, she hurried on.

"So I was thinking maybe you and I could go for a drive after. You know. Just to talk."

My jaw went slack. Apparently, Laura had not left all her *Englisch* ways behind. Such boldness flew in the face of the traditions we held so closely. Did the bishop know of her forward behavior? Did her family?

I eyed her with a stern expression. "I will ride home with my family, as always."

Her face fell, and I knew I'd hurt her feelings. I experienced a twinge of regret but left her standing there before she could reply. Better to bruise her ego than to offer a kind refusal—which I had done last Sunday regarding her invitation to the singing—that could be misconstrued as softness toward her.

After I'd placed the dog's food near the door, I cut a wide path around my family and the visitors. A few moments later I slid onto the passenger seat of Robbie's car. Laura watched openly as the car turned around. When we were on the road, I relaxed against the back of the seat.

He glanced sideways at me. "That girl's sweet on you."

I looked at him sharply. "Why do you think that?"

He laughed. "It's obvious, dude. She was batting her eyes and swinging her skirt back and forth."

"I am *not* sweet on her."

Apparently, he understood from my tone that I didn't wish to discuss Laura King further. He did not mention her again during the rest of the drive.

Fourteen

March gave way to April, and the weather continued its gradual warmth. Though our fields were not yet ready for planting the crops that provided the bulk of our family's income, we prepared the soil in the family garden for early produce. Onion sets, garlic, leaf lettuce, beets, and turnips were all planted in neat rows of cultivated soil. Ever conscious that my family might resent my absence during the important work of planting, I stayed home and did my share of the work. But I missed my time at the potter's wheel.

On a sunny day in mid-April, I joined Aaron in the garden after breakfast. We stood on the grass, the toes of our boots touching the soft soil.

"Early cabbage today," he said. "Then peas on Thursday, I think."

"We need to watch the boys more closely." I pointed toward a garlic clove, which had been planted yesterday, lying on top of the soil midway down the row in front of us.

"*Ach*, I thought I had."

He strode between the even rows and squatted before the errant clove. I watched as he sank his hands into the soft dirt, forming a four-inch hole. He set the clove carefully, almost lovingly, and then covered it with the rich soil. For a moment afterward he remained on his haunches, his gaze sweeping across the garden. The look of satisfaction on his face resonated deep inside me. Is that how I looked when I cupped my hands around a lump of clay, pushing and moistening and then forming a bowl or a platter that would one day rest on a family's table?

He rose and returned with careful steps to my side, where we resumed our examination of the garden.

"You have not been to Strasburg in more than a week. You miss your work there."

And I thought I'd done such a good job of masking my feelings.

"There is more important work to be done here," I said.

"Work, *ya,* but not more important." He glanced at me sideways. "At least not to you, I think."

I smiled and said nothing.

Aaron clasped his hands behind his back in an imitation of *Daed,* though I doubted he was aware of it. "The family can plant the garden. We have plenty of hands to make the work light. If you want to go to your shop, no one will fault you."

Becky and Saloma, and even *Mamm,* might disagree. Though no one had mentioned Laura or any other single woman within my hearing, I knew they had not yet given up their plans to see me matched with one of the eligible girls in our district. I knew they somehow blamed my growing interest in ceramics for my lack of cooperation.

From his pursed lips and held breath, I knew my *bruder* had something else to say. I remained silent and did not have long to wait.

"Have you considered becoming a potter yourself? As an occupation, I mean."

The question surprised me, though it shouldn't have. At first I'd considered pottery an engrossing pastime, a pleasant way to spend the winter months when the farm was not so demanding. Only recently, when orders for my candleholders began to come in regularly, did the idea occur to me that pottery might become something more than a hobby. But surely that was a fluke. Surely a man could not make a career out of canisters with holes in them, however decorative.

"I am not nearly good enough to make a living. Elias has been a potter his entire life, as was his father before him."

Aaron smiled. "You are not exactly old, Seth. You have a long time yet to devote to learning. And this Elias does not have sons to take over his business when the time comes, does he? At least, you have not mentioned sons."

Elias did have sons, three of them, but he had told me that, to his disappointment, not one shared his love for the clay. Nor did his daughters' husbands. The only one of his family who cared for the business he loved was Leah, and she admitted to having no skill.

Perhaps he would consider an apprentice, someone to take over one day when he was ready to hang up his clay-stained apron. The idea excited me. Not that I could ever hope to achieve Elias's skill at the wheel.

I narrowed my eyes and peered at Aaron. "Not long ago you told me I would always have a home here. Have you changed your mind? Do you want me to leave?"

"No!" He shook his head with such vehemence that his hat slid sideways. "I meant what I said. You are family, and family is for always. But you seem…" His gaze rose to the sky as he appeared to grasp for a word. "You seem calmer when you are making pottery. Almost at peace, or as close as I have seen you since the accident."

An astute observation, and one that rang true as soon as I heard the words. How odd that I hadn't noticed it myself.

Now that he'd spoken his mind, Aaron seemed eager to dismiss the subject. "It's something to think about. But I hope you will help with the planting. I will need you then."

"*Ya*, of course."

"This year will be our last to grow tobacco." He spoke in the low tone of one confiding a secret and tossed a defiant glance toward the house. "Next year, we will switch to soybeans."

Aaron and *Daed* had disagreed for the past few years about our cash crop. Aaron claimed, and I privately agreed, that selling tobacco condoned an addictive habit that a conscientious man should not promote. Our father argued that Hostetlers—and many other farmers in

Lancaster County—had grown tobacco for years, and those who used it were adults and could make their own decisions. Also, soybeans would not bring the price of tobacco, so the switch would result in less money for the family. Out of respect, Aaron had not pushed the issue even after he took over management of the farm. I'd wondered several times how long he would wait before insisting.

"I'm glad." I nodded my approval. "It's the right thing to do."

With a grateful smile, he strode off in the direction of the barn.

I stayed where I was for a long while, considering the conversation. Working with clay did make me…if not happy, then at least satisfied. To take a lifeless, formless lump and watch it change as it spun on my wheel quenched an uneasy thirst inside me that had been with me so long I no longer noticed it.

Perhaps I would speak to Elias. Ask his opinion of my abilities and whether or not I would ever be able to achieve anything close to his level of skill. If he thought my work worthy, perhaps he would be interested in formalizing our teacher-student relationship.

And if so, what of Leah? Would she feel threatened at the idea of an outsider taking an official place at her *grossdaadi*'s side?

I returned to Plain Man's Pottery the next day after more than a week's absence. Robbie did not hide his pleasure at being asked to drive me again, and when I entered the shop, even Leah seemed pleased to see me, though it was hard to tell given the sarcasm of her greeting.

She straightened from kneeling before a lower shelf, eyebrows arched. "Look who decided to show up today. I thought you'd deserted us."

Was there a touch of hurt in her caustic tone? Maybe, but I wasn't given the opportunity to wonder long because Elias hurried through the curtain. When he caught sight of me, a huge smile wreathed his face.

"My student returns." He clapped his hands with obvious delight. "The work has been lonely without you."

"It's planting time." I shrugged. "My family needed help with the garden."

"*Ya, ya,* my Lily is planting too. I hired some boys to help with the heavy work, but she is a hard worker herself, my Lily."

It occurred to me that I did not know where Elias and his wife lived. "Do you have a farm?"

"No, just a bit of property. Enough for a garden and a shed for the horse." He beckoned me toward the back. "Come. You are a blessing from *Gott* today. I have more work than I can do myself."

I glanced around the store, spying three of my candleholders, and then settled my gaze on Leah. "More orders for candleholders?"

"A few," she acknowledged, and then she smiled. "I had to take mine down off the website because people kept trying to order one exactly like it."

I followed Elias into the workshop. We moved together with a silent harmony in assembling our tools, retrieving the day's clay from the storage closet, filling our bowls with water. It reminded me of the way the women in my family worked together in the kitchen.

An attack of nerves overtook me as we stood side by side at the wedging table. I had determined to speak with him today about my future, but during the night fear had seized me. What if I didn't possess the talent to make a living as a potter?

"What is it?" He kept his gaze fixed on his hands working the clay. "There is a question trying to burn its way out of your mouth."

I couldn't help but laugh at his perceptiveness, which lessened my tension. "*Ya,* there is." My laughter ended, and I mimicked him, keeping my gaze on the wedging. "Do you think I have the makings of a potter?"

He looked up at me, surprise coloring the heavy creases around his eyes. "You *are* a potter, Seth. Do you not throw pots?"

"I mean a real potter. A skillful one, like you."

He studied me a minute. "Do you not realize that, except for the large planters we did last month, your work has brought more money into this shop than mine?"

Now it was my turn to be surprised, but I discounted the claim with a shake of my head. "Only because *Englisch* people have taken a liking to my candleholders, and Leah sets such a high price on them." I turned the clay in my hands and inspected the bottom. "I think I would like to make pottery as a business, as you do, but I don't know if I have the talent, and I am sure I have not mastered the skills I need to be a good one."

Elias deserted his clay and turned to face me. "Am I not teaching you the skills?"

"I am your student, yes, but I would like to be more." I could not meet his eye. "I would like to be your apprentice."

His deep laughter filled the room. Unsure whether or not I should feel offense at being laughed at, I tried not to look hurt while he got control of himself.

"Young Seth, you *are* my apprentice. How can you have worked with me all these weeks and not know that?"

"I am?"

He spread his hands wide to indicate the workshop. "Do you see any other students vying for my time? Do you see anyone else's work for sale in my store?" He sobered and placed a hand on my sleeve. The unusual contact forced me to stop my work and look him in the eye. "I will make a promise. For as long as *Gott* grants me time on this earth, I will teach you the skills you need to know."

A thrill of pleasure shot through me. "*Danke,* Elias. I will work hard."

"That I know. I have a feeling the apprentice will soon overtake the master." Before I could react to that, he slapped at the clay I'd wedged. "Let us begin by learning a new skill. Forget candleholders today. I will teach you the chattering technique for a flat-form bowl. For that we need to wedge more clay."

Unable to suppress a smile, I did as my teacher instructed.

I was working on my third flat bowl when Leah stuck her head into the workroom. "You have visitors, Seth."

I could not imagine who would ask for me here. For one horrified moment I thought perhaps Laura had decided to make another bold attempt at gaining my attention and formed a silent prayer. *Not her. Please not her.*

I washed my hands and, after wiping them on a clean towel, followed Leah into the showroom. Relief washed over me when I recognized one of the two *Englisch* women waiting there.

"Amanda."

Robbie's mother turned from her examination of a large bowl, her features brightening. "There you are. Jackie, this is Seth Hostetler, the man who made that beautiful votive holder in my family room."

The other lady, elegant-looking in the *Englisch* way, gave me a pleasant nod.

"Jackie and I are out doing some shopping, and we thought we'd drop by to see some of your other pieces." Amanda picked up the bowl in both hands and turned it over. "This is one of yours, isn't it? I recognize the mark on the bottom."

"Yes. That is one of mine."

"Jackie, look at the coloring. I've never seen that combination before."

While the two inspected the bowl, I stood next to Leah, uncertain what to do. I wanted to leave these two in her care, but this was Robbie's mother, who had been kind to me and my family when *Mammi* was released from the hospital.

Her friend looked up at me. "Do you think you could make a set of salad plates to match this?"

The glaze was one I'd experimented with, combining a muted violet with a soft white called coconut. The result was not what I'd hoped for, but apparently it appealed to Amanda's friend.

I nodded. "I can do that."

"Oh, good." She set the bowl on the sales counter. "Could you make eight?"

When I agreed, Leah took the bowl to store in the back so I would have a model from which to work. Amanda dug in her pocketbook and extracted a folded piece of paper. Judging by the ragged edges, it had been torn from a magazine.

"Another reason I'm here is because I saw this and fell in love with it." She unfolded the page and spread it out on the counter. The picture was of an *Englisch* living room with brightly colored furnishings. With a white-tipped fingernail, she tapped on a vase. At least, I thought the object was a vase, though of a decorative kind that would detract from the natural beauty of any flower arrangement. "Do you think you could make something like that?"

Leah returned as I studied the object. The body was a perfectly circular ball, attached to a flat, triangular base with column-like pillars. At the top, a fluted opening protruded from the sphere. The piece itself was bright blue, though ovals carved into the side of the round part had been painted in a variety of colors. I thought it very ugly.

"Wow," Leah said. "That's quite a contemporary design."

Contemporary. Yes, that perfectly described this object. And, I realized as the image of her dining room rose in my mind's eye, Amanda's entire house. Another word I would use was *fancy*. As in, not Plain.

This vase would fit in Amanda's house perfectly.

"I have never made anything like that," I admitted, though my mind was already planning how I would approach the job. The base and support columns would pose no problem, nor would the fluted opening. The sphere, though, would be a challenge.

"Oh." She gave a short sigh. "Well, no problem. I thought I'd ask."

"*Daadi* could do it." Leah looked up from the picture. "Elias Beachy, my grandfather," she explained to Amanda.

"He is my teacher," I added.

Amanda grinned. "Maybe he could teach you how."

Creating a piece like this would definitely require a different skill than I had yet learned. The idea appealed to me, though the piece definitely wasn't one I would have chosen to attempt. Of course, neither were the candleholders. They had been a profitable accident.

"I make no promises, but I will try." I picked up the page. "May I keep this?"

"Of course." A broad smile settled on her features. "And if it doesn't look exactly like that, don't worry. It might be even better. After all, it's art."

We arranged for them to return in two weeks' time to pick up their pieces. The salad plates would be ready far more quickly, but I wanted to give myself plenty of time to work on the fancy vase.

When they'd gone, Leah folded her arms and eyed me. "You are definitely good for business."

Ducking my head, I returned to the workroom to finish my flatform bowls.

The salad plates were finished within a few days, as I'd expected, but Amanda's ugly vase proved more challenging. Over the next two weeks I created no less than four fancy vases, but none of them looked similar enough to the picture for me to be satisfied. Elias exercised great patience, as always.

After the fourth failure, I lost my temper. I threw my sponge into the water bucket with force and raised my voice. "You finish it! I can't do this."

My teacher's serene expression did not change. "If I finish the piece for you, you have learned nothing. Now, you will take a walk to calm yourself, and when you return you will try again. Next time use a lighter touch."

I took his suggestion, breathing deeply of the fragrant April air, and tried again.

Finally, I achieved a result I felt Amanda would approve of. I glazed the piece the same bright blue color she favored. The placement of the decorative ovals did not match the picture, but in that I took pleasure in creating my own design. That part of the vase, at least, held a subtle beauty of which I approved.

The day before she and her friend were to pick up their pottery, I painted the ovals. Leah had ordered the bright, garish colors, for we did not stock glaze in such hues. I mixed them thick, and set about applying them with a paintbrush. They would be ready for the final firing that night.

I was hunched over my work when the curtain behind me parted. Assuming Leah had entered the room to watch me work as she sometimes did, I didn't bother to look up until I'd finished painting a yellow oval.

When I straightened, I was surprised to discover that my observer was not Leah.

"Bishop Beiler." I set my brush down and stood. "I did not expect you."

"Apparently not." He did not immediately meet my gaze but inspected my work closely. The corners of his mouth turned downward, giving him a stern and disapproving look that I had not often seen.

Finally, he looked up. "You made this?"

With a glance at my vase, I nodded. "It was a commissioned piece." I snatched up the magazine page, which by now was stained with dried clay and rainbow-hued glaze. "An *Englisch* woman asked me to make it for her."

His eyes moved from the vase to the picture and back again. "They do look alike."

If that was supposed to be a compliment, it was grudgingly given. My defenses went up, and my posture stiffened. "I think she will like it."

Looking away from the vase, he glanced around the room, actually turning in a circle to see every corner. "So this is where you spend all of your time."

"This is where I am learning my craft, *ya*."

"Your craft." Now he waved toward the vase. "Is that what you call this?"

Rarely had I seen my bishop express such disdain. I sucked in a long breath and battled a flare of temper. He had no inkling of how hard I'd worked on this piece. I changed the subject.

"My teacher, Elias Beachy, is outside tending the wood kiln. I would like you to meet him."

I headed toward the doorway, but he stood stiffly in place. "I met him when I arrived. A good man. And a good potter. I looked at his work in the showroom."

So he had met Leah as well. Had she reacted to the arrival of an Amish bishop with her customary scowl? Or did she not realize who this man was? I pictured her now, standing behind the counter on the other side of the curtain, where she could not help overhearing this conversation.

"I saw your work as well." He met my gaze, and now made no pretense of hiding his disappointment. "Your teacher's work is beautiful. Yours is fancy."

I bristled. Leah had insisted on my trimming and glazing my four failed attempts to create Amanda's vase, declaring them to be lovely enough that an *Englisch* customer would buy them. I'd complied because I'd come to appreciate her intuition when it came to pieces that would appeal to buyers. And also because I could see that, even though they were not Plain, they had turned out well. Amanda would call them art.

So far two had sold, and I'd gasped when Leah told me the outrageous price they'd brought.

When I could reply in a calm tone, I said, "Not all of my pieces are fancy."

"*Ya*, I saw some nice bowls and plates and pitchers." With that admission, the man's rigid posture softened. His expression lost the stiff disapproval and took on the concern that lay more easily on his face. "Seth, I am worried for you. You spend much time here, and not much at home."

Had someone in my family complained to our bishop? No, I couldn't believe that. They'd all seemed pleased with my announcement that I would become a potter instead of farming the land. Even *Daed*, who naturally would like to see his sons follow the same path he had taken through life, had expressed his approval with my choice.

"I spend so much time here because I am learning the techniques I need for the profession I have chosen."

"This is what you would do with your life?" He waved a hand toward my vase. "Create objects that have no use, no purpose? Do you think this pleases our Lord, Seth?"

Ya! I wanted to shout. How could anything that gave pleasure to a kind person not be pleasing to *Gott*, who loves all His creation, Amish or not? But was I to argue with my bishop? That would definitely not please the Lord. I countered with a question of my own.

"Do you expect that everything an Amish man makes be for Plain use only?" I could reel off a list of businesses within our own district that contradicted that view. Noah's animal carvings, for instance. The birdhouses James Troyer made and sold at the Amish craft stores across Lancaster

County. Even the crops we raised were not for Amish use only, but sold for a profit to anyone who had the money to buy them.

Bishop Beiler shook his head, and his expression softened further. "No, of course not. And your work is not the reason I came today. If you want to make…" He looked at my vase, over which I now felt a bit protective since it had suffered an attack. Clearing his throat, he continued. "If you want to make fancy things for the *Englisch* to buy, that is your decision. Though I prefer the bowls and mugs that are beautiful in their own way while also having a purpose."

Because I agreed with him, I remained silent.

"The reason I came to talk to you is because there has been some concern expressed about the time you are spending with the *Englisch*."

Was it my imagination, or did I hear a soft gasp from the other side of the curtain?

I shook my head. "I do not understand. Elias, my teacher, is Amish."

"No, not him. It is your driver, the *Englisch* boy."

"Robbie?" I plucked at my beard, my thoughts whirling. Who would have complained about Robbie driving me?

The words were on my tongue to relay what I suspected about Robbie's troubled past, and his mother's concerns and gratitude that driving me gave him a purpose and a way to help. But before I could speak, the bishop continued.

"I have nothing against the boy. You are my concern." He peered at me closely. "You are a full-grown man. You should have your own buggy and drive yourself."

Now I knew where the complaint had come from. Laura King. My teeth clamped together, and I had to restrain myself from grinding them. Or if not Laura, then her *mamm* or *daed* or someone who hoped to see us together.

I could not force my jaw to unclench. "I am not interested in…" I stopped myself before I spoke her name. "…buying a buggy."

Compassion shone in my bishop's eyes, and he nodded slowly. "I understand the reason. But *Gott* cannot heal you from something you hold to so tightly."

Tears stung my eyes, and I turned quickly away. The words had hit their mark. I wanted to flee, to run from the room where I could gasp in great gulps of air that might dissolve the boulder that had lodged in my throat. No, I wanted to grab a lump of clay and slap it on the worktable and wedge it with fury until the tightness in my chest eased.

Bishop Beiler waited, kindness wafting from him in palpable waves. He truly did desire my healing. He wanted to see me married and living the happy life of an Amish family man. I understood that. But could he not see that a buggy would not heal me? Why didn't anyone except me see the truth? How could I ever live in peace when two wives had died because of me?

But if a buggy would satisfy him and the others in my community, then I would buy a buggy.

Once I was sure I could speak, I faced him. "Okay. I will buy a horse and buggy." But so that there would be no confusion, I added in a stern voice, "But I will *not* drive Laura King."

From the sudden widening of his eyes, I knew I'd guessed the source of today's errand correctly.

The curtain parted, and Elias entered the room, followed by Leah carrying the lunch basket.

"Bishop Belier, you are in time to share with us a rare treat." He beamed. "I know gluttony is a sin, but once you taste my wife's cooking you will understand why it is a sin I struggle with daily."

The bishop held up his hands. "No, I could not impose."

"Impose?" Elias appeared outraged at the thought. "You are my apprentice's bishop, and my guest. Sharing our meal is surely not an imposition." A grin crept onto his face. "You have never tasted anything like my Lily's chicken pie."

"Chicken pie?" Interest erupted on the bishop's face. "Well, in that case…"

FIFTEEN

Planting time was nearly upon us. Aaron had plowed in the fall, but soil hardened beneath a long winter's layer of snow and must be prepared. Aaron and Noah began the work on our fields with the disc harrow. By weekend they would smooth the soil with the cultipacker. My *bruder* told me that my help with the planting would be appreciated the following week, providing the weather held.

Though tempted to delay buying a buggy until after planting was accomplished, once the decision was made, I didn't want to wait. *Daed* seemed more eager than I, and he managed to discover several buggies for resale throughout the county. I arranged for Robbie to drive us around on a Thursday, and I spent Wednesday trimming all my thrown pots so I could take the day off without unfinished tasks weighing on my mind.

The selection of a buggy could be an ordeal. Each district had its own approved style, so not just any buggy would do. The buggies of some of the eastern districts had brown tops, something which would not be permitted in ours. Thankfully, all the districts of our affiliation had agreed on a standard design that included several styles based on the required size. That meant I had a good chance of finding a suitable buggy in the area without having to pay the price for a new one.

We drove north first, to a farm outside of Ephrata.

In the front seat, I twisted around toward *Daed.* "How did you hear about this one?"

"From Leon Schrock. His brother-in-law's cousin has a friend who bought a bigger buggy for his family." He stabbed a finger at the window. "There. That is the place."

Robbie slowed and turned onto the dirt path leading up to the house. I knew the moment I spied the buggy that I would not buy this one. It was small and carriage style, and looked far too much like the one I had bought for my Hannah. The one beneath which she and our unborn child had died.

But *Daed* exited the car the moment it rolled to a stop. What could I do but follow him?

The young man who owned the carriage came out of the barn, smiling and telling *Daed* the history, how he had bought it from another man in his district who had also outgrown it. I followed them around the buggy, inspecting the wheels and the bench, my stomach churning all the while.

The door to the house opened, and a smiling woman appeared. "Werner, invite them in for coffee and sweet rolls."

My heart skipped a beat when I caught sight of her round belly. A pregnant woman rode in this open carriage? I almost bought the thing on the spot, just to keep her out of it. But then I spied another buggy parked beyond the barn, a solid one, properly enclosed. *Daed*'s comment came back to me, that this man had bought a bigger buggy for his growing family.

I found I could not speak, but instead I caught *Daed*'s eye and shook my head. Muttering my thanks to the young man, I hurried toward Robbie's car, heart pounding double time to my footsteps.

"You don't like that one?" Robbie asked.

I didn't trust my voice, so I merely uttered a closemouthed, "Uh-uh."

Daed joined us soon after. "That is not the one for you. The axle clips were worn and would need to be replaced."

He continued on at some length about deficiencies I hadn't looked closely enough to notice, and I was glad to let him carry the burden of the conversation. We'd driven several miles before my heartbeat returned to normal.

Our next stop was Farmersville, but even a casual observer could see that the amount of work required to repair that buggy made the low price far less appealing. From there we visited New Holland, and then on to Intercourse. Those two were probably fine buggies, and the prices were not bad, but I could not develop any enthusiasm for either. When we got back in the car, even Robbie could tell that *Daed*'s temper was becoming short because he kept glancing at him in the rearview mirror.

"I begin to think you do not intend to make a purchase today," he grumbled from the backseat.

I kept my face forward, but the words worked on me. Truly, there had been nothing wrong with the last buggy. Why had I not wanted to buy it? Was I letting my fears get the better of me?

I knew the answer to that. In every buggy we had seen, I imagined a ghostly figure seated on the front bench. Stupid, *Mammi* would have said, and she would have been right. My fears were stupid. The buggy had not been the cause of the accident. It had been the fault of the *Englisch* teenagers who drove like maniacs, and mine for not protecting my wife better.

The sound of paper rustling came from the backseat.

"There is another nearby," *Daed* said. "Turn left at the next intersection."

Robbie did, following a series of turns until we arrived at a large Amish dairy farm. A fine herd of cattle occupied fenced fields behind the house. Clothing hung on a line in the yard, swaying in a light breeze. The woman who pinned them up apparently enjoyed order, for the clothing formed a neat row, beginning with the longest dresses and decreasing evenly in size to small white squares that looked like hand towels.

A man in the field began walking toward us as Robbie parked the car.

Daed and I got out, and this time my driver did too. I glanced around but didn't see a buggy.

"Maybe he already sold it," I said to *Daed*, who nodded.

When the man approached, he introduced himself with a friendly smile. "Welcome. I am David Miller."

"Silas Hostetler. This is my son, Seth, and our driver, Robbie Barker. You are kin with Kurt Miller, a minister in my district."

David nodded. "Kurt is my cousin."

"He mentioned to me that you have a buggy to sell." *Daed* made a show of looking around the yard. "But maybe not?"

"*Ya*, I do. It's behind the barn."

We followed him around the two-story structure, where we found the buggy. I knew at first glance that I would buy it, not because it was any better than the last two we'd seen, but I'd grown weary of looking. Still, I followed *Daed* and David around, inspecting the wheels and axles. I opened the door and glanced at the benches—two, which would seat four adults comfortably—and ran my hand across the dash rail.

"It is a fine buggy." I closed the door. "Why do you wish to sell it?"

The man's expression did not change, but his eyes became sad. "It belonged to my *daadi*, who passed on this winter."

We did not reply for a respectful moment, and then *Daed* clasped his hands behind his back. "How much are you asking?"

"I thought to get fifteen hundred."

A fair price for a buggy in such good shape. I was prepared to pay two thousand or even more. *Daed* looked at me, his eyebrows arched in a question, and I nodded. "I will buy it."

Looking pleased—though not nearly so pleased as my *daed*—David said, "Come inside, and I will write the bill of sale. I am sorry my wife is not here to offer you something to eat, but she has gone into town."

Daed and David started toward the house, while I went to the car to get my money pouch.

Robbie followed me. "How are you gonna get that thing home? I hope you're not planning on towing it behind my car." He laughed.

"I will come back and bring my *bruder's* horse." I glanced at the sun, which was not yet overhead. There was still plenty of daylight. "Maybe even today."

Ahead of us, David stopped and turned. "Are you looking to buy a horse as well?"

"In time." I had discussed the matter with Noah, who was agreeable to letting me use his Wilbur until I found a suitable horse of my own. "I thought to buy one at the mud sale in May."

"I have a horse for sale, also belonging to my *daadi*. He has pulled this buggy for more than five years."

He pointed at the field beyond the barn, where a lone horse grazed near the fence. My pulse stuttered. The gelding bore such a resemblance to Lars that for a moment I thought it might be the horse my Hannah had loved. I knew that could not be, because I had sold Lars to a man in Drumore. Besides, this horse was several years older, and stood at least a hand taller than Lars. But he bore a white star on the center of his forehead, and even a smattering of white on his croup.

I approached the fence, and when the animal caught sight of me, he raised his head. Without hesitation, he came toward me, arriving at the fence at the same time as me. He put his head over the top rail, examined me with a friendly eye, and then gave a soft nicker. I rubbed the white star on his forehead, and when I stopped, he nosed my hand in a blatant plea for another caress.

Robbie had come up behind me. "I think he likes you, dude."

"Orion likes everyone."

I faced David, who had also joined us. "Orion?"

He shrugged. "My daughter named him after a star because of—" He tapped on his forehead.

"Orion." I turned back to him and indulged him with another rub. "I will buy him."

Daed cleared his throat. "If the price is a fair one," he said to David, while giving me a stern look.

"Is twelve hundred dollars a fair price for the horse and gear?"

I could probably find a horse for less at the upcoming mud auction, but the price was fair, especially with the addition of the gear. Besides, Orion had already made himself mine just by looking like Lars, only with a gentler nature. Hannah would have loved this horse, that I knew. And that was enough for me.

I faced David. "*Ya,* it is a fair price. I will buy him."

Daed frowned, and I could tell he thought the purchase of this horse a mistake. But the next moment he shrugged. "It's your decision."

With a final rub on Orion's forehead, Robbie and I once again headed for the car.

When *Daed* and David were out of earshot, Robbie gave me a troubled look. "I guess this means you won't need me to haul you around anymore, huh?"

The worried creases on my young friend's brow touched me. Whatever problem haunted him from his past had not yet been resolved, though I thought he was now closer to finding his peace. Driving me had played a part, but if it was time for me to move forward, maybe it was time for him as well.

"Not every day," I answered softly. "But I hope for longer distances I can still call you."

That seemed to please him, though the lines did not disappear completely. "Of course. Anytime."

I opened the door and pulled my money pouch from beneath the seat. I opened it and pulled out a stack of bills.

Robbie eyed the money. "Don't tell me we've been riding around with twenty-seven hundred dollars in cash."

"Only five hundred," I assured him. I showed him my checkbook. "A bit of cash is always appreciated."

"Yeah, I'm with you on that."

We walked toward the house side by side. At the door, he drew a deep breath, and I paused before entering.

"I'm gonna miss you, Seth."

Were those tears in his eyes? Compassion stirred in my chest. Though it was not my habit to embrace another, I put an arm around Robbie's shoulder and squeezed.

When I'd released him, I said, "We will see each other still."

"Yeah." He sniffed and rubbed his eyes with the back of a hand. "Uh, you go on in. I'm gonna go take another look at your horse."

He left without waiting for an answer. I watched him retreat, his hands shoved in the pocket of his jeans, shoulders hunched forward. Among the *Englisch* I had a few acquaintances, but no real friends. At least, I had not thought so until that moment.

I would miss him too.

Driving myself forced a change in my schedule. The ten-mile trip that Robbie drove in fifteen minutes would take me close to ninety. I awoke early the next morning and finished the milking before Saloma had the morning meal ready. Grabbing a couple of hot biscuits right out of the oven, I slapped on several pieces of bacon and took my breakfast with me.

The sun had fully risen by the time I hitched Orion to my new buggy, but I was grateful for the windscreen as a protection against the morning chill. Though I'd driven home yesterday, *Daed* had been seated beside me. Today was my first time to drive alone.

The biscuits remained wrapped in a towel. How could I eat when thoughts of Hannah hovered in my mind and turned my stomach into a churning mass of grief? If only I'd had a buggy like this one instead of the courting carriage, she would still be here. She might even be seated beside me, holding our baby in her lap.

Our baby.

Now my memory dredged up Rachel from the depths, and the babies we had lost.

How I missed Robbie and his chatter that kept my mind on the day ahead instead of the ones that lay behind.

With my heart thudding and pain pounding in my head, I nearly turned Orion around. There was too much time for thinking during this drive. Every *clip-clop* of the horse's hooves represented a memory. They marched through my mind and left a searing trail of pain.

Gott, *I cannot do this.*

Before my anguished admission had faded away, an idea occurred to me. Why should I not move to Strasburg? My job and my teacher were there. Not until the planting was over, but when that was done I could rent a room from someone. Surely, there was an Amish family somewhere with a spare room or empty *daadi haus.* In fact, it was the only thing that made sense. Why had I not thought of it before?

Was this idea a nudge from the Lord? Coming so close on the tail of my prayer, it seemed likely.

And then something else occurred to me. A ninety-minute ride each way would give me time to pray. Instead of obsessing over tormented memories, I should make use of the time by focusing my thoughts in prayer. I'd been so busy recently that I had not spent much time in conversation with the Lord.

Pleased with my plan, I put it into action.

❦

Orion maintained a steady pace, and we arrived at the shop before anyone else. My mood was much lighter after a lengthy time in quiet meditation, and I chuckled as I unhitched him and led him to the small pasture out back. Perhaps I didn't need to rise quite so early tomorrow.

As I latched the gate, Leah's car pulled into the parking lot. She got out and headed toward me. "Looks like you found a good one," she said as she approached.

At first I thought she meant the buggy, but her gaze was fixed on my horse. He had walked away, inspecting the grass in the center of the small space, but he trotted back to us when he saw her. Leah received the same greeting I had yesterday, and she laughed as he nosed her hand.

"He sure is friendly." Her smile as she gave his neck a brisk rub held not a hint of restraint. She was an attractive woman, with a delicate curve to her cheek and a sparkle in her eye.

"That's one reason I bought him."

"One reason?" She looked at me. "What's the other?"

I touched the white star. "He reminds me of another horse I used to have."

The *clop-clop* of Elias's horse interrupted our conversation before my thoughts could once again become morose. He hopped down from his buggy and waved toward mine.

"I see your search was successful."

"*Ya*. It was a *gut* day."

I helped him unhitch his buggy, and together we watched as Orion and Elias's mare greeted one another. Alert for any signs of tension in either horse, I was relieved when after a minute they nosed each other, a sign of affection. They seemed content in each other's company. A good thing, because they would spend a lot of time together.

After checking to make sure the trough held plenty of water, the three of us headed toward the shop.

Leah pulled a key from her handbag and fitted it in the door's lock. "I imagine Robbie wasn't pleased that you found a buggy so quickly."

"No, he was not."

"I feel sorry for him. Sometimes he doesn't act like he's very happy. Strange, because his mother seems like a nice person, so I assume he comes from a good home." She opened the door and we followed her inside.

I considered telling her what little I knew about Robbie's troubled past, but I decided against it. Though I knew Leah had grown fond of the teenager too, talking about a friend behind his back was something I would not do. I knew how it felt to be the topic of gossip.

Instead, I spoke to my teacher as we made our way to the workshop. "I came to a decision on the drive this morning."

"Oh?" He flipped the light switch, and the windowless area brightened.

"When the planting is finished, I will look for a place to live near here."

Interest showed on his face. "You will move to Strasburg?"

"*Ya*. I am not needed at home, and that way I can spend more time at the wheel."

"Your family will miss you." He peered at me. "And I think you will miss them too."

He was right on both accounts. My absence would bring about another change in the household, which still felt unsettled after *Daed* and *Mamm*'s move to the *daadi haus*. The whole family would feel the change, but most of all the children would miss their *Onkel* Seth, and *Mammi* would miss her *kinskind*.

"I will not be far away, and it's for the best." I went to the shelf where we kept the tools and retrieved mine. "Perhaps you know of someone in this district who has a place to rent?"

"I most certainly do." He pounded a hand on his chest. "Me."

I stared at him, surprised. "You have never mentioned renting a room in your house."

"Rent? *Phaw!*" His hand waved in the air. "We have three empty rooms upstairs. Why should my apprentice not have one?"

Leah entered the workshop. "Did I just hear you offer Seth a room in your house?" She ducked her head and gave him a stern look. "Without even consulting *Grossmammi*?"

He dismissed her with another wave. "*Ya, ya,* I will ask, but she will approve. She will be happy for another mouth to feed."

For a moment I wasn't sure if I liked the idea of living with my teacher. We worked well together, but to work *and* live under the same roof? In the next instant, I nearly laughed out loud. I'd done the same all my life, working and living with my family. In the short time since I'd met him, Elias had become almost like family to me.

I glanced at Leah, who was studying me with a speculative look. Her comment from a few weeks ago came back to me. She ate dinner with Elias and Lily almost every night. What would she think of sharing meals with me? Of sharing her family with me? It would almost be like—

I halted the thought, my pulse quickening.

"Would you mind?" I asked the question quickly, to stop the unnerving turn my thoughts threatened to take.

"Me?" She shrugged. "Why would I? It makes perfect sense. And *Daadi* is right. *Grossmammi* will be thrilled. She will spoil you like you're her own grandson."

Grandson. Yes, that is what I would be. Like a grandson. Which would make me like Leah's *bruder*. Her Amish *bruder*.

"Talk to her," I told Elias. "If she approves, then I will accept your offer. But I must pay rent."

His lips pursed as he thought, and then he brightened. "Rent you will pay, but not in money. Instead—"

I held up a hand. "I know." Leah joined in, and we spoke in unison. "Throw more pots to sell."

We all laughed, beginning our workday on a pleasant note.

Sixteen

I refused to drive my buggy on the following church Sunday.

"It makes no sense to take three buggies," I told my family over breakfast. "I will ride with Aaron as usual."

My announcement upset the women, which confirmed my suspicions. They'd hoped I would drive so I could offer to take Laura or some other unmarried girl home. Saloma and Becky exchanged a loaded glance, and *Mamm* frowned at me across the table.

"We will be too many because we are all going today." She dipped her head toward *Mammi,* who would return to church for the first time since her surgery.

"Then I will ride with Noah. There is plenty of room in his buggy, and only three to ride."

Becky spoke up. "We thought *Mammi* could ride with you in your buggy. It would be more comfortable for her and not crowded."

"I have never felt crowded before," *Mammi* said.

Mamm's lips drew into a tight line. Using more force than necessary, she stabbed at a bite of hotcake with her fork. "The twins are growing bigger every day."

Mark and Luke both sat straighter and smiled at each other.

Mammi leaned forward to see around Becky and catch Noah's eye. "May I ride with you? Sadie will fit nicely between me and Seth, with room to spare."

Becky opened her mouth, and for a moment I thought she might refuse the request. But then she closed it again without speaking. To insult her own *grossmammi* by refusing her a ride would be inexcusably rude.

Noah seemed oblivious to the unspoken frustration being exhibited by the women around the table. He finished chewing his sausage and then said, "*Ya,* of course you can ride with us."

The look *Mamm* gave *Mammi* would have withered a lesser woman, but *Mammi* maintained an innocent expression as she sliced off a bite of hotcake. I thought she, too, must have been unaware of the women's scheme, until she looked up at me and slightly winked.

I hid my smile behind my coffee mug.

When we arrived at the Zooks', I hopped out and then helped *Mammi* down. When I would have released her, she clung to my arm.

"Will you walk with me, Seth? I may need help up the stairs."

Noah went to park the buggy, and Becky took Sadie ahead into the house. *Mammi* made a show of leaning on my arm and walking slowly. Too slowly.

I studied her through narrowed eyes. "I have seen you go up and down the stairs at home with no help. And yesterday when you and Sadie were in the yard, I noticed you moved well."

"Truth be told, my hip feels better than it has in many years. I think I might take the doctor's advice and have the other one done."

"Are you sorry you agreed to move to the main house, then?"

"A little." A second later she shook her head. "No, not really. Change is never easy, but sometimes it is good. Like your move to Strasburg. It will be sad to have you gone, but it is a good change."

My family had reacted with varying degrees of surprise to my announcement. Aaron and *Daed* seemed to have expected it, while *Mamm* burst into tears and had to be reassured that I would still come out to the farm for family gatherings and Sunday dinners.

"If your hip feels so well, then why am I helping you as if you are an invalid?"

A small smile deepened the wrinkles around her mouth. "I wanted to speak to you. You know Joan hopes you will take to that girl, Laura King?"

I snorted. "Not her only, but it seems Saloma and Becky too."

"Well, not me." I looked at her, surprised by the vehemence in her voice. "The wildness is not yet gone from that one."

Judging by the boldness with which Laura had pursued me, I agreed. But I couldn't help defending the girl a little because I felt somewhat responsible for her return to the Plain life.

"Maybe marriage will help her settle."

"That I do not doubt, but she is not the wife for you." She tilted her head to gaze up at me. "Your wife will have a level head on her shoulders."

I heaved a sigh. Not once had I wavered in my insistence that I would not marry again. Why did no one believe me?

"Please tell me you do not have someone else picked out." My voice sounded weary in my own ears.

"There is no one in this district I would choose for my *kinskind*. Perhaps in your new district you will find her." She held more tightly to my arm. "How I will miss you when you are gone."

"I will visit often," I promised.

We arrived at the house then. She released me and walked up the stairs with no assistance. At the top, she turned a grin on me. "That is all I wanted to say. Look for a wife with a level head."

She disappeared inside.

I was still standing there, shaking my head, when a familiar voice called my name. I turned to find Josiah striding toward me.

"I heard you bought a buggy," he said by way of greeting.

I wasn't surprised. News had a way of spreading through the district quickly. I nodded.

"*Das gut.*" He peered closely at me. "It is progress, *ya?*"

My insides went tight. Progress toward what? I didn't ask the question because I didn't want to hear the answer.

Josiah seemed intent on telling me anyway. "I hope this means you are feeling better and ready to make plans for the future."

I answered stiffly. "I have made plans. Have you not heard? I am moving to Strasburg to devote myself more fully to learning the craft of ceramics and pottery."

"I have heard that." An enthusiastic smile appeared. "And that you are skilled already. One day soon I will come to see your work."

A family approached. We both greeted the Yoders as they entered the house, followed by a stream of others.

Josiah took my arm and pulled me to one side. "There are some who will be sad not to see you so often."

Because we had been friends for so long, I knew he didn't refer to himself. Or to my family.

I tore my gaze from the stare he fixed on me. "Oh?"

Never one to hem and haw, he got to the point. "You know Laura King is taken with you."

I answered through clenched teeth. "How could I not know, since she has enlisted the help of everyone in the district to make sure I do?" I gave him a pointed look. "Including my friends."

He had the grace to look ashamed, but only for a moment. "Seth, it has been more than a year. You need to think about getting married again."

Words snapped out of my mouth at a volume I did not intend. "Who are you to tell me what I need?"

The people filing toward the house turned their heads our way, and I drew a deep breath to try to calm myself.

"I am your friend."

"If you were my friend," I ground out, "then you would respect my grief over the loss of *two* wives."

"I do, truly. But you cannot continue to live in the past."

Angry heat shot down my spine. "Two wives, Josiah. Both dead. I will not kill a third."

I would have given anything to take back those words. Understanding dawned on his face, followed closely by something that fanned my anger even hotter. What right did he have to pity me?

"Seth, you did not kill Rachel or Hannah. If you feel responsible, there is something wrong."

I raised my hand, which trembled with the effort to control my voice, and shook my finger in his face. "Do not speak to me of them again. You do not know anything about my feelings."

When I would have strode away, he grabbed my arm. With a violent shake, I threw off his grip.

In a flash, his own anger replaced the pity in his eyes. "If that is your true feeling, you should talk to the bishop or someone who can help you." His mouth tightened. "I cannot."

Turning on his heel, he stomped away from me.

I did not move until the last person had entered the house. Then I marched away with long, determined strides. A church service was no place for the rage simmering inside me. I would walk home and pray for *Gott* to cool the fires that smoldered in my mind.

I couldn't banish the conversation with Josiah from my thoughts. During the ride to work on Monday morning, his words played over and over, which derailed my determination to spend that time in prayer. Was there something wrong with me? The speed with which anger overtook me as we talked was disturbing. No, the emotion had been stronger than anger. I'd felt nearly blinded with rage. In that respect, Josiah was right. A man should be able to control his feelings.

But Josiah did not understand my guilt. No one did. Of course I had not *done* anything to kill either Rachel or Hannah. I knew that. My fault lay in inaction. With Rachel, I had not insisted on taking her to the hospital. I had let her tearful pleas for home birth to persuade me. But who was the husband, the head of the family? Had I forced her, she might still be alive. My failure to act had contributed to her death.

A car passed my buggy, and Orion's pace remained steady. A good horse, this one. If only I had chosen a gentle one like him last year.

Lars had been another failure on my part. I should have insisted on a different horse, one with a calmer temperament, no matter how taken Hannah had been with Lars.

I removed my hat and scrubbed at my scalp, as if that could dislodge the disturbing thoughts. Logic told me I was not the cause of the accident that killed Hannah. Those *Englisch* teens bore the majority of the fault. But I could not shake the certainty that, had I made different decisions, my second wife might not have died.

The battle still raged in my mind when I arrived at the shop. Leah's car sat in the usual parking place, but I had arrived before Elias. I unhitched Orion and turned him out in the pasture, my hands itching to wedge clay and mold it into something useful. A pitcher today, perhaps, to match the cups I'd trimmed yesterday.

Leah greeted me with a bright smile which I returned halfheartedly. Her smile faded into concern.

"Is something wrong?"

I halted on my way toward the workshop. "Why do you ask?"

Her lips twisted. "Because you're carrying a storm cloud on your face."

My chest heaved with a bitter laugh. "It's nothing. Driving from home gives me too much time for thinking. The sooner I move to Strasburg, the better."

"Changing where you live won't stop you from thinking." A scowl settled on her face. "Trust me in this. I know."

I so wanted to ask what had happened to her. I almost did, but she spoke first.

"It's girl trouble, isn't it?" I must have looked surprised. "When a man looks as disturbed as you do, a girl must be involved. Is it the runaway who came home? The one who likes you?"

"Laura King."

"Laura. I'd forgotten her name. She flirted with you at church yesterday." She ducked her head to catch my eye. "Am I right?"

That, at least, had been one benefit from my flare of temper. I'd been spared Laura's flirting and possibly another invitation to drive her somewhere.

"No, because I did not go to church."

"Really? I thought you said yesterday was a church Sunday."

"It was."

Her expression became openly curious, which was not customary for the normally taciturn Leah. We had become friends after weeks of seeing each other and eating together, but she rarely pried into my private life, as I did not hers. Just then, though, she seemed genuinely interested.

I heaved a sigh and shifted my coat from one arm to the other. "The women in my family schemed to throw us together yesterday, but I would not let them manipulate me."

I described the conversation over breakfast. When I got to the part where *Mammi* came to my rescue, she said, "I think I would like your grandmother."

"I am sure of it."

We shared a smile, and then her brow creased. "You said you didn't go to church, but you rode there with your grandmother?"

Looking away, I struggled with how to answer. "I...argued with a friend before the service began. So I left." My face heated at the admission that I could not control my temper.

"Let me guess. Your friend agrees with your mother that you should marry Laura King."

I gave her a sharp look. Leah was smart. I'd known that from the beginning. But until that moment I hadn't realized that she was also more perceptive than most.

As if my bubble of reserve burst, I found myself pouring out my frustration. "I do not understand why everyone wants to see me married. Do they not hear me when I say I will *never* marry again? I have loved two women. That is more than enough for any man."

"And they both died." She spoke the words I held back. "You feel responsible, is that it?"

My hands itched for activity. I clenched them into fists. "I *was* responsible."

Her voice lowered to barely above a whisper. "You told me how they died. Neither one sounded like your fault."

"But maybe if I'd acted differently…" The words choked me. Never before this moment had I given voice to the guilt that tormented me.

"That kind of thinking will drive you crazy, Seth. You weren't responsible." Her voice grew even softer. "Just like I wasn't responsible."

I looked up to see her running a finger down the scar on her face, her gaze tortured and unfocused. Never had she looked so young, so vulnerable. Thoughts of myself fled, and I fought the impulse to cross the space between us and gather her into a protective embrace.

The door opened, and Elias entered. The moment between us shattered at the sound of jingling bells.

"*Guder mariye*," he called in his cheerful voice.

"Good morning."

Leah matched his tone. I peered at her and marveled that her expression had changed in an instant. Gone was the raw emotion I'd glimpsed, though the smile she gave her *grossdaadi* appeared a touch rigid.

She picked up a piece of paper and handed it to him. "The electric bill. It's higher than usual."

He barely glanced at it before setting it on the counter. "*Ya*, well, we run the kiln more than before." Grinning at me, he rubbed his hands together. "It is time to get to work, my apprentice."

Leah did not meet my eye as I passed by, following Elias into the workshop.

Aaron set Wednesday as the day planting would begin. With our four-row planter, purchased two years ago, he expected to have the cornfields completed in four days. The tobacco seedlings had been delivered two days past, and were currently hardening beside the field where they would grow to maturity. Transplanting them would begin Monday. Our tobacco setter was an old one, only two rows, and required three people to operate. The process was slower than that of planting corn, but we grew only a few acres of tobacco, so he allocated two days for that task. I would be gone from the shop for a week.

On Tuesday I finished trimming all my greenware and readied them for the bisque firing. I also glazed everything in the bisque trays, unwilling to leave any work that Elias would have to finish for me. I worked late, and when I left the shop, Leah was already gone.

The sun had sunk low on the horizon by the time I hitched Orion to the buggy. My thoughts centered on Leah during the trip home. Our talk the day before had changed something between us. There was now an awkwardness that hadn't existed before. Whenever I remembered my confession of guilt, my cheeks burned. Why had I not kept my thoughts to myself?

Yet in an odd way, I felt my pain was safe in Leah's keeping. Even with the awkwardness, I sensed a new closeness whenever our eyes met. I found myself wanting to return to that moment before Elias interrupted our conversation. If I had asked then, would she have confided in me? Not only about the scar on her face, but the reason she left the Amish?

Another question burned in my mind. Would she ever consider returning?

The reason behind that question lay at the base of the awkward feelings I felt in her presence. I didn't want to consider why.

The timing of Aaron's planting could not have been better. When I returned to the shop after a week's absence, maybe things between us would be back to normal.

The sun was nothing but a dim glow in the west by the time Orion and I arrived home. I brought the buggy to a stop beside Aaron's and hopped out. Noah's buggy was not there. A twinge of concern plagued me as I hopped to the ground.

The door to the *daadi haus* opened and *Daed* emerged. The twins followed, and when they caught sight of me, they raced past him. My concern deepened. Why were the boys in the *daadi haus* instead of in their own bed? "*Onkel* Seth, we get to spend the night with *Grossmammi* and *Grossdaadi*!" Luke shouted, skidding to a halt in front of me.

Not to be outdone, Mark elbowed him out of the way. "We will have our own beds!"

"Cushions on the floor," Luke reminded him.

"That will be fun," I told them.

Daed approached, and I searched his face. The worry I found there twisted a knot in my stomach.

"Go back inside and tell *Grossmammi* that Seth is here. He will be hungry for supper." When they sped away, he spoke in a gravelly whisper. "Saloma's baby is coming."

Alarm buzzed in my head. "It's early, is it not?"

"*Ya,* she is early by several weeks."

I did a quick calculation. "The baby is due in June. That is more than three weeks. Is she going to the hospital?"

When he shook his head, pain began throbbing in my temple.

"Noah has gone for the midwife. Joan and Becky are with Saloma. Come and pray with the rest of us." He turned toward the *daadi haus.*

"Midwife?" My shout filled the air around us. "A woman in labor before her time needs to go to the hospital!"

His brow creased with a heavy frown. "That is not for you to say. Now come and pray."

"It *is* for me to say! She needs help before it is too late."

I took off at a run toward the main house, my father calling after me. Blood roared in my ears, propelled by my racing heart. As I reached the door, I was dimly aware that *Daed* had hurried as quickly as his shuffling gait allowed for the *daadi haus.* Fine. Let them pray. I would not stand by and watch my *bruder's* wife die in childbirth.

Bursting through the door, I shouted as I dashed up the stairs. "*Mamm,* get her dressed. She is going to the hospital."

I burst into the bedroom Saloma shared with Aaron, to find three stunned faces turned toward me.

Disapproval descended on *Mamm's* features. "Get out, Seth. This is not proper."

"I care nothing for being proper."

She winced at my volume, but I turned to Saloma. She lay in bed, pillows propped behind her. Sweat gleamed on her brow and plastered her unbound hair to her head.

Becky jumped up from her chair and rushed at me. "What is the *matter* with you?" She placed her hands on my chest and shoved. "Leave!"

Hardly aware of my actions, I grabbed her wrists and forced her arms down. My gaze fixed on Saloma, I pleaded. "Please come with me to the hospital. This baby comes too early. The doctors will help you. Please."

Hands grabbed me from behind, and I found myself pulled forcibly from the room. Becky slammed the bedroom door. I whirled and found myself looking into my *bruder's* furious face. "You have no business here."

"Why won't anyone listen to me?" I threw my head back and yelled toward the ceiling. "Why won't anyone help her before it's too late?"

His grip on my arms firm, Aaron propelled me down the stairs with a force I had never seen in my peace-loving *bruder.* A lifetime of farm work had given him such strength that I could not twist away from him.

When we reached the living room, he whirled me around to face him. "She. Is. My. Wife!" He ground out the words, his jaw clamped shut. "Not yours."

My head felt as if it would explode. Pressure throbbed in my temples, and Aaron's face blurred as tears filled my eyes.

"Then help her—" I choked on the words.

His chest heaved several times, and finally he released my arms. He spoke in an even tone, though still with force. "The midwife told us it is not uncommon for second babies to come sooner, especially after twins. She will be fine."

"But what if the midwife is wrong?" A sob squeezed my voice tight, and I did not even care.

Understanding softened his gaze. "Seth, it is Saloma upstairs. Not Rachel. You know that, *ya*?"

Of course I know that! I wanted to shout. But I couldn't force any sound from my throat.

Footsteps sounded on the stairs. Turning, I saw Saloma, supported on either side by *Mamm* and Becky. She still wore her nightdress.

"I think Seth is right." A shudder rippled through her body, and she closed her eyes for a moment. When she opened them again, she spoke to Aaron. "I want to go to the hospital."

Such relief washed over me that my knees threatened to give out. I fumbled for a chair and sank into it.

Aaron crossed the room to stand before his wife. "Are you sure?"

Her gaze slid past him and locked on to my face. "I am sure."

Mamm spoke then. "Seth, will you fetch Kevin? The hour is late, but I think he will be willing to drive us."

Nodding, I launched myself out of the chair and left the house, sending a heartfelt prayer of thanks toward the night sky.

SEVENTEEN

I paced in the hospital waiting room like a nervous husband.

When I'd banged on Kevin Cramer's door the night before and explained our need, he had immediately put on his shoes and coat. Doris Cramer told me she would pray for Saloma, which touched me nearly to the point of tears. They were good people, the Cramers. Mennonite, which was as close to being Amish as an *Englisch* person could get.

By the time Orion and I got back home, Aaron was helping Saloma into the car. *Mamm* also insisted on going, but Becky would stay home with the children. No one protested when I slid onto the front seat. After my emotional outburst, they were probably afraid to question me. If they had, I would not have had an answer. All I knew was I could not stay home, waiting through the night for news that could not come until the next day when a phone call to the Cramers would be possible.

Mamm sat on a chair in the corner of the waiting room, alternating between bowing her head in prayer and casting cautious glances at me. I avoided looking at her. Now that we had delivered Saloma safely into the hands of a doctor, shame had begun to creep over me. My behavior was inexcusable. The rage that had overtaken me frightened me. I had laid forceful hands on Becky when she tried to shove me from the bedroom. Unforgivable. I'd struggled with Aaron to escape his grip. Intolerable. I had even shouted at my own *daed*. In short, I had sinned against those I loved most, and guilt burned like acid in my gut.

The clock on the wall read four thirty when Aaron finally entered the waiting room wearing a green paper outfit. *Mamm* hurried across the room to stand at his side. He looked exhausted, his eyes red and his skin drawn.

But he wore a huge grin. "A girl. I have a *dochder*."

I closed my eyes against another disturbing wave of tears. He would not smile with such pride if the news was bad.

"She is okay?" *Mamm* clasped her hands beneath her chin. "She is healthy?"

The grin faded. "She is healthy but very small. Only four pounds six ounces. They have taken her to the Neonatal Intensive Care Unit and say she must stay there for a few weeks." He crossed the floor to stand in front of me, holding my gaze. "The doctor said if we had not been here, she would most likely have died."

My *bruder* grabbed me in a hug and pulled me close. The embrace, so uncharacteristic for us, took me by surprise. Then I wrapped my arms around him and clung until I had a firm grip on the tears that threatened.

"*Danke*, Seth," he whispered before releasing me.

I swallowed a few times and then asked in a husky voice, "Saloma is okay?"

His smile returned. "She is fine and also grateful. We are both thanking *Gott* for you."

Shaking my head, I released a pent-up breath. "I behaved like a crazed man. I sinned against my family and need to ask your forgiveness." I included *Mamm* with a glance in her direction.

"All is forgiven." Aaron's gaze dropped away for a moment before returning to my face filled with concern. "But we are worried about you. Such behavior is not like you, Seth."

Mamm stepped close to my side, nodding.

What could I do but agree? They were right. If I could not control my temper, another outburst might lead to worse sin than fighting with my family.

"There is a favor I would ask of you," Aaron said.

If he had a suggestion for taming a wild temper, I wanted to hear it. More likely, the planting lay heavy on his mind. With his wife and new *dochder* in the hospital, he would feel torn between his duties to them and to the farm. Of course I would do whatever I could.

"*Ya,* sure. Anything."

"Saloma and I talked about it just now, and we are in agreement." He drew in a breath and held my gaze. "If it would not be painful for you, we would like to name the baby Rachel."

I lost my struggle with my tears. Rachel, *my* Rachel, would be honored in the precious life of this tiny new baby. With salty rivers pouring from my eyes, I managed to utter a hoarse, "I would like that very much."

Word of Saloma's early delivery spread through our district as if it had been picked up by the wind. By noon the following day, a team of farmers arrived with their own equipment, ready to pitch in and help a friend in need. With relief, Aaron left the organization of the planting in the hands of our bishop and returned to the hospital to spend time with Saloma and little Rachel. Bishop Beiler handed off overseeing the cornfields to Kurt Miller and James Troyer, while he directed the teams who would plant the tobacco.

I took my place at the tobacco setter, feeding seedlings into the planter alongside Daniel Schrock, while Noah sat in the driver's seat and guided our horse up and down the straight furrows. Josiah and his *daed* started at the opposite end of the field, and by the time the sun set on Thursday, we were finished.

After a mere two days of work, all our corn and tobacco were planted.

At the end of the day on Thursday, we bid goodbye to our neighbors. Noah and *Daed* and I stood in the yard, watching as the last of the farm equipment pulled off of our property.

"Sometimes," my *daed* said, "it is very good to be Amish."

I could not agree more.

I returned to my pottery job on Friday. When I entered the shop, Leah looked up from her computer, surprise coloring her features.

"What are you doing here? We didn't expect you for another week at least."

Warmth for my district had done a good work on me in the past two days. The anger that lately hovered at the edges of my temperament felt far removed. Or maybe it was the sight of little Rachel, looking tiny but healthy in her incubator, which I had been granted just the night before.

"We finished early. And we had a baby."

I could not help taking credit. I felt responsible for Rachel somehow and didn't bother to question the feeling. Speaking with an enthusiasm that I saw gradually reflected in Leah's face, I related the events of the past few days.

When I finished, she was smiling broadly. "I am so glad, Seth. You saved that baby's life."

I dismissed that with a snort. "I might have found a more peaceful way to do it."

That brought a laugh—a genuine one that not only showed on her face but shone through her eyes. In that moment she looked truly happy and as peaceful as I felt.

A question rose in my mind, and I voiced it without thought. "Will you ever return to the Amish?"

Her expression slammed shut. She stiffened. "Why would you ask such a thing?"

I drew in a breath and held it. Why, indeed? It had seemed a natural question, given the warmth of feeling I held for my family and my friends today. And for her. But apparently my question struck a nerve with her.

I shrugged to make light of the situation. "I just wondered, is all."

But inside me, the question burned. If Leah were Amish, what would that mean for our relationship?

"No." She answered with certainty, jerking her head sideways. "I will never return."

I accepted her answer with a nod, and though disappointment threatened my happy mood, I left her in the showroom with no further comment. Determined to put the disturbing conversation out of my mind, I went about setting up my supplies for the day.

Bishop Beiler's visit a few hours later did not surprise me as it had before. In truth, I had expected him to initiate a conversation two days ago, while we worked together to plant my family's cash crops.

I'd just finished trimming a platter, one of a matching set of tableware with which I was particularly pleased, when he entered the workroom through the curtain. Elias looked up from his wheel. A pleasant greeting on his features died when he spied the bishop's serious expression.

The bishop addressed Elias before me. "I would speak with Seth in privacy, if you do not mind."

"*Ya*, of course."

My teacher made as though to rise from his wheel in order to leave us alone, but I waved him down. The thought of being confined within the walls of the workroom with a stern-faced bishop set my insides to trembling.

"Can we walk while we talk?" I looked to the bishop, who nodded approval.

We left the shop, and I avoided Leah's inquisitive glance when we passed her.

Outside, the May sun lay hidden behind a layer of clouds. The promised rain would be good for the crops we'd just planted, but not great for a stroll down the street. I hoped the rain would hold off for as long as it took for the bishop to deliver the lecture I expected.

He walked much as my father would, with his hands clasped behind his back and his gaze, partially hidden beneath his round-brimmed hat, fixed on the horizon in front of us.

"I have heard disturbing things, Seth. They leave me concerned for you."

The question of who had spoken with the bishop crossed my mind. My father, or my brother, or perhaps even my mother? I rejected the thought as not worthy of consideration. Given my behavior, whoever had talked with Bishop Beiler had been justified.

I matched his pace, our steps falling in unison on the pavement. "I understand your concern." I paused to swallow. "In fact, I share it."

He glanced sharply at me. "Do you? That makes my task easier."

"Your task?"

He came to a stop and turned to face me. "You carry a heavy burden, Seth. One I have tried to understand but failed. So I want you to speak with someone else. Someone who can help you."

In an instant I knew what he was asking. I started to shake my head, but he stopped me with a raised hand.

"I know of a counselor who understands our ways. He is Mennonite and respectful of the Plain lifestyle." He held my reluctant gaze. "I want you to talk to him."

My instinct was to refuse. With all my heart, I wanted to shout, "What good will talk do?" But the guilt of my uncontrollable temper lay heavy on me, and so I nodded. "I will talk to him."

"*Gut.*" Bishop Beiler produced a piece of paper from somewhere within his coat. "Here is his name and number. Call him today, please."

I clutched the paper in my hand. Though we had not reached a crossroad physically, we turned on the road and began our journey back to the shop.

"If I may voice one more concern," the bishop said, his gaze fixed ahead of us, "I would ask about the woman who works with you."

My head jerked toward him. "Leah? She is my teacher's granddaughter."

He nodded. "I understand that. And even a casual observer can see that she has suffered much." Though he did not glance at me, I felt the weight of his regard. "I must caution you against feelings for her. She has made her choice for her future, and her choice is not compatible with yours."

Apparently Bishop Beiler had detected the developing friendship existing between Leah and me. His warning served a purpose that he had not intended. Though I saw the truth of his words—that a relationship between us was impossible—for the first time I acknowledged reality.

I was attracted to Leah, and I thought maybe she shared the attraction. And that attraction was apparent to outsiders.

We walked on a few steps before I could manage an even reply. "You have no need for concern."

"Still." He stared straight ahead. "I have heard of your plans to move here, to live with your teacher, who is this woman's *grossdaadi*. I cannot help but feel concern for one of my flock."

"She is *Englisch*. I am Amish." I stopped on the road and faced him. "That will not change."

"If she could be persuaded—"

I held up a hand to cut him off. "She will not."

He heaved a sigh and we resumed walking. "What a shame you have no feelings for Laura King."

Why must everyone continually throw her at me? Was it not enough that she threw herself at me? The peace of the last few days began to crumble, and I clenched my jaw against a sharp reply.

When I said nothing, he continued. "The bishop of this district is a good man. May I speak to him of my concerns for you?"

In other words, he would make sure my new bishop was aware of my history, my temper, and my stubborn refusal to comply with everyone's wishes in the matter of taking a wife. I would come to my new district with my past already there before me.

Such conversations between bishops were probably common. I supposed I should feel honored that he had asked permission first.

I gave it grudgingly. "If you feel you need to, then you must."

We reached the shop, and he bid me goodbye. I stood in the parking lot, watching until his buggy became a distant black spot on the road. Our conversation replayed itself, disturbing on many counts. Talking to a stranger about my failures would not be easy. Why had I agreed to call the Mennonite counselor? Because I had promised, I would keep my word, but I dreaded the task.

Beyond that, the bishop's perceptive comment about my feelings for Leah sat like a heavy stone in my mind. When had my feelings changed? At first I'd felt nothing but pity for her, and maybe a little defensive at her obvious mistrust of me, displayed in caustic comments and hard expressions. Over the past two months her tongue had softened, and now she smiled in my presence more often than she frowned. More, she had a kind ear into which I had poured some of my inner turmoil. If she were Amish, I might be tempted to ask to drive her home. Maybe then she would open up to me, as I had to her, and discuss the traumatic event that left her scarred and bitter.

I kneaded a knot in the base of my skull, my decision to never marry again at the forefront of my thoughts, firmer than ever. It was a good thing Leah was *not* Amish. If she were, I would be forced to reject her friendship as firmly as I did Laura's bold attempts. Leah's determination to remain *Englisch* made it possible for us to continue to be friends. A good thing, as I was about to move in with her closest family.

The bishop's concerns about Leah resolved in my mind, I entered the shop, eager to immerse myself in work.

❧

That afternoon, Leah left the shop to run errands in town. I finished forming the platter I had thrown, and when I was satisfied, straightened from my work.

"May I use the telephone?" I asked Elias.

He did not even glance up from the bowl taking shape on his wheel. "Of course. You do not need to ask."

Thanking him, I went to the shop and called the number written in Bishop Beiler's neat handwriting. The woman who answered the phone listened to my hesitant request for an appointment with Dr. Phillips.

"You're in luck," she told me. "He just had a cancellation. Can you come on Monday at three o'clock?"

So soon? I had counted on having a week or so to grow accustomed to the idea of talking about my private pain with a stranger.

On the other hand, the less time I had to fret, the better.

"Yes, I can come then."

She took my name and then asked for insurance information.

"I am Amish."

"Oh, okay." She did not sound at all surprised. "Then you'll have a discounted price for the session because we don't have to mess with insurance forms. Can you give me a phone number where we can get a message to you if we need to?"

I provided the number for the store, jotted down the address of the counseling office, and then hung up. My next phone call was to a familiar number I knew without looking.

"Hey, Seth," Robbie said when he answered. "It's good to hear from you. Everything going okay?"

My mood lifted at the sound of his voice. I had missed him.

"*Ya,* everything is good."

The door opened, and Leah entered. She spared me a surprised glance as she made her way to the counter.

I said into the phone, "I have an appointment in Lancaster on Monday at three o'clock. Can you drive me?"

"Oh, man, I've got a thing at two, and it won't be over until around three." He sounded distraught. "Let me make a call to see if I can change it."

"No, don't change your schedule. I will find another driver."

"Dude, I hate that. I told you I'd help whenever I could."

"You have helped, many times." I poured assurance into my tone. "And I will call you again, I promise."

"Well…if you're sure."

"I am."

We said our goodbyes, and I disconnected the call. The distance between Elias's shop and the office in Lancaster was close to fifteen miles. I'd much rather make the trip in a car than spend so much time on the road.

Leah had been standing at the edge of the counter, eavesdropping on my conversation.

"I'll drive you to Lancaster on Monday," she offered. "*Daadi* can cover the shop by himself for a while."

It was on the tip of my tongue to accept, but Bishop Beiler's warning returned to me. Was driving in a car, a man and woman alone, the same as driving a girl home from church in a buggy? Perhaps not, but the two were too similar for my comfort.

I fixed a polite smile on my face. "No, but *danke* for the offer."

She narrowed her eyes and studied me for a moment. Then she shrugged. "Suit yourself." Picking up an envelope from the counter, she waved it in the air. "I forgot the electric bill, and it's due today."

When she'd gone, I stared at the closed door for a long moment. After my conversation with the bishop and the realization that my feelings for Leah could be deeper than I was comfortable with, a barrier to our friendship had been erected. Only in my own mind, perhaps, but it left me sad.

I once again picked up the phone. If Kevin Cramer couldn't drive me, then I would make the trip by buggy.

EIGHTEEN

Breakfast on Saturday was a solemn meal. Saloma's absence upset the twins, who had never spent more than a few hours away from her. Aaron had stayed at the hospital with her and baby Rachel Friday night, so his chair sat empty as well. To make matters worse, this was to be my last meal while living under the Hostetler roof. *Mamm* wore a somber expression, and *Daed* refrained from his typical morning talk of the Almanac's predictions for the weather. *Mammi* cast more than a few tearful glances across the table in my direction. Even Sadie seemed affected by the solemn atmosphere. Her little lips formed a frown, and she whined when Becky tried to coax her to taste a biscuit.

"But who will milk the cows?" Luke fretted, pushing his eggs around on his plate without eating.

"*Onkel* Noah will," I said.

Noah nodded and spared the child a kind smile.

The twins had requested to sit on either side of me today. I placed a comforting hand on Luke's shoulder and another on Mark's. "Perhaps he will need help. You are almost four years old. Time enough to learn milking."

Mark straightened, his expression eager. "Can we, *Onkel* Noah?"

He nodded. "It is a good idea, I think. We will ask your *daed* when he comes home."

I squeezed gently. "But take care around Delilah. She likes to use her tail as a whip. I will have a talk with her before I leave, and tell her to behave herself around my nephews."

The boys' cheerful nature, and the idea of milking a cow, won out. They both brightened and began to eat.

A twinge of regret surprised me as I looked around the table. My move was the right thing for me and for my family. It wasn't as if I were moving to Ohio or somewhere far away. Still, things would be different when I visited. The children would grow accustomed to the newness sooner than I would, and that saddened me. I would become the visiting *onkel.* Sadie would not even remember a time when I lived here, and what would I be to baby Rachel? I battled sorrow as I finished breakfast.

I did not have much to move. My clothing fit into a bag *Mamm* gave me, and the few personal items I owned—books and the like—were placed in a wooden box and set on the back bench of my buggy.

I promised to return the following week for the Sunday meal and said goodbye to my family, who lined up to wave as I flicked the reins and Orion took me away.

No. He was not merely taking me *from* somewhere. He was taking me *to* somewhere. A new home, and a future I viewed with a great deal of satisfaction. With that thought, I steered him onto the road and headed for Strasburg.

At the end of the workday, Orion and I followed Elias's buggy out of the parking lot. Leah's car passed us on the road, and we covered the short distance to my teacher's house at an easy trot. We took Star Road past the dairy farm, where herds of cattle grazed in pastures on both sides of the road. A series of homes lay beyond, some with long, freshly planted fields behind them. I spied Leah's car in front of a white house up ahead, and then saw her standing in the yard beside an Amish woman in a lilac dress and white apron.

As the horses slowed, I examined Lily Beachy with interest. Strange to think I had worked with Elias for two months and not met his wife. I'd certainly eaten enough of her cooking, but either Elias brought the lunch basket with him in the morning, or if the meal was to be served hot, Leah went to pick it up. A glance around the large yard revealed one possible reason. Mine and Elias's were the only two buggies, and I saw no horse in the pasture behind the house. With their only buggy at the shop all day, she had no transportation.

I pulled Orion to a stop beside Elias's buggy in front of a large shed and jumped to the ground. Lily hurried toward me, her face wreathed in smiles, while Leah trailed behind. Joining her, Elias took his wife by the arm and drew her forward.

"Meet my apprentice, Seth Hostetler. Seth, this is my Lily."

"*Velkumm* to our home, Seth."

"*Danke,* Lily, for opening your home to me."

"Your home from this moment on. I have your room ready." She gestured toward Orion. "You men see to the horses, and then bring your things in. I hope you are hungry because I have made a special meal for Seth's first dinner with us. Pork tenderloin with cheese potatoes and beans and chow-chow, and for dessert, *schnitz* pie."

My belly was still full from the bountiful lunch she had provided. No wonder Elias carried such a wide girth. If Leah ate here every night, how did she manage to maintain a slender figure?

I opened my mouth to protest, but Elias cut me off.

"Ah, Seth." He beamed in my direction. "You have never tasted anything like my Lily's *schnitz* pie."

Was there ever a man prouder of his wife's cooking than my teacher? Laughing, I could only reply, "I look forward to it."

We set about unhitching the buggies and settling Orion in his new home.

At just past two o'clock on Monday, Leah stuck her head into the workroom and announced, "Your ride is here."

Kevin had arrived earlier than expected. I hurried through the process of cleaning up, hating to leave him waiting.

"I will be back before the shop closes," I told Elias.

My teacher eyed me with an openly inquisitive expression. I had not confided the nature of my appointment, though I'd fielded many curious invitations to explain. The idea of speaking with a counselor about my volatile emotions was one I found more than a little embarrassing, and I was not yet ready to tell anyone. If the outcome of today's appointment resulted in more sessions, then I would feel I owed Elias an explanation. Until then, I merely nodded a farewell and left him to his work.

To my surprise, the driver waiting for me in the showroom was not Kevin, but Doris Cramer. She held one of my vases—not fancy, but a beautiful one such as any Plain person might use for flowers cut from their spring garden—and was inspecting it closely.

She looked up when I appeared, clearly impressed. "You made this?"

A blush threatened to heat my cheeks as I nodded.

"What is the price?"

Leah started to answer, but I spoke quickly. "If you like it, it's yours."

I received a sharp look from Leah, but she held her tongue.

Doris returned the vase to the shelf with care. "I couldn't accept it without paying."

I crossed the room in two strides, picked up the vase, and pressed it into her hands. "The price is thirty dollars, which is what I would pay you for driving me today. So if you will accept it in trade, we are even."

Behind Doris's back, Leah gave me a tight-lipped glare. I knew that she knew the price she had set on that vase was one hundred twenty dollars. Though I thought that figure outrageously high, we had already sold several similar to it.

The smile on my driver's face was reward enough for me. "Done." She hugged the piece close to her chest, and gave me a narrow-eyed look. "But I think I got the better end of this bargain."

Leah softened enough to wrap the vase in newspaper with something that approached a pleasant expression.

As she did, I said, "I expected Kevin. I hope he is not sick."

"No, but a job came up, and he needed to be there to oversee the painters at the start. I hope you don't mind my taking you."

Kevin Cramer owned a house painting business and employed several men from my district. Or my former district, as of two days ago. On occasion Doris had driven my family, especially in pleasant weather, which was her husband's busiest time.

"Of course I do not mind."

The irony struck me even as I spoke. I felt uncomfortable letting Leah drive me alone in her car, but not a twinge of difficulty in accepting Doris's offer. The reason lay not in the fact that Doris Cramer was *Englisch* because Leah was too. Doris was a married woman, but I would not lie to myself that the reason lay there. No, there was a different reason, one I did not wish to think about at the moment, so I focused instead on Doris.

"I'm glad. Kevin said your appointment would last an hour, and that's perfect timing for me. I want to go by the hospital for a short visit with Saloma. I have a gift for the baby."

"She will like that."

"Here you go." Leah handed the wrapped vase to its new owner. "I hope you enjoy it."

"I'm sure I will." She beamed as she headed toward the door.

I stepped ahead of her and held it open as she exited.

When I started after her, Leah grabbed my arm. "That's an expensive ride you're getting today," she whispered.

I matched her tone. "You do not approve?"

She shrugged. "It's your vase. But I would have taken you for free."

How could I reply to that? No words came. Our gazes locked together. The blue of her eyes seemed to darken as I watched. She stood not a foot away from me, so close I smelled the clean scent of the soap that clung to her. Though I tried to pry my gaze from hers, I was pulled deeper into the blue depths.

She seemed to realize that she still held my arm and released it quickly, breaking the moment that had grown uncomfortably intimate. I stepped back, shocked to realize that I had begun to lean toward her.

"You'd better go," she said, her voice husky. "Or you'll be late for your appointment."

My thoughts in turmoil and my pulse beating like a drum, I left the shop.

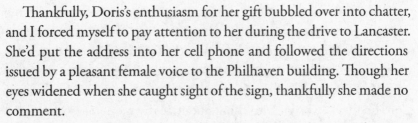

Thankfully, Doris's enthusiasm for her gift bubbled over into chatter, and I forced myself to pay attention to her during the drive to Lancaster. She'd put the address into her cell phone and followed the directions issued by a pleasant female voice to the Philhaven building. Though her eyes widened when she caught sight of the sign, thankfully she made no comment.

By the time she dropped me off at the entrance to the counseling center, I'd managed to banish thoughts of Leah and instead had developed a full-fledged attack of nerves for the upcoming appointment.

"We're a little early." She turned an apologetic grimace my way.

"It is fine." I opened the door. "Tell Saloma I said hello."

I stepped into a pleasant room, furnished with a blend of Amish and *Englisch* chairs and couches. Bushy plants in baskets grew here and there, and several small tables, placed between the furnishings, held Bibles besides an assortment of magazines. An *Englisch* man seated in a padded chair glanced up at me and then returned to the magazine in his lap.

Two young women smiled at me from behind a long counter facing the door, one dressed Plain and wearing a Mennonite *kapp*. When she spoke, I recognized her voice as the one I'd heard on the phone.

"Hello. Are you here for an appointment?"

I approached the counter. "*Ya*. I am Seth Hostetler," I told her in a hushed voice. "I am early."

Her smile widened. "That's actually a good thing. Since this is your first visit, I have some paperwork for you to fill out." She handed me a clipboard with forms on it and a pen stuck beneath the clip. "You can ignore the section about insurance. Bring it back to me when you're finished."

Nodding my thanks, I selected a wooden chair. I filled in my name and address, and listed *Daed* as my contact, with the Cramers' phone number. The second form was a list of questions, and some of them left me shifting uncomfortably. Though I was able to truthfully check the box marked "No" when asked if I had ever considered suicide, my pen hesitated over the question concerning emotions I could not control. But what good would this appointment do if I was less than honest?

I checked "Yes."

A beautifully carved clock on the wall read fifteen minutes before three when I handed the clipboard back to the Mennonite girl.

"Have a seat, and we'll call you back when Dr. Phillips is ready for you."

Before I returned to my chair, I selected a Bible from the nearest table. I might as well have left it there. The words swam before my eyes, my jangled nerves robbing me of the ability to focus.

A door to the left of the counter opened, and a man with an untrimmed beard and broadfall trousers appeared. His gaze swept past me and settled on the other man. "Carl, are you ready?"

Carl tossed his magazine on a table and exited the waiting room.

A few minutes later the door opened again. I closed the Bible, expecting to hear my name called. Instead, I received a shock when a familiar figure stepped through the doorway.

"Robbie!"

The young man jerked to a stop, his eyes going round. "Seth. Wh-what are you doing here?"

Several things became clear to me at once. The *thing* he had mentioned on the phone, the reason he could not drive me today, was an appointment here at Philhaven. A counseling appointment. The day we'd shared a lunch of sub sandwiches he had mentioned a counselor who advised him to take a year off before attending college. I assumed he meant a school guidance counselor, but apparently not.

My mouth too dry to answer, I might have been glued to my seat. I stared at the young man, whose throat convulsed with the nervous gulping I had not seen since shortly after his first visit to our family farm. His hands trembled with such violence that he splayed them for a moment, staring as if in horror, and then he shoved them into the pockets of his jeans.

Robbie's obvious nerves acted as a soothing agent on mine. Compassion for a young man I was fond of swept through me. Whatever the trouble of his past had been, he apparently wished to keep it private—a feeling I completely understood.

Rising from the chair, I clutched the Bible in one hand and attempted to answer in a normal tone. "This is the appointment I called about."

A man appeared in the doorway behind him, slender and not much taller than *Mammi*. He wore black-rimmed glasses, and a frown lay heavy on his clean-shaven face as he stepped to Robbie's side.

"I knew I was meeting a new client today, but until just now I didn't know who it was." He held aloft a slender folder as he peered through his glasses at me. "You are Seth Hostetler."

I nodded.

"It's nice to meet you. I'm Sam Phillips." The frown cleared, and he stepped forward with his hand extended. "Robbie has mentioned driving you and your family." I shook his hand, and he turned his head to speak to the girl behind the counter. "Angela, will you show Seth into my office? I'm going to step outside for a moment."

As the Mennonite girl left her chair, Dr. Phillips escorted Robbie out the main door so quickly I didn't have a chance to say goodbye. Thoughts whirling, I followed Angela down a short hallway. At the mention of an office, I'd expected a desk and perhaps a file cabinet. Instead, I was led into a comfortable room, smaller than the one out front, but similarly furnished. Muted gray paint covered the walls, and a tan carpet felt soft beneath my feet.

"Would you like anything?" Angela smiled at me. "Water or coffee, or a soft drink?"

I declined, and she left me alone in the room. Again I selected a straight-backed wooden chair, much like the ones in the living room at home. I had not waited more than a few minutes before Dr. Phillips returned.

He closed the door behind him, talking while he took a seat in a padded armchair. "I'm sorry about that. I wanted to assure Robbie that anything he and I talk about remains strictly between us." He peered at me through his glasses. "And I want you to know the same. No part of any conversation we have will be repeated to Robbie or anyone. And if you would prefer to see someone else, I will refer you to one of my colleagues."

For a moment I wasn't sure how to reply. "Is it not common for people who know each other to see the same…counselor?" The word felt odd on my tongue, especially when I was the one seeing a counselor.

"It's quite common, actually. One person refers another, and so on. But if I'd known you were coming, I would have discussed it with Robbie first and made sure he was comfortable with the arrangement." His features scrunched. "I certainly wouldn't have scheduled your first appointment directly after his, and I would have avoided a surprise encounter in the waiting room."

The answer showed a sensitivity to Robbie's feelings that I appreciated. As to his question, I wasn't sure how to answer. I didn't mind in the slightest talking to Robbie's counselor. My discomfort lay in talking to *any* counselor. This one looked professional and disturbingly *Englisch* in a pair of zippered slacks, a light blue shirt, and dark blue tie. Not like the man I'd first seen.

"My bishop said you were Mennonite." I left the question unspoken.

"I am, though my church is not as conservative as some in this area." A grin appeared on his face. "You would feel more comfortable talking to me if I grew a beard and wore suspenders?"

In truth, I would. But this man's honesty and easy manner had already begun to settle my nerves. Now that I was here, I might as well finish the appointment.

"I think I will withhold judgment and see how today goes." I managed a smile to soften my words, but I meant them. And my hesitation had nothing to do with Robbie.

"Fair enough." He opened the folder and extracted the forms I had filled out. "Let's start out by going over your questionnaire, and we'll see where that takes us."

During the drive home, Doris must have sensed my need for thought, for she didn't resume the chatter of the first trip. She described her visit with Saloma and expressed her disappointment that she did not get to see baby Rachel, who was not permitted visitors in the neo natal unit. After that she fell silent.

I stared out the window, watching the Pennsylvania countryside roll past. My conversation with Dr. Phillips—or Sam, as he insisted on being called—rolled around in my mind. He'd expressed the opinion that, while not normal, my uncontrollable fits of anger were at least under-standable after the devastating losses I had suffered. I left his office armed with material about post-traumatic stress disorder that he hoped I would read before our next appointment.

When I arrived, I wasn't at all certain there would be a second appoint-ment. But before I left, I stopped at the counter and asked Angela to schedule one for the following week. This time I asked for a different day, and though I didn't mention my desire to avoid another encounter with Robbie, I think she sensed the reason for my request. At least, I hoped so.

We arrived back at the shop to find the parking lot nearly full. Doris pulled to a stop as close to the door as she could.

"I'm glad I got my vase when I did." Her gaze briefly scanned the cars. "Otherwise someone else might have bought it."

"I could always make another for you, and I will be happy to make anything else you want. I appreciate your time in driving me."

"Anytime, Seth. Really."

I got out of the car and stood watching as she exited the parking lot. I hadn't asked her about driving me to my next counseling appointment. Normally, I would call Robbie, but now I wasn't sure if I should. I needed to think about that.

Inside, customers crowded the small showroom. Both Elias and Leah were there, talking with them and answering questions about various pieces. They spied me with obvious relief.

"Here's our other potter now," Leah told the woman who held a crock I'd crafted. "He can tell you all about it."

Though I'd much prefer to escape to the workroom and sink my hands into soothing clay, I arranged a smile for our customer while Leah headed for the cash register, where another lady waited to purchase a set of bowls.

On her way past me, Leah leaned close and hissed in my ear, "Don't you dare give this one away."

The caustic comment did much to relieve my fears that our earlier encounter would make things awkward between us. Apparently, she was prepared to ignore it, and I was happy to oblige.

Thirty minutes later Elias closed the door behind the last customer. He faced us with a broad smile. "A few more days like that, and we will have to hire more help."

"I wouldn't go that far," Leah said, "but we definitely made enough to cover the bills for a while." She speared me with a sharp, if slightly teasing, look. "And it would have been more if Seth would resist the impulse to give away our inventory."

I raised a hand in a promise. "I will make another vase to replace it."

Though she didn't answer, an easy grin settled on her features as she rounded the counter and picked up a stack of mail. She pulled off the elastic band holding the bundle together and began sorting through it.

"That was a garden club from Lancaster who decided to visit us as an outing." Elias raised his eyebrows. "One of them mentioned seeing your work at the home of a friend, Amanda, and was disappointed that we had no more unusual pieces of a similar sort for sale. Perhaps you should throw a few more fancy things for us."

That was not the first customer who had mentioned Amanda's recommendation. When she picked up the fancy vase I'd crafted, her delight with the piece had been almost embarrassing. Apparently, she'd been quite vocal about her satisfaction with my work. Robbie's mother had certainly been good for our business.

I opened my mouth to voice the thought, but stopped when Elias's expression changed. His face creased with concern, he fixed a gaze on something behind me.

I turned to find Leah staring at an envelope. Grasped between a finger and thumb, she held it away from her, her arm extended to its fullest length, with a look of sheer repulsion on her face. While I watched, blood drained from her cheeks, leaving her skin as white as bleached flour.

"What is it?" Elias took a step toward her, his alarm apparent. "Leah, tell me what is wrong."

Color returned to her then, a deep purple stain that raced upward from her neck until even her forehead seemed to radiate heat. Instead of answering the question, she grasped the envelope with the other hand and, with vicious, jerky gestures, ripped it in two. She continued to shred it until the remaining pieces were nothing more than a pile of confetti. These she grabbed in a fist and, whirling, tossed them into the trash can.

"I-I have to leave."

Elias and I watched, his expression as helpless as I felt, as she snatched her handbag from beneath the counter and nearly ran for the door.

"We will see you at dinner, then," Elias called after her.

"I'm not hungry tonight."

The door slammed on her last word. Seconds later we heard an engine roar and watched as her car peeled out of the parking lot.

Nineteen

On Tuesday Elias and I arrived at the store to find Leah already stationed behind the sales counter. My friend had disappeared in the night and was replaced by the stern-faced *Englisch* woman I'd met on my first visit to Plain Man's Pottery. She wore her hair unbound, and it fell forward, shielding her face as she bent over her accounting ledger. We received barely a glance when we entered. Elias and I exchanged a look, his expression sad, mine no doubt displaying my confusion.

Dinner the night before had been a quiet meal. Leah's absence, and the news of her reaction to the mysterious letter, doused even Lily's normally talkative manner. That husband and wife knew the cause of their granddaughter's distress was obvious by the troubled glances they exchanged, but no one ventured an explanation, and I didn't feel free to ask.

"Good morning," I said as I slipped around her on my way to the workroom.

She mumbled a reply without raising her head.

Elias stopped beside her and covered her hand with his. A silent message passed between them, ending when the tiniest of smiles made a brief appearance on her tight lips. As though satisfied, he nodded and followed me.

Though my teacher's typical exuberance was somewhat dampened, he managed something resembling his usual cheerful countenance. "No bowls or vases today," he announced. "It is time for my apprentice to learn a new technique. We will make a double-walled vessel. A teapot, perhaps."

The opportunity to learn something new brightened my spirits, and I began setting out our tools.

⁂

Over the next week, a gradual change occurred in Leah. She lost the grim, hard expression and smiled more often, though I sensed that whatever had disturbed her regarding the letter still hovered beneath the surface. She returned to dinner at her grandparents' table, and the atmosphere at the Beachy house once again reflected Lily's cheerful demeanor.

After church on Sunday—where I received a warm welcome by my new district—I declined to join the community meal. Instead, I climbed into my buggy and pointed Orion toward Upper Leacock to fulfill my promise to return home for a family dinner.

The greeting I received would have warmed even the coldest heart.

The twins charged out of the house, shouting, "*Onkel* Seth is here!"

Sadie raced to keep up with them, and the three halted and bounced like human balls until my buggy came to a full stop.

Dismounting, I swept all three of them up in turn, tossing Sadie high in the air, a thrill of delight racing through me at the sound of her childish squeals of delight.

"Have you missed me?" I asked after I'd deposited her beside her cousins.

"*Ya*," the boys chimed in unison while Sadie nodded.

"But we are grown up now." Luke's chest swelled. "We help with the milking every day. I pet Caroline's nose so she will be happy while *Onkel* Noah milks her." He sobered. "Delilah does not like her nose petted."

I laughed. "No, I suppose she does not."

"And I fetch for him the empty pails," Mark told me importantly.

"*Das gut,*" I said. "I am sure you are big helpers."

Sadie shoved her way in front of the boys. "I got eggs."

Another thrill shot through me, this one with a twinge of sorrow. She spoke in a full sentence with no baby babble. I'd been gone only a week, and already she had grown.

Mark awarded her a look of disgust. "*Ya,* but you broke three."

Anger puckered her little face, and she might have answered, but I swung her up again into my arms. "That is okay. You boys have broken your share of eggs. Sadie will learn to be more gentle, *ya?*"

She put her arms around my neck and squeezed, and an empty place in my heart filled.

The door to the main house opened, and my family filed out to greet me. Even Saloma was there. The welcome I received almost made me glad I had moved away, and *Mammi's* eyes were not the only ones that flooded with happy tears.

"Where is baby Rachel?" I asked, glancing toward the house.

Saloma bit her lip. "In the incubator still." When I would have voiced concern, she shook her head quickly. "She is healthy but still too small to come home. Doris drives me to the hospital every day, and I can even hold her for a while."

"Why are we standing out here while dinner is growing cold inside?" *Mamm* spread her arms to shoo the family toward the house as if they were chickens. "Aaron, help Seth unhitch his horse, and make quick work of it."

While we did, my *bruder* brought me up to date on the progress of the crops, the farm, and the family.

"*Daed* heard of a farm near New Holland that may be up for sale in the fall. Noah and Becky are praying they will be ready by then to buy."

I eyed him as we slid the collar off of Orion's neck. "You will have your hands full here when they leave."

He shrugged. "It is the way of things. If this year's crop pays as it should, I can hire help when I need. Between *Daed* and Saloma, they can manage most things with the livestock. In a few years the boys will be old enough to be of real help." He peered at me over Orion's back. "I hope I can still count on my *bruder* to lend a hand every now and again."

Grinning, I said, "The good thing about throwing pots is the work is not dependent on the season. I can take time off every now and again to help my family."

When Orion was comfortably settled in the horse pasture and becoming reacquainted with Rosie, we headed for the house. Walking side by side with my *bruder*, I was glad I'd skipped the community meal at my new district.

⸎

When Robbie arrived on Tuesday to drive me to my second counseling appointment, he didn't come inside. He pulled his red car up to the shop's front door and waited with the engine running.

I'd considered asking Kevin to take me, but only for a moment. Even though I no longer saw Robbie often, the boy was my friend. I wanted no awkwardness between us.

Leah looked up from her task of dusting the display shelves. Today she wore her hair braided in a long rope, and it swayed almost to the floor as she bent over to apply her dust cloth. I'd come to view her hair as an indicator of her mood. When she felt especially introspective and unhappy, her long hair swung free. I'd seen her let it fall forward, covering much of the scar on the right side of her face. She acted open and most friendly when her hair was pulled back into a bun, like an Amish woman's. Today's long braid spoke of a quiet and even serene mood, but with a touch of defiance against Plain ways.

Straightening, she stared out the window. "I wonder why he isn't coming inside. He used to come in to talk with me while you cleaned up."

The change in routine told me he still felt uneasy from our chance encounter in the Philhaven waiting room. I hadn't mentioned the incident to Leah. In fact, I hadn't confided any details about my appointment at all. Though I detected curiosity in her expression when I announced that I had a second one scheduled for today, neither she nor Elias had asked the nature of my trip to Lancaster. For that I was grateful. I still found the idea of seeing a counselor embarrassing. A man should be able to resolve his own issues without involving others. If I admitted that I could not, would they think me weak?

In answer to Leah's comment, I said, "It's a good thing I'm already washed up and ready to go then. I'll be back in time to help close up the shop."

Again, curiosity colored her features, but all she said was, "See you then."

Outside, I slid onto the passenger seat and snapped my seat belt.

With a quick glance in my direction, Robbie mumbled, "Hey."

Without waiting for a reply, he put the car in gear and left the parking lot. His grip on the steering wheel, along with the convulsive movement of his gulping throat, told me much. Regret flooded me, and I longed for the return of our easy friendship.

"How have you been?" I asked.

His answer was a shrug.

I tried for a casual tone. "Your mother has sent many of her friends to the shop. She certainly has helped Elias's business. We are grateful."

A quick nod, but the silence continued.

We covered a few miles. What could I say to put the boy at ease? I was no good at small talk and in fact disliked pointless chatter. If a man had nothing to say, then say nothing. But if there were words to be spoken, then speak them.

"If meeting me in the waiting room last week upset you, I am sorry." I didn't look at him, but out of the corner of my eye I saw him stiffen. "I was as surprised as you."

For a moment I thought he wouldn't answer, but then he drew in a breath.

"It was kind of a shock," he admitted.

"For me too." I hesitated. Should I tell him of my embarrassment at seeking help for my uncontrollable temper? "I have never seen a counselor before and only made the appointment at the request of my bishop."

"Sam's great." His grip on the wheel relaxed a fraction. "He's been my therapist for about a year."

So I'd been correct last week. Sam was the counselor who had advised

Robbie not to go to college. Was it also Sam who instructed him to become a driver for Amish people? An odd suggestion for a counselor to make of a teenager.

"If you are uncomfortable with me talking to your…therapist—" The unusual word felt awkward on my tongue. "—I will ask for someone else."

"No, I think Sam's the right guy for you." Robbie shot a quick glance my way. "Besides, he won't tell us anything about each other. He promised."

"He made the promise to me as well."

"So we're good."

I didn't disagree, but the mood in the car didn't feel *good*. If he did not mind my seeing his therapist, then why was he still gulping with nerves? And why had he not met my gaze once?

At least the awkward silence had been broken, and Robbie seemed determined not to see it return.

"So how's your family? Your grandmother doing okay?"

"*Ya,* she is good. And I have a new niece."

"Really? That's cool."

I relaxed against the seatback and set about updating him on the happenings of the Hostetlers.

Robbie left me at the front entrance of Philhaven, promising to return in an hour. I entered the building without the nervous flutter that had accompanied me the week before. Though I still found the idea of counseling uncomfortable, at least I knew what to expect this time.

Angela greeted me by name, and I wrote out a check. Therapy sessions were not inexpensive, even with the discount for having no insurance. How many bowls would I have to sell to pay for one appointment?

I didn't even have time to sit down before Sam appeared in the doorway.

"Come on back, Seth."

We shook hands when I approached, and then we walked side by side down the short hallway to his office. I seated myself in the same chair as before. He took the corner of the couch, my questionnaire from last week lying open on the cushion beside him.

"Robbie drove me today," I told him.

"Oh? And how did that feel?"

I considered before answering. "Awkward. But better toward the end of the drive."

He gave a smiling nod and then changed the subject. "Did you have a chance to read the information I sent home with you?"

I did, though my brain had struggled with the idea of identifying myself with the situations described in the material. Did I truly have an *anxiety disorder*? I couldn't deny the symptoms of pounding pulse and racing heart, and the idea of a similar event triggering a re-experience fit my situation exactly. I knew now the source of my hesitancy to drive a buggy, and I felt some pride that I'd conquered that reluctance. I could now drive without my heart threatening to pound through my rib cage. And the sight of Saloma in early labor naturally triggered the traumatic emotions associated with losing Rachel.

"*Ya*, I did. But I read nothing about outbursts of temper and how to control them."

"Symptoms present differently in individuals. As to how to control them…" He crossed one leg over the other and wrapped his hands around his knee. "It takes time. The first step is to understand what causes the outbursts. Then we will work on coming up with a coping strategy."

Unfamiliar words, but they made sense. "*Ya*, that sounds like a good plan."

He peered at me through his glasses for a long moment. "You realize that we need to talk about the traumatic experiences themselves, and especially your feelings concerning them. That won't be comfortable."

My stomach tightened, immediate proof of his words. I managed a nod.

"Why don't you start by telling me about the accident that resulted in your second wife's death?"

I want to leave now. Get out of this chair, go through that door, and never come back. The idea arose in my mind, so strong that I had to fight to stay seated. If I truly had post-traumatic stress disorder, what good was dredging up the situation that caused it? Wouldn't it be better to put it behind me, to look ahead and not backward?

But the accident refused to stay behind me. It rose constantly to torment me in the present. If I did nothing, it would continue to haunt my future as well.

Resolved, I described the day my Hannah died. In halting words at first, my recounting of the day eventually came faster. Details I had not realized I recalled poured out, such as the color of Hannah's dress, and the way Lars had nuzzled her hand while we showed him off to Josiah and Ella. The way she slid close to me on the bench. I could almost feel the length of her thigh resting against mine.

The details of the crash itself remained as vivid in my mind as if they had occurred that morning. Had I not seen them over and over for the past year? The mocking laughter of the *Englisch* teenager. The sickening lurch when our courting carriage's wheels left the pavement. Lars's high-pitched screech and the smooth wood of the brake lever in my hand. And Hannah's scream. That, especially, echoed in my mind.

Sam's soft voice broke into my description of the accident. "So you tried to grab her, but you couldn't."

"Our fingers touched. I-I was holding on to the brake lever." I swallowed, my throat desert dry. "If only I'd let go…"

"Then what?" he prodded. "What would have happened if you had let go?"

I closed my eyes, the scene more alive in my consciousness than Sam's office. "I would have been able to reach her."

"And would that have stopped the carriage from crashing?"

Maybe! I wanted to shout the word, but honesty prevented me. I shook my head. "By then we were too far off balance." I realized my hands were trembling, and I tightened them into fists. "But if I had not applied the brake at all, the horse might have recovered before we tilted."

"So you feel responsible for the accident."

His words lay between us like a pointing finger. An accusation. Not in his tone, but in my ears.

I nodded, acid churning in my stomach. "*Ya*. I feel responsible. She was my wife. I should have protected her."

He made no judgment but merely nodded. "Guilt is a powerful emotion." He paused, and when I said nothing, continued. "And what of the people in the car? Surely some of the blame lies with them."

Hot anger flickered to life in the back of my skull. The sound of the boy's voice, his derisive laughter, rang again in my ears.

"Some of the blame lies with them." The bitterness in my voice surprised me, and gave the words volume.

Sam's expression did not change. "You might even say most of the blame."

It was true. Had those *Englisch* boys acted respectfully, had they driven responsibly, my Hannah would still be here.

My jaw remained clamped shut.

"Seth, your anger toward those boys and your own feelings of guilt are perfectly normal. You wouldn't be human if you didn't experience violent emotions after a traumatic situation like that."

I shot out of my chair, unable to sit still. Instead of going to the door, where my impulse to escape might be too much to resist, I approached the room's single window and jerked back the curtain. Outside a tree covered in tiny green apples stood so close, its branches nearly brushed the glass. I noticed that only in passing, my mind busy processing Sam's words.

"I do not feel normal."

"Maybe that isn't the right word. *Explainable* might be a better one."

I didn't turn, and silence stretched long. The ticking of a clock on the top of a bookshelf grew loud.

"You are a man of faith, aren't you?"

Surprised at the question, I did face him. "You know I am. I am Amish."

"Then you believe the teachings of Jesus?"

Impatience for the question clutched at me. "*Ya,* of course."

"Then you also know the power of forgiveness."

I stared at him a long moment. I knew the power of my anger, and that I resented having to forgive those unruly *Englisch* drivers. Their irresponsibility had killed my Hannah and our unborn baby.

"I know it here." I touched my forehead, and then I moved my hand to my chest. "But I do not feel it here."

His smile held such compassion that my heart twisted in response. "So, you think forgiveness is a feeling?"

I understood both the question and the point he was trying to make. At least a hundred sermons on forgiveness, delivered by the ministers and Bishop Beiler, rose in my memory. Forgiving someone required a decision, and an action as a result of that decision.

But how could I make a decision to forgive when I felt nothing but fury toward the people who had taken my Hannah from me? I could not. I *would* not.

Sam must not have expected an answer to his question. When he spoke again, his tone was lighter. "That's a topic for a future session, I think. Come, sit back down and let's talk about your first wife." He glanced at the paper beside him. "Her name was Rachel, right?"

I allowed myself to be lured back into my seat to continue the session.

With a third session scheduled, I exited the building to find Robbie leaning against the trunk of his car, smoking a cigarette. His height and lanky frame struck me anew. Had he lost weight? He looked thinner than usual, or maybe it was because the weather had finally become warm enough that he wasn't wearing a bulky jacket.

As I approached, he dropped the cigarette on the pavement and crushed it beneath his tennis shoe.

"I have never seen you smoke," I said.

"I don't usually. Mom hates it." He jingled the keys in one hand. "But every so often a cigarette tastes good."

I held the same opinion as Amanda. Josiah took up smoking during our *rumspringas*. I tried it a few times, but my lungs revolted. I refused to allow Josiah to smoke in our car. When he was ready to separate himself from the world, cigarettes were the thing he found hardest to leave behind.

We got into the car, and though I smelled the acrid odor of smoke clinging to Robbie's clothing, thankfully I detected none in the car. Apparently, he confined his smoking to outside, as Josiah had done.

When he started the engine, the radio came on. Usually Robbie turned it off while he drove me, but today he left it on, the music loud enough to make talk difficult. The boy's convulsive gulping had returned, and his clutch on the steering wheel was so firm that the car jerked when he made the turns. What had happened to the friendly manner on which we'd parted an hour before? After the session with Sam, I had too much on my mind to try to draw him out of his fit of nerves. Instead, I watched out my window as we left town, the buildings and houses becoming fewer and farther apart. In the countryside, I scanned freshly planted fields, herds of cattle, and pleasant farm houses, many with laundry hanging on lines to dry in the sunshine.

When we turned onto Star Road, Robbie broke the silence.

"Seth, there's something I want to tell you." He shook his head, the gesture jerky. "No, I really don't want to. But I have to."

In the months we'd known each other, I'd never seen Robbie look so nervous. His jaw bulged repeatedly as he clenched his teeth. He sat forward, his spine rigid and not resting against the seatback. The muscles in his neck stood out like cords beneath his skin.

Just looking at him, the knots that had appeared in my stomach during the therapy session pulled even tighter. Whatever he wanted to discuss, the topic was bound to be unpleasant. With my mind full of painful past events, I wasn't sure I wanted to hear another stressful thing.

"If this is something you don't want to discuss, then don't. We'll have many other opportunities to talk."

He jerked a quick look at me. "I hope so."

Plain Man's Pottery came into view on the horizon, but instead of driving there, Robbie applied the brake and pulled to a stop on the side of the road, partially in the buggy lane. The radio ceased abruptly when he shut off the engine. He didn't turn, but instead continued to face forward with a white-knuckled grip on the steering wheel.

"This isn't my first car, you know."

The comment took me by surprise. "No?"

He gulped a few times. "No. I bought one the summer before my senior year. It was a piece of junk, really, but Mom and Dad made me save up my own money, and it was all I could afford."

He stopped and seemed to expect a reply. I grasped for an appropriate comment. What about buying a car would make the boy so nervous? "A good plan, forcing a young man to pay his own way. A friend and I also bought a 'piece of junk' when we were younger."

A quick nod, and then he asked, "Want to know what happened to that car?"

I gave the response he expected. "*Ya*. What happened to it?"

"I sold it. Something happened, something terrible, and I couldn't stand to look at it anymore."

I didn't know how to respond, but Robbie did not seem to expect me to. He began talking, the words pouring out in a flood, as though he could not say them fast enough.

"My buddy and I went out partying the night before, doing some stuff we shouldn't have been doing, you know? We drank a bunch of beer, and then we got ahold of some coke."

I assumed he wasn't referring to a soft drink.

"That stuff wires you up, you know? We didn't sleep all night, just hung out and partied, and before we knew it, it was, like, lunchtime the next day. I knew I was gonna catch all kinds of grief when I got home, so we hopped in my rusty old car and took off, driving like a bat outta you know where, and still kind of buzzing, and all I could think about was how I was gonna get grounded for life. And my buddy Justin, he snorted more of that stuff than me, and he was acting crazy."

I went still. My limbs became heavy, as though paralyzed. Two wild *Englisch* boys driving a rusty car? Blood raced through my veins, propelled by a heart that pounded so hard I couldn't force a breath into my lungs.

"And there we were, d-driving down the-the-the road—" Choking tears stuttered his speech. "And up ahead there were all these b-b-buggies, and I started honking the horn, and Justin rolled down his w-window and—" He collapsed forward over the steering wheel and sobbed freely. "We passed them, and I took him home and then I went home. It wasn't until the n-next day I found out about a buggy crash on that road, and I…"

Everything went dark. Robbie's voice sounded as though it were coming from far away. I was aware that I sat in the car, that he continued to talk, but I was no longer listening.

Robbie Barker, the young man I'd befriended, had killed my Hannah.

Hot rage surged through my veins. My hands clenched into fists. I had to get out of that car, to get away from him. I threw open the door and leaped out, blood roaring in my ears. The car, Robbie's second car, had been bought because his first car was the one he used to kill Hannah. I slammed the door as hard as I could, and then, hardly aware of my actions, I struck the window with my fist. Glass cracked and spidered, and pain shot from my fist up to my hammering head.

Robbie jumped out of the car on the other side, face blotchy and tears streaming. "Seth, I'm sorry. I'm so sorry. You don't know how terrible I feel—"

"How terrible *you* feel?" My shout filled the air and rose into the sky.

He ran around the car toward me. "I didn't mean it that way. I know my feelings don't matter."

Though my hand throbbed, I couldn't manage to unclench it. As the boy approached, all I wanted to do was smash his face with my fist.

Gott, *I need help!*

I began to walk—long, quick strides that would take me away from the one who had killed my wife and baby, who had stolen my happiness and left me crippled with rage. If I didn't get away from him soon, I wasn't sure I could control myself.

He ran after me. "Seth, please. I'm sorry. Please talk to me."

I whirled on him, and my fury must have showed in my face because he halted.

"So this is why you wanted to drive me. To make up for *killing* my wife?"

I spat the word, and it struck him like acid. His face crumpled.

"And this is why your mother spent so much money buying my pots and sending others. Does she think she can buy my forgiveness?" I stepped toward him, and he took a backward step. "Does she think her money can buy my Hannah back?" He shook his head, but when he would have spoken, I cut him off by a hand slashing through the air between us. "Get away from me." I ground the words out through gritted teeth. "Never come near me again."

I left him standing in front of his car. My boots pounded the road so hard they might have crumbled the pavement to gravel. I could not go into the shop, not while my brain buzzed with emotions I did not know what to do with. Instead, I passed it by and kept walking.

TWENTY

Twilight had almost turned to night by the time I arrived at the Beachy home. I stepped into the yard and saw my buggy parked beside Elias's. We rode to work together since I'd moved, and I usually drove, as I had that morning. He'd brought Orion and the buggy home from the shop, and I headed first toward the pasture to check on the horse. He trotted over to greet me and nuzzled my hand with his nose, blowing warm, grass-scented breath into my face.

Sometime during my three-hour walk the fiery rage had ceased to roar, but it had become a smoldering anger deep in my soul. I was not sure I would ever be able to douse that fire completely, nor did I care to try. But at least I thought I could manage to speak politely to Elias and Lily without fear of my emotions erupting.

When I headed for the house, I spotted Leah's car parked on the other side. Usually she left after washing the dinner dishes, and that would have been at least an hour ago. Had they held the meal, waiting for me to come home? Guilt stabbed at me. I should have stopped somewhere and found a phone to call the shop and let them know I would be late.

I'd no sooner stepped around the buggies when the front door opened and Lily, holding a kerosene lamp, appeared.

"*Ach,* there you are finally." She bustled outside and met me in the grass, lifting the lamp to peer into my face. "And you are well?"

Remorse washed over me. I hadn't thought they would be concerned for my welfare.

"I am well," I assured her. "I am sorry to have worried you. I...went for a walk."

Leah had come up behind her, and I saw Elias standing in the doorway, silhouetted by more lamps burning inside the house.

"A walk?" The sarcasm in Leah's tone weighed a ton. "For three hours?"

I met her gaze. "I had a lot to think about."

Lily studied my face a moment longer, and then she lowered the lantern. "Well, you are home now, and I think starving. I kept your dinner warm, and we have saved our dessert so you would not have to eat alone. Come." She headed for the house.

Relieved that they had not delayed their own dinner, I started to follow her, but Leah stepped in front of me.

"We'll be there in a minute," she told her grandmother.

Lily hesitated, but then with a nod she went into the house. Elias closed the door behind her.

Leah studied my face, her eyes narrowed. "*Grossmammi* and *Daadi* were really worried."

"I am sorry." I hung my head.

"We thought maybe you were in a wreck or something, so I called Robbie to find out what happened."

At the mention of his name, my head shot up. My anger must have been apparent, for she nodded.

"He told me the two of you had argued, and you stormed away."

"Did he tell you what we argued about?" I winced at the acid in my tone, but her expression remained placid.

"No, only that he'd done something that hurt you, and you would probably never be able to get over it."

"He's right."

She stood still a moment, and then she folded her arms across her chest. "Well? Are you going to tell me about it?"

"I—" My throat closed. I wasn't at all sure I could, or should, talk about the day's revelation. My anger smoldered, and it would not take much to fan it into a full flame.

And yet, my insides still felt as if a fuse had been lit, and if I did nothing, I would eventually explode.

"Robbie Barker killed my wife."

The words felt like bombs as they left my mouth. Clearly, Leah had not expected them, because she gasped, her hands flying to her face.

I began to talk, to tell her everything. For the second time that day, I described the day Hannah died, my devastation at losing a second wife, and my helplessness against the rage that at times overtook me. I touched on my own guilt as well. She shook her head and would have interrupted, but I did not allow her the opportunity.

Sometime during my tirade, we gravitated toward the porch and perched on the edge while I paced in the grass before her, my words continuing to flow as if a tidal wave had been let loose in my soul and I would drown if it did not wash itself out. Once the door cracked open, and I was aware that Leah waved a hand behind her back, telling whoever would have interrupted to leave. The door closed again.

The torrent finally ended. Exhausted, I collapsed onto the porch beside her, my eyes burning as if with tears, though I had none left to shed. We sat quietly for a long time, while stars winked into view in the night sky above us.

When she spoke, her words were not at all what I expected.

"Well, clearly, that therapist is not acting in your best interests."

I looked at her. "Sam?"

She nodded. "He obviously knew about Robbie's involvement in the accident that killed your wife. If he had an ounce of ethical reasoning in his brain, he would have referred you to someone else the minute he found out who you were."

Though her words made sense, I found myself wanting to defend Sam. He had promised to keep my confidence and Robbie's as well. So far I had no reason to believe he had broken his promise.

But had he known that Robbie would confess to me today? Was that why, during our session, he had urged me to consider forgiveness? His relationship with Robbie was a long-standing one, whereas I had known him only a week. Would he push me—however gently—in a direction that served Robbie's interests over my own?

It occurred to me that I didn't care if that were true or not.

"I will not go back to him," I told Leah. "How can I, since he is the one who urged Robbie to befriend me, to offer to drive me, knowing all the while that Robbie is the reason for my pain?"

Her lips twisted, the scar standing out starkly in the white moonlight. "I've seen my share of therapists. There are good ones out there, but you have to wade through a lot of muck to find them."

I almost laughed at her descriptive phrasing. Wading through muck was an apt picture of my emotional state.

She shifted sideways on the porch and faced me. "Seth, I'm really sorry for all you've suffered today. Believe me when I say I really do know something about what you're going through."

Though the light was dim, something shone from deep in her eyes, something painful and full of anguish. I believed her. She had experienced trauma, just as I had. She didn't need an external scar to stand as proof of that.

When I made no reply, she said in a quiet voice, "You can talk to me anytime. I don't have a single answer for you, but I have a friendly ear."

She reached forward then and covered my hand with hers. The gesture was probably meant to be comforting, if a bit forward, but the intent was spoiled when I hissed in pain.

Her touch became light, her expression concerned. She gently took my wrist and pulled my hand toward her, into a ray of light shining from the window in the house. "What's wrong with your hand?"

I heaved a silent laugh. "An un-Amish display of temper. I broke Robbie's car window with my fist."

Satisfaction settled on her features. "Good. He deserves it, and more." She looked up at me. "But if this is not better by tomorrow, I am driving you to the emergency room to have it x-rayed. You might have broken something."

The door behind us opened for a second time, and Leah snatched her hands away from mine.

Lily stood in the doorway, looking at us sternly. "Seth must come and eat now. Else he will faint from hunger, and such a big man he is, the three of us together will not be able to drag him inside."

With relief, I realized my laugh was not forced. I climbed to my feet and helped Leah stand—with my good hand—with a warm feeling flooding through me at the smile shining on her face. I'd been betrayed by one friend that day, but another friendship had deepened.

The curtain surrounding the hospital bed on which I sat opened with the metallic sound of rings sliding across a rod. The emergency room doctor, a likable young man with a ready smile, entered carrying an X-ray.

I'd awoken in the morning with my hand swollen and my fingers bruised purple. Leah took one look at it and insisted on driving me to the hospital. Elias agreed. I'd been to Lancaster General Hospital more often in the last two weeks than in the previous ten years, not a trend I wished to continue.

"I have good news and bad news." The doctor placed the X-ray on a white panel hanging on the wall behind me and flipped a switch. The panel lit, showing a picture of the bones in my hand. "The bad news is that you have a fracture. The good news is that it's just a hairline fracture in the fifth metacarpal."

"That is good news?" A break of any kind spelled disaster for a potter.

The doctor gave me a sympathetic look. "If it were worse, you'd need surgery to repair it. This is actually a fairly common break. It's called a boxer's fracture." His expression became stern. "I hope you didn't punch a person."

"No. I punched a car."

A grin appeared. "I think the car won."

I could not muster an answering smile. "How long before I can use my hand?"

"Around six weeks before the bone is fully healed." He switched off the light and removed the X-ray from the panel. "I don't think we need to cast it, but I am going to splint your hand and forearm. It's important to keep your pinkie finger immobilized."

A flicker of hope appeared in the dark gloom of his pronouncement. "Only my little finger? So I will be able to use the rest?"

His expression became stern. "Not for several weeks. The hand and wrist are a complex system of bones, muscles, and tendons. Move one, and they all move." He picked up a chart, glanced inside, and grimaced. "You're a potter. I understand your concern." Hesitating, he chewed on his lower lip a few seconds. "Tell you what. Come back in three weeks and we'll take another picture. If the bone is healing well, I'll splint only that finger. That'll give the rest of your hand time to heal from the trauma and those contusions will be gone. Maybe some limited usage by that point will be okay."

Several weeks of not using my right hand. Wedging, throwing, and trimming would be impossible.

A nurse arrived carrying a box from which the doctor removed a splint. He fitted it on my hand. My pinkie and the next finger were completely covered. The splint wrapped around my wrist and several inches up my forearm. The doctor secured it with Velcro straps.

"Keep that on all the time. Use an ice pack for 20 minutes every couple of hours for the next day or so. Ibuprofen for pain. And prop your arm on a pillow when you're sitting." He jotted something down on the chart, and then he smiled up at me. "I'll see you in three weeks. In the meantime, no more boxing."

When he'd gone, the nurse gave me papers with the instructions and pointed me toward the waiting room. Leah looked up from a magazine when I entered.

I held up my splinted hand. "Broken."

"I figured." She stood and picked up her handbag. "Are you ready?"

With a glance toward the hallway leading to the rest of the hospital, I asked, "Do you care if we try to see my niece before we leave?"

"Sure."

I asked directions of the woman behind the check-in counter, and we found our way to the Delivery Pavilion. There we approached another counter, and the girl seated there slid open a window.

"I would like to see my niece, who is in the Neonatal Intensive Care Unit."

She shook her head. "I'm sorry, but we don't allow visitors in that area." My face must have fallen, because she gave me a sympathetic smile. "Who is your niece?"

"Rachel Hostetler." That was the first time I'd spoken the baby's full name, the same as my Rachel's.

The girl brightened. "Oh, Saloma's baby. She's here now. Hold on a minute."

I glanced at Leah while the girl picked up a telephone and pushed buttons. She explained that Saloma's brother—I didn't bother to correct her—was here and would like to see the baby. A few moments later she replaced the receiver and smiled at us.

"You can't go into NICU, but they are going to let Saloma take the baby into the regular nursery for a few minutes, so you can see her through the window."

We followed her directions to the nursery, a long glass window with a curtain on the inside. Before long a nurse dressed in brightly decorated scrubs opened the curtain. She smiled and held up a finger, indicating we should wait.

The nursery was full of bassinets, most of them occupied.

"Look at that one." Leah pointed toward a bundled infant wearing a blue knit hat. "He's so tiny."

I read the card. "He was born only last night."

She touched the window with a finger, pointing. "That one over there was born today. Aw, he's crying."

The nurse weaved through bassinets, picked up the crying baby, and took him to a rocking chair on the far side of the room.

A door in the corner opened and another nurse appeared. She held the door, and Saloma stepped through carrying a bundle of her own.

When she caught sight of me, a broad smile lit her features, and she made her way to the window. Once there, she pulled back the blanket, so I could get a better view of my niece.

"I take it back," Leah whispered. "That boy looks like a giant compared to yours."

My throat closed around any reply I might have made. The baby in my sister-in-law's arms was the most beautiful infant I'd ever seen. Her tiny face appeared slightly bigger than an apple, with a delicate nose and pink rosebud lips. If unwrapped from the blanket, I thought I could hold her entire body in both my hands. Her eyelids fluttered open, and I stared into dark blue eyes.

"She's precious," Leah said.

I could not take my eyes off of her. Baby Rachel. My own Rachel would have fallen in love with her in an instant. As I had. I looked up at Saloma and mouthed, *She is beautiful.* Grinning, Saloma nodded.

Long before I was finished gazing at her, the nurse approached Saloma and said something. With a smile at me, Saloma tucked the blanket back around little Rachel's face. She waved goodbye and left.

Not until the door closed behind her did I turn away from the window to find Leah staring at me, a smirk on her lips.

"You're besotted."

I did not bother to deny it. "Do you blame me?"

The smirk became a grin. "Not a bit. She's a beautiful baby. I think I'm a little smitten myself."

Leah and I didn't talk much on the ride back to Strasburg. The radio played, and she hummed along with several of the songs. Apparently, she didn't share my discomfort at driving alone with me in her car. Elias must not have thought the arrangement inappropriate either, or he would have suggested calling another driver this morning. Was I the only one who thought the situation compared to courting? The only thing that kept the situation from being improper was Leah's firm assertion that she would never return to the Amish. Riding with her meant no more than riding with Doris.

I reminded myself of that many times during the short drive.

Back at the shop, I apologized to Elias for the injury that would keep me from my work, but he dismissed my concerns.

"There is plenty of work to keep a one-armed potter busy. You can still glaze, can you not?"

Since glazing involved dipping bisque pieces into the tinted liquid, I could do that with one hand. "*Ya,* I can glaze."

"So I will throw while you operate the kilns and glaze." He shrugged, as though that settled everything.

Though I would itch to do more, perhaps I would not be completely useless around the shop.

"For now, would you go outside and stoke the firebox?" He peered at my injured hand. "But do not lift large logs. Only do what you can with one hand."

With a longing glance at my wheel, I left the workroom. Leah was busy at the short file cabinet where she kept all the paperwork. She spared an absent smile for me as I passed and then returned to her work.

Outside, I checked the firebox. Yes, more fuel needed to be added. The wood supply had been recently replenished, and I approached the woodpile against the back of the shop. The first piece I picked up proved heavier than I expected, and it slipped from my grasp, barely missing the toe of my shoe. I spared an unkind thought for Robbie, the cause of all my problems.

In the act of bending down to retrieve the log, I stopped. The mere thought of my former *Englisch* driver brought a bitter taste rising in my throat. I would dislike him for the rest of my life, but Robbie wasn't the cause of *all* my problems. I'd broken my own hand because I couldn't stop the rage that had taken possession of me upon hearing his confession.

And he'd done nothing to contribute to my first wife's death. Nor had he forced me to purchase a horse that was clearly not suited to pulling a buggy.

With a firm grip on the log, I carried it to the kiln and added it to the coal bed, wincing against the heat. My discussion with Sam yesterday gnawed at the edges of my guilt. He'd spoken of the power of forgiveness. Well, I couldn't forgive Robbie. Nor could I forgive Sam for deceiving me. Leah was right. The counselor was unethical.

Once the firebox was fully stoked, I headed toward the front of the building. As I rounded the corner, the postal truck pulled into the parking lot. I altered my course to greet the letter carrier. We'd developed a casual acquaintance over the past few months.

"I'll take the mail inside," I told him. "No need for you to get out."

"Thanks, Seth." He handed over a bundle wrapped in a rubber band, and then noticed my splint. "What happened to your hand?"

Half a dozen replies came to mind, but I settled on, "I broke it."

"Sorry about that." He put his truck in gear and left.

Turning toward the shop, I glanced down at the bundle. An official-looking letter on top was addressed to Leah. When I saw the return address, I nearly stumbled.

The letter was from the Adult Parole Authority of the Ohio State Penitentiary.

Twenty-One

I lingered up front, fiddling with a display of bowls while I watched Leah out of the corner of my eye. How would she react to the letter? She set the bundle of mail on the counter and continued her work with the files. Eventually, I could find no excuse to stay longer and stepped through the curtain to return to the workroom.

I was not surprised when I heard the door close a short while later. Leah had left the shop without a word to anyone.

Elias peeked through the curtain and then turned to where I was mixing a bucket of glaze, his expression mystified. "Leah is not here. Did she say where she was going?"

"No." I continued to stir and did not look up.

"Perhaps she had an errand to run."

Should I tell him about the letter? I wrestled with the question for a moment before coming to a conclusion. Elias was more than her employer. He was her grandfather.

"She received another letter in the mail that might have upset her." I glanced up. "It was from the Ohio State Penitentiary."

Elias closed his eyes, emotions playing across his face in rapid succession. Understanding. Pain. Concern. A moment later he opened his eyes to reveal a deep sadness in their brown depths.

Questions burned in my mind. Was Leah on parole? Had she received the scar while committing a crime? Was her bitterness gained while serving a prison sentence? That would explain why many of her relatives rejected her. I couldn't make myself believe her capable of a crime terrible enough to require such a severe punishment, but she had once mentioned being sinful and unrepentant, which was why her former bishop had forbidden anyone to eat with her.

Elias left the workroom, and a moment later I heard his low voice. No customer answered, so he must be using the telephone.

When the glaze was thoroughly blended, I tapped the paddle on the rim of the bucket to shake off most of the droplets and then carried it to the sink. I was rinsing it when Elias returned.

Worry deepened the lines in his face. "Seth, may I take your buggy to town?"

"*Ya*, of course." I did not have to ask why, for he told me.

"Leah has received upsetting news. I must go to her. You will watch the shop?"

Oh, how I wanted to ask the nature of the news, but instead I merely nodded. To ask might have put him in the position of betraying his granddaughter's confidence, which I would not do. Instead, I followed him outside and helped hitch Orion to the buggy.

Customers came and went sporadically over the next several hours, so I didn't get much glazing done. I'd learned to operate the cash register only the week before, which was fortunate because several people made purchases. I did my best to answer their questions about each piece, but I was not outgoing by nature and tended to be quiet around strangers.

Elias returned late in the afternoon, wearing sorrow like a second skin. He offered no explanation but set about wedging a lump of clay with a focus that I recognized as a troubled mind working itself out through industry. Had I not done the same thing? In fact, I would be doing so myself if I hadn't broken my hand.

My concern for Leah had grown throughout the hours of his absence, and I couldn't stop myself from asking, "Will she be coming back?"

"Tomorrow." He continued to knead the clay, though it looked ready for the wheel to me. "But only for a few hours to show us how to make out the bank deposits while she is gone."

"She is leaving?"

"For a few days."

His lips formed a tight line through which I sensed I would get no further details.

Mystified, I returned to the showroom and left him to his work.

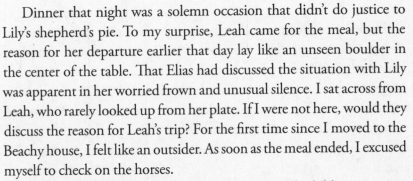

Dinner that night was a solemn occasion that didn't do justice to Lily's shepherd's pie. To my surprise, Leah came for the meal, but the reason for her departure earlier that day lay like an unseen boulder in the center of the table. That Elias had discussed the situation with Lily was apparent in her worried frown and unusual silence. I sat across from Leah, who rarely looked up from her plate. If I were not here, would they discuss the reason for Leah's trip? For the first time since I moved to the Beachy house, I felt like an outsider. As soon as the meal ended, I excused myself to check on the horses.

Orion trotted over to the fence when I approached, blowing in my face and tossing his head in a plea for a caress. With a quiet laugh, I obliged. Elias's mare maintained a safe distance, as though she had not yet decided whether I was trustworthy.

Thankfully, the temperature remained pleasant that evening. I intended to stay outside until Leah left so they would have plenty of time to discuss whatever they needed to talk about.

With something like a shock, I realized I'd been so concerned about Leah during most of the day that I hadn't once felt the smoldering anger over Robbie's confession. Or even the familiar guilt that had been my constant companion since Rachel's death. For the span of a few hours, the absence of those tormenting thoughts rendered me almost light headed.

As thoughts will do, the reminder called them back to shatter the delicate peace I'd enjoyed. My right hand ached, another reminder. I hardened my heart against the image of Robbie's face, blotchy and streaming tears as he apologized. As if mere words could erase years of anguish.

Footsteps approached behind me, and I turned to find Leah striding across the grass. She wore her hair loose tonight, and it hung in gentle waves over her shoulders and down her back. Orion deserted me to beg attention from the new arrival. She obliged without smiling.

"You didn't have to leave the house," she said, her gaze fixed on the horse.

"I thought you might want to speak with them alone."

"That's what I figured." She shook her head. "Thanks, but there's nothing to talk about. I'm going, and they don't think I should. End of discussion."

Her drooping shoulders and the sad gaze she fixed on Orion moved me to compassion. There were many layers to the woman standing beside me, but vulnerability was not one I had encountered before. I longed to know about her past, but mostly my heart ached to offer what comfort I could. Last night I had unburdened myself to her. Perhaps she would like a friendly ear as well.

"You are going to Ohio?" At her sharp look, I explained. "I saw the return address on the letter you received before you left today."

Understanding dawned on her face. "Yes. I've been invited to attend a parole hearing at the prison."

A hearing. The reason for the invitation dawned on me. The letter had not come to Leah because she was on parole. It was to inform her of a hearing for someone she knew. Shame that I had, however briefly, considered her capable of committing a crime washed through me. Though I didn't know much about prisons or criminals, I did know that when an inmate was being considered for parole, certain people were able to attend. Family members…and victims.

Leah turned abruptly and walked away from the fence. I hesitated. Should I follow her or leave her alone with her thoughts?

No, living alone gave her plenty of time for thinking. I followed.

When I came alongside her, she slowed but didn't stop. We walked down Elias's short driveway, turned onto the street, and headed in the direction of the ceramic shop. The sun had dipped below the horizon, but the clouds overhead still reflected its light in a dazzling display of color.

"I was nineteen when it happened." She spoke without turning her head, her gaze fixed on the sunset. "My friend and I were walking to the store to get an ice-cream cone. A car stopped, and the man inside offered us a ride." We covered a few steps. "Naturally, we said no, and he drove off. But on the way home, he came back. There was a stretch of road that was pretty deserted, and I think he must have been waiting for us to get there. He stopped his car beside us, in the middle of the street."

I did not look directly at her but watched from the corner of my eye. Her hands became fists at her sides. A terrible suspicion crept over me about what happened next. Should I stop her, tell her she didn't have to relive that moment for my benefit? But I knew, as few else do, that she had already relived it a million times in the years since. I remained silent and let her talk.

"We should have run. I don't know why we didn't. Too surprised, I guess. He grabbed Moriah and shoved her in the front seat. I started screaming and lunged toward the car, trying to grab her and pull her out." A bitter laugh escaped her lips. "A lot of good that did. He swung around and I remember thinking, *He's going to hit me.* Then everything went black."

My stomach churned. I could not have managed to eke a sound through my tight throat even if I'd been able to think of something to say.

"When I woke up, I was alone in the backseat of his car. I sat up and saw..."

Her voice squeaked, tight with tears. She stopped on the road, and I faced her then. Her eyes were distant, fixed on the past. I had never seen such torment in anyone's face.

"You do not have to tell me any more," I said softly.

She continued as though I hadn't spoken. "I looked out the window and saw him. He had Moriah pinned on the ground, and she was screaming and struggling. I had to stop him. I looked around for something to use and found a beer bottle on the floor. Before he even knew I was there, I hit him with it. It broke on his head but didn't knock him out." Tears flowed down her cheeks. "He left Moriah and turned on me. He called me…terrible things, and then he took the broken bottle from me."

Her hand rose, and she rubbed a finger down the scar on her cheek.

I closed my eyes to hide from the agony on her face. Against my will, my mind conjured the scene. What kind of man would harm two young girls? Would attack them and cut them? Sickened, I opened my eyes to find Leah's gaze focused on me.

"At least I stopped him from hurting Moriah. He cut me and was about to do it again when she hit him from behind with a log." Her lips twisted into a smirk. "That knocked him out. We left him on the ground and took his car to the hospital. Neither of us had much familiarity with driving, but Moriah had done it once during her brother's *rumspringa*, so she managed to get us away from there. I was bleeding too badly. He'd driven us way out in the country, so it took a while to figure out where we were."

"Did the police find him?" Dumb question. Of course they did. How else would he be in prison?

She nodded. "The hospital called them, and Moriah described where we left him. He wasn't there anymore, but they found him not far away."

We had walked all the way to the ceramic shop. The sun had truly set by then, and darkness cloaked the familiar building.

Leah stopped at the entrance to the empty parking lot, and her shoulders heaved with a silent laugh. "Looks like long walks are the thing to do when you're upset about something. You yesterday and me tonight."

"If only walking would lead us away from the things that trouble us."

"If only," she echoed. "But some things can never be left behind."

The words from a dozen sermons rose to mind. "And yet our Lord would have us live peaceful lives."

The look she gave me could have pierced metal. "Is that supposed to make me feel better?" Her nose curled. "Peaceful lives. How very *Amish* of you."

I could have taken offense at her sneering tone but chose to answer mildly. "I am Amish, as you know."

She planted her hands on her hips, anger showing in her glare. "Do you think Moriah and I should have let that animal attack us without a struggle? That's what the Amish are all about, aren't they? Turning the other cheek. Nonresistance and all that."

The fire with which she spat the words took me by surprise. In the next instant, I realized I should not have been. Another reason for Leah's ongoing bitterness became clear.

"Is that what your district said?" I asked.

"Of course not. Most everyone didn't speak of the incident at all. Like, if they ignored it, it never happened." Her chin shot upward, defiance clear on her face. "I refused to let them ignore me. The bishop and the ministers said I had to forgive him, the man who attacked us." She barked an unpleasant laugh. "Not only that, they advised me not to testify in court about what he had done, and said instead I should pray for him every day."

So that was her sin, the one about which she was unrepentant. She had refused to forgive her attacker, which was one of the basic tenets of our faith. Did not the Lord Himself say if we refuse to forgive another, we will not be forgiven either?

"You went to court anyway."

"Of course I did. I'm glad too. If I hadn't, he would have hurt other girls, and they might not be as fortunate to get away from him as Moriah and I were." Her jaw tightened, and her eyes hardened. "He ruined my life, and I hate him. I will not stand by and do nothing while he gets out on parole, either. I want him to stay in prison where he belongs."

She looked fierce, and yet I saw her chin quiver. The vulnerable young woman was still there, hiding beneath the angry facade, desperately fighting the pain that had been inflicted on her. Could she not see what was so clear to me? That the hatred to which she clung was hurting her even worse than the attack?

Without speaking, we turned toward Elias's house and began the trek back. Leah walked with a quick, determined step, seemingly as eager to be done with this conversation as I was.

A question still remained unanswered. If I didn't ask it now, I might never find her in a mood to talk about her traumatic past again.

"What of Moriah? Did she go to court with you?"

Scorn gave an acid edge to her tone. "Of course not. She obeyed the bishop like a good little Amish girl. She forgave our attacker. Then she went to the classes and was baptized a few months later." Her gaze slid sideways to meet mine for a moment. "When I went *Englisch,* Moriah even came on one of the visits to try to convince me to come home. Wrote letters too. In fact, she's still writing letters. Last month she told me she had corresponded with *him*—" The venom in her voice left no doubt as to who she meant. "—and told him she had forgiven him long ago. She urged me to do the same. And then do you know what she did?" I was not given a chance to answer. "She told him to write to me!"

The source of the upsetting letter she received last week became clear. "She gave him your address?"

Anger gave her feet speed, and though my legs were longer, I almost had to trot to keep pace with her.

"No, she's not that stupid. He sent a letter to the victim advocate office, and they forwarded it. They put his name on the return address, which is how I knew to tear it up without reading it. That's another reason I'm going to Ohio. I want to make sure they *never* send me anything from him again."

She could not even read a letter from her attacker, and yet she would face him in a hearing? And alone?

I asked my question as gently as I could. "Are you sure it is wise to go to this hearing?"

She looked at me as though I'd lost my mind. "I'm not going to the hearing. I never want to lay eyes on that animal again. Besides, the hearing isn't until next month. The victim advocate's office is going to arrange for me to meet with the parole board on Friday. I can give them my opinion in advance."

I didn't point out that she could probably accomplish both goals over the phone or by writing a letter. No doubt Elias had already tried to convince her not to go and failed.

We didn't speak again until we reached Elias's house. When I would have gone inside, she stopped me.

"Listen, I'm sorry if I offended you with my comments about the Amish." She hung her head. "I guess I figured you'd understand after all the stuff that happened with Robbie yesterday."

The words pierced my ears like darts. Yes, our situations were similar, but to liken Robbie to the horrible man who had inflicted such cruelty on two helpless teenagers felt…wrong. I wasn't prepared to defend Robbie, but the comparison jarred me.

"I-I was not offended," I managed to reply. "I am honored you trust me enough to speak your mind."

A smile softened her eyes. "I do trust you, Seth. Thank you for understanding."

When she went inside, I hung back. I needed a moment to clear my thoughts. Were we alike, Leah and I? Though our situations were different, we shared the experience of a traumatic past. Was she, too, suffering from post-traumatic stress disorder? Sam would probably say yes. She'd spoken before of seeing many counselors, who had no doubt told her the same thing. But we had followed different paths as a result of the devastation that occurred to us. She chose to reject her faith, the very thing that could provide the peace God promised those who followed Him. While I had chosen to stay, to embrace the hope afforded by serving God through our Plain lifestyle.

Or had I?

Twenty-Two

Leah came to the shop on Thursday long enough to show Elias and me how to complete the daily bank deposit. She looked very *Englisch* today, with her hair once again hanging loose, and wearing jeans and a T-shirt. The atmosphere between us was strained. I knew the fault lay with me, and more than once I saw her watching me with unspoken questions in her eyes. We had confided in one another, and that should have drawn us closer. Instead, I had tossed most of the night on my bed, unable to sleep, plagued by questions I didn't want to answer.

Would unforgiveness eat at my soul until one day I, too, became bitter and sour? Was I already that way and didn't recognize the fact? Were the uncontrollable fits of rage a result of unforgiveness or PTSD—or maybe both?

More than that, my feelings for Leah could no longer be denied. She had opened her life to me and shared a pain I knew she shared with few. I ached for her and wanted her to be happy. Not just that, but I longed to be the one to restore her happiness. To be the cause of her happiness.

When I courted Rachel, I had experienced all of the giddy, palm-sweating emotions of youthful love. Then I met Hannah, and our love had a dreamlike quality. To think that someone so beautiful and kind wanted to share a life with me was almost more than I could believe. My grief over losing Rachel lay like an open wound in my soul, and *Gott* had sent Hannah to heal me. How could I not be grateful? I'd been granted another chance at life.

I felt neither of those things for Leah. Our relationship had nothing to do with physical attraction, though I had no doubt if I let my guard down for an instant, that aspect would come. Through the night, whenever my eyes closed, I envisioned a different aspect of the woman I'd come to know over the past few months. I pictured Leah scornful and smirking. Soft and smiling. Blue eyes dark as rain clouds, telling me how her district would not eat with her. Thoughtful after she read my letter to Laura King. Angry on my behalf when I told her of Robbie's confession. The multiple facets of Leah haunted me through the long night.

Never before had anyone opened their soul to me as she had done. What she revealed to me was painful. She'd shown me a heart every bit as tormented as my own. And never before had anyone understood me so thoroughly. If she were Amish...

That *if* lay at the foundation of my distress. If Leah were Amish, I could love her. And if I did, she would die, as the others I loved had done.

All of that I tried to put out of my mind while she showed us where she kept the banking ledger.

When she felt that we had been thoroughly trained—which came near to offending me, as though she thought me too dim-witted to fill out a bank deposit slip—she picked up her car keys from the counter.

"I'll be back on Sunday. If you have any questions in the meantime, call my cell. Leave a message if I don't answer, and I'll call you back."

"*Ya,* we will." Elias wore his concern for his granddaughter heavily this morning. From the redness of his eyes, I assumed he had not slept much either. "You will call here when you get to Youngstown, so we know you are safe?"

She gave him a tender smile. "Don't worry, *Daadi.* It's less than five hours' drive. I'll be fine."

He fidgeted with the waistband of his trousers, his deep frown giving him an older appearance than I'd yet seen. "You are sure you will not stay with Amos and Beulah? They would be happy to have you."

Now she rolled her eyes upward, but the kind smile remained in place. "Sugarcreek is almost a hundred miles from Youngstown. Besides, I don't want to cause them any trouble. If I stay with them, you know how the rest of the family will act." He opened his mouth to protest, but she held up a hand to stop him. "I made a reservation at a nice hotel, very safe and secure. And yes, I will call when I get there."

She wrapped him in a hug, and I heard her whisper, "*Ich liebe dich, Daadi.*"

The endearment, especially uttered in Pennsylvania Dutch, moved me nearly as much as it did Elias. He returned her embrace, which was unusual in front of an outsider. Either his concern for his *kinskind* was so powerful that he did not care that I saw, or he had accepted me as part of his family. Either way, my vision blurred, and I turned away, blinking hard to clear my eyes.

Then she stood before me. For one horrifying moment, I thought she might embrace me as well.

"Would you walk with me to the car, Seth? There's something I'd like to ask you."

What could I do but nod and follow her outside?

We reached her car, but instead of opening the door, she turned and leaned against it, her gaze searching my face.

"I made you mad last night with my jabs at the Amish, didn't I?"

I shook my head and hurried to say, "No, you did not."

Her head tilted sideways. "Then why are you so distant today? You've barely looked at me all morning."

What could I say? *Thoughts of you robbed me of sleep all night.* That would be the truth. Instead, I rubbed at my eyes. "I am sorry. I didn't sleep well." *Or at all.*

For a moment she studied me. Then she heaved a breathy laugh. "Neither did I. We talked about some pretty heavy stuff, huh?"

With that I could heartily agree. "*Ya,* some heavy stuff."

Her gaze traveled to the store behind me. "I'm glad they have you, Seth. Watch out for them while I'm gone, okay?"

With a solemn nod, I said, "I will."

She turned and opened the car door but then paused. Eyes lowered, she said, "Say a prayer for me, would you? I have a feeling this isn't going to be easy."

At the sight of her bowed head, her hair falling forward to hide her face, something in my chest twisted. The urge to pull her into an embrace, much as she had just done to Elias, was so strong I fought to keep my arms at my sides.

"*Ya,*" I promised. "I will pray for you."

The flash of a smile was the only response I received. Then she slid into the car and shut the door.

I didn't move until her car had driven out of sight.

※

Without Leah, a pall hung over the shop. Though she called several times to assure us that she was safe and well, Elias continued to wear a worried frown and worked in silence. He turned out piece after piece, beautifully crafted tableware that I fired and glazed in a variety of hues. When she returned, Leah would be thrilled with the amount of new stock for our shelves.

When she returned…

I managed the showroom, talked with the customers, dusted the shelves, handled the sales, and tried not to think about Leah's return on Sunday. Though I missed her, in a way her absence relieved me. I hadn't realized how often I spoke with her during the day, or how I looked forward to the curtain parting and her peeking through to see how our work progressed. How I gauged her mood by her hair and her expression, and how her attitude affected my own. The realization disturbed me. An Amish man should not be so preoccupied with an *Englisch* girl.

Nor could I banish thoughts of Robbie. Whenever I absently tried to use my right hand or bumped it against the counter, anger burned in my chest. Thoughts of his deceit obsessed me, and when I became aware of my own scowl, I was reminded again of Leah.

The circling of thoughts such as those could drive a man crazy.

That Sunday was not a church day. At the breakfast table, I told Elias and Lily, "I am going to visit my family today. I might be late, so don't hold dinner for me."

Lily paused in the act of removing an empty platter from the table. "Leah will be home by then. I am cooking her favorite. Chicken and dumplings."

Elias, whose mood was much improved today with Leah's impending return, spoke in something close to his cheerful self. "You've never tasted anything like my Lily's chicken and dumplings."

Laughing, I told her, "If I am not back, will you save a dumpling or two for me?"

When she promised, I excused myself from the table to hitch Orion to the buggy.

The drive to Upper Leacock was not a pleasant one. Though I had prayed much of the night, I could find no peace concerning my feelings for Leah or the anger that continued to plague me over Robbie's actions and subsequent betrayal. *Die Bibel* urged me to forgive. Our *Confession of Faith* instructed us to "bring forth fruits meet for repentance" because it is only through repentance and forgiveness that a man will find God's peace. I knew the command and the reason for it. But how could I conquer feelings over which I had no control?

Instead of going to my family's house, I steered Orion to another farm. When I spied Bishop Beiler's buggy parked in front of his barn, I breathed a relieved sigh. Because it was not a church Sunday, he was home. I left Orion near the barn and approached the house. Before my foot touched the porch step, the door opened.

"Seth!" The bishop greeted me with a wide smile. "Welcome. Come inside." He turned his head and spoke over his shoulder. "Sarah, Seth Hostetler is here. Have we something to offer him?"

Sarah appeared at his side holding their young grandson on her hip, while another child hugged her leg. She also beamed at me. "*Ya*, I have cinnamon cake and will make coffee."

Manners dictated that I should accept the offer of hospitality, but my stomach churned with the reason for my visit. I held up a hand. "*Danke,* but I ate a large breakfast." I peered at the bishop. "I do not wish to intrude on your Sunday, but I would like to talk with you."

"It is no intrusion." With a glance at his wife, who nodded and retreated into the house, he stepped outside. "The weather is nice. We can sit outside where it is quiet, *ya*?"

I followed him around the side of the house, where two benches sat angled in the grass, surrounded by a garden blooming with flowers. A bird feeder hung from a post nearby, swaying gently from the activity of a pair of feasting robins. The bishop gestured for me to sit on one of the benches, and he took the other.

"What have you done to your hand?" He nodded toward the splint.

"I broke it." I did not elaborate. Now that we sat face-to-face, nerves threatened to rob me of words. How should I begin? "I will not keep you long from your family."

He waved a hand in dismissal. "I have plenty of time for those who want to talk to their bishop."

"I am no longer in your district," I reminded him.

"I have known you since you were born, Seth. You will always be a sheep of my flock no matter where you live." He rested an arm across the back of his bench. "Have you done as I requested and called the Mennonite counselor?"

My lips tightened at the mention of Sam, the unethical counselor. "I have met with him twice. That is partly why I am here. He is not a *gut* therapist."

His expression became inquisitive, but he made no reply.

I could not filter the anger from my voice as I described the encounter with Robbie in Sam's office, and then the next therapy session. I went on to describe Robbie's confession. Sometime during my tirade I launched myself from the bench, frightening away the robins, and began to pace in front of Bishop Beiler. My volume rose until I was nearly shouting.

When I reached the end of the story, where I stormed away from the sobbing young man, I fell silent. The bishop's expression had remained attentive, though it had grown more somber as I talked.

He spoke in a quiet voice. "Is that when you broke your hand?"

I had forgotten to mention that part. I ducked my head. "*Ya.* I punched the car window."

The confession of yet another display of temper brought an assault of shame. I returned to the bench, propped my elbows on my thighs, and dropped my head into my hands. "After we visited Laura King, you told me that such anger is not pleasing to God."

"That is still true today."

"I know." My head snapped up, frustration again giving my words volume. "But what am I to do with an emotion I cannot control?"

He replied mildly. "What did the counselor say?"

"He spoke of the power of forgiveness, and said forgiveness is not a feeling. But I am not going back there. He is more concerned with Robbie's well-being than mine."

"Why do you say that?"

I set my teeth together. "It's obvious. A friend who has seen many therapists said he should have refused to see me as soon as he realized who I was. He did not."

He fingered his beard for a moment. "Or perhaps he felt he could be of more help to you because he already knew something of your past. As long as he did not share your confidences, or the *Englisch* boy's, I see no unethical act."

"Why did he urge me to forgive the *Englisch* teenagers responsible for the accident on the same day he knew Robbie would confess? That proves he felt more concern for Robbie than me."

The bishop nodded slowly. "That is one conclusion. Another may be that he hoped to prepare you for the coming blow."

That reason had not occurred to me. I would give it thought later, when I could concentrate without anger boiling inside me.

"He is right about forgiveness." Bishop Beiler leaned forward, arms resting on his knees. "About its power to heal, and that it is not a feeling. Forgiveness begins by speaking the words."

"But anger *is* a feeling!" I knew I was shouting again, but I didn't care. "How can I combat a feeling with words only?"

"With prayer, Seth. With much prayer." Compassion softened his features. "Think of the Happening."

The mention sobered me. Every Amish person knew the term referred to an event we did not care to discuss, the time when a disturbed *Englisch* man held Amish girls hostage in a schoolhouse in Nickel Mines and shot them before killing himself. The Happening had taken place not fifteen miles from where we sat.

"You know as well as any that we forgave. Many of us attended the man's funeral and reached out to his family." He held my eyes in a direct gaze. "Do you think the parents of those girls *felt* forgiveness in the first days after the Happening?"

I shook my head. How could they?

"But they forgave anyway because that is what our Lord asks of us. They prayed. And the next day they forgave again, and they prayed again. Every time they felt the anguish of their loss, they forgave again and they prayed again." He shook his head. "Forgiveness is not a wand to wave and make everything right. It is an action that must be blended with prayer, and it must occur over and over."

"And is their anguish gone, after more than ten years of forgiving and praying?" I sounded like Leah at her most bitter.

He did not take offense but answered truthfully. "Probably not, but they have something better." He straightened. "They have the peace that only comes from living a life of obedience to *Gott*."

The idea of forgiving Robbie soured my stomach. I slumped forward. "I am not as good as those parents. I cannot forgive the boy who killed my Hannah. The words would choke me."

"Do not underestimate our *Gott*, Seth. When He commands us to do a hard thing, He also gives us the ability to accomplish it." When I did not reply, he continued. "I have a feeling that forgiving the boy is not the most difficult thing *Gott* would have you do. There is someone else you need to forgive."

I looked up to find him watching me closely. "Who?"

He smiled and said softly, "He will tell you when the time is right."

Bishop Beiler stood and waited for me to do the same. Apparently, our meeting was over, and I still had not talked to him about Leah. I realized I didn't want to. He had already warned me about developing feelings for her. What else could he say on the matter? Besides, I had enough to ponder from this conversation already.

Twenty-Three

I intended to go to my former home from the Beilers', but with the conversation still playing itself over in my mind, I couldn't inflict my sour mood on my family. Instead, I gave Orion his head. We traveled east on PA-23 toward Lancaster. Perhaps if I paid a visit to the hospital they would allow me to see baby Rachel again. If the sight of that tiny infant did not calm my anger, nothing would.

Best to steer clear of thoughts about forgiving Robbie. I had banished him from my life and preferred to do the same with my thoughts. Instead, I considered the bishop's comments about Sam.

Had he truly acted unethically, as Leah said? During our first session he did offer me the opportunity to see another counselor, and I declined. At the time I liked the fact that he displayed sensitivity to both my feelings and Robbie's. If I had known of Robbie's past, as he did, I would have felt differently. I would have insisted on talking to the other Mennonite therapist—the one I had seen in the waiting room.

Sometimes my ninety-minute buggy ride seemed to last an eternity. Not so today. I was still debating whether or not Sam had acted unethically when I looked up with a start and realized we had entered Eden. The road where the Barkers lived lay less than a mile away. We would pass it in a matter of minutes.

As we approached, I acted on a whim. With pressure on the reins, I turned Orion onto the Barkers' street. The lawns were greener than they had been on my visit at the end of March. Flowers bloomed in many well-tended gardens, and the trees had leafed out. To my left, a handful of golfers took advantage of the sunny afternoon.

Though we rode through pleasant surroundings, pressure built in my chest the closer we got to the Barker home. What was I doing here? To forgive the reckless act that had killed my wife? I was not prepared to speak the words Bishop Beiler urged. I did not mean them, would never mean them, so to speak them would be a lie.

Yet when we approached the house, I steered Orion into the circular driveway. Perhaps if I confronted him again, I could at least put to rest my questions about Sam. I saw no evidence of Robbie's red car, but the doors were closed on the huge garage.

Invisible bands tightened around my chest, and blood pounded in my ears. I couldn't do this. I flicked the reins, directing Orion to continue all the way around the circle and take me away from this place.

The double front doors opened, and Amanda stepped onto the porch. Our eyes met, and then her expression crumpled into tears. When she began descending the steps toward me, what could I do? Drive away and leave her crying in the yard? I pulled the reins and applied the brake, and Orion came to a halt.

Amanda approached the buggy and stood there, her arms wrapped around her middle and tears streaming down her face. Though I could barely force breath into my lungs, I opened the door and climbed down.

"Oh, Seth." The pain in her tone moved me, but I ignored a wave of pity. "I don't know why you're here, but I want to apologize. I should have told you that night you came to dinner." She swallowed, shaking her head. "I-I just couldn't. It needed to come from Robbie."

I nodded agreement but remained silent.

"I know how upset you are. Robbie told me about the other day. I wish I could tell you how sorry I am." She hugged her waist tighter, choking back a sob. "But please don't think I was trying to buy forgiveness for my son. Every piece I bought was because I loved it. And I've sent my friends there because your work is beautiful and unique."

My words, shouted in anger, came back to me. I'd forgotten the accusation. Looking at her now, crying in front of me, I believed her.

"I am sorry for saying that. I shouldn't have insulted your kindness. I was...upset."

"You had every right to be." She wiped her eyes, leaving black makeup smeared across her face. "Did you come to talk to Robbie?" Hope radiated from the face turned up to mine.

"I..." My throat closed. "I do not know why I am here."

"Please." She placed both hands on my arm. "I am so worried about him. He's improved so much since he started driving for you, but now..." She glanced over her shoulder, and lowered her voice. "He said yesterday he didn't deserve to live. We're afraid to leave him alone."

I couldn't have been more shocked if she had slapped me. Would Robbie consider harming himself? The image of him as I'd seen him last rose in my mind's eye. The anguish of his sobs, his pleading as I stomped away. Yes, a tormented person might wish to take his own life. As angry as I was with him, I would never wish that. What purpose would Robbie's death serve? It wouldn't bring back Hannah but would only add another tragedy to the already unbearable weight of her death.

"I'll talk to him." Though what I would say, or how I would speak through the tightness of my throat, I didn't know.

A fresh wave of tears ran down her face. "Thank you. He's inside."

She already had a grip on my arm, and now she tugged me toward the house. A man stood in the open doorway. How long had he been watching us?

Amanda didn't release my arm until I stood before him. "Seth, this is my husband, Michael."

I shook the hand he extended.

"I'm glad to finally meet you." He searched my face. "Though I'm sorrier for the circumstances than I can say. Please come inside."

Stepping aside, he gestured for me to precede him into the house.

"Should we do something for your horse?" From the perplexed

expression on Amanda's face as she stared at Orion, I guessed she didn't often have Amish visitors.

I glanced at him standing calmly, no doubt tired from the trip. There was no place to tether him, and though I knew he would wait for me, I spared a hope that he would not eat their lawn. "He would appreciate a bucket of water if you have one."

"I'll take care of that." Michael left and headed around the side of the house.

I followed Amanda inside and noted in passing that my vase now stood in the center of the glass dining table.

"Robbie is upstairs in his bedroom," she explained as she led me to the large great room where we had eaten dinner. "Have a seat and I'll get him."

When she left, I stood in the center of the room. This place did nothing to put me at ease, with its *Englisch* furnishings and photographs nearly covering one wall. How could people find the mishmash of items comfortable? Objects covered the surface of every table—remote control units and magazines and figurines. A large cabinet in the corner held more things—painted plates and fancy statuettes and gleaming crystal miniatures. I selected a chair covered in deep red leather and perched on the edge, the knots in my stomach so tight I feared they might never untangle.

I hadn't noticed the wall of photos on my last visit. A glance revealed Robbie at various stages of his life—a baby with a thick shock of dark hair sitting in the center of a blanket, a skinny boy smiling with a gaptoothed grin, a young man who looked more like the one I knew, dressed in a suit and tie.

A huge clock on the wall ticked in the silence, and the sound grated across my nerves. What was taking so long? Perhaps Robbie no longer wished to see me. The idea ignited the familiar anger. What right had he to refuse a visit from me? I had to exert an effort not to leave the house.

The click of Amanda's heels descending the stairs reached me, though I heard nothing else. Was she returning to tell me Robbie would not come down?

Then he entered the room behind his mother, barefoot. At first sight of the boy, I rose from my chair, my gaze glued on him. The change in the past five days shocked me. I'd wondered on Tuesday if he'd lost weight; today I was sure of it. His cheeks appeared sunken, his jaw sharply angled and clearly visible beneath a thin layer of skin. Beneath a thin T-shirt, his collarbones protruded sharply. His hair had not been combed in several days, I suspected. He watched me through dull eyes.

No wonder the Barkers were worried about their son.

Amanda gave us both a nervous smile. "Can I get you something to drink? Water, or a Dr Pepper?"

Robbie made no response, as if he had not heard the question. He stood as still as one of the statues in the corner cabinet, his stare fixed on me.

"No, thank you," I told Amanda.

"Okay. Well, then. I'll step outside and help Mike with that water for your horse."

When she'd gone, neither of us moved. The clock marked the passing of many seconds.

Finally, when I could no longer stand the silence, I voiced the thought at the front of my mind. "You look terrible."

Surprise flashed onto his face, replaced by a bitter scowl. "Yeah, well at least my outsides match my insides."

When another silence threatened, I said, "I would like to sit."

He dropped onto the sofa, also of red leather, while I returned to my chair.

"Did you do that on my car window?" He pointed toward my splinted hand.

"*Ya.*" I considered apologizing for breaking his window but decided against it. I was not ready to apologize to this young man for losing my temper. Maybe I never would be.

"Why are you here?" He sat rigid, his arms stiff at his sides. "Do you want to break the other windows? You can, you know. Or my jaw, if you want." He gulped several times. "You have the right."

I drew in a deep breath against the anger that threatened to darken my vision. How dare he make a flippant comment? Though when I looked closer, I knew he meant the words literally.

I didn't deny his claim. In his world, an injury deserved retribution. But not in my world.

"I don't want to break your windows or your jaw. I want to talk about the day my Hannah died."

He couldn't meet my gaze. "I've already told you what happened. It was totally my fault. I..." More gulping. "I killed her."

Though the words shot through me like a flaming arrow, I kept my tone even. "And afterward you felt remorse."

"Well, yeah. Wouldn't you?" He glanced up for a second.

"What of your friend? The one who shouted out the window?"

"Justin?" His lip curled. "He didn't feel remorse if that's what you're asking. He said the whole thing was an accident, and we didn't want any-body to die, so we shouldn't feel guilty." He snorted. "He's at Penn State this year, but I heard he's about to flunk out because he's spending too much time partying and not enough studying."

So the other boy took no responsibility. He continued with his wild ways.

Robbie straightened, planted his feet on the floor, and clasped his hands between his knees. He looked me directly in the eye. "We should have gone to the police and reported what happened. I've almost done it, like, a million times. At first nobody knew except me and Justin. I fig-ured you told the police what happened, and they were probably look-ing for an old green Chevy. For weeks I expected the cops to show up at the door and arrest me."

I shook my head. "The police came, but no one told them the car was a Chevy. I don't know much about car models."

"I'll still confess if you want me to." An earnest gaze fixed on me. "I don't know what they'd do to me, but I'll go to jail if that's what you want."

"What good would that do? Would that bring my Hannah back?" When he would look away, I ducked my head to hold his eye. "Amish believe in the justice of God more than the justice of man."

"Yeah, that's what Sam said too."

Now that he had brought up the counselor, I could ask a question that had disturbed me since my talk with the bishop. "Did Sam know you planned to confess to me that day?"

"No. I didn't know myself."

I sat back. So my assumption that Sam urged me to forgive Robbie because he knew what was coming was not correct. Did that mean I was wrong about Sam's intentions toward me as well?

Robbie kept talking. "I've been practicing with Sam for months. You know, planning out what to say when the right time came. But I just couldn't do it anymore, you know? Drive you around, pretending like that day never happened. It was okay when I first started, and you were just an Amish dude I'd hurt. But then…then I started thinking of you as a friend. It was, like, eating at me. I had to get it out in the open."

"Did Sam suggest that you drive me?"

"Are you kidding? He tried to talk me out of it." He lunged off the sofa and paced to the window. "I've been going to him for months, every week, and all we do is talk. I was sick of talking. It wasn't getting me anywhere, you know? And for a while I thought I was right. Helping you made me feel better. My parents understood. They were proud of me for trying to make up for my mistake, even if it was just a little." He faced me. "I mean, I know nothing can make up for causing that accident. But I had to do something, didn't I?" His shoulders slumped. "Turns out Sam was right. I was trying to make myself feel better, but I wasn't being straight with you, so I made everything worse."

He returned to his seat, folded his arms, and buried his face. His words fanned the ever-present fury in my soul. I wanted to shout at him, *Yes, you did make everything worse!* To twist the knife of guilt so he would know the pain his actions had caused.

Then I noticed his heaving shoulders. Silent sobs wracked his too-thin body. These were tears from an aching heart. I recognized them because I'd shed so many myself.

In an instant, my fiery rage receded, doused by a wave of pity so strong tears sprang into my eyes. Yes, I had suffered deeply from my loss. But watching Robbie, I knew his suffering went just as deep. Three lives had ended that terrible day—Hannah's, mine, and Robbie's. Was that not enough?

I left my chair and sat on the couch beside him. Were I *Englisch,* I would have laid a comforting hand on his heaving back. Instead, I sat quietly, lending the comfort of my presence while his sorrow played out. For a long while I doubted he knew I was there, but gradually the wrenching sobs slowed.

"Robbie." He looked up, and the agony in his eyes twisted my heart. "You were wrong to deceive me, but you meant it kindly."

His head shook violently. "Th-that doesn't m-make it right."

"No, it does not." I drew a deep breath, my chest expanding to its full extent while I gathered strength to speak the words I'd never thought to say. "But I…I forgive you."

They came out much easier than expected. In fact, as they left my body, I felt an unexpected lightness, as if a weight had begun to lift.

He still shook his head, so I spoke again, this time more freely. "I forgive you."

Utter disbelief showed on his face. "But, Seth, I *killed* your wife. I lied to you. I hurt you. You can't forgive me. I don't deserve it."

What answer could I give? What he said was true. A teaching from *die Bibel* came to mind.

"If a man receives only what he deserves, we are all doomed. Instead, we forgive each other, and God forgives us." Looking into those tortured, red-rimmed eyes, I realized another truth that must be spoken. "The hardest part of all, I think, is that we must forgive ourselves, as God forgives."

He gulped. "How can I ever make it up to you, Seth?"

"Do you think driving me to town will erase my grief?" The familiar anger threatened to flicker. With an effort, I tamped it down. Bishop Beiler's wisdom returned to me. Forgiveness was not a wand to be waved. It was an act to be done day after day. Sometimes, like now, minute after minute. I said it again. "I forgive you. That is enough. You do not have to do penance anymore, Robbie. Forgive yourself and go on with your life."

The impact of the words I'd just spoken struck me. Suddenly, I knew what the bishop meant. Forgiving Robbie was not the hardest task I had before me.

An urgency to leave overtook me. I needed to be alone, to think and to pray. I rose, and Robbie did as well. We stood awkwardly a moment, and then he did something very *Englisch*. He threw his arms around me.

"Thank you, Seth. I'm a lousy friend, but you're a good guy."

What could I do? Stand there frozen with my arms at my sides while this suffering boy expressed friendship? I returned his embrace.

"I would rather have a lousy friend than none at all." I pulled back and laughed to cover my embarrassment at the physical display. "And to prove that I am still your friend, I will ask Lily Beachy to cook for you a *schnitz* pie, and I want you to eat every bite. You are too thin."

We left the house to find Michael and Amanda sitting on the front porch, watching Orion munch happily on their lush green lawn.

Michael waved aside my apology. "Don't worry about it. Who cares about a little grass?"

Amanda studied her son's face, her expression anxious. She offered me a tentative smile. When I returned it, tension wilted from her posture.

Though they urged me to stay for dinner, I made my excuses and climbed into my buggy. As I pulled out of their driveway, I looked back. The three of them stood clustered together, heads bowed, arms around each other.

I had much to consider during the ride home. Seeing Robbie's agonized guilt brought my own into sharp focus. Forgiving him had taken an effort, but once done, I had proved the bishop's wisdom true. A peace I had not felt in more than a year had descended on me. Perhaps I would again fight anger in the coming days, but *Gott* truly had given me the ability to do what I had not thought possible.

But that peace was not enough. Guilt still ate at me. So many regrets plagued me. My sins of inaction that resulted in Rachel's death. My indulgence of Hannah in buying Lars, and my reactions to the horse's skittishness that resulted in her death. How could I forgive myself for those? But now that I had tasted the peace that comes from forgiving, I hungered for more. As the bishop said, it would take many times of saying the words, and many hours of prayer.

I set about the task that very moment.

⁂

I did not visit my family but instead returned home to the Beachys'. Though the time was not yet three o'clock, Leah's car sat in the driveway. I unhitched Orion and brushed him down after his exertion, keeping a close eye on the door in hopes that she would come outside and tell me about her trip. When my horse had been safely returned to his pasture, I went inside.

The aroma of roasting chicken set my stomach to rumbling. Breakfast had been a long time past, and I hadn't stopped for lunch.

Lily turned from the stove, her expression happy. "You are home in time for dinner!"

Seated at the kitchen table with the Bible open before him, Elias awarded me a grin. "I knew you could not resist my Lily's dumplings."

At the counter mixing dough in a large earthenware bowl, Leah glanced up at me. "Good call, Seth. You'll love them."

A smile flashed onto her face, strained and tight, before she returned to her work. I looked at Elias, my eyebrows arched. He gave a quick shrug and a slight shake of his head. Though I knew he was relieved to have Leah safely back, the worried lines had not left his brow. Had things not gone well in Youngstown?

Lily seemed determined to force a cheerful atmosphere. "How is your family? And what news of the precious *boppli*?"

I pulled out a chair and sat. "I didn't visit my family as I intended. Instead, I had a matter to discuss with Bishop Beiler."

Though interest appeared on my teacher's face, he didn't say anything. Nor did Lily, though she looked as if the effort of biting back a dozen questions was almost more than she could handle. Leah did not even turn from her bowl but maintained her stiff posture.

"I was going to visit the *boppli* at the hospital," I told Lily, "but instead I stopped in Eden to see Robbie Barker."

At that, Leah jerked around and fixed wide eyes on me.

I hadn't discussed Robbie's revelation with Elias, so he merely nodded and asked, "We have not seen much of the boy since you bought your buggy. How is he?"

"He is…" How to answer truthfully? Especially with Leah's openly curious stare fixed on me. "…not *gut*."

"That is sad." Lily opened the oven door and peered inside. "Is he sick?"

An image of the hollow-faced young man loomed in my mind. "*Ya*, he has been sick. But I think my visit cheered him."

"*Das gut*." She pulled a tray of chicken from the oven and set it on top of the stove. "Leah, fetch for me a fork, please."

Leah did, though she kept a hard stare fixed on me. Mumbling something about her car, she hurried from the kitchen. We heard the front door slam a second later. Lily and Elias looked after her, their expressions stunned.

"What happened in Youngstown?" I asked.

Elias shook his head. "She has not said."

"Go after her, Seth," Lily said. "You are her friend. Maybe she will talk to you."

From the hard glare she had given me before she left the room, I doubted it. But I rose from the table and followed her outside.

I found her standing at the fence, rubbing Orion's neck. She didn't turn, though I was sure she heard me approach.

"You forgave him." Her voice was flat. "You talked to your bishop, who told you to forgive him, and then you went and did it."

"*Ya*. I did."

She jerked her head toward me, her glare piercing. "He lied to you and pretended to be your friend." Her voice came out in a hiss. "He killed your wife."

I winced at the sharpness of the words. "That is true. And the guilt has eaten him like a cancer from the inside."

"Good!" At her shout, Orion started and then retreated to the center of the pasture. "He ought to feel guilty. And you have every right to be furious with him."

"*Ya,* I do have the right," I said softly. "But to what end? His mother said he has talked of taking his own life. Would another tragedy make the first one easier to bear?"

She bit her lip, her brow wrinkled. I knew she had been fond of Robbie, no matter how angry with him she was on my behalf.

"I would hate to see that," she admitted. "But he still ought to pay for what he's done."

"He has paid." My firm tone did not appear to convince her. "By forgiving, I have not only freed him but freed something in myself."

Now she sneered. "How very *Amish* of you."

She climbed up on the bottom rung of the fence and hung her arms over the top. Probably sensing her mood, Orion kept his distance, his stance cautious as he watched her.

I decided to ignore the comment she obviously intended as an insult and turned the conversation. "How did your meeting go?"

"Fine." She clipped the word short.

"Hmm." I rested one arm across the top fence plank, my body turned toward her. "You do not act as though it was fine."

"He's not getting out on parole, and that's what I wanted."

There was more to the story. I knew that from her rigid posture and the nervous tapping of one toe against the fence plank.

"So your testimony convinced them?"

She gave a bitter laugh. "Actually, no. Turns out they were going to deny his parole anyway, so it was a wasted trip."

"Then why are you unhappy?"

For a long moment I thought she might not answer. Then she drew a shuddering breath. "Because of the reason he's being kept in prison. Turns out Moriah and I weren't the first girls he attacked. After the trial where I testified, others read about it in the newspaper and came forward. He's been convicted of two more counts of sexual assault." She turned her head toward me. "I was trying to keep him in prison so nobody else would suffer, but they already had."

I didn't understand. "But you stopped him from harming others. If you hadn't testified against him, he would have been free to continue his attacks."

She turned fully toward me then. "Don't you understand? Those two girls were *Englisch*. How many Amish girls has he assaulted and got away with it because they said nothing?" Her chest heaved, and her face flushed red. "They acted like Moriah, like good Amish girls, and forgave him. And now they're living with the memories, tortured with flashbacks, and—"

She flung herself away from the fence and ran toward the shed, where she rested her arms against the side and buried her face in them. The posture was so like Robbie's earlier that I ached for the agony she must feel.

I wanted to point out that she did not know if her suspicions were true. She did not know if the man had committed any other attacks, and therefore she was torturing herself with something that might not have happened. But how could I reason against a fear that could never be proved? I could only speak of what I knew to be true.

I went to her side. "You are wrong, you know."

Her head jerked up. "About what?"

"If he did attack other Amish girls, and if they have truly forgiven him, then they are not tortured. *Gott* promises peace to those who follow Him."

"Oh, please!" She glared at me. "Don't you dare preach the Bible to me, Seth Hostetler. You don't know anything about me or what I'm going through."

"No, but I know what I have gone through." I held her gaze, brittle as it was. "I have forgiven, and I have felt God's peace."

"You know what?" She jerked away from the shed and drew near to me, fury in the face that hovered inches from mine. "You make me sick. You're as bad as Robbie. You wormed your way into my family, the only people who love me and accept me. You pretended to understand, to be my friend. But it was all a lie. You're here to ruin my life by spouting your Amish garbage at me."

If I'd thought before that my temper had been tamed, I was wrong. My pulse pounded, fury roaring in my ears at her unjust accusations.

"Are you so self-centered to think that I work for Elias because of *you?*" I snapped back.

"It doesn't matter why you came. You're here, aren't you?" She waved violently toward the house.

By panting deep gulps of air, I managed to control my tone. "I *am* your friend, Leah, no matter what you think. But if I am ruining your life, I will not stay."

Before she could answer, I spun on my heel and stomped toward the road. Would she follow me? I half expected it, but she did not. I prayed as I walked, a constant stream of pleas to *Gott* for a return of the brief peace I'd received earlier.

Peace did return, and along with it, a decision. The emotions between Leah and me ran too high. They were improper and not pleasing to *Gott.* The best thing I could do was make good on my words to her. I would leave Elias's house and his shop, and return home to my family's farm.

Twenty-Four

My family welcomed me back, as I knew they would. Though there were many unasked questions around the dinner table that night, the children's enthusiasm at *Onkel* Seth's return more than made up for the worried glances from *Mamm* and the others.

"Will you take over the milking again?" Mark asked.

I glanced at Aaron, who shrugged. "I might," I told the boy.

"I will pet Caroline's nose for you," Luke promised.

"That will be a big help."

My farewell to Elias weighed heavily on my heart. He had accepted my explanation that I had mistaken my desire to make pottery my life's work without question, though his sad expression told me he suspected that was not the true reason. Lily had cried openly and begged me to visit often. I did not commit. Leah, who had left the house while I walked off my anger, would not appreciate my presence at her family's table. What her grandparents guessed about her role in my abrupt departure remained unspoken.

After dinner, I left the house under the pretext of checking on my horse. Aaron followed me out and fell into step beside me, the puppy Laura had given us following at our heels.

He wasted no time in coming to the point. "I cannot help but wonder at your decision. Farming has never appealed to you."

I scanned the tobacco field, neat rows of green plants lining the rich soil. "It's not a bad life."

"Hmm."

"I thought of asking if I could build another house beside the *daadi haus*. A small one. It would not take much land."

He clasped his hands behind his back. "You're welcome in the main house. I have told you that. When Becky and Noah leave, we will have more than enough room."

I had no heart for listing the reasons. He would only say I was not underfoot, though I felt differently.

"But if you really want to build a house, Seth, of course you may. Or perhaps you could build a workshop instead."

"A workshop?"

"To make pottery." He looked at me. "You have a gift for the work. Would *Gott* not want you to use such a gift?"

It was an idea worth considering. If I could work the clay, perhaps I would find contentment here, living with my family. I nodded slowly. "I'll pray about it. But tell me, how is baby Rachel?"

He brightened. "*Gut*. She gains weight every day. The doctor thinks we can bring her home next week."

And I would be there to welcome her. The thought lifted my spirits.

When we returned to the house, *Mammi* waited outside. "I would speak with you alone," she told me.

Aaron went in as I eyed her uneasily. The events of the day had left me confused and tired. I didn't relish discussing them with anyone.

She peered up at me. "Something has changed. You are different."

Surprised, I laughed. "I am the same Seth as before, *Mammi*. Your *kinskind*."

But she shook her head. "There is a light in your eye that I have not seen in years. And also a sadness." She narrowed her eyes. "A new one."

Ever the perceptive one, my *grossmammi*. I saw I would not escape this conversation without some sort of explanation. "So much has happened, and I am too tired to tell it all tonight. But I found the boy responsible for the accident that killed Hannah, and I have forgiven him."

The corners of her lips turned upward. "That explains the light." Then she sobered. "And what of the sadness?"

"The decision to leave my work and my teacher was not an easy one." Though certainly true, I didn't feel inclined to offer any further explanation. She waited, clearly expecting me to continue. Instead, I changed the subject. "And what of you? How is the exercise for your heart?"

She allowed herself to be distracted. "Bah! I walk miles and miles, and when I complain about my bad hip, I get no sympathy. The doctor gave me weights to lift, and Joan stands over me, counting to make sure I do exactly the right number. Worse, Saloma and Becky conspire against me in the kitchen." Her features fell. "No more fried chicken or pork chops. Instead, they bake everything. And only a dollop of gravy for my biscuit."

I smiled. "They take good care of you, then."

"Just you wait." She scowled. "They force the whole family to eat this new healthy diet. You'll be sorry you've come home when you see how they ration the bacon in the mornings."

I patted my belly. "It will be good for me. I've enjoyed much rich cooking lately."

We entered the house together, and I looked forward to a pleasant family evening.

I fell back into my old routine with no effort. Little had changed in my absence—a fact I found comforting. True, *Mamm* and *Daed* no longer ate every meal at the big house, but they still spent much of the day with the rest of us, cooking and working and reading as they always had.

Rachel's homecoming was a joyous occasion. I asked Robbie to drive her and Saloma home, and my heart warmed to hear the joy in his voice as he accepted. When they arrived in Amanda's Lexus, the whole family lined up to welcome them. I had two causes for rejoicing that day. First, that my young friend looked healthy and happy, grinning widely as he opened the door and helped Saloma out.

The second was the bundle Saloma carried. Though still the tiniest baby I'd ever seen, she had filled out considerably from the day Leah and I watched her through the nursery window. Holding her became a favorite occupation for all of us, even the children. I relished my time in the rocking chair, gazing down into her perfectly formed features. Leah's words returned to me often. *You're besotted.* I was—and not ashamed of the fact.

My thoughts centered on Leah more often than I wished, and that didn't diminish as the weeks passed. May became June, and still I awoke to find her on my mind. I discussed my distress with no one but Sam, to whom I had returned at Bishop Beiler's urging. Sam listened, ever attentive, but he offered no solution. Because he respected the Plain ways, he knew as well as I that there could never be a relationship between us.

Mamm and I were weeding the garden the day Leah arrived at my house.

"Who is that?" On her knees before the bean plants, *Mamm* straightened and looked over my head.

When I turned and spotted the car rolling down our driveway, my heart stuttered. Mouth dry, I managed to say, "That is Leah, Elias Beachy's granddaughter."

She climbed to her feet. "Then I had best tell Saloma to put on coffee. I wonder if she has any cobbler left from last night." Leaving her kneeling pad on the ground, she left the garden.

I did not move.

Leah's car pulled to a stop, and I heard *Mamm* invite her inside. I couldn't make out the reply, but *Mamm* waved toward me before entering the house. Leah started in my direction, her gaze locking on to mine.

She looked almost Plain today, with her hair pulled back into a proper bun and in a dress that fell below her knees. With the addition of an apron and *kapp,* she could be mistaken for an Amish woman. I drank in the sight of her, glad when I saw the ghost of a smile on her lips instead of a scowl.

"Hello," she said as she drew near.

I don't know what possessed me, but I replied in *Dietsch.* "*Guder mariye.*"

She acknowledged the greeting with a breathy laugh. "If that was to remind me that you're Amish, you shouldn't have bothered." She gestured at my Plain clothing. "You look every bit the part, as always."

Was that a jab at my faith? I detected no sarcasm in her tone, so I decided to take the comment at face value. "*Ya,* well, that is what I am."

Her expression sobered. "I know."

I climbed to my feet and dusted the dirt from my hands. "Your *grooss-seldre* are well?" I almost cringed at my continued use of *Dietsch.* "Your grandparents."

"I know the word. They're fine. They miss you, though."

"And I them."

"I hope it's okay that I came." She half turned toward the house. "Will your family mind?"

Instead of answering, I crossed the rows of carrots and radishes until I stood before her. She raised her chin to look up at me.

"Why did you come, Leah?" When her name left my tongue, my stomach fluttered.

"To talk to you." For a long moment we stared into each other's eyes, but then she looked down. "And to show you something."

I had not noticed until then that she held a folded paper in her hand. I started to reach for it, but she jerked it away.

"First, we talk." Her head turned as she glanced around our yard, but we had no benches or chairs as Bishop Beiler did.

"Would you like to go inside so we can sit?"

She shook her head. "I...I'd rather talk privately."

Was that a tremble in her voice? Could it be that the strong, tough woman before me suffered from an attack of nerves?

Compassion washed over me, and I said in a soft voice, "Follow me."

I took her to the barn and set the milking stool in the center of the open doorway, where we could be seen by anyone looking our way but overheard by no one. Then I upended an empty milk can and perched on it.

Once settled on the stool, she fidgeted with the paper for a moment. "I've thought about you a lot." My pulse sped up. Did I haunt her thoughts, as she did mine? As though she'd startled herself, her gaze flew up to mine. "I mean, about our conversation. The one about forgiveness."

Disappointment stabbed at me, unreasonable though it was. I managed to reply calmly. "What have you thought?"

"Oh, a gazillion things." She heaved a laugh. "First, how infuriating you were. And how you didn't understand anything about what I've been through." The laughter faded. "But then I realized how self-centered that was because you've been through some terrible things too."

"I should not have said that. I lost my temper."

Her gaze flickered upward. "I *am* self-centered, Seth. In so many ways. And once I realized you were right about that, I thought maybe you were right about a few other things too. And…well…"

She extended the paper toward me. I took it and unfolded it. At the top was a name and address at the Ohio State Penitentiary. No salutation or date followed, merely two lines in her neat script.

I forgive you.
Leah Beachy

I refolded the paper and returned it to her. "Will you mail it?"

"I haven't decided." She stood and went to lean against the door frame. "I thought writing it would make me feel better, like you said. Instead, I feel sick. Will that creep think I'm saying what he did is okay?"

"Does it matter what he thinks?"

Her mouth opened to make a quick reply. Then she shook her head. "No. What he thinks doesn't matter at all."

How I wished Bishop Beiler were there. He could speak to these things so much better than I. But she had not come to the bishop. I formed a quick prayer.

"I do not think forgiving means the sin was okay." I spoke slowly, articulating thoughts as they occurred to me. "I think forgiving is what we do when we can no longer stand the pain of not forgiving."

Her head tilted sideways. "That's pretty profound."

Actually, I thought so myself and whispered a prayer of thanks.

"You know what I hate?" She didn't wait for me to answer. "I hate thinking about it all the time. I hate the way that day haunts me, and depresses me, and makes me want to scream. It's like he's still hurting me, you know?"

I said nothing, but my mind was a flurry of prayers. I had no answers for her. Only *Gott* could heal a tortured heart.

She straightened and slapped the letter against the palm of her hand. "Yes. I'm going to mail it." A tense smile curved her lips. "And then I'll probably throw up, but I'm going to mail it."

I couldn't help smiling. "I will pray that you do not throw up, but that you'll find peace instead."

A look of longing settled on her features. "Seth, will you come back? *Daadi* and *Grossmammi* miss you a lot." Her voice became husky. "And so do I."

Which was precisely the reason I could not return. My heart ached so that I feared it might stop beating altogether as I shook my head.

"I cannot," I whispered.

I offered no explanation. Did she guess the reason? That I could not face her every day, listening for her voice, relishing her rare laughter, sharing the companionship of family meals?

If so, she gave no indication other than a nod. Though her eyes were downcast, I saw a tear slide down her cheek in the second before she walked away.

I followed her to the car, where she cleared her throat and spoke without looking up.

"Please tell your family I appreciate the offer of hospitality, but I need to get back to the shop."

My family. They had been unusually absent. Not even the children had come out to see our visitor. Had they sensed our need for a private conversation? I glanced at the house to find four faces watching us through the kitchen window. They quickly drew back.

"I will tell them."

When her car turned onto the road, I returned to the garden. There were weeds to pull. Perhaps ripping them from the ground would help to calm my raging thoughts.

Tweny-Five

*D*ear Leah,

 I carry a burden in my heart, and the peace I've felt since forgiving Robbie is out of reach until I share it. I think you already guess the reason I cannot return to the shop. You and I cannot be friends. It is not proper for an Amish man to have such feelings for an Englisch woman as I have for you.

 There is a deeper reason. I have loved two women in my life, and both have died. I will never marry again. I no longer think that I caused their deaths, though I did for a long time. But I cannot risk another loss. I am certain I would not survive it.

 You once told me if you received a letter like the one I wrote Laura King, you might have returned home. Maybe you did not say that exactly, but I remember your expression. I have tried to think of ways to convince you to return to the Amish. Not because of me, but because I do believe you will be happier living the Plain life you were *raised in. Then I realized that what I said to Laura is as true for you as for her. This is a decision you must make on your own. I will pray that you make the right decision for you.*

    Seth

I read my letter a dozen times by the light of the candle on my bedside table. Would mailing it finally put an end to the longings that plagued me? Just writing the words and laying out the reasons that a relationship between us would never be possible brought me a remnant of the peace I so desperately needed. Every word was true. I *did* want Leah to return to the Amish for her own good. Though she gave every indication of embracing her *Englisch* life, why would she remain fascinated with reading books about the Amish? She told me herself she liked them because they reminded her of her peaceful childhood. I wanted that for her again.

The part about losing my wives…well, that was true too. Though my struggle against the guilt that I was responsible for their deaths continued to be prominent in my daily prayers, I knew I had made the best decisions I could at the time. Would I change them given the choice? Of course. But Leah's words in the barn had resonated in my heart. Dwelling on my past mistakes gave them the power to continue to torture me. I was tired of living a tortured life.

After one final review, I picked up the pen and added a line.

P.S. After I mail this letter, I will probably throw up.

Satisfied, I slid the letter into an envelope, addressed the front, and then blew out my candle.

A tail whipped across my cheek, the sting so sharp even through my beard that I cried out. Mark and Luke, watching me milk Delilah from the safety of the barn doorway, both giggled.

I raised my head from her side and rubbed my cheek. "Do you see why I call her Devilish Delilah?"

At the mention of her name, the cow turned her head to look at me. Was it my imagination, or did a smirk lurk in those chocolate eyes?

The sound of an engine reached me.

"A car is coming," Luke announced.

An *Englisch* visitor? Though an hour of daylight remained, visitors rarely arrived in the evening.

"It's a blue car," Mark added, proud that he knew the color.

My lungs snatched a breath and held it. Though my instinct was to leap up and run to the barn door to see the car, I forced myself to stand calmly, remove the half-full milk pail from beneath Delilah's udder, and set it safely out of reach of her hooves. Only when I had retrieved my hat and placed it on my head did I stride through the straw toward the entrance.

When the boys and I emerged from the barn, Leah was already standing beside her car. She caught sight of me. Even across the distance, her eyes drew mine like magnets.

"Boys, go in the house."

My voice, husky with emotion, must have held enough of a command that they did not argue. The door opened before they reached it, and Saloma appeared to take them inside. Somewhere in the back of my mind I spared a thought of gratitude that she didn't come outside to greet our guest, as manners dictated, but followed her sons into the house and shut the door.

I couldn't take my eyes from Leah as I walked toward her. She again wore the modest dress and had pinned up her hair in the Amish way. Was she here because of my letter, mailed a week ago?

She met me halfway across the distance, halting a few feet in front of me. Her eyes moved as she searched my face, and then her gaze returned to mine.

A smile quirked the corners of her mouth. "*Gut'n owed.*"

She greeted me in *Dietsch*? My surprise must have showed because she laughed. "You didn't expect that, did you?"

My shoulders heaved with an answering laugh. "No, I did not."

Questions spun in my mind. Why would Leah, who scorned all things Amish, speak in our native language? Was she here in response to my letter? A possible answer to both lay at the edges of thought, but I refused to hope it was true.

Instead, I asked the safest question I could. "Elias and Lily are well, I hope?"

"They are, though they still miss you."

"And I still miss them. The business goes well?"

She nodded. "We've sold all of your pieces. You received the check for them?"

"*Ya,* I did."

Meaningless talk. Impatience danced in my stomach. I noticed then that her hands were clasped at her waist, fingers entwined but fidgeting. Was that a display of nerves? The idea gave me the confidence to voice the question that burned to be asked.

"Why have you come, Leah?"

She lowered her gaze. "That was a good letter. Thank you. Or rather—" She flashed a grin up at me. "*Danke.*"

Hope rose in my heart. Another *Dietsch* word could mean only one thing. I could not stop the slow spread of a grin. "You are returning to the Amish."

Her smile nearly blinded me. "I am. I've already met with the bishop, and he'll announce my intentions to the congregation on Sunday. That's why I'm here. I wanted to ask if you will come to church with us. I...I'd like you to be there."

"*Ya,* gladly." My feet threatened to bounce like Mark's and Luke's when they were excited. Leah was coming home! "What made you decide?"

"You, of course."

The impact of her words struck me. Joy drained from me as quickly as it had arisen, and I took a backward step. "A decision as important as this cannot be made for someone else."

"Oh, stop it." A shade of her former scorn surfaced. "I don't mean I'm coming back *for* you but *because* of you. I thought a lot about what you said. And…prayed about it too." She leaned against the car and looked out over the fields beyond our house. "I haven't been happy since I went *Englisch*. A lot of that had to do with forgiving the man who hurt me, but once I mailed that letter I realized there was so much more. I was raised to be Plain. That's where I feel—" She drew in a breath, her gaze focusing once again on me. "That's where I feel the peace you're always talking about. God's peace." A smile once again appeared. "That's so much better than a microwave."

As she spoke, relief flooded me. This was not a decision she had made lightly. She was returning to the Plain life for the right reasons.

"So it's a good thing you moved out of *Daadi's* house…because I moved in today." She patted the hood of her car. "I figured it was only fitting that the last time I drive, I come here."

"I'm glad." Such an understatement for the joy that swelled in my chest.

She cocked her head sideways. "So does this mean we can be friends again?"

I studied her. Did the question hold more meaning than the words implied? I answered cautiously. "*Ya*, we can be friends."

Heaving an exasperated sigh, Leah shoved herself off the hood of the car and planted herself in front of me, hands on her hips. "Seth Hostetler, you listen to me. That whole thing about losing a third wife is just, pardon the pun, *plain* stupid."

My war with anger was far from over, and at her words the familiar spark flared. "My feelings are not stupid."

"Of course they aren't. But some feelings are stronger than others."

How well I knew that.

Even if I'd been able to speak, she didn't give me the chance. "I read your letter over and over, and I know what you didn't say. You love me, but you're afraid you'll be hurt if something happens to me." The scar on her cheek turned pink, and her lips quivered. "Ask your bishop what *die Bibel* has to say about love." She stepped closer, her gaze holding mine. All the sass left her voice, which lowered to a whisper. "It's stronger than fear, Seth. Between the two of us, we can overcome your fear."

Warmth spread from my chest like a wave throughout my body. Was she saying what I thought? "Do you love me?"

Her eyes softened, and tears glistened in them. "Of course I do. Now are you going to kiss me or not?"

I was not sure who kissed who, but in the next moment our mouths met. Emotion jolted through my body as my lips caressed hers, lingering over the place where the scar marred one corner. She would always bear the mark of the tragedy, but only on the outside. God had healed her heart, and though I hardly dared to believe it, that heart beat for me.

The door to the main house burst open, and *Mammi* flew down the porch stairs, waving her arms and shouting. "*Ach! Vas in der velt? Vas duhscht?* Get away!"

At her shouts of *What in the world?* and *What are you doing?* guilt shafted through me, and we jerked apart. My *grossmammi* descended on us like a lion defending her cub. In a flash I knew what had happened. My family, spying through the kitchen window, assumed I was being seduced by an *Englisch* woman. Though I knew *Mammi* would never harm a soul, I stepped in front of Leah to provide a protective shield.

"*Mammi,* it's okay." Grabbing her arms, I gently lowered them and held them at her sides. "This is Leah, the granddaughter of my teacher Elias, who has come to tell me of her decision to return to the Amish."

Outrage drained from her face as understanding dawned. She straightened. "Ah. Well." She stepped back from me and brushed at her apron, and then she sidestepped so she could see Leah. A gleam appeared in her eyes—the same one that I'd seen in *Mamm*'s eyes whenever she mentioned Laura King. "In that case, come inside and be welcome."

From the way her mouth twitched with a smile, Leah recognized the look as well. "Sadly, I must get home. Someone is coming this evening to buy my car." She rested a hand on the hood. "But I would like to extend the invitation to you and your family to visit our church meeting on Sunday, when my bishop will present me to the district. And afterward, my *grossmammi* would be pleased if you will stay and enjoy supper with us."

Mammi smiled. "I will make my pumpkin rolls."

With the twitch of a grin, I told Leah, "You have never tasted anything until you have tasted my *grossmammi's* pumpkin rolls."

We shared a laugh, and then I opened the door for her. The soft touch of her lips still tingled on mine, and I would have kissed her again except *Mammi* did not leave my side. Together, we watched Leah drive away.

As we turned toward the house, she gave a satisfied nod. "I think that girl has a good head on her shoulders."

⁂

My entire family traveled to Strasburg to see Leah presented to her new Amish community. She stood in the front of the room, flanked by the bishop and ministers, a *kapp* covering her hair and a Plain dress falling below her knees. As her bishop announced that she had made her confession and been accepted into the community, such joy swelled in my heart I could barely contain myself.

On my left, Elias wiped a tear from his eye, while on the other side of the room Lily cried openly if quietly.

When the service was over, and we filed out of the house into the bright June sunshine, so many people crowded around Leah to welcome her that I lost sight of her. My family and I stood to one side, waiting for Elias and Lily to lead the procession to their house for the meal.

Sadie tilted her head to look up at Becky. "I ride with *Onkel* Seth?"

"Me too," shouted the twins in unison.

With a knowing glance at me, Becky shook her head. "*Onkel* Seth will have no room in his buggy for nieces and nephews today."

When the last well-wisher drifted away, I approached Leah. "May I drive you home?"

A smile lit her face. "I hoped you would ask."

It was not without a twinge that I helped her climb into my buggy. Would there ever come a time when I no longer had to fight that particular fear? As I climbed up after her, I formed a prayer—the only weapon I had at my disposal. And the best.

Elias went first, and I steered Orion onto the road after his buggy while my family followed behind. How could I not remember another day when I left church with a woman I loved at my side? But I did not have time to think about it, for Leah slid close.

"*Grossmammi* is so excited to have a big family dinner. She has been cooking for days."

I anticipated the meal with pleasure. "I've missed her cooking for sure."

"Well, on Monday you can start enjoying it again."

I had decided to return to my job as Elias's apprentice. "That will make the long drive from home worthwhile."

She pressed closer to my side. "Is that the only worthwhile thing about working with us?"

A teasing response came to mind, but we had a serious matter to discuss. "That is not even the best thing." I looked down at her. "You are."

Leah smoothed her dress. "You know I will take the classes in the fall."

"*Ya,* that is what I heard the bishop say."

"And then I will be truly Amish." She was playing coy, her eyes downcast but with a smile twitching her lips.

I played along. "That is the way it works."

"And then after that…" She let the comment dangle.

After the fall baptism came the wedding season from October through December. Couples to be married generally kept their intention secret until just before their wedding, but that did not mean they didn't select the date far in advance.

Leah gave up the pretense of coyness. She turned on the bench and faced me. "Are you going to make me propose to you, Seth Hostetler?"

I arched my eyebrows. "Do you intend to propose to me?"

"If you don't, then I do."

Leaning forward until we were so close her breath tickled my cheek, I whispered. "I do too."

I covered her lips with a kiss that set my insides buzzing.

EPILOGUE

September, the following year

I stood in the doorway of the hospital room, quiet so my wife would not hear me. Would I ever get enough of watching her? The soft, flickering light from the quilt-patterned candleholder she'd brought from our home gave her skin a warm, glowing appearance that mirrored the warmth in my heart. How beautiful she was, and never more than at this moment as she gazed at the bundle in her arms, murmuring in the tender tones of a mother for her child.

Though I'd made no sound, she looked up. When she caught sight of me, she gave me a smile as bright as sunlight, and for a moment I could not breathe.

"Come here," she whispered. "He is sleeping, and his little mouth is moving as though he's trying to smile."

I entered the room and lowered myself gently to sit on the side of the bed. "Infants less than one day old do not smile," I told her.

"Others may not." Love shone in the eyes she fixed on him. "But ours will be so happy, he will smile all the time, beginning now."

My empty arms itched to hold him, and I reached for him. Leah carefully handed him to me, and I cradled the precious baby. My son. A gift from *Gott,* who had already blessed me abundantly, so much more than I deserved.

May you never be afraid, my son. I formed the blessing in my mind, as a prayer. *May you always be happy. May you live in the peace that comes from the* Gott *who loves you.*

Little Eli's eyelids fluttered, and a soft, breathy coo caressed my ears. His lips, the same shape as the ones I loved to kiss, twitched in his sleep.

"I think you are right," I whispered. "He is smiling."

My son, may you always smile.

Discussion Questions

1. Though Seth has lived in his family home for most of his life, he feels like an "extra." Name several reasons he may harbor these feelings.

2. Seth's family and Amish district believe one year is long enough for him to grieve Hannah's loss. How do they let him know that they believe he has grieved long enough? Do you think there is a specific time period for grief after the loss of a loved one?

3. When Laura King ran away from home, the people in her community wrote many letters to convince her to return to her Plain life. What was different about Seth's letter to her? Can you think of any ways that difference may apply to your life?

4. How is Seth's guilt and grief evident in his everyday life and attitudes?

5. Robbie Barker is also tortured with guilt. How does his reaction to his personal guilt differ from Seth's?

6. In what ways does Seth blame himself for aiding in the

deaths of both Rachel and Hannah? Is his self-recrimination correct? How are his feelings of guilt resolved?

7. What does Seth find so appealing about pottery? Name several ways working with Elias helps Seth heal.

8. What are the sources of Leah's bitterness? If she hadn't moved away from her previous district, do you think she would have eventually returned to a Plain life and her Amish beliefs?

9. Seth describes forgiveness this way: "I think forgiving is what we do when we can no longer stand the pain of not forgiving." Discuss your reaction to that statement.

10. Identify several ways in which the characters in *The Amish Widower* practice forgiveness. In each case, who was affected, and how?

ACKNOWLEDGMENTS

Several years ago I wrote a series called The Amish of Apple Grove (coauthored with Lori Copeland). Those books were set in the Wild West when the Amish weren't the only people who wore long dresses and rode around in wagons, and they were infused with a wacky kind of humor. Writing a serious story about the Amish of today presented an entirely new challenge for me. But I believe that's how the Lord stretches us, by presenting us with challenges and assuring us with an "I'll help you." He most certainly did help me with this book, and I thank Him from the bottom of my heart.

I'm also grateful to a bunch of others, including...

Kathleen Kerr from Harvest House Publishers, who invited me to write this book. Kathleen, you have encouraged me through many books and in so many ways, both professionally and personally, and I thank God for you.

Kim Moore from Harvest House Publishers, who also has helped me through many books. For this one I am so appreciative that she gave me the freedom to write the story I believed in, and worked with me to make it the best it could be. Kim, you are the most awesome cat lady in the world!

Georgia Varozza, an excellent editor who shared her in-depth knowledge of the Pennsylvania Amish culture. Thank you for instructing me in so many subtleties that made this story richer.

The entire team at Harvest House Publishers, far too many to name, who work so hard to release God-honoring books. I'm thrilled to be part of the Harvest House family!

Wendy Lawton from Books & Such Literary Management, my friend and agent, whose advice is based on godly wisdom and a knowledge of the publishing industry that astounds me.

Mindy Starns Clark, for her wonderful book *Plain Answers About the Amish Life*, and for answering my emailed questions quickly and thoroughly. And a special thanks to Mindy and Susan Meissner, the writing team who wrote the first three books in the Men of Lancaster County series. Ladies, well done! I'm honored to have the opportunity to follow your lead with this book.

James Robertson, potter *extraordinaire*, who spent many hours teaching me the basics of throwing pots. James, you were my Elias during the research for this book, and I thank you.

John Zogg, a friend and an extremely creative potter who read this book to make sure I didn't say anything stupid about pottery. Thank you, John, for tearing up in the right places, and for telling me about boat anchors.

Anna Zogg and Marilynn Rockelman, for brainstorming Seth's story. Anna also read my very rough first draft and made some excellent suggestions, and she's the one who suggested the candle canister idea for Seth's artwork. I love your enthusiasm and your creativity, my sister-in-Christ.

The members of the Utah Christian Writers Fellowship for their enthusiasm for Seth's story, and especially Leslie Coleman and the late Jim Cook, for pointing out specific elements that made the book so much stronger.

The members of the Capital City Round Table, for helping me decide, and especially Ray Peden, author of *One Tenth of the Law*, for telling me, "Just do it!"

The group at the Bear Lake Cabin, for listening to me whine and complain and ponder and consider when we should have been relaxing in the mountains. Patti Chauza, Annie Baker, Melissa Mondragon, and Sandie Coffman, you have no idea how I value your encouragement, your ideas, your advice, and your friendship.

My mom, Amy Barkman, for teaching me about true forgiveness. Considering the theme of this story, that is an incredible acknowledgment.

My husband, Ted Smith, for his patience and support, and for answering 1001 questions about pigs and cows and milking and plowing and planting. And for loving me. You can't imagine how much I love you in return.

Soli Deo Gloria.
Virginia Smith

About the Author

Virginia Smith is the bestselling author of thirty-one novels (and counting), an illustrated children's book, and more than fifty articles and short stories. An avid reader with eclectic tastes in fiction, Ginny writes in a variety of styles, from lighthearted relationship stories to breath-snatching suspense. Her books have been finalists for many literary awards, and two of her novels received the prestigious Holt Medallion Award of Merit.

A firm believer in research, Ginny immerses herself in the lifestyles of her characters in order to write the details of their lives believably. Her dedication to research has taken her many places, from the depths of the Caribbean to the cages of African porcupines while volunteering as a zookeeper. During her research for *The Amish Widower*, she took pottery lessons and managed to produce a few acceptable pieces amid many clay disasters. She fell in love with the craft and plans to continue her lessons.

Learn more about Ginny and her books at
www.VirginiaSmith.org.

**Meet the other Amish men in
The Men of Lancaster County series.**

Tyler Anderson
A groom-to-be who has to make a decision
between two very different women.

Jake Miller
A blacksmith who loves to fix things,
but can he fix a broken heart?

Clayton Raber
A clockmaker who is a gifted craftsman,
but he hides a devastating secret.

Enjoy the following excerpt from *The Amish Groom* from
bestselling authors Mindy Starns Clark and Susan Meissner.

One

The surface of the pond was glassy smooth, a deep liquid oval beckoning through the trees. I headed down the path, my dog at my side. When we reached the clearing, Timber darted forward, chasing a duck into tall reeds. I came to a stop right at the edge of the water, work boots and pant cuffs damp from the morning dew, and paused to take it all in.

This secluded little farm pond was always so striking, so peaceful, but never more so than at this time of day, when the sun was just coming up—not to mention at this time of year, when the trees lining its banks offered riotous bursts of reds and yellows and oranges among the green. Whatever the season, I could never get enough of it. The fish that darted in and out of sight below. The dense and rocky overgrowth on all sides. The weeping willow at the far end, its branches dangling down to the water, tickling the surface.

I set down the tools and other items I was carrying and then turned my face upward just as the sun broke across the stillness. I watched as the horizon lost its sleepy purple cast, turning auburn. There wasn't a cloud in sight, and I knew a perfect day lay in store for my cousin Anna's wedding. As if on cue, Timber barked from somewhere off to my right, reminding me that there was much to do between now and then. Time to get to work.

Not far away, the old wooden rowboat rested upside down on the grass where I'd left it the last time I'd used it, the oar tucked securely underneath. I flipped it over and brushed out a few spiders who'd been living inside. Then I put the oar and the stuff I'd brought into the small craft and slid to the water. When it was all loaded, I glanced around for Timber and was glad to see that although the duck had flown off, the yellow lab was now fully occupied with sniffing his way around the pond's perimeter.

I placed one foot in the boat's hull and gently pushed off with the other, the small vessel cutting through the water with ease. When it slowed about ten feet short of my goal, I lowered the oar into the water and paddled toward the buoy that floated near the center of the pond. As I did, I breathed in the new morning air, filling my lungs with its earthy, October fragrance.

According to my grandmother, this pond had been my mother's favorite place to go when she was young and wanted to be alone with her thoughts. She had come here often, and I had a feeling I knew why. When the morning sun slashed across the top of the trees on mid-autumn dawns like this one, I could see my reflection in the water as clear as in the mirror in my bedroom back at the farmhouse, as if there were another me beyond the surface, looking back. I was always drawn to that other place, to the what-ifs of it all. No doubt my mother, who was so full of wanderlust, had felt the same.

Easing the boat alongside the buoy, I brought it to a stop once the floating brown orb was within easy reach. I rested the dripping plank beside my feet, gave the straw hat on my head a pat to make sure it was secure, and then slid my hands into the cold water, feeling under the buoy for the rope. Grasping it, I began to pull slowly upward, working my hands along the taut line, wishing I'd thought to wear gloves for a better grip. The more I pulled up, the slimier it grew, coating my palms in a nasty brown goo that smelled of mud and dankness and rot.

I'd known last spring that something needed to be done when the ice began to melt away and I'd spotted more than a few silver, bloated bodies floating sideways in the black water. Too many fish had not survived the winter, which confirmed what I'd suspected for a while, that there was a problem with the aerator.

Not that this pond mattered all that much in the grand scheme of things. No one ever even bothered with it except me anyway—and, in her youth, my mother. Hidden among the trees on a far back corner of my grandparents' farm, it was no longer necessary once wells were dug on the farm, but that didn't mean it was unimportant—at least not to me—or that it could be ignored. Busy with my work in the buggy shop, I'd managed to put off dealing with the issue for months. But now that fall was here, and another winter just around the corner, I knew it was time to get this thing repaired.

As I pulled on the rope, an old airstone emerged from the surface, with long strands of what looked like seaweed dangling down from its round head. I put it into my lap—wetness, slime, and all—pressed my elbow against the boat's rim to hold the tubing in place, and then grabbed the wrench to disconnect the rusting adapter. After considerable effort, I finally broke the valve free. The rest of the installation was easy by comparison, and soon I had the new diffuser attached and ready to go, while the old one lay in a puddle at my feet.

I released my elbow hold on the tubing, gripped the rope, and began lowering the new diffuser into the water a little bit at a time.

I wasn't sure how long it would take for the bubbles to start appearing at the surface, but I didn't mind sitting in the boat, waiting. My time was usually spent in quiet reflection, standing on the bank, but being here in the middle of the pond was giving me a unique vantage point, so I took in the scenery, gulping it down like liquid to a thirsty man.

For years I'd been coming to the pond once every few weeks or so, but lately I'd found my way down here almost daily. As blessed as I was to have this place where I could escape and contemplate life in private, I knew the increase in frequency didn't bode well. My mind had become such a jumbled mess, and it seemed all I wanted to do was be alone to think and pray and try to make sense of the conflict raging inside of me.

Much as my mother had done, long before I was born.

Not far from the path, a cluster of rocks and boulders formed a natural sort of sitting area, and I often imagined her as a young woman, perched there and doing the very same thing, begging God for clarity and direction as she tried to soothe her troubled soul. She had been just eighteen years old when she turned her back on the farm for good, leaving behind her parents and siblings and the Amish life she no longer wanted. She'd thrown in her lot for a life among the *Englisch*, eventually marrying my dad, moving to Europe, and giving birth to me.

Then she died, suddenly and unexpectedly, when I was just six years old.

After that, I had been her family's consolation prize, so to speak. The little boy with the football jerseys and blue jeans who had known a smattering of Pennsylvania Dutch but otherwise hadn't a clue what it meant to be Amish. At my newly widowed father's request, my grandparents had taken me in right after the funeral, an arrangement that was supposed to have been temporary. But here I was, all these years later, still in the same place, living on the same farm my mother had lived on, sleeping in the same room that had been hers, and spending time at the same pond that had drawn and captivated her. I had accepted my lot and the fact that my dad found a new life with a new wife—and even a new son—without me. I'd see them now and then, but for all intents and purposes *Mammi* and *Daadi* were more like parents than grandparents to me. For that matter, the aunt and uncles I'd grown up with—Sarah, Thom, Eli, and Peter—were more like sister and brothers. Even Jake, who was a mere six months older than I, was technically my uncle, even though we felt and acted like brothers.

That very first day I arrived, I had traded in the jerseys and jeans for broadfall trousers and plain white shirts and had been raised Amish from then on. My dad had remained peripherally involved in my life even after he remarried and became a father a second time, but I had now been living here, on this farm, for seventeen years. At twenty-three, I was on the verge of big decisions that would determine the rest of my life, my future, my path—whether *Englisch* or Amish.

And I'd never been more perplexed.

Before she left here for good, my mother had been confused as well. I knew that much from what I'd been told by her brother Thom, who had been sixteen at the time. As a child, I hadn't known much about my mother at all, or at least not the person she was when she lived in this world. She had never talked much about her years growing up Amish. I don't remember her telling me about the house, or the smell of the horses' tack, or the sounds the buggies made when their wheels rolled on pavement, or how quiet the dark was on winter nights.

Most of what I knew about my mother I had learned from my aunt and uncles and from *Daadi* and *Mammi*. They told me she loved peaches and jonquils and her horse, Nutmeg, and the first snowfall. That she liked surprises and twirling and laughter.

Even though she had never joined the church, they would always see her as Amish. I looked Amish too, but lately it seemed as though underneath the Plain clothes and the hat and the language, there was a different man. Rachel Hoeck, who was the closest friend I had besides Jake, said I was as Amish as any man born right here in Lancaster County. I grew up here. I went to school here. I'd worked in my grandfather's buggy shop since I could tighten a bolt. I was on the verge of church membership and baptism. At twenty-three I was more than old enough to take my vows as an Amish adult—vows of commitment to the Amish life and vows of marriage to an Amish bride. Those faraway years when I lived in the *Englisch* world were just that, Rachel would say—far away. But how could she know? I'd never brought her here at the crack of dawn. She'd never seen the man in the pond who stared back at me with questioning eyes. Then again, if she did see him, I knew what she would say to me.

That is just your reflection, Tyler. That's you. The Amish man I love.

And I would want to believe her.

But there would be this tugging inside me, as there was every time I came to the pond now, pulling at all that I knew to be true of me. As though a loose thread was in the grasp of something or someone who wanted to yank it free...

My thoughts were interrupted by the subtle sound of a hundred tiny bubbles breaking on the surface.

A beautiful sight. The diffuser was doing just what it should.

I rowed back to shore, returned the rowboat and oar to the tall grass, and whistled for my dog. Then I gathered my things and started up the path toward home, Timber trotting alongside. I knew I should have felt good. After all, the aerator was working again, it was a beautiful morning, and God's presence was everywhere. But up ahead, as the farmhouse came into view, I felt a surge of emotion I couldn't even name. Loss? Joy? Hope? Fear?

Maybe all of the above, simultaneously?

My mind again went to my mother and one of the few memories I had of her, the first time she ever told me about this pond. We'd been far from here—a world away, in fact—but the way she talked, that small body of water had come as alive as if I'd been standing on its banks myself.

I had been in my bed, crying because there was a thunderstorm outside and lightning was scissoring over the house as though it wanted to slice me in two. My mother was sitting on my bed, trying to convince me the storm couldn't hurt me. Then, to take my mind off what was happening outside the window, she began telling me all about the pond, her favorite place on the farm where she grew up. She went on and on, finally concluding her elaborate description with the words, "You can see a different world in the water. It's like there's always another place besides the one where you are."

I hadn't known what she meant by that, but I remember asking her if there was thunder and lightning at that other place too.

She chuckled softly. "Every place has something about it we would change if we were in charge."

Swallowing hard, I closed my eyes now as I walked, trying to picture my mother's pretty face from that night, her gentle hands as she smoothed the covers around me. But then a voice echoed across the silence and the image tumbled away, back to the unseen place where I kept all of my memories hidden—or at least my memories of her.

"Tyler!"

I opened my eyes to see Jake watching me from where he stood in the drive, arms crossed over his chest. He and I were supposed to have loaded some additional benches we'd made in the buggy shop into the wagon first thing so that right after breakfast we could deliver them over to the Bowmans' farm for Anna's wedding. But my task at the pond had taken longer than I'd expected, leaving him to do the loading all by himself. I felt guilty, as I knew my errand could have waited for a more appropriate day. To be honest, I had probably just used the diffuser replacement as an excuse to get down to the pond this morning and have a little time to myself.

I gave him an apologetic smile and a shrug, and though I could tell he was about to lay into me, when he saw that my shirt and pants were covered in dark, slimy mud, he hesitated and then simply grinned.

He and I both knew that whatever my *grossmammi* doled out once she saw what I'd done to my clean clothes would be payback enough.

Stepping inside, I tried to soften the blow by warning her first.

"Just so you know," I called out as Jake and I paused in the mudroom to remove our hats, jackets, and boots, "changing out the diffuser in the pond was a lot messier job than I'd expected."

"Oh, Tyler, no," she replied from the kitchen. "You didn't fall in, did you? Your *grossdaadi* told you not to trust that old rowboat."

"No, nothing like that."

I stepped around the corner to see her at the counter, spooning out scrambled eggs from the pan. The aroma of coffee and peach strudel wafted past my nose, and I realized I was starving. I'd fed Timber before going to the pond but hadn't eaten a thing yet myself.

She didn't even look up to see me, so Jake let out a low whistle as he pushed past to go to the table. "Wow, Tyler. Nice going on your clothes there! Did you leave any mud in the pond?" He whistled again, dramatically.

Of course, at that *Mammi*'s head snapped up. She took in the sight of me, her eyes narrowing.

"Just for that, no strudel," she said. When Jake burst out in a victorious laugh, she gave him a sharp, "I'm talking to *you*, young man. No strudel for troublemakers."

Lucky for me, she hated tattling even more than she hated extra work on laundry day. I grinned, though I didn't dare make a sound in return lest she come down on me as well.

"I'll rinse everything out as soon as I take it off," I told her.

"See that you do," she replied, returning her attention to the food preparations in front of her.

I flashed Jake a "gotcha" look. He snagged a corner of the strudel when *Mammi's* head was turned and tossed it into his mouth with a smirk that said "gotcha back."

Ten minutes later, I had returned to the kitchen, cleaned up and ready for the day, relieved that the mud had rinsed right out. I spotted *Mammi* still standing at the counter and Jake sitting at the table. He was sipping coffee but otherwise waiting to dig in until everyone else had convened here too. I heard *Daadi* come in the back door as I was taking my seat, and once he'd hung up his hat and jacket, he joined us in the kitchen and crossed the floor toward his wife.

Daadi always greeted my grandmother the same way when the morning's first chores were done and it was time for breakfast and devotions: kissing her cheek and speaking in the softest words, meant just for her, saying, *"Gud mariye, meiner Aldi."* Good morning, my wife.

Mammi smiled the way she always did. *"Gud mariye,* Joel."

I loved how tender my grandparents were with each other in these first few moments of the day. Like most Amish, *Daadi* didn't give *Mammi* kisses in front of people, or fuss over her in a personal kind of way, especially not in public. But their morning custom made me feel good about the start of the day, and it always had. It was strange and wonderful to think my mother probably saw them do this same thing every morning of her life too.

Daadi brought a mug of coffee to the table and took his seat at the end. "Beautiful sunrise over the pond this morning?" he asked, letting me know in his gentle way he'd seen me heading to the place I always went when there was much on my mind.

"Sure was," I replied, adding nothing else, not even about the diffuser repair. He knew as well as I did that that wasn't really why I'd gone out there.

I avoided his gaze, watching as *Mammi* brought a plate of sausages to the table. We bowed our heads for a silent prayer, and the topic of the pond was dropped. That was fine with me. I had always felt free to share even my most troubling thoughts with my grandfather. But I wasn't ready to have *that* conversation.

Not yet, anyway—and especially not with him.

TWO

After breakfast Jake and I drove the wagon a short distance over to my aunt Sarah and uncle Jonah's farm to deliver the extra seating we'd constructed for the wedding. We'd helped to get everything set up the day before—clearing out some of the furniture from the main room of the house and filling the space with all of the benches from our district's bench wagon. The Bowmans still lacked a few more rows, though, and as none of our neighboring districts had benches to spare thanks to weddings of their own, last night Jake and I had ended up doing some quick carpentry work in the buggy shop, making the extra benches ourselves. Today we were back to deliver them, with just two and half hours to go before the festivities would start. When we arrived, we greeted Anna and then went right to work with the help of her brothers, Sam and Gideon, carrying the supplementary benches inside and setting them up.

This was one of the earliest weddings of the season, and intentionally so, according to Rachel. As the youngest of four children, Anna had grown tired of being the last of everything, so she wanted to be among the first of the courting couples to marry this year. Rachel was Anna's best friend and had been talking about this event for weeks.

At least she hadn't used it as an opportunity to put pressure on me,

I thought as Jake and I lifted down another bench from the wagon, though she certainly had every right to. Rachel and I had been a couple for years, long enough for her—and everyone else, for that matter—to assume we, too, would end up married.

Though we hadn't begun courting until we were in our teens, we'd been friends long before that. I first met Rachel when I was ten and she was nine. She had come from Ohio after her grandfather died and her parents moved to Lancaster County to take over his dairy farm. Rachel was the youngest of three daughters—all honey-brunettes with a sprinkling of freckles—but she was by far the prettiest. Her eyes were a vivid blue, easily rivaling the bluest cornflower ever to sprout.

When she first moved here, she was just a new girl to tease—all in good fun, of course. Jake and I couldn't resist, and we told her all sorts of tall tales, the biggest being that he and I were twins. Though we looked almost nothing alike, she believed us until she learned that he was a Miller and I an Anderson.

"How can you be twins if you have different last names?" she'd asked one day during her second week there.

"That's so people can tell us apart," Jake replied with a perfect deadpan.

After a long moment, her eyes narrowed, and then she turned on her heel without a word and marched off to speak to the teacher, knowing we were pulling her leg and ready to settle the matter once and for all.

"Tyler?" For the second time today, Jake's voice pulled me out of a memory.

"Huh?" I asked, blinking.

He was lifting down his end of the final bench, waiting for me to do the same. "I said, 'What's going on?'"

"What do you mean?"

"You're a million miles away. What gives? You okay?"

"Of course. I'm fine." Or I would be if he would mind his own business.

We carried the last bench into the house together and slid it into place. After that, Sam and Gideon went out to handle some other chore, leaving Jake and me to finish up. We both looked around at the room, transformed now from a living area to a church, and began to shift things a bit to allow a little more leg room between rows.

Nearby, the large kitchen area was bustling with women, including Anna and her mother and various relatives, helping to prepare the wedding feast. If I'd been in there with them, I would have been stepping on people's toes, bumping into their backs, and generally making a big mess, but they worked together seamlessly, thanks to years of practice.

"I know what it is," Jake said suddenly, pausing to look my way as I was tugging a bench into place.

"What *what* is?"

He glanced toward the kitchen before lowering his voice so only I could hear. "Why you're so nervous and distracted today. It's because you know that this time next year we'll be slinging benches around for *your* wedding."

He laughed.

I didn't.

"Oh, come on, Tyler," he prodded in a soft voice. "I don't know why you're not *already* married. And neither does anyone else."

I glared at him, gesturing toward the kitchen and the women who might overhear his words.

"I'm serious!" he said, moving closer now so he could speak even more softly. "You're getting up in years, you know?"

"I'm twenty-three."

"Which is high time to take that next step. And you'll never find a better match for you than Rachel."

Now it was my turn to pause. Why didn't he get it? I spoke through gritted teeth, telling him I was not going to discuss it with him, but he kept talking as if he hadn't even heard me.

"You know she's perfect for you. *She* thinks you're wonderful." He put the emphasis on "she," meaning, of course, that Rachel thought it even if no one else did.

"Funny," I snapped.

Jake moved to the end of the row. "It's time to take that next step, buddy, just like Tobias will today with Anna. I know it and you know it. Most of all, Rachel knows it."

Unsure how to reply, I leaned down and made one final shift, intentionally pushing the bench at Jake's knees. He yelped as he tried to avoid the impact.

"Sorry," I said in a loud voice, glancing toward the kitchen and giving an "everything's okay here" wave to the two women who had turned to look. "Guess I didn't see your legs there, buddy. Must need to get my eyes checked."

"Get your brain checked, you mean." Jake sat down to rub his knee and whispered, "I'm only saying what you need to hear."

"No," I hissed, "you're only saying a bunch of stuff that's none of your business."

I was saved from further harassment by the appearance of Jonah Bowman—Anna's father and my uncle—who came in from outside. "We're all finished here," I said. "Anything else we can do for you?"

"*Ya*. Before you go, can you cut some more logs for cooking? We use propane in the house and in the wedding wagon, but I also borrowed three big cookstoves that we have going out back." Glancing toward the kitchen, he added, "I thought I had enough wood, but I may have underestimated the need."

We all shared a smile, knowing that the women in there would have an absolute fit if they ran short of fuel before they were finished roasting all the chickens this day would require.

"Happy to do it."

Jake and I went outside to the toolshed, grabbed some axes, and then made our way to the woodpile, where we pulled out logs of birch and oak and began breaking them down into smaller, stove-sized pieces. Across the driveway from us, the barn's big doors were open to the sun, and I could see people milling around inside, setting up for the reception.

We chopped for a while, quiet except for the thwack of our axes and the crisp splitting of wood.

"I guess I'll let you off the hook—for now," Jake said finally, pausing to wipe the sweat from his forehead. "But just let me say that I really am glad you have Rachel."

"Thank you," I replied, relieved he was willing to let it go.

Then he added, "After all, you'll need *someone* to fill the lonely hours once I leave tomorrow."

I couldn't help but smile as I reached for another log and placed it on the chopping block. "Oh, yeah? You think I'll be counting the days till you get back?" I slammed the ax down, splitting the log neatly in two.

"Absolutely. Mark my words. You're going to miss me while I'm gone more than you can imagine."

"Uh-huh," I said, leaning down to pick up the larger of the two pieces and placing it on the block to split it again. "More likely, I'll forget all about you. You'll come back in four months' time, and we'll have to be reintroduced. I'll be all, 'What's that? Jake who? I suppose you do look kind of familiar…'"

I grinned, he smirked, and together we continued working side by side, the only sounds our occasional grunts and the steady rhythm of our task. I was glad he had dropped the discussion of Rachel, but I would have liked to avoid this topic as well. We both knew that his teasing words held more than a little truth. I couldn't imagine what the next months were going to be like without Jake around. He was headed to Missouri for blacksmithing school, something he'd been looking forward to for a long time. Though Jake had always labored alongside me in *Daadi*'s buggy shop, his first love was the horses that pulled those buggies. Shoeing took skill, craftsmanship, and a level of trust between animal and man that few people appreciated. I did, but only because Jake had been talking about it since we were kids.

Now that he was going to become a blacksmith, he'd be the first of the Millers to leave the buggy trade. His older brothers, Thom, Eli, and Peter, all worked in the buggy shop, as did some of their sons. On a busy day, there could be a dozen of us in there. Now it would be eleven.

"So I suppose you're all packed," I said, clearing my throat.

He smiled at me. "Just about."

"You probably won't want to come home," I said, pretending that wouldn't bother me in the least.

We both knew it would, though. Low-key guys like me didn't have a lot of close friends. But since the day I'd come to live here seventeen years ago, I'd had Jake, the best friend of all.

"Are you kidding? Of course I'm coming back. You might forget me, but the horses in Lancaster County won't. They need me."

"At least the horses, if not the ladies," I teased.

Before he could respond, we both heard the distinct clip-clop of hooves behind us. Turning, I spotted a familiar market wagon coming our way, a sight that always filled me with inexplicable warmth. I watched until it rolled to a stop nearby. My eyes met those of the driver, and then she softly said my name. Hers was the sweetest voice I knew beyond that of my mother's echoes.

Rachel.

She climbed down from the wagon, a casserole dish tucked under one arm.

"*Guder mariye,* Tyler. *Guder mariye,* Jake," she said. She smelled like a summer morning, like sweet pea blossoms. The ties of her *kapp* flitted in the slight breeze like butterflies.

We tipped our hats, and she and I shared a smile. As Anna's closest friend, Rachel was one of her two *newehockers,* or attendants, so I wasn't surprised that she had come early.

"*Mariye,* Rachel," I said. "You're looking pretty today."

Blushing, she was about to respond when Jake interrupted.

"Got a full load here?" he asked, moving to the back of the wagon and peeling up a corner of the tarp to peek underneath.

"*Ya.* The last of the dishes and table linens."

"Okay. We'll get them into the barn once we're done here."

"*Danke,* Jake."

He took over with the horse, leading it toward the hitching post nearest the barn as Rachel turned back to me and spoke in a softer voice.

"How's Anna?" she asked, her eyes sparkling. "Excited, I bet."

I glanced toward the house and admitted I didn't know, that we hadn't really taken the time to speak—other than a quick hello—since I'd arrived.

"*Ach,* well, she's probably busy in the kitchen. Guess I'd better get in there too."

"Guess you'd better," I said, but then neither of us made a move to go. Instead, we just stood there, our eyes locked. Rachel really did look especially beautiful today, her cheekbones a rosy pink, her skin perfect cream, her lips soft and full.

"What?" she whispered, giving me a sexy smile, as if she could read my mind.

"Nothing," I said, a twinkle in my own eye. She and I both knew that what I wanted more than anything in that moment was to give her a kiss.

"All right you two, enough with the googly-eyes," Jake said, returning to the woodpile. "Tyler, get over here. We're not done yet."

I tipped my hat again and Rachel gave me a wink before she turned and headed for the house.

Jake was right: Rachel really was the perfect woman for me. So why did I keep putting things off?

I returned to my work—lift, place, *thwack*, split—my mind racing despite the calming scent of fresh-cut wood that wafted up from every chop. Rachel had been so patient with me thus far, but how much longer would she wait before giving up on me—on us—for good?

Reaching for another log, I thought again of that time long ago, back when we were children in school. After the "twins" incident and our teacher told her that Jake was my uncle, not my brother, I had expected Rachel to be mad and to keep her distance.

Instead, it seemed our deception had only fueled her curiosity. That night she must have put two and two together and begun to wonder that if I was being raised by my grandparents, then where were my *real* parents?

She came to me in the schoolyard after lunch the very next day, concern etched into her face. "Do you not have a mother and father?" She was practically crying.

"Everybody has a mother and father," I said, pretending I was not moved by her concern for me. "You can't be born without parents."

She was unfazed. "Are they...are you an orphan?"

I frowned. "No, I'm not an orphan."

"So where are they?" Her eyes glistened.

Even then, I hadn't known how to explain. What could I say? My mother had died. She was gone for good, living now in a place very far away, as she had since the moment she'd passed. But what of my dad? I had seen him just twice in the past three years. At the time Rachel asked me that question, he was in Japan, by choice, on an extended tour that would keep him gone until I turned eleven. And even though I knew he was very much alive, most days he seemed just as far from me as my mother was.

"They're not here," was all I said. Then I'd walked off in search of someone to play with who already knew my story and didn't need to ask stupid questions.

But Rachel wasn't giving up that easily. The next day, she tried again, this time taking a seat on the swing beside mine and saying, "Tell me about your mother. What was she like?" Obviously, someone had filled her in, at least a little bit. Otherwise, she wouldn't have put it quite that way.

I wanted to rebuff her, but again, her question left me silent and confused. What *had* my mother been like? Did I even know anymore? I still had some memories of her, of course, but Rachel had asked me not for memories but for a description.

Sitting on the swing, my toes digging a rut into the dry, dusty ground at my feet, I tried to picture my mom. I could barely recall her face by that point, though I could still hear the faintest echoes of her voice, sometimes in English, sometimes in the Pennsylvania Dutch she'd grown up speaking.

What else?

I remembered her smile, from when we lived in Germany and I found three *pfennigs* in the street as she and I walked to the *backerei* to buy bread.

I remembered her eyes, from when she watched me blow out the candles on a cake she'd baked for my birthday—white frosting with sprinkles on top, just like I'd asked for.

I remembered her long brown hair, flowing out behind her as we pedaled down the street together on our bicycles.

Of course, that had been back when we still lived in Germany. I couldn't remember moving out of our house in Heidelberg or the long airplane ride to the States, but I remembered my mother calling her parents once we were settled into our new home in Maryland to tell them we had returned from overseas at last. I remembered that conversation well, remembered hearing her say that we wanted to come for a visit. But then after she hung up the phone, she just cried for a long time. And that visit never happened. I never even met my grandparents, in fact, until the day of the funeral, the day they took me home and my old life came to an end and my new one began.

"My mother?" I said finally, turning to Rachel. "She was smart and funny and nice and everybody liked her." Glancing her way, I couldn't help but add, "She wasn't *Amish*, you know. Neither is my dad."

I could still see Rachel's face in that moment, the hurt in her big blue eyes. I could still feel the shame burning my cheeks, shame at the way I had said the word "Amish," as though it was something to be disdained, as though I wasn't wearing Amish clothes myself or living an Amish life, day after day, in my grandparents' Amish home.

Once again she had walked away without a word. That was on a Friday, and I felt bad all weekend long about what I'd said. When I saw her again that Monday at school, I was ready to apologize. But before I could, she simply came up to me and gestured across the playground toward the swings. We ran there together, and that time we didn't just hang still but instead tried to get ourselves going. By pushing off with our feet and pumping our legs, over and over—leaning back, stretching out, leaning forward, curling under—we eventually went so high we were nearly perpendicular to the ground.

"We're going to swing to the moon!" she cried.

"We're going to swing to the sun!" I responded.

"We're going to swing all the way to heaven!" she said. "All the way up to your mother!"

I glanced at her, but she wasn't making fun. She wasn't even pretending, really. She was just trying to make me feel better, to say something kind. That was the first I became aware of Rachel's gift for compassion.

"All the way up to heaven," I agreed, and in the look we shared as we soared toward the sky, I knew all would be well between us from that moment forward.

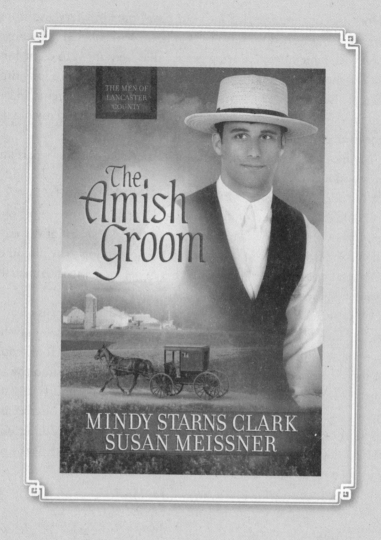

THE MEN OF
LANCASTER
COUNTY

The
Amish
Groom

MINDY STARNS CLARK
SUSAN MEISSNER

The time for wondering is over.
The time for commitment is now.
And yet...

Tyler Anderson is torn between two worlds—Amish and *Englisch*. Born to an ex-Amish mother and an *Englisch* father, he is raised as a military kid until his mom passes away and his dad places him in the care of his Amish grandparents. Now 23, Tyler knows it's time to commit to the Amish church for good. Still he hesitates, unsure if he'll ever truly belong.

Rachel Hoeck has been patient as she waits for Tyler to make up his mind and become her husband. But as much as Tyler adores Rachel, he can't be certain this is God's plan for his life. Conflicted, he prays for direction and peace—only to find himself being pulled to the outside world yet again. During a stay with his father's second family in Southern California, Tyler meets a free-spirited young woman named Lark, putting his future with Rachel even more in question.

As pressure mounts on both sides, will Tyler choose to stay with Lark and remain an *Englischer*? Or will he find his way back to Rachel and become her Amish groom at last?

❧

A poignant novel of the search for identity and lifetime love, nestled between a beloved Amish community and an exciting modern world.

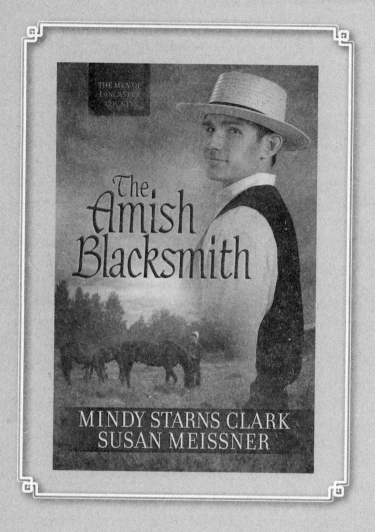

THE MEN OF
LANCASTER
COUNTY

The
Amish
Blacksmith

MINDY STARNS CLARK
SUSAN MEISSNER

Does time really heal all wounds?

Six years ago, Priscilla Kinsinger's mother died in a tragic accident, plunging the teenager into a grief so intense she was finally sent to live with relatives elsewhere. Now an adult, Priscilla has returned to Lancaster County hoping to find peace at last with her *mamm*'s death, for which she has always felt responsible.

Talented horse-gentler Jake Miller, an apprentice blacksmith for the Kinsingers, is soon at odds with the beautiful but emotionally complex Priscilla. He much prefers the lighthearted, easy-going ways of Amanda Shetler, the local young woman he's been courting. But his boss is Priscilla's uncle, so when the man asks Jake and Amanda to help his niece reconnect with community life, they have no choice but to do just that.

Surprisingly, as Jake spends time with Priscilla, he finds himself drawn to her. Just as he fixes troubled horses, he wants to "fix" her too by convincing her she was not to blame for her mother's death. What he discovers instead will challenge everything he believes about the depth of emotion, the breadth of forgiveness, and the true nature of love.

A tender novel of friendship, love, and the power of trusting God to change hearts and lives, set in the close-knit Amish community of Lancaster County.

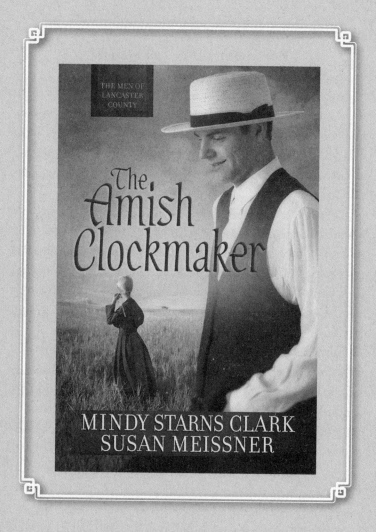

THE MEN OF
LANCASTER
COUNTY

The
Amish
Clockmaker

MINDY STARNS CLARK
SUSAN MEISSNER

Only Time Will Tell

Newlywed Matthew Zook is expanding his family's tack and feed store when a surprising property dispute puts the remodel on hold—and raises new questions about the location's mysterious past.

Decades earlier, the same building housed a clock shop run by a young Amish clockmaker named Clayton Raber. Known for his hot temper, Clayton was arrested for the murder of his beloved wife, a crime almost everyone—including his own family members—believed he'd committed, even after charges were dropped. Isolated and feeling condemned by all, Clayton eventually broke from the church, left Lancaster County, and was never heard from again.

Now the only way Matthew can solve the boundary issue and save his family's business is to track down the clockmaker. But does this put Matthew on the trail of a murderer?

A timeless novel of truth, commitment, and the power of enduring love, where secrets of the past give way to hope for the future.

To learn more about Harvest House books and
to read sample chapters, visit our website:

www.harvesthousepublishers.com

HARVEST HOUSE PUBLISHERS
EUGENE, OREGON